D1357389

6090418000

Colin Falconer was born in North London. He has worked in TV and radio and as a freelance journalist. He has been a novelist for the last twenty five years, with his work published widely in the UK, US and Europe. His books have been translated into seventeen languages. He currently lives in Australia. Visit his website at **www.colinfalconer.net**

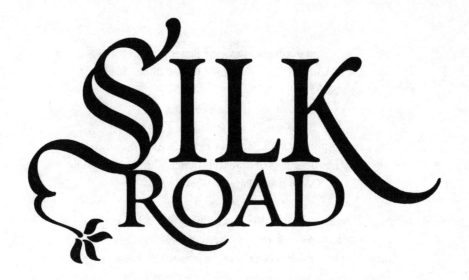

SILK ROAD

COLIN FALCONER

CORVUS

First published in Great Britain in 2011
by Corvus, an imprint of Atlantic Books Ltd.

9 8 7 6 5 4 3 2 1

A CIP catalogue record for this book is available from
the British Library.

Hardback ISBN: 978-0-85789-108-2
Trade paperback ISBN: 978-0-85789-109-9
E-book ISBN: 978-0-85789-119-8

Printed in Great Britain by the MPG Books Group

Corvus, an imprint of Grove Atlantic Ltd
Ormond House
26-27 Boswell Street
London WC1N 3JZ

www.corvus-books.co.uk

Acknowledgements

The story of *Silk Road* was many years in the making and I would like to thank those who finally got it into print. Firstly my agent Patrick Walsh, whose enthusiasm for my story saw it from his submission tray into the hands of the wonderful Anthony Cheetham at Corvus, Atlantic.

I would like to thank everyone at Corvus who worked on the project with me, particularly Nic Cheetham and Rina Gill, who both championed the book, and also my wonderful editor, Laura Palmer, who took it through, line by line. My thanks also to Richenda Todd for her comments and suggestions on the typescript. Thank you all. A special thank you also to Tim Curnow, my lifelong friend, who has been with me through thick and thin and knows this story, and the story of the story, better than anyone.

I would also like to thank the driver who took us out to the caves at Turpan and got us down off the hairpin cliffs after the steering rod on the 4WD broke. I wish I remembered his name now. Traumatic amnesia perhaps. Also many thanks to the bus driver out of Urumqi who somehow missed all that oncoming traffic despite driving on the wrong side of the road with his headlights on. Maybe less whisky at the rest stops next time?

This book is for my bella Diana, who mended my wing
and showed me how to fly again.

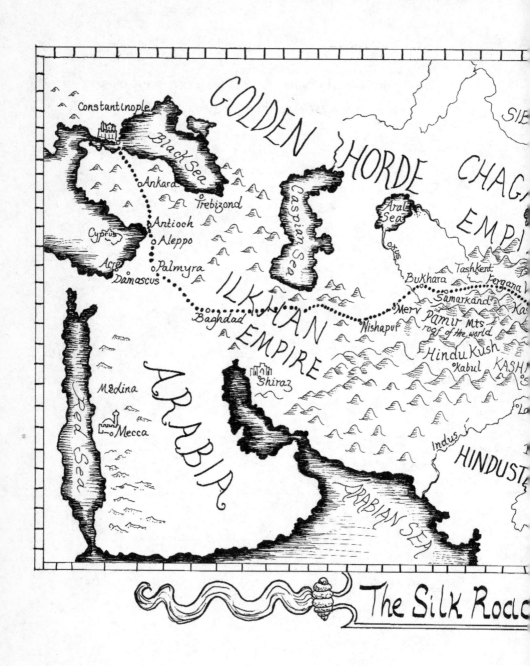

Lake Baikal

MONGOLIA

MANCHU

Altai Mts

Qaraqorum
Gobi Desert
Xanadu
Great Wall
GORYEO

HAI
Tien Shan mts
Flaming mts
Gaochang
Kuqa
Aksu
Turpan
Kumul
Anxi
EMPIRE
Dadu
YELLOW SEA

Taklimakan Desert
OF
CATHAY
Yellow River
Lanzhou
Chang'an
Nanjing
Zin'an

un Lun mts
Chang'an
Yangtse

KUBLAI KHAN

TIBET
Lhasa
SONG EMPIRE

Himalaya
PACIFIC
OCEAN

Ganges

PAGAN
KINGDOM
Pagan

Bay of
Bengal

Dadu - 'Great Capital' - also called Khanbaliq - 'Residence of the Great Khan'
(now Beijing)
Xanadu - now Shan-tu
Zin'an - now Hangzhou.
Kumul - now Hami

PROLOGUE

✠

Lyon, France
in the year of the Incarnation of Our Lord 1293

THEY FOUND HIM in the cloister, lying on his back with ice in his beard. He was half-conscious, muttering about a Templar knight, a secret commission from the Pope, and a beautiful woman on a white pony. His fellow monks carried him back to his cell and laid him on the hard cot that had been his bed for the last twenty years. He was an old man now and there was nothing to be done. His eyes had the cold sheen of death. A brother went to fetch the abbot so that the old fellow might make his last confession.

✠

It was cold as death in the room. The abbot knelt down beside him. Somewhere in the forest a fir bough crashed to the ground under its burden of snow. The old man's eyes flickered open at the sound and the yellow glimmer of the candle was captured in the lens of his eye. His breathing was ragged in his chest and the abbot wrinkled his nose at the sour smell of it.

He whispered something; a name perhaps, but it was unintelligible.

'William,' the abbot murmured, 'I can hear your confession now.'

'My confession?'

'You will be absolved of all sin and this night you shall see our Blessed Saviour.'

William smiled, a ghastly grin that chilled the abbot to his soul. William, who had come to them in such mystery, would leave them now in the same manner. 'Water.'

The abbot lifted his head and moistened his lips from a wooden bowl. So cold in here. William's breath rose to the ceiling in a thin vapour, like a spirit leaving the body.

'The Blесséd Saviour will not see me.'

'You must make your confession,' the abbot repeated, anxious now that it be done before the soul was taken.

'I see the Devil. He warms the brands for me.'

The abbot felt a thrill of dread along his spine at his invocation of the Beast. 'You have lived a holy life. What do you have to fear from Beelzebub?'

William raised a hand from the bed, touched the sleeve of the abbot's robe. 'Come closer,' he said. 'Come closer and I shall tell you . . . precisely . . . what I have to fear.'

PART I

Saracen Moon

Acre to Aleppo
1259–1260

I

✠

Fergana Valley
in the Chaghadai khanate of the Tatar
the Year of the Sheep

SHE HAD ALWAYS dreamed she could fly.

She imagined that the earth was laid before her, as in the eye of an eagle, could feel the updraughts of the valley in the sweep of a wing, could believe for that moment that no silver bond tied her to the earth . . .

Khutelun reined in her horse, turned her face to the north wind, the cold burning her cheeks. The snow peaks on the Roof of the World had turned a glacial blue in the late afternoon sun. Below her, in the valley, the black yurts of her tribe huddled like thieves on the brown valley. Nothing stirred on the plain. She was alone up here, alone with the great silence of the steppes.

This is my birthright, on the back of a good horse, my face burned by the wind. But if my father has his way I will be given to some upstart boy who will give me his babies and have me tend his yurt and milk his goats and I will never ride at the head of my father's *touman* again. I am born to the wrong sex, with the heart of a stallion and the tail of a mare.

If I had been born in the body of a man I would be the next khan of the high steppe. Instead my consolation is that one day one of my sons will rule the high grasslands. Even for this I must one day go to pasture with a man.

The thought of submitting herself made her feel sick inside.

Of course she wanted children of her own. She also hungered for the physical comfort of a man, and lately she had listened to the lewd chatter of her married sisters with more than a passing interest. But to take a husband – though she knew that one day she must – would consign her to his yurt forever.

Her father had found a new suitor for her, the son of a khan from north of Lake Baikal. It was her father's duty and it was also good politics. But as a Tatar woman it was also her right to refuse, as she had done many times before. This time, however, she had made a bargain with him. If he found her a boy who could prove he was worthy of her by besting her on horseback, then she would submit to marriage.

It was not outright refusal.

She heard a faint cry and looked up, saw a falcon flick its wingtips in the face of the wind.

Look at her brothers. Gerel was a drunkard and Tekudai had the brains of a goat. They could not match her in wits, or in spirit.

I was born to be more than a receptacle for some man's seed.

She made a promise to herself then, shouted it to the Spirit of the Everlasting Sky. But her words were lost on the wind.

II

✠

KHUTELUN'S FATHER, QAIDU, had made his camp that winter in the Fergana Valley, below the Roof of the World. Black crags rose into the sky on every side, like the fists of the gods, the slopes below dotted with silver poplar. To the north, a high col cupped a dark lake. Above it loomed the ridge called The Woman is Going Away.

The night before he had placed the headless bodies of two white goats on its crest. To win the challenge, Khutelun, or her suitor Jebei, must be first to place one of these carcasses at the door of his yurt.

Everyone had gathered to watch the spectacle: the men in their fur coats and felt caps; the women clutching snot-nosed children. There was an eerie silence. Breath from a thousand mouths rose in the still morning air.

Jebei's escort mounted their horses and waited, a little way off. Their broad-shouldered Mongolian ponies stamped their hooves in the dawn cold.

Jebei himself had the body of a man but the face of a boy, and his quick, untidy movements betrayed his nervousness. His father watched him, frowning.

Qaidu strode from his yurt, went to his daughter and placed a hand on her horse's mane. She was tall and slim for a Tatar, but the slenderness of her body was hidden under her thick coat and boots. She wore a fur-lined cap and there was a scarf wrapped around her nose and mouth so all that was visible was her eyes.

'Lose,' he whispered to her.

The dark eyes flashed. 'If he deserves me, he will win.'

'He is a fine boy. You do not have to ride your best.'

Her pony stamped its foot in excitement, eager to begin.

'If he is as fine a boy as you say, my best will not be good enough.'

Qaidu frowned at her defiance. Yet he wished Tekudai or Gerel had inherited some of her spirit. He looked around at the silent, bronzed faces. Most of the women were smiling at his daughter. They wanted her to win.

'Whoever brings me the goat has their will!' he shouted and stepped back.

Jebei nudged his horse forward so that he stood head to head with Khutelun. He smiled and nodded at Qaidu. He thinks he can win, the old man thought. He does not know my daughter.

Qaidu raised his right fist in the air. When he brought it down the race was under way.

A hard gallop through the crowd, then out beyond the yurts, towards brown hills dusted with white. Jebei stood in the stirrups, riding hard, the wind in his face. His pony's hooves drummed on the frost-hard plain. He looked over his shoulder, saw Khutelun's horse veer suddenly away; in moments it was two hundred paces distant, heading towards the steepest slope of the mountain.

He wondered if he should follow her. The broad shoulder of the col loomed above him. He had decided on the cleanest way up the ridge when he walked the course the previous day. Too late to change his mind now. What was the girl doing? Perhaps she had chosen a longer way; it must be her strategy to ensure he would win. He kept straight for the col.

She did want him to win. Didn't she?

✛

Khutelun grinned as she imagined Jebei's confusion. Really, he had no choice. If he followed her now he would put himself behind her in the race and he could not close the gap between them unless her horse fell. What else could he do but keep to the obvious course?

She rode around the spur towards a defile in the cliff called The Place Where the Ass Died because of the steepness of the slope. Her horse's hooves slipped on the loose shale. She urged him on. She knew his pumping heart and sinewy muscles were equal to it. How many times had she ridden this path before, in other races, for sport?

Poor Jebei.

III

✠

Khutelun picked her way back down the mountain, the carcass of the goat hanging limp from her right hand, bloodying her horse's flank. Jebei sat astride his own black mare, waiting for her, a grin on his face. So he had followed her after all. It was immediately clear to her what he planned to do. He thought she was weak and that he could wrestle the goat from her, here in the defile, where no one could see them.

She reined in her horse.

They stared at each other. 'You are not as stupid as you look,' she said to him.

'Would it be so bad to be the wife of a khan?'

'I am the daughter of a khan. I am content with that for now.'

He held out his hand. 'You may be swifter on horseback but you are not as strong. Do you think you can pass me with your burden?'

Her shoulders sagged in defeat. She had not thought he would have the wits to trap her this way. She walked her horse forward and held out the kid's carcass.

'Wait,' he said. 'Before I take my prize, I must know what I have won. After all, I have never seen your face. Perhaps I might not want your goat.' The women of the steppe were not veiled, for they were Tatars before they were Mohammedans, yet she had always taken care to keep her scarf of purple silk coiled around her face, both to irritate and intrigue him. He waited as she reached for the silk with her free hand and pulled it aside.

He stared at her. 'But you're beautiful,' he said.

Beautiful, she thought; well, so men tell me. A worthless gift for a Tatar princess. Beauty is the gift of submission.

'I'm also stronger than I look,' she said and with one fluid movement of her right arm and hips she swung the bloodied carcass of the goat into his face and knocked him out of the saddle. He lay groaning on the frost-hard rock.

Khutelun did not spare him a glance. She walked her horse over him and trotted back through the defile.

✢

Qaidu stared at the dead goat lying at his feet. He nudged it with his boot, almost as if expecting the lifeless meat to spring to life. Finally he looked up at his daughter. 'So. You won.'

'Jebei is a fool.'

Qaidu looked at Jebei's father, sitting stone-faced on his horse, by providence too far away to hear this summation of his son's character. 'He is the *son of a khan*.'

'The wind blows cold on princes and goats alike.'

Khutelun saw her brothers watching from the doorway of her father's yurt, their disappointment at the outcome of the contest plain to read. 'If only Tekudai was more like you,' Qaidu said to her under his breath. Khutelun grinned beneath the purple scarf. He could not have paid her a higher compliment.

✢

After Jebei had left the camp with his father and escort, to return to the frozen wastes of Lake Baikal, the clan decided to rename the defile where Khutelun had won her ride. From that day it was no longer known as the Place Where The Ass Died.

It became, instead, The Place Where the Ass Was Felled by a Goat.

I V

+

the Templar fortress at Acre
in the year of the Incarnation of Our Lord 1260
the Feast of the Epiphany

JOSSERAN SARRAZINI, ALONE and on his knees. A single oil lamp burned in the pre-dawn darkness of the chapel, its flame reflected in the black and gold image of the Madonna above the altar. This giant with close-cropped chestnut hair bowed his head, lips moving silently in prayer as he asked for absolution for that one sin for which he could not forgive himself.

In his mind he was far from the dusty streets and olive presses of Palestine; instead he heard the creaking of snow-heavy boughs, the smell of damp furs and the chill of cold stone walls.

'I knew it was wrong but I could not resist,' he murmured.

It had happened one morning soon after the feast of the Nativity. She had wanted to go riding in the forest and, at his father's request, he had agreed to escort her. She rode a chestnut mare, its disposition as haughty and silken as her own. Ever since she had come to live with Josseran and his father at the manor, scarcely a friendly word had passed between them.

She gave him no outward sign that his presence made any deeper impression on her than did her groomsman's.

They rode deep into the forest and her mare found a rabbit's burrow and stumbled. She fell from her horse and lay still on the frozen ground. He leaped from his own mount, fearing she had broken bones. But as he bent over her, her eyes blinked open, wide and black as sin, and he felt his belly turn to warm grease.

She smiled. He would never forget it.

She said that it was just her ankle that was hurt, and commanded him to help her back into the saddle of her horse.

Was the temptation irresistible or was it simply that he did not resist? Even as his arms went around her he felt the heat of her body and on an impulse he tried to snatch a kiss from her lips. He thought she would push him away, but instead she pulled him on top of her. He groaned, unable to stop himself. His manhood, as yet untried, was hard as oak and the frost-hard ground might as well have been a bearskin rug and a feather bolster.

Suddenly and to his great astonishment, he was inside her.

And what did he now remember of their encounter? Just the drumming of blood in his ears, the stamping of the horses as they pawed at the hard ground, the salt taste of her hot tongue in his mouth.

She racked him on the sweet stretching of her intimate flesh. Her lips were drawn back from her teeth in a grimace that was more pained than pleasured. Like an animal.

He tried to hold back from the peak but he was swept along with it, cursing his youth and inexperience. He spilled himself quickly, the oily warmth emptying his belly, leaving him hollow and weak.

She pushed him roughly away and he lay panting on his back, staring at the washed blue sky, feeling the cold frost melting into his cambric shirt. She pulled down her skirts, limped to her horse and remounted, without his assistance. Then she rode away, leaving him there with the juices of their bodies smeared on his thigh.

If it had been one of the servant girls there would have been no harm in it. But she was not. When he finally dragged himself to his feet he heard the Devil's laughter ringing in his ears and the weight of guilt had already settled in his belly like an ingot of lead.

On the way back through the forest he cried for what he had done. Yet within an hour of his return to the castle he was plotting to do the Devil's work once more.

V

✠

WILLIAM OF AUGSBURG had been in the Holy Land for just two days and he was scandalized.

Acre was part of the Crusader state of Jerusalem and he had come here expecting to find a bastion of piety; instead the knights and lords charged with the protection of this sacred place disported themselves no better than Saracens.

He had arrived on a Venetian merchant galley a few days before. As he stood on the poop beside the captain, watching the great fortress rise from the sea, he was overcome. Here was Palestine, 'Outremer' – 'Over the Sea', as the Franks called it – the sacred birthplace of Our Lord. At last he would step in the footprints of the prophets. He gripped the wooden rail, his knuckles white.

My Lord, my God, let me serve Thee. Let me die for Thee, if it is Thy will.

The sails whipped in the wind as the helmsman leaned on the long tiller. Sailors clambered up the rigging to their positions on the fore and main masts. As they entered the harbour, he watched the waves send sprays of foam high up the walls of the great fort.

Beyond the Crusader turrets and barbicans William saw the domes of the Mohammedan mosques and the towers of the minarets. Their presence served as a reminder that even here the Lord was under siege. The Saracen halls had long since been consecrated as Christian churches, but the thick castle walls were all that lay between the pilgrims and the godless hordes. With Jerusalem lost, Acre was a symbol of hope to everyone in Christendom, an outpost of God among the heathen.

And he was to be its saviour.

But the heady promise of his arrival had not been fulfilled. Far from being an outpost of the sacred, the city was just another stinking, hot Saracen town. The narrow streets were crowded with heathen, the turbans and chadors of the Jews and Mohammedans bobbing everywhere, the alleys choked with their filth and excrement, the stench that rose from the cobblestone alleys almost tangible. The bazaars were clamorous from dawn to dusk with the jibber-jabber of the hawkers.

The swarthy, hook-nosed Mohammedans stared back at him from under their keffiyehs, their hawk eyes glittering with venom. He felt sullied by their looks, if not threatened, for the Templar sentries stood watch at every gateway of the city, distinctive in their white surcoats with red cross pattée.

The number and brazenness of the heathen astonished him. But it was the lords of Acre themselves who confounded him, as they would any good Christian. The palaces in which they lived were decked with marble, the walls furnished with silk carpets and high ceilings. They lived lives of sumptuous decadence, an offence to any God-fearing Christian.

They had even insulted him on the evening of his arrival by offering him a bath.

They wore loose silk robes and sometimes even turbans, in imitation of the Saracens. Their wives dressed like Muslims, with veils and jewelled tunics and flowing robes, and they employed kohl and perfumes like the common houris of Damascus.

It was hardly what he had expected to find when he left Rome.

The holy cause in Outremer had met with disaster upon disaster over the last two decades. Jerusalem, which had been wrested from the infidel at the urging of the Pope two centuries before, was once more lost to the Saracen, sacked by a horde of Turks in the pay of Sultan Ayub in 1244. It was just a decade ago that Louis IX of France had himself taken up the Cross to save the Holy City from the heathen but his expedition had found disaster in the Nile delta and Louis himself had been taken prisoner and held for ransom.

William had thought to find those beleaguered garrisons yet in Christian hands – Acre, Antioch, Jaffa, Sidon – expending all their might and energy on the recapture of the Holy City. Instead they seemed more taken with commerce, trading openly with the Saracens and keeping friendly relations with them. The merchants of Genoa, Pisa and Venice even battled with one another over trade routes.

The great mosque of Acre had been converted, quite properly, into a Christian church, but to William's horror he discovered a side chapel that had been set aside for the Mohammedans to worship in. He had been further outraged to discover that the mosque at the Oxen's Well had not been consecrated at all and that the Mohammedans still prayed there openly; there was a Christian altar *alongside* that of the heathens.

The city was not the repudiation to the Saracen that he had expected to find. There were even prostitutes and vendors of hashish on the streets.

But he was on the Pope's special embassy and he could not allow the decadence that had insinuated itself here to deter him from his commission. And judging by the news he had just received, he had not a moment to lose.

✛

The Kingdom of Jerusalem was governed by a monarch, with the aid of a council made up of the leading barons and churchmen of the realm. But there had been no council for two years, as the Crusader states of Acre and Tyre were at war over the succession.

For three years now, the Tatar armies had been making their way westwards, had torn down the mountain citadel of the dreaded Hashishim at Alamut, and had then sacked Baghdad, where they had massacred countless tens of thousands, fouling the air so badly with the stench of corpses that even their own soldiers had to withdraw from the city. Now, under their prince, Hülegü, they had reached the gates of Aleppo in Syria.

After Aleppo, the Holy Land lay open to them.

Perhaps that would get the barons of Jerusalem out of their *baths*.

VI

✠

A MARBLE CHAMBER with vaulted ceilings, the walls hung with silk carpets. It opened on to a shaded courtyard with a fountain bubbling at its centre. On the other side there was a fine view of the winter sea. An onshore breeze raised whitecaps under a washed blue sky. In Rome there would be snow on the fir trees and ice in the wells.

The barons sprawled on divans, in their Saracen robes, while olive-skinned women in silk qamis, their wrists and ankles adorned with gold bangles, served them sherbets from silver jugs. There were little tables with copper salvers of melons and figs for their further refreshment. Other Saracens played drums and lutes in a corner of the room.

They all watched William stamp across the room, every inch a Dominican in his black and white habit and tonsured blond head.

'Brother William,' one of the them said, after his commission from the Pope had been read, 'I am sorry we are not properly ready to receive you. We have no bed of nails prepared, just these soft cushions, I fear.'

There was a bubble of laughter.

William ignored the jibe. In the last few days he had come to expect no less from this rabble, despite their noble birth. He looked around at the great gathering: counts and constables, bailos and barons, a handful of Venetian merchants – fops and sodomites the lot of them – as well as the patriarch of Jerusalem, Reynald.

A surfeit of jewels and indolence. Only one sober presence, that of Thomas Bérard, the Englishman, Grand Master of the Knights Templar. He had with him an escort of ten soldiers, who waited, a silent but ominous presence, by the door, distinctive in their white surcoats with the splayed red cross pattée on the left breast. They had cropped hair and wore beards, in contrast to the long hair and clean-shaven faces of the other nobles.

The Templars were the best soldiers in Christendom. Unlike the other knights and lords they owed their loyalty to no king; they were answerable only to the Pope himself. Yet because service in the Order guaranteed remission for all sins, the Templars also attracted rapists, heretics, even murderers to their ranks.

Malcontents and assassins. He didn't trust any of them.

Especially that giant with the chestnut beard, lounging against the wall, his face creased in a smile of detached amusement. William detested him instantly.

Geoffrey of Sargina, the bailo, brought the meeting to order. He described the latest news from the East and the sweeping gains the Tatars had made in the last few months.

'The question that faces us,' he concluded, 'is whether we confront these Tatars as a threat to our own sovereignty in these lands, or embrace them as allies in our fight against the Saracen.'

'Perhaps we are a little tardy,' one of the barons said, sucking on a fig. 'Bohemond of Antioch has already rushed to submit to this Hülegü like a dog begging for scraps.'

Hugues de Pleissy, Bohemond's representative at the meeting reacted angrily. 'It is a prudent alliance, no more! In return for his cooperation Hülegü has offered to march with him to retake Jerusalem!'

'Retake it, yes. But will he let us keep it?'

Count Julian was their host here in Acre. It appeared to William he spent more time fighting to stay awake than fighting for God. He lounged on the divan and offered them all an unctuous smile. 'Bohemond got what he wanted. Hülegü has granted him extra territories.'

'Which the Tatars have looted and burned just the same.'

'The Tatars claim their khan has the right to universal domination!' another of the barons shouted. 'It is blasphemous! It is as much an affront to the Christian Church as the presence of the Saracen in the Holy Sepulchre!'

Thomas Bérard, the Templar, was the voice of sweet reason itself. 'Our position here is not strong. If we treat with them we may yet turn the tables on the Saracens.'

'Treat with them?' one of the barons shouted. 'Are we to forget what they did in Poland and Hungary? It is only two decades since they laid waste half of Christendom and burned and raped their way almost to the gates of Vienna. And you say treat with them? It is like getting rid of an unwanted dog by inviting a bear into your house!'

William had been just a child when these events had taken place, but he had heard the stories. The Tatar hordes had appeared without warning in the East, cutting a swathe through vast tracts of Russia, laying whole cities to waste and slaughtering tens of thousands. They took Moscow, Rostov and Kiev, and then decimated the armies of Poland and Silesia. At the battle of Liegnitz they had cut an ear from every corpse and worn them as necklaces as they rampaged on through Hungary and Dalmatia.

A plague of black rats followed the Tatars into Europe. It was said at the time that the devil horsemen had sprung from Hades itself, to punish those who had not been faithful to Christ. Everyone in his home town of Augsburg had taken sanctuary in the church, thinking it was the time of the final judgement.

But just as suddenly the Tatars disappeared, riding back the way they had come.

'These Tatars are not men,' one of the Venetians was saying. 'They eat their prisoners. The women they ravish until they die and then they cut off their breasts as dainties. They eat snakes and drink human blood.'

'Did you hear what they did at Maiyafaqin?' another said. 'They took the emir as their prisoner and cut pieces of his flesh away, toasted them over a slow fire and forced them down his throat. It took him hours to die.'

'Of course we have never stooped to such barbarous acts in Outremer,' the giant with the chestnut hair said.

The conversation stopped for a moment and the others stared at him, unsettled by this pricking of their own consciences. But Bérard did not reprimand him. Instead he smiled indulgently into his beard. 'They also say that this Hülegü's general is a descendant of one of the Three Kings who brought gifts to Our Saviour. Indeed, did not William of Rubruck report that Hülegü's own wife was Christian?'

William remembered this Rubruck, a Franciscan monk who had

been sent as emissary to the Tatars by King Louis. He had travelled through Russia to the Tatar capital some five years before and returned with tales of Christians living among the barbarians.

What credence could be given to his claims was another matter.

Anno von Sangerhausen, Grand Master of the Teutonic Knights, spoke next. He had no love of the Templars but on this point at least they were of one mind. He slapped his leather gauntlets into the palm of his hand impatiently. 'I say we offer them a parlay.'

Geoffrey of Sargina stroked his chin, disturbed by the clear divisions among them. 'Before we decide on this, I must tell you all some further news. We have received, under flag of truce, a message from the Saracens, from their prince, Baybars. He wishes to offer us an alliance against the Tatars.'

'Of course he wishes it,' Bérard exploded, laughing. 'He doesn't want his ear on a Tatar belt!'

'I say we do not make alliance with either of them,' Count Julian said. 'Let their two armies fight each other. When they are both exhausted we may think again. Side with the victor if he is yet strong; crush him if he is weak. Then, whatever happens, we cannot lose.'

And so it went on, hour after hour, until the shadows crept across the courtyard and the first bright stars appeared on the velvet horizon. William felt his frustration growing. Privately, he agreed with those that said that the Tatars were as much an abomination as the Saracens. But he had his sacred commission from the Pope himself and, regardless of the outcome of this meeting, he must see it through.

'So, what say you, William?' Geoffrey of Sargina said at last, appearing physically exhausted by the arguments that had raged around him for the last two hours.

'My opinion in this is of no account,' he said. 'I am not here to sanction your actions. I have on my person a letter from the Pontiff for the prince of the Tatars, to be delivered by my hand.'

'And what does it say?' Geoffrey demanded.

'I have been charged to bring the letter to the Tatar prince, not to the bailo of Jerusalem. It is also my trust to bring the reply direct to the Holy Father in person. Further than that, I cannot say.' William was delighted to see the anger and dismay on the faces of the nobles around him. 'The Holy Father has also charged me with preaching the doctrine of our faith to the Tatars,' he went on, 'and he has given me the authority to establish churches and ordain priests among them.'

'The Pope thinks he can convert the Tatars?' Count Julian said, his voice choked with disbelief.

'I do not deem to know the mind of the Holy Father. But, like you, he has received reports that there are Christians among them and feels that it is time to exercise God's will and bring all believers into the arms of the Holy Mother Church.'

They all muttered into their beards. Christians they might be, but not all of them regarded the Pope with the veneration that they might.

A gloomy and profane silence fell on the discussion.

'What of Prester John?' someone said.

Prester John was the legendary priest-king, a descendant of the Magi, who many believed would come from the East to save Christendom in its darkest hour. His name had first been spoken in Rome 150 years before.

'Isn't he a little old to save us now?' the giant Templar muttered.

William glared at him but the Templar stared him down. 'Some believe that John may have been vanquished by the Tatars,' William went on, 'and that their king then married John's daughter. It is their descendant who now sits on the Tatar throne and this is why we hear talk of Christians among them. We may yet find our salvation there.'

'It is a possibility we should not ignore,' Geoffrey said.

Thomas Bérard nodded. 'If Father William wishes to arrange a meeting with this Hülegü, then we shall be happy to accommodate him, as our charter requires us to do.'

'What do you suggest?' Geoffrey asked him.

'We can arrange for him to be escorted to Aleppo under flag of truce to deliver his message. One of my own knights can serve him as escort and interpreter. This man might also serve as our spy, so that we may better know the mind of this Tatar before we proceed.'

Geoffrey nodded, thoughtfully. 'Do you have someone in mind for this charge?'

'Indeed, I have,' he said. 'He speaks Persian, Arabic and Turkic, and is as accomplished at diplomacy as he is at arms.' Bérard smiled and looked over his shoulder at the giant knight with the chestnut hair. 'May I present to you Josseran Sarrazini. This man I would trust with my life.' Then he added: 'He may even save yours, Brother William. If it suits him.'

☨

When they left meeting Bérard took Josseran aside. 'Try not to slit his throat the moment you are outside the castle walls.'

'Why would I do that?'

'I know what you think of churchmen like him.'

'I came here to fight for God not the Dominicans. But I also took an oath of obedience and if you say I must escort this fool on his errand, then that is what I shall do.'

'You have almost completed your five years of service. You could ask to be relieved of this duty.'

Josseran thought about it. For a moment he was almost tempted. A long journey in the company of a Dominican friar was not a proposition he relished.

'I have nothing to hurry back to France for. I am not sure I know how to take up my former life. Besides, France is full of men like this William now. At least here there is only one.'

☨

The smells of the city were themselves an assault on the senses. Gasping from the stink of ordure, Josseran took two more paces along the alley and smelled jasmine; taking a deep breath he caught a whiff of offal left to dry in the sun on the bare brick window of a butcher, but then was immediately seduced by the heady scent of cardamom and cumin at a spice merchant just another step further on.

Veiled women, arms jingling with gold hooped bracelets, hurried past him, hugging the walls. The huge brown eyes behind their veils betrayed hate and fear in equal measure. Long-bearded Armenians in blue turbans and barelegged water carriers jostled him and he was as careless of them as he would have been of any French burgher or peasant in Troyes.

☩

The street was so steep it was like a stone ladder, but he could have found his way along it blindfold. He ducked his head into a dark vaulted passageway, emerging suddenly into a small square court-yard, fringed with yellow sand. Three servant girls were squatting on straw mats spinning wool. They looked up as he entered, but he was a familiar presence here, and they quickly returned to their work.

A broad square of red cloth had been stretched over the court to shade it from the worst of the midday sun, but the heat radiated from the whitewashed walls like a brick oven. A rampart looked out over the harbour where the tips of yellowed sails drifted past, but the sea offered up only a scrap of breeze.

The light was intense. It was the one thing that he would miss when he returned to Burgundy. Even on its fiercest summer days the light was never like this.

The striped curtain that had been drawn across the door was flung aside and Simon stepped out. He looked like a bear in a djellaba and skullcap, and was almost as tall as Josseran himself. His salt and pepper ringlets and beard framed a broad smile.

'Friend,' he said and embraced him. 'Come inside. Drink tea with me.'

It was blessedly cool inside, the thick stone walls keeping out the worst of the heat. It was dark, and redolent with the frankincense that burned in copper censers hanging from the ceiling. There were rich carpets on the walls and the floor. Simon clapped his hands and a woman brought tea and a tray of almonds.

'So, you are leaving us?' Simon said.

'You know already?'

'All everyone does in this city is gossip. I probably knew about the envoy from Rome before you did.'

'Then I did not need to come and bring you the news.'

Simon clapped him on the shoulder. 'You came because we are friends and you wanted to say goodbye.'

Doves fussed and fluttered around the window. 'I am going to miss this,' Josseran said.

'I will still be here when you return.'

Josseran shrugged his shoulders. If I return.

Simon must have known what he was thinking, for he said: 'Is it dangerous, what you are about to do?'

'Being a Templar is always dangerous.'

'Not as dangerous as being a Jew.'

Josseran smiled. 'You are probably right.'

'Before I forget!' Simon said and jumped to his feet. He opened an iron-banded chest in a corner of the room and took out a small crimson velvet pouch. He handed it to Josseran. 'For your protection on your journey.'

'What is it?'

'Something of no use whatever to a Jew like myself.'

Josseran loosened the drawstring. A heavy crucifix fell into the palm of his left hand. He held it towards the light. It was made of burnished copper and inset with garnets. 'How did you come by this?'

'It was given to me as part of a transaction I made a long time ago. It is very old, I believe, five or six centuries, perhaps more. The man who sold it to me said his father found it many years ago near a convent high in the Languedoc. He believed it has a certain magic to it.'

'Why did he sell it?'

'He was dying and he had no further need of magic. He wanted the money instead, to give to his concubine. Would you like it?'

'I should never shun good fortune, or a gift from a friend.'

'Now you have both.'

Josseran put the cross around his neck. It felt curiously warm against his skin. Then they drank tea and sampled sweetened almonds from an enamelled dish and Simon tried to explain to Josseran the rudiments of al'jibra. At home, Josseran thought, I should drink myself senseless on ale, tear at a joint of beef with my teeth and talk endlessly about jousting. Perhaps I am getting soft living here.

He said goodbye to his friend and made his way back up the alley towards the castle. How strange that I should feel so at home here among these hawk-eyed traders and veiled women. I speak Latin more often than I speak French and Arabic more than I speak Latin. His best friend was not a soldier but a heathen and a usurer and, thanks to him, he knew the Talmud, the Q'ran and the Kabbalah as well as he knew the Gospel. He had found more kinship with a man whose ancestors had murdered Jesus than with his own kind.

He feared he was becoming a stranger to his fellows and a foreigner to his friends. But should he not return from Aleppo he yet hoped to find heaven. At least there he might find a corner where he belonged.

VII

✠

Fergana Valley

THE STEPPES WERE dusted with snow. The air was brittle, under a sky of endless blue. Two figures, wrapped in furs, were silhouetted against the morning sun, their broad-shouldered ponies at the walk.

'You had to win,' Tekudai said. 'He would have made as fine a husband as any other. Father wanted it. His father wanted it. I think perhaps *you* even wanted it. But no. You had to win. You always have to win.'

She ignored him. Her breath formed white clouds on the air.

'You have to get married some time,' he said, pressing her.

He is jealous, she thought. It burned in him, this envy, for he was not like Gerel. Gerel was drunk on black koumiss all the time. He cared for nothing else. Tekudai was a warrior with a warrior's soul. But simple. He had neither the brains of a general nor the athleticism of a good horseman. She knew she had been favoured by the gods with both and it rankled with her brother that she was the better hunter and the better horsewoman.

And that she was their father's favourite, as her mother had been. Her father had three other wives now, as well as concubines, in the Tatar custom, but it was still Bayaghuchin he grieved for.

She had died when Khutelun was ten years old. Bayaghuchin had been Qaidu's first wife. Khutelun remembered her as strong and straight and with a temper to match. She was a woman in the mould of a true Tatar; it was said that even Chinggis Khan had been afraid of his wife. But Khutelun had not only inherited her mother's fire; she had her gifts as a seer as well.

Suddenly there was movement on the steppe. Two marmots, ground squirrels, perhaps two hundred paces distant, whistled in perplexity at the appearance of these intruders in the vast emptiness.

One scampered underground, the other hesitated, head jerking quizzically, tail erect.

Khutelun had her bow to her shoulder first, the arrow already in her right hand, her movements so swift and practised it was as natural to her as blinking. Her first arrow – there would not have been time for a second – took the small creature cleanly through the skull, death swift and merciful. More food for the pot that night, some meat for the winter stew.

Tekudai had yet to draw back his own bowstring. He replaced the arrow in the wooden quiver at his waist. Their eyes met.

He hated her.

VIII

✠

the Templar fortress at Acre

A SARACEN MOON rose over the lighthouse, a perfect crescent. Josseran stood on the parapet, staring at the sleeping city. He could hear the rush of the ocean against the rocks below.

The great monastery of San Sabas loomed in the darkness, on a hill between the Venetian and Genoese quarters. It had been abandoned by the monks who lived there several years before and had immediately become a point of contention between the two rival merchant communities. Each had tried to gain possession of it, first by legal wrangling in the Haute Cour, then by force. Pitched battles in the street had led to a full-scale civil war, with the barons and military orders being forced to take sides. The survival of the Crusader states themselves, after all, depended on the sea power of the Italian merchants.

The war had culminated in a naval battle off Acre just eighteen months before in which the Venetians had sunk twenty-four Genoese ships. An uneasy truce had been patched together by the Pope. But the dispute still simmered, with the Genoese having now abandoned Acre for Tyre, to the north.

We were supposed to be fighting the Saracens.

Josseran picked out other landmarks in the darkness: the tall, graceful silhouette of St Andrew's Church; the palace of the governor in the Venetian quarter; the cathedral of the Holy Cross; the Dominican monastery in Burgos Novos; and in the distance, on the northern walls, the Accursed Tower and the Tower of St Nicholas.

He knew this city now better than he knew Paris or Troyes. Five years he had been in Outremer and he barely recognized himself as the zealot who had first stepped on these shores, fervent, conscience-weary, afraid. On leaving France he had secured a loan of two thousand shillings from the Templar preceptory to make his way to Acre. In return he had pledged his properties to the Templar lodge should he not return from his pilgrimage.

Five years!

He had changed so much. At home he and his fellow Franks had dressed in furs and gorged themselves on beef and pork. He rarely washed his body, believing that he would make himself sick with chills. What a savage I was! Here he ate little meat and supped from copper salvers of oranges, figs and melons, drank sherbets instead of mulled wines. He bathed at least three times a week.

He had been taught from a child that the Mohammedans were the embodiment of the Devil himself. But after five years in Acre he sometimes wore robes and turbans in the Saracen manner, and had learned from these same devils a little of mathematics and astronomy and poetry. The Temple even kept Mohammedan prisoners as artisans or armourers and saddlers. Over time he had formed tentative friendships with several of them, had come to see them as men like himself.

I don't know if I can ever go home now. I don't even know where my home is.

His regime as a Templar was strict. In winter his day began just before dawn; after prime he would check his horses and their harnesses, inspect his weapons and armour and those of his sergeants-at-arms. Then he would undertake his own training and that of his men: the constant practice with lance, mace, sword, dagger and shield. He would eat his first meal at noon and not sup again till the evening. He would recite a dozen paternosters each day, fourteen every hour, and eighteen for vespers. It was the life of a warrior monk.

He had thus made his pilgrimage, done his penance, almost served the five years of his pledge. The chaplain said he was forgiven all his sins. So why then did he still feel this heaviness in his heart? Soon it would be time to return to France and resume the patrimony of his father's lands. He should be more eager for that homecoming.

He heard a footfall on the stone in the darkness and turned around. His hand went instinctively to his sword. So many assassins in this accursed city. 'Put away your sword, Templar,' a man said, in Latin.

He recognized the voice. The Dominican friar, William.

'They told me I would find you here,' he said.

'I often find comfort in the night.'

'And not in the chapel?'

'There are fewer hypocrites up here.'

The friar came to stand at the battlements and looked towards the harbour, his face in silhouette. The Dominicans. *Domini canes*, as some wits would have it, 'the bloodhounds of the Lord'. The order had been founded by the Spaniard, Guzmán, the one they now called St Dominic, during the crusade in the Languedoc. They had set themselves the task of eradicating heresy and bringing Europe under the heel of the clerics.

They had the Pope's ear. A Dominican had held the position of Master of the Sacred Palace, personal theologian to the Pope himself, since the days of Guzmán. In 1233 Gregory IX had entrusted them with the holy work of the Inquisition.

They were all meddlers and murderers, in Josseran's opinion. The one thing you could say about them was that they were not hypocrites like the bishops and their priests; they did not get their housemaids pregnant and they kept to their vows of poverty. But they were cruel and joyless creatures. The tortures and burnings they were responsible for in the Languedoc were simply unspeakable. All done in the name of God, of course. Josseran hated every single one of them.

'It seems we are to be companions,' William said.

'It would not have been my choice.'

'Nor mine. I have heard of the vices and treachery of Templars.'

'I have heard the same things said of priests.'

William gave a short, barking laugh. 'I have to know. Why were you chosen?'

'You heard what Bérard said of me. I know how to use a sword and I ride passably well. And I am skilled in certain languages. It is a gift it pleased God for me to possess. Do you have anything besides Latin?'

'Such as?'

'It is hard to make any commerce in Outremer unless you speak a little Arabic.'

'The language of the heathen.'

Josseran nodded. 'Our Lord spoke Latin, of course, when he

strolled through Nazareth.' William did not reply and Josseran smiled to himself. A small victory. 'So you speak only Latin and German. A fine ambassador the Pope has chosen for the East.'

'I speak French passably well.'

'That should be useful in Syria.'

'If you are to be my interpreter I expect you to serve me faithfully.'

'I am to be your escort, not your servant.'

'You should know that I shall tolerate no interference in my plans.'

'Should I get in your way, you can always go on alone.'

William reached out his hand and touched the crucifix that hung on a silver chain at Josseran's throat. Josseran knocked his hand away.

'A pretty piece,' William said. 'Where did you get it?'

'That is none of your business.'

'Is it gold?'

'Gilded copper. The stones are garnets. It is very old.'

'It is just that you do not appear to me to be a man of much piety. And yet you have come here to fight in Christ's army. Why the Templars? They shelter all sorts of criminals, I hear.'

'I may not be a man of much piety but you do not appear to be a man of much diplomacy. And yet they have sent you here as an ambassador.'

'I hope your master knows the kind of man in whose hands he has entrusted my life.' William turned on his heel in the darkness. Josseran scowled. Priests! But the charter of the Templars required that he guard him well and endure his arrogance all the way to Aleppo. With God's speed the journey should take no longer than a month.

He turned back to the night and its stars, wondering where fate might bring him by the time the moon waxed full.

IX

✠

THE NEXT MORNING, at dawn, Josseran arrived at the wharf with his sergeant-at-arms, one Gérard of Poitiers, and provisions for the journey. He brought three horses. His big war horse, his destrier, he left behind but he had brought his favourite white Persian, Kismet. Gifts for the Tatar prince were locked in an iron-bound money chest; there was a damascened sword with gold quillon and motifs in Arabic script, an ebony inkstand ornamented with gold, a suit of chain mail, a mail helmet, some gauntlets of tooled red leather and a handful of rubies. He also had a quantity of golden Arab dinars and silver drachmas at his disposal, to use as he saw fit.

They boarded the two-deck galley and joined the captain on the poop deck. The morning was still and the flag with its red cross pattée hung limp at the stern rail. Their supplies were unloaded from a creaking wagon. The packhorses that would carry them were led up the gangway, followed by the servants he had brought to mind them and cook the food.

Finally William appeared, a sombre presence on a fine morning in his black-cowled robe. His face was grey.

'I trust this morning finds you well,' Josseran said to him.

William produced a perfumed handkerchief from his robe and put it to his nose. 'I do not know how any man can bear the stench.'

Yes, the stench. It was true, it was intolerable. It came from below, from the Mohammedans manacled to the oars on the slave deck, their own faeces lapping around their ankles in the bilges.

'I have found since I have been in this land that a man may grow accustomed to any vileness,' Josseran said. He turned and murmured to Gérard, who stood beside him. 'Even that of churchmen.' Well, not quite. The idea of chaining men to galley benches offended him as much as it did the friar.

'I fear my stomach will revolt,' William said.

'Then it behoves you to remove yourself to the side,' Josseran said and led him to the starboard rail of the galley. A moment later they heard the friar revisiting his breakfast.

The sounds of the morning – the booming of a drum, the flat slap of the slave master's whip, the clank of manacles – mingled with groans. The oars dipped for a moment, seawater glistening on the blades, then moved in time with the great drum as the galley sliced across the smooth waters of the harbour towards the mole.

Josseran looked back at the colonnaded piazza of the Venetian quarter, its three broad gateways open to the sea, the *fondachi* flying the Golden Lion pennants. Beside the Iron Gate, the old Genoese warehouse presented a sheer wall to the harbour. The chain was lowered and their bow cut between the breakwater under the shadow of the Tower of Flies. Their captain set their course towards Antioch. Josseran stared at the familiar barbicans of the Templar fortress on the Dread Cape. He had the uneasy feeling that he would never see them again.

✝

Josseran and William spoke little on the sea journey north. There was a palpable air of tension among the crew until they had passed Tyre, for the Genoese and Venetians were still raiding each other's merchantmen and no one could be sure that even a Templar galley might not be attacked. The soldiers prowled the rigging, crossbows slung over their shoulders, their faces grim.

Josseran was gratified to note that the good friar spent most of his time bent over the stern, heaving bile into the ocean. He was not accustomed to finding satisfaction in other men's discomfort but William somehow invited it.

The Dominican arrived in Antioch stinking and foul. As they stood on the dock at St Symeon even Kismet twitched her nostrils at the smell of him.

'You should have no trouble finding a bath house, even in Antioch,' Josseran said to him.

William stared at him as if he had spoken a blasphemy. 'Are you mad? You wish me to catch the vapours and die?'

'In this climate we find such indulgences welcome, even necessary.'

'Indulgence is all I have found among you and your kind thus far.' He staggered on to the wharf.

Is he going to stink like that all the way to Aleppo? Josseran wondered. This is going to be a long journey.

X

✠

Antioch

THE BYZANTINE WALLS had been built by the Emperor Justinian,
one spanning the river Orontes, two more winding up the precipi-
tous heights of Mount Silpius to the citadel. In all there were four
hundred towers commanding the plains around Antioch.

Prince Bohemond may have negotiated a truce with the Tatars
but on first impression Antioch did not seem a city at its ease. There
were soldiers everywhere, and fear was etched into the faces of the
Mohammedans in the medinas. Everyone had heard what had
happened at Aleppo and Baghdad.

Bohemond's welcome was cool. He had no love for the Pope or
any of his emissaries. But Josseran was a Templar and no one in
Outremer wanted to offend one of *them*.

From the citadel Josseran looked back over his shoulder, at the
whitewashed villas that clung to the slopes of Mount Silpius below,
descending to the cramped and twisted streets of the city. Through
the haze that clung to the plain he could just make out the glimmer
of the sea at St Symeon.

They were escorted to Bohemond's private audience chamber. It
was sumptuously furnished, but the most remarkable thing about it
was not the silk kilims on the floors or the silver ewers, but Bohemond's
personal library. The walls were lined with thousands of beautifully
bound books, many of them in Arabic, learned books on such arcane
matters as alchemy and physic and what Simon called *al'jibra*.

Tools of the devil, William said.

Bohemond was seated on a low divan. Before him was a table
piled with fruits. There was a huge carpet of lustrous design on the
floor, its centrepiece a hanging votive light, woven in crimson and
gold and royal blue. A fire blazed in the hearth.

'So I hear you are going to convert the Tatars to Christ!' Bohemond jeered at William by way of welcome.

'*Deus le volt*,' William answered, using the words that had sent the first crusade to the Holy Land. 'God wills it.'

'Well, you know that Hülegü's wife is Christian,' he said.

'I have heard these rumours.'

'Not rumour. It is true.'

'And this Hülegü himself?'

'The Tatar himself is an idolater. I have treated with him person-ally. He has eyes like a cat and smells like a wild goat. Yet he has humbled the Saracens in their own cities, something we have failed to do in one hundred and fifty years of war. He seems to do well enough without God on his side.' There was a sharp intake of breath as William reacted to this blasphemy. Bohemond ignored him and turned to Josseran. 'And what of you, Templar? Are you simply escort for our friar here, or do you Templars wish to make alliance with them, as I did?'

Josseran wondered at this remark. Did he have a spy behind the walls at Acre? 'I am just a humble knight, my lord,' Josseran answered.

'I have yet to meet any Templar I would call humble.' Bohemond got up and went to the window. He watched a shepherd boy scramble after his goats as they scampered through the olive groves below the citadel. 'What do they say about me in Acre?'

Josseran imagined he already knew the answer to his question, and so he told him the truth: 'There are some who call you wise, others who call you traitor.'

Bohemond kept his back to them. 'Time will show that it is wisdom, not treachery, that spurred my actions. This is our one opportunity to rout the infidel from the Holy Land. You will see. Hülegü and I will ride side by side through the gates of Jerusalem.'

'If he enters as a baptized Christian, the Pope will join the thanks-giving,' William said.

'If the holy places are returned to us, what does it matter?' Bohemond said. When William did not answer, he added: 'You have requested a guide and a dozen soldiers. So be it. My men will escort you to Aleppo where you may meet with the prince Hülegü. You will see for yourself that we have nothing to fear from him.'

'We thank you for your service to us,' Josseran said. Nothing to fear? he thought. Why then does my prince Bohemond look so afraid?

✛

They dined that evening at his court, and the next day they set off from Antioch with a squadron of Bohemond's cavalry at their back, the wagons containing their stores and the gifts for the Tatar trundling behind. Their Bedouin guide, Yusuf, rode at the van as their caravan wound its way into the hills heading east, to Aleppo, and an uncertain tomorrow.

XI

✠

Fergana Valley

'A RIDER CAME this morning, from Almalik,' Qaidu said. From his expression, Khutelun knew the news was all bad.

Qaidu sat facing the doorway of the yurt. On his right, the side of the mares, were his sons; on his left, the side of the cattle, Nambi, Qaidu's third wife, and Khutelun herself. Two other wives were also present, for it was the Tatar way for the advice of women to be sought on all matters but war and hunting.

The yurt was heavy with smoke and the smell of mutton fat. A branch cracked in the fire.

'Möngke, our Khan of Khans is dead,' Qaidu said. 'He died fighting the Soong in China, four moons past.'

'Möngke? Dead?' Gerel repeated. He was already drunk. Too much koumiss. Always too much koumiss.

There was a long and dreadful silence. Möngke's death meant that none of their lives would ever be the same. With the passing of a Great Khan the world would change irrevocably. Möngke had been Khaghan, chieftain of chieftains, for as long as he could remember.

'Möngke is dead?' Gerel repeated.

None of them minded that he was drunk; it was not a matter of shame among them. But drunkenness was not a great virtue in a chieftain, a khan. Let's hope he will never become one, Khutelun thought.

'You have been summoned to the *khuriltai*, the council?' Tekudai asked.

'Yes. All khans of the Tatar have been called to Qaraqorum for the election of our new Khaghan.'

'Möngke is dead?' Gerel said again, slurring the words. He

47

frowned and shook his head, as if he could not make sense of the words.

'Who will it be?' Nambi asked, ignoring her stepson.

Qaidu gazed into the fire. 'Hülegü has been absent from Qaraqorum now these ten years, warring in the west. Of Möngke's other brothers, only Ariq Bőke has the heart of a Tatar. Khubilai, Chinggis Khan's grandson wants to be Khaghan, but he has been in China too long.'

There was a loud, snorting sound, like a camel at a well. Gerel was asleep, snoring loudly.

'I fear Möngke will be our last Khan of Khans,' Qaidu said.

They fell silent again, in dread of their father's pronouncement.

'Berke is far to the north, in the Russias, with the Golden Horde. He will never return and he will not bow to the rule of his brothers. Hülegü, also, has carved out his own kingdom in the west and I doubt that he will bend the knee at the *khuriltai*. Our great people is dividing and in that there is peril for us.' He looked at Khutelun, his daughter, the shaman, the seer for the clan. 'Tonight you must commune with the spirits,' he said. 'You must see what they wish for us to do.'

☩

Khutelun, her head uncovered to the wind and her sash around her neck, stood alone on the ridge called The Woman is Going Away.

She knelt nine times, the customary way, in honour of Tengri, Lord of the Blue Sky. She sprinkled mare's milk on the ground as offering to the spirits who lived on the mountain, spilled more in the fast-flowing stream as sacrifice to the water sprites.

Afterwards she returned to her yurt where the embrace of the koumiss and hashish enveloped her like a mother's arms, and she danced in the sweet and cloying darkness, alone with her ancestors and the great star that blazed through the smoke hole in the roof. The shadows swayed and clawed; the moaning of the wind was a thousand voices of the dead, raised again to life by the rhythm and rattle of the shaman's drums.

But all the smoke-dreams would show her of the future was a man with hair the colour of fire, riding a horse as white as ice and as large as a yak; behind him were two other men, one dressed in black, the other in white with a cross the colour of blood emblazoned on the breast.

And in the dream the man with the fire-hair returned from the mountain with the body of a white goat and he laid it at the feet of her father and claimed Khutelun as his own.

XII

✠

the road to Aleppo

SHADOWS DANCED IN the olive trees behind the orange glow of the camp fire. A log crackled and tumbled into the flames in a small shower of sparks. The horses twitched at their tethers, and there was the low murmur of talk as William and Josseran and Gérard huddled together for warmth.

Bohemond's soldiers were asleep, except for two men that Josseran had posted sentry on the perimeter of the camp. The servants were huddled under the wagons. Yusuf, the old Arab guide, was the only other soul still awake at this hour of the watch, but he had sensed William's enmity and kept himself a little apart, out of the firelight.

Gérard, a lean young man with sparse hair and a wiry beard, spoke rarely, and contented himself with stirring the fire listlessly with a long stick.

William stared at Josseran. On the journey from Antioch the knight had taken to wearing a makeshift turban, which he wrapped around his head and his face to protect it from the wind and the sun. 'You look like a Saracen,' he said.

Josseran looked up. William's lips had cracked, and the skin on his face was already peeling from the effects of the harsh sun on his fair skin. 'And you look like a boiled peach.'

William saw Gérard smile.

'I am still curious about this cross you wear.'

'It was given me by a friend in Acre. A Jew.'

'You are friends with Jews?' William hissed. It confirmed his worst suspicions.

'He has been my language teacher this last five years.'

'Because a Jew is a teacher does not make him a friend. How long have you been in the Holy Land, Templar?'

'Five years.'

'A long time to be away from the company of civilized men.'

'The Jew who gave me this cross is one of the most civilized and learned men you will ever meet, priest. He taught me both Arabic and Turkic, without which you might as well be a dog barking here in Outremer. Besides, how may I be so far from civilized men when I am in the holy land where Our Lord was born?"

A fine speech, William thought. Why then, did he feel as if he was being mocked? 'Is that why you are here, to be closer to God?'

'I was told that the Holy Land needed knights like myself.'

'Indeed. The Holy Land is our sacred trust. That so many of the holy places are still in the hands of the Saracens is a foul stain on our honour and our faith. It is the duty of every good Christian to win them back.' He saw the expression on the knight's face and it irritated him. 'Is that not your belief, Templar?'

'I have been here five years. You have been here not five days. Do not tell me my duty in the Holy Land.'

'We are all here to serve Christ.'

Josseran stared moodily into the fire. Finally, he said: 'If one may serve Christ by killing men, slaughtering women and children, then Gérard and I shall surely shine resplendent in heaven.'

He saw another look pass between the two Templars.

'What do you mean by that?' William said.

Josseran sighed and tossed a stick on to the flames. 'I mean my duty in the Holy Land lies heavy on me, Brother William. I came here thinking to reclaim the Holy City from the Turk. Instead I have seen Venetians run their swords through the bellies of Genoese in the streets of Acre itself, and I have seen the Genoese do the same to the Venetians, in the monastery of St Sabas. Christian killing fellow Christian. How does that serve Christ? I have also seen good Christian soldiers rip children from their mother's wombs with their swords and I have seen them rape women and then cut their throats. These particular innocents were not occupying the holy places but were simple Bedouin fetching their sheep from the pastures. All done in the name of Our Saviour.'

'The Holy Father, as you know, was most offended to hear of the strife between the Venetians and Genoese, for he believes, as you do, that our warlike efforts should be turned against the infidel and not each other. But as for these innocents, as you call them . . . we kill sheep and pigs without sin. To kill a Saracen is no greater stain on the soul.'

'Sheep and pigs?' Gérard shifted uneasily and gave Josseran a warning glance.

But Josseran could not help himself. 'Do sheep and pigs have good physic? Do sheep and pigs know astronomy and the movement of the stars? Do sheep and pigs recite poetry and have their own music and architecture? The Saracens have all these things. I may dispute with them on religion but I cannot believe them to be just sheep and pigs.'

Astronomy and the movement of the stars? The Pope had made it a blasphemy to reach into the secrets of nature. It was clearly an unlawful invasion of the sacred womb of the Great Mother. On his last visit to Paris he had seen a family of Jews dragged from their house and beaten by a mob because they had been discovered secretly translating Arabic texts dealing with mathematics and alchemy.

'The heathen believe the world is round, in defiance of the laws of God and of heaven,' William said. 'Do you believe this, too?'

'All I know is that though they may not have faith, they are not animals.' He looked at Gérard. 'Tell him what happened to you.'

'When I was in Tripoli, I was kicked in the leg by a horse,' Gérard said. 'The leg became infected and an abscess formed. A Templar surgeon was about to cut off my leg with an axe. One of my servants sent for a Mohammedan doctor. He applied a poultice to the leg, and the abscess opened and I soon became well. You understand, Mohammedan or no, it is very hard for me to hate that man.'

'You have a blasphemous tongue, Templar. It was God that healed you. You should give thanks to the Lord, not the heathen.'

'I am tired of talking to priests,' Josseran said. He walked away and lay down on a blanket under the trees. Gérard followed.

William sat alone in the guttering firelight. He prayed to God for the soul of the Templar, as was his duty, and prayed also for strength for what was to come. He prayed long into the night, long after the fire had settled to embers, for he was deathly afraid of facing this Hülegü and he did not want the others to know.

XIII

✠

THEIR PROCESSION SNAKED across the hills, past villages with curious beehive-shaped mud-brick houses. Yusuf rode in front, Josseran and Gérard behind, the packhorses and carts spread along the trail behind them, Bohemond's soldiers at the centre. William followed at the rear, head stooped, already exhausted by the journey.

Josseran found a grim satisfaction in the priest's suffering.

They followed an old paved Roman road that cut through the rocky wastes, as it had since the days of the Book. Josseran was glad of Bohemond's soldiers, for the country was perfect for ambush, and he was sure they were being watched from the hills by Bedouin bandits. Not that he supposed they looked much like a rich Christian caravan, certainly not from their dress.

He and Gérard wore simple tunics made of *mosulin*, a fine cotton the Crusaders traded from the Turks in Mosul, and they had Mohammedan scarfs wrapped around their faces to keep the sun from burning their skin. Josseran had offered similar comforts to Brother William, who insisted instead on keeping the heavy woollen cowl he had brought with him from Rome. His face was already beet red.

They enjoyed their suffering, his lot.

By late afternoon, their journey had settled to drowsy fatigue; Gérard and William dozed in the saddle, lulled by the heat of the sun on their backs, the creak of the wagons and the dull clip of the horse's hooves. The stony Syrian hills stretched away all around them.

They smelled them before they heard them. Their ponies reacted first, twitching and stamping their hooves. Yusuf reined in his horse and twisted in the saddle.

'What is wrong?' William shouted.

They appeared suddenly and from nowhere. Their helmets

flashed in the sun, their red and grey standards whipped from pennant lances. Yusuf shouted an oath. His eyes were wide, like a horse running from a fire.

But the horsemen had already outflanked them, in an expert pincer movement, executed at the gallop. Gérard instinctively reached for his sword but at a sharp command from Josseran he sheathed it again. Bohemond's soldiers, too, had been taken by surprise and sat docile in their saddles, watching.

Josseran looked around at the friar. William sat calmly in the saddle, his face a mask. 'Well, Templar,' he shouted over the thunder of hooves, 'let us hope your Grand Master's faith in you was not misplaced.'

Kismet stamped her feet, excited by the charge and the foreign scent in her nostrils.

The horsemen whooped like devils as they completed the encirclement and then rushed towards them. There were perhaps as many as a hundred in the squadron. For a moment it seemed they would gallop over them but at the last moment they reined in their broad-shouldered ponies and stopped.

Then there was deathly silence, save for the occasional snort of a horse and jangle of traces. Josseran spat out their dust.

So. These were the dread Tatars.

Their stench was more horrible than their appearance. Their cheeks were the colour of boiled leather and without exception they had dark eyes that seemed to slant, and coarse, straight black hair. They wore little body armour, either a coat of mail or a cuirass of leather covered with iron scales. Each soldier had a lobster-tail helmet of leather or iron and a round, leather-covered wicker shield. In hand-to-hand combat they would be no match for a heavily armoured Frankish knight, Josseran thought. Yet he supposed, looking at the bows they carried with them, and the box-like quivers of arrows on their belts, they would never allow a superior enemy to get up close.

Their horses were scarcely bigger than mules; ridiculous, ugly animals with blunt noses and large shoulders. Was this really the most feared cavalry in the world?

One of the Tatars, wearing a gold-winged helmet, walked his pony forward and looked them over. Their officer, Josseran supposed. His eyes were golden and almond-shaped, like a cat. He had a wisp of a black beard and carried a battleaxe in his right fist.

'Who are you?' he said, in passable Arabic. 'Why do you approach Aleppo?'

Josseran removed the scarf he had coiled around his mouth and he saw a moment's surprise in the eyes of the Tatar officer at seeing his fire-gold beard. 'My name is Josseran Sarrazini. I am a knight of the Order of the Temple, assigned to the fortress of Acre. My lord is Thomas Bérard, Grand Master of the Order. I have been sent as ambassador to your prince, the lord Hülegü.'

'And what of the crow perched on the brown skeleton behind you?'

The crow. Josseran smiled. In his black habit, it was exactly what William looked like. 'He is a fellow ambassador.'

'He does not dress like one.'

'What does he say?' William said.

'He wishes to know our business.'

'Tell him I have a missive for his lord from the Pope himself.'

'Be patient and let me do the talking for us.'

'My name is Juchi,' the Tatar officer said. 'I will escort you to Aleppo. Hülegü, Khan of all Persia, will meet with you there.'

Josseran turned to William. 'They are going to take us to Aleppo to meet with Hülegü.'

'Good,' William said. 'I have had enough of this horse and your company already. I do not think I could stand another day of it.'

XIV

✠

THEY HEARD ALEPPO long before it came into view.

The city was in its death throes. Only the citadel, with its great barbicans and paved glacis, perched on a rock high above the town, still resisted the Tatar onslaught. Below the fortress, the town itself was already in the hands of the invaders, who had exacted swift retribution for the people's intransigence. Smoke rose from the gutted remains of the mosques and madrassahs, the pale blue sky merging with the yellow haze, streaked with smoke from burning fires.

It was the greatest siege army Josseran had ever seen. Herds of sheep and goats and packhorses and camels seemed to fill the entire plain. Even from a distance the booming of the Tatar kettledrums seemed to make the ground itself vibrate. He heard the braying of horses and camels and the screams of men fighting and dying below the walls as another charge was flung at the gates of the citadel.

'This could be Acre,' Josseran murmured. If their great enemy could be routed so easily, what chance would they stand against the barbarians?

They rode through the streets of the old bazaar, passed the smoking, blackened timbers of a merchant warehouse. The cobbles below their horses' hooves were slick with blood. The Tatar massacre had been chillingly efficient. Men and women and children lay where they had fallen; many of them had been beheaded and mutilated. The corpses had bloated in the sun and were covered with swarms of black flies that rose in murmurous clouds at their passage.

The stench of death was everywhere. Josseran thought he was accustomed to it, but even he had to swallow back the bile in his throat. William put a sleeve across his mouth, began to gag.

The Tatar soldiers stared at them with pure hate. They would rather cut our throats than parlay with us, Josseran thought, A regiment of Armenian foot soldiers trotted past, urged on by a Tatar drummer mounted on the back of a camel, beating a *naqara*, a war drum. This is why Hülegü found the alliance with Bohemond so useful, Josseran thought. He needs cannon fodder for the walls.

The dark, brooding presence of the citadel loomed above them. The sun had fallen behind the barbican, throwing the streets in shadow.

Squadrons of Tatar archers, armed with crossbows, were firing volleys of flaming arrows over the battlements. Nearby, huge siege engines had been drawn up. Josseran counted more than a score of them, great ballistae that hurled massive blocks of stone the size of houses. The walls of the fortress were pocked and battered from the daily assaults.

'Look!' Gérard hissed, pointing.

Instead of stones the engineers were loading one of the lighter siege engines, a mangonel, with what appeared to be small, blackened melons. It took him some moments to realize what they were: not melons, or stones, or weapons of any kind. They were loading the sling with scores of human heads. They would not bring down the Saracen walls but he could imagine the effect these grisly missiles would have on the defenders' morale.

The sling was released, with a hiss, and its gruesome cargo arced towards the burning walls.

A detachment of horsemen approached them through the smoke, the now familiar red and grey standards whipping from pennant lances.

Bohemond's soldiers had already dismounted and were kneeling beside their horses. Josseran and the others were slow to respond so Juchi's men dragged them from their saddles.

'What is happening?' William shrieked.

Josseran made no effort to resist. It was pointless. The Tatars forced them to their knees. From somewhere behind him he heard their guide, Yusuf, sobbing and begging for his life. William began to recite a prayer, the *Te Deum*.

Beside him Gérard had his face pressed into the dirt, a Tatar boot on his neck. 'Do they wish our heads for their catapults?' he whispered.

'If they do,' Josseran answered, 'the friar's will make a particularly fine, heavy one. It may even make the breach in the wall that they have been hoping for.'

He could feel the drumming under his knees from the hammer of the horses' hooves. Were they to die then, their faces in the dirt?

XV

✠

THE HORSEMEN STOPPED no more than twenty paces away; to a man they were armed with battleaxes and iron maces. Two of the Tatars walked their horses forward. One of them had a gold winged helmet and a leopard-skin cloak.

Hülegü.

Juchi fell to his knees. He said something to the khan and the general who attended him in a language Josseran had never heard before. Josseran used the moment to study this Tatar prince who had so easily accomplished what the Christian forces had failed to achieve – even with God's help – for almost two centuries; the rout of the Mohammedan world. He was an unlikely scourge, a small man with a smooth rounded face, a pug nose, and those same curiously almond-shaped eyes so distinctive of the Tatars.

This was not the meeting he had anticipated. He had imagined a great pavilion, where he would be presented before Hülegü's throne in formal court, not like this, thrust face-first into this blood-reeking street.

The sounds of the battle carried to him from the gates of the citadel, not two crossbow shots distant. A blast of trumpets signalled another attack, followed by the screams of men dying, and dying badly.

Hülegü's general addressed him, in imperfect Arabic. 'My captain says you are an ambassador from the Franks. You have come to make a treaty with us?'

'My name is Josseran Sarrazini. I have been sent by Thomas Bérard, Grand Master of the Order of the Temple, from his fortress at Acre in the Kingdom of Jerusalem. We have a common enemy, namely the Saracens, and my lord ventures to send his congratulations on your many successes and extends his hand in friendship.'

The general began to laugh, even before he had finished. Hülegü listened to the general's translation, his face impassive, and then spoke again in the strange new language.

'Our khan is not amazed that your lord extends his hand in friendship,' the general said, 'otherwise he may find it cut off.'

Josseran swallowed his anger at this insulting reply. But pride is not easy to maintain when you have your face next to the ground. 'We have no quarrel with your khan,' he answered carefully. 'Indeed, we may find common cause.' Josseran thought of Rubruck's reports that Hülegü's wife was Christian, that the Tatars had paraded a wooden cross through the streets of Baghdad. 'We Franks, too, are Christian.'

'What is going on?' William hissed.

William, of course, could not know that Josseran had just proposed the very treaty that so many of the Haute Cour opposed. It was a decision that had been reached by Thomas Bérard alone, on behalf of the Templars, before Josseran had left Acre. It would not be the first time the Templars had made a treaty independent of the other states. Yet this was the most dangerous game of any they had played. Once you took a bear about the neck, Josseran thought, you had best be sure you had a firm grip.

'He wishes to know what we want here,' he said to William.

'Have you told him I have a Bull for him from the Pope himself?'

'I doubt if this creature has even heard of the Pope, Brother William.'

'Then you must explain to him that the Pope is the leader of the Christian world and has sent me here to bring him and the rest of these barbarians to salvation!'

Josseran turned away. He intended no such thing. The Tatars might have their heads at any moment and he had no wish to die like this, grovelling at some savage's feet. He had promised himself that when he finally met his end it would be with a sword in his hand, in the service of Christ. It would at least make some recompense for his sins.

Hülegü was watching them, and Josseran imagined he saw uncertainty on his face.

'My lord Hülegü wishes to know what is this common cause you speak of,' the general asked.

'The destruction of the Saracens.'

The general laughed again. 'Like this, you mean?' He waved a hand in the direction of the town. 'As you can see we have destroyed the Saracens without the help of your Grand Master, as you call him.'

'Now what is he saying?' William shouted again, almost trembling with frustration.

'I do not think he is interested in us overmuch.'

'But he must hear the Bull from the Holy Father!'

Hülegü whispered something to his general. 'What is that creature and what does he say?' the general asked.

'He is one of our holy men, my lord.'

'Does he have magic to show us?'

Josseran was startled by the question. 'Magic? I fear he does not.'

The general passed this information to Hülegü, who seemed disappointed. There was another long conversation between the two Tatars.

'The great khan wishes to know if your lord will become his vassal, as the lord of Antioch has done, and pay him annual tribute.'

Josseran masked his surprise. This was not the relationship as Bohemond had described it. 'What we seek is an alliance against the Saracen. In return for our military aid we would have Jerusalem . . .'

Hülegü did not wait to hear the rest. He murmured a few words to his general and turned his horse away.

'The great khan says he cannot talk to you of an alliance. That is something only Möngke, the Khan of all Khans, can decide. You will be escorted into his presence. You may take your holy man with you. The rest of your party will stay here as hostage until your return.'

The general spoke rapidly to Juchi in the Tatar tongue and then he wheeled his horse away and followed the khan back to the walls of the citadel, their escort following in tight formation. The audience had been brutally swift, and was now, apparently, concluded.

They were all hauled back to their feet.

'What is to happen?' William shouted. 'What has taken place?'

'He says he does not have the authority to hear us. It seems there is a lord even higher than he. We are to be taken to him.'

'Where is this lord? How much further must we travel?'

'I do not know.'

He saw Gérard and Yusuf staring at him, their eyes wide. Unlike William, they had understood all that had been said.

'So,' Juchi laughed. 'You are to see Qaraqorum.'

'How many days travel is it?'

'Days?' The officer repeated what he had said to the rest of the Tatars and there was a howl of laughter. He turned back to Josseran. 'If you ride hard you might be there in four moons. With that elephant you ride you will be fortunate to arrive in eight!'

Josseran stared at him. Four *months*? It might take a man on a good horse so long to travel from Toulouse to Constantinople, the very breadth of Christendom. But eight months, twice that distance, heading east through and beyond the land of the Mohammedans, was simply inconceivable! They would fall off the edge of the world!

'And if we do not wish to go there?'

The Tatar laughed again. 'What you wish is of no account. It is what the khan wishes. And if he wishes it, then it is done.'

William was tugging at the sleeve of his tunic. 'What did they say? You must not make mystery of this!'

Eight months in the presence of this damnable churchman! If he survived. 'Just get on your horse,' he growled. 'We are going east. To some place called Qaraqorum. That's all I know.'

XVI

✠

Fergana Valley

A SKY AS grey as a corpse, mountains hidden behind a veil of cloud, with sleet drifting across the steppe. Wooden wheels crunched on the frost-hard earth. Two carts arrived, laden with tribute from the Kazaks at Almalik: furs of ermine and sable and two young girls for the harem.

Qaidu watched their arrival astride his favourite horse, the black stripes on its hind legs singling it out as a mare not long tamed from the wild herds that still roamed free on the northern steppe. A corona of fur wreathed his head and there were droplets of ice in his beard. He looked at the stacked furs and the two girls shivering on the back of the cart, his eyes hard rather than greedy, assessing their value as tribute with the practised gaze of a conqueror.

'Do they smell?' he said to Khutelun, turning his gaze to the women.

'They are sweet enough,' she answered. 'But although they are the prettiest of their women, they are only a little more comely than the yaks they have been herding. The Kazak are not a pretty people.'

Qaidu nodded, but she could see his mind was not on the women, but on politics.

'Chinggis's grandson Khubilai remains in Cathay fighting the Soong,' he said, reading the question in her eyes. 'Ariq Böke has called again for a *khuriltai* in Qaraqorum.'

'You will go?'

He shook his head. His gaze focused on the grey horizon, contemplating the uncertainty of a future without their Khan of Khans. 'I think it is better I stay here.'

She knew what he was thinking: if there was going to be blood-shed it was better to stay here and protect his own fief. 'A rider came from Bukhara this morning with news,' Qaidu said. 'There are ambassadors passing here on their way to Qaraqorum. We are asked to escort them as far as Besh Balik. I want you to lead that escort.'

Khutelun felt a surge of pride at being chosen before either of her brothers for the task. 'You will bring them here first, until the weather is better. But you will not take them to Besh Balik. Instead I want you to take them all the way to Qaraqorum.'

'Why?'

'So you can give Ariq Böke my support in the *khuriltai*. I cannot be deaf and blind to everything that happens.'

'I am honoured you trust me with this task, Father.'

'I have always trusted you, daughter. You are the ablest of all my children.'

It was the greatest compliment he had ever given her. If only I had been a son, she thought, I could have been khan. 'These ambassadors,' she asked him. 'Where are they from?'

'They are from lands far to the west. Barbarians. It seems they wish to prostrate themselves at the feet of our Khan of Khans.'

'But we have no Khan of Khans.' The process of the *khuriltai*, she knew, could take perhaps two or three years.

Qaidu shrugged. 'If we have no Khan of Khans,' he answered, 'then they will have to wait in Qaraqorum until there is one.'

PART II

The Roof of the World

Aleppo to Kashgar
northern spring,
in the year of Our Lord 1260

XVII

✠

How LONG HAD they been travelling? He had lost count of the weeks. Or was it months?

They had taken the great desert route from Aleppo, mile upon mile of hard gravel, the lonely province of goats and Bedouin shepherds. The Tatars had insisted they leave behind their carts with the heavy iron chests of provisions and the suit of chain mail Josseran had brought as a gift for the Tatar khan. The other gifts Josseran packed into a waterproof leather bag and carried on his horse. He himself wore the damascened sword.

William still clutched a leather satchel that he had brought with him from Acre. Josseran wondered what treasures he had decided were indispensable to his mission. A thumbscrew and a hair shirt perhaps.

Although it was yet winter the days were warm and William, unaccustomed to the heat and fatigued by the rigours of the journey, swayed from side to side on his mount. He will not last eight more days, never mind eight months, Josseran thought. They were all tortured by the flies that clustered at the corners of their eyes and mouths whenever they stopped to rest. Eight months! Josseran thought. Impossible. Juchi must have been trying to torment them.

✠

'I want you to teach me to speak Tatar,' Josseran said.

'You would find it too hard,' Juchi said, in Arabic.

'It sounds very much like Turkic and I already speak that well enough. I think you will find I have an aptitude. And we have nothing else to do on this interminable journey.'

'Where do you want me to start?'

'I already know Hello is *Salam*. Thank you is *Rèqmèt*. In the morning you say *Qaiyerle irtè* to each other. At night it is *Qaiyerle kiş*.'

Juchi laughed, delighted. 'Excellent. My men think you are as stupid as your horse, but they have underestimated you. Very well, Barbarian. As you say, we have nothing better to do while we ride. I will tell you a few words as we ride, and we shall see who learns to speak Tatar first, you or your horse!'

✠

One evening, not long after they had set out from Aleppo, one of the Tatars was bitten by a scorpion. He spent that entire night sobbing with pain, and died early the next morning. The incident chilled William to the marrow.

But visions of his Christ helped him endure. If this was to be his cross, his purgatory, then so be it. He would welcome his tribulations as scourge for his impure thoughts.

Horse dung clung to their damp clothes; the atmosphere inside the tent was ripe with it. William wiped his eyes, which were streaming, smarting from the fire smoke.

'You think they will eat us next?' he said to Josseran.

He had heard the legends about these people; that they drank blood and ate dogs and frogs and snakes, even each other. Watching them now, it was not difficult to imagine. He stared in disgust at the mess of sheep's intestines on the soaking grass in front of him. The Tatars laughed and encouraged him to eat as they wrenched tubes of offal from the steaming pile of guts with grease-blackened fingers. The rest of the animal, the fleece, the head and bloodied bones lay in a heap to one side.

The owner of the yurt had slaughtered the animal in their honour. Josseran had never seen an animal killed in such a fashion; the man had simply thrown it on its back, pinned it down with his knees and slit its belly with his knife. He had then thrust his arm into the animal's twitching guts up to his elbow and squeezed off the aorta, stopping the heart. In a few moments the sheep's head had flopped to the side and it died, with barely a drop of blood spilled.

Their method of cooking the beast was just as brutal. Only the stomach contents were discarded; everything else, the tripe, the head, the offal, the meat and the bones were tossed in boiling water.

William felt faint with hunger but his stomach rebelled at eating any of the pink and parboiled mess in front of him.

Juchi carved off a piece of almost raw meat from the carcass with his knife and thrust it in his mouth. William could hear small bones crunching between his teeth. Grease glistened on his chin.

There was a goatskin bag at the doorway. Juchi lurched to his feet and poured some of the liquid from the bag into a wooden bowl and thrust it into William's hands. He motioned for him to drink.

It was what they called koumiss, the fermented mare's milk that they drank with every meal. This at least was not unpleasant, now he had become accustomed to it. It was clear and pungent, like wine, and slightly effervescent; it left an aftertaste of almonds.

William lifted the bowl to his lips and downed the contents in one gulp. Immediately he clutched at his throat, gasping for breath. His insides were on fire. The Tatars burst into laughter.

'You have poisoned him!' Josseran shouted.

'Black koumiss,' Juchi said. He patted his stomach. 'It's good!'

And so nothing would do but they forced William to drink more, standing in front of him and clapping their hands at each swallow. He knew what they were doing. This black koumiss was as strong as sack and William knew that soon he would be as drunk as they were. After he had downed several cups of this foul liquor they tired of their game and sat back down on the wet grass and resumed their meal.

'Are you all right, Brother William?' Josseran asked him.

'Will you join me ... in prayer?' he answered. His tongue felt suddenly twice the size and he realized he had slurred his words.

'My knees are already blistered and raw from your constant supplications.'

'We should ask for divine guidance ... so that we may win these people for the Lord.'

The Tatars watched him as he fell on his knees beside the fire and lifted his clasped hands to the sky. Their eyes followed the direction of his gaze to the smoke hole and the single evening star that hovered above the yurt.

'God's bones, just stop it,' Josseran told him. 'They are not at all impressed with your devotions. They think you are afflicted.'

'The opinion of a Tatar does not trouble me.'

It was true. For the first time in weeks he was no longer afraid. He felt strong, invincible and charismatic. William called loudly on the Lord to come among them, guard their souls and lead their barbarian escorts to the one true way.

When he had finished Josseran was still grimly chewing on a piece of raw offal. 'How can you eat this disgusting mess?' William said.

'I am a soldier. A soldier cannot survive without food, no matter how displeasing it may be to the palate.'

William took a coil of cooked gut in his hand, feeling the slimy texture of it. He felt his gorge rise. He stood up and left the tent, shaping to toss the offal at a pack of dogs.

But then the world began spinning around him and he fell, dead drunk, on his back.

✝

William woke before dawn. He heard the baying of a wolf somewhere in the night. There was a dull ache behind his eyes. He reached for the crucifix at his throat and murmured a silent prayer. He knew that if he failed in this, the redemptive mission of his poor life, there could be no deliverance.

XVIII

✠

It was a cold, grey morning. Below them was a lake, the colour of steel. The slopes around them were wreathed in dark cloud. Occasionally, between breaks in the overcast, they glimpsed the jagged teeth of the mountains that stretched across the horizon, their peaks capped in snow and ice.

Juchi crouched beside the fire outside the yurt. He seemed unaffected by the cold. He wore thick-soled felt boots, like all the Tatars, and a thick wrap-around gown that they called a *del*, tied with a broad sash of orange silk. He had not yet put on his fur-lined cap. His head was almost completely shaven, like all the rest, with just a tuft of hair at the forehead and two long braids behind each ear.

He was roasting the head of a sheep on the end of a long stick. He turned it over the coals. When all the hair had been singed off he put it on the ground and began to extract meagre pieces of charred flesh and marrow with the point of his knife.

Breakfast.

'How long before we arrive in Qaraqorum?' Josseran asked him, in the language of the Tatars.

Juchi grinned. 'Very good. You said you had an ear for language. I thought it was just boasting.' He probed with his knife in the eye socket to find another tender morsel. 'Qaraqorum? If we ride hard and if the weather is favourable . . . perhaps summer.'

Josseran felt his spirits dip. So they had not been toying with him after all. 'Still so far?'

'Qaraqorum is at the centre of the world. Here we are still at its very rim.'

William emerged from the yurt, staggering slightly, his skin ashen. 'How did I find my bed?' he said to Josseran.

'I carried you there. You had fallen in the grass.'

The friar absorbed this information in stolid silence. Josseran expected a murmur of thanks, at least. 'I see you are learning their jabber now.'

'Is that not a good thing?'

'You are a traitor and heretic, Templar.'

'How so?'

'You banter with them constantly yet you have not informed these heathen of the missive I bear from the Holy Father. Is it not true you offered to make truce with these devils?'

'I am your escort and interpreter. That is all.'

'Do you take me for a fool?'

Josseran turned away. He saw Juchi toss the remains of his breakfast into the fire, where the head popped and sizzled.

'How I long for a good piece of roast hogget,' William said and stumbled away to find his horse.

✟

Josseran was worried about Kismet. The pace of their journey had wasted her. Since reaching the mountains there had been less feed and now she was no more than a skeleton. She struggled on, her spirit undaunted, but he did not think she could survive much longer.

At first he had thought the Tatar mounts ridiculous. They had thick necks and a dense coat and were barely taller than the pony on whose back he had first received instruction as a child. When he saw these supposedly fierce Tatar warriors on these yellow-brown mules, he could scarcely believe this was the cavalry that had laid waste half the known world.

He had been forced to revise that opinion. These squat, ugly beasts could ride forever at a gallop and even with the snow thick on the ground they were able to find their own feed, pawing at the ice with their front hooves to chew at the frozen and blackened vegetation beneath and somehow draw sustenance from it.

The packhorses Josseran had brought from Acre had long since died.

It had been a harrowing journey, day after day, week after week, in the saddle, their escorts setting a murderous pace. There was only one way a Tatar knew how to ride and that was at a gallop, taking just a few minutes' rest every two hours. Sometimes they would travel up to fifty miles a day.

Each of them had brought with him from Aleppo at least five horses, the bridle of each one loosely knotted around the neck of the horse on its left, the last animal in the line led right-handed by the rider. They used each horse for two days before resting it.

Josseran had been given his own string of Tatar ponies. But their flat hammering run left him saddle-sore and exhausted after the easy gallop of the Persians he was accustomed to riding, and Kismet herself could not keep up, even unsaddled.

The Tatars employed short stirrups, made of leather, and stood in the saddle, hour after hour, their sinuous legs never seeming to tire. Josseran had tried to imitate them but after a few minutes his thigh muscles cramped and so he let himself sag in the hard, wooden saddle and was jolted and shaken until his bones rattled. By noon every day the pain had settled into his joints; first his knees, and then his spine, until by late afternoon it seemed that his whole body was on fire.

But these Tatars seemed more at ease on horseback than they did on their short bow legs; he had even seen them sleep in the saddle. They controlled their mounts by pressure of their calves on the horse's flanks, and because they could ride without using the reins they could even fire arrows at full gallop. This was why they wore such light armour, he realized; they had no interest in conventional hand-to-hand combat. They could let their arrows do their killing for them, at a distance. Even the Templars would not stand a chance in battle against cavalry like this.

He had never known warriors like them. They were able to survive on so little. Sometimes they would pass the whole day without stopping for food. And such food. It invariably consisted of a few chunks of boiled mutton, eaten almost raw.

He had always prided himself on his strength and endurance, but he had come to dread the mornings and the prospect of another unrelenting battering in the saddle. There were times he even wondered if he would survive to see this legendary Qaraqorum. As for William, his skin had turned grey, and Josseran had to lift him off of his horse at the end of every day. But, sure in his faith, he gave himself up to it again each morning like a true martyr.

And as long as the damned friar could endure it, so could he.

XIX

✞

WHAT JOSSERAN HAD seen of these Tatars so far had persuaded him that an alliance was not only advisable, it was essential. No Christian army could defeat them on horseback, or even halt their advance, certainly not with the forces they had in Outremer.

If the Crusaders could not defeat the Tatar cavalry on the battle-field, their only alternative would be to take refuge behind the walls of their castles. But if the number and size of the Tatar siege machines he had seen at Aleppo was any indication, then even Acre and Castle Pilgrim might not long withstand them.

Yet Qaraqorum was so far away. By the time they sat down to finally talk with this Khan of Khans, there might not be a Christian or Saracen left alive in the Holy Land to strike the treaty.

✞

After they crossed the Elburz Mountains into Persia he saw for himself the consequences of resistance.

At the caravan city of Merv not a building was left standing. Chinggis Khan had laid the city waste many years ago. After the population surrendered, he had ordered that each Tatar soldier must slay three hundred Persians by his own hand. The command was applied to the letter. Later he burned the great library, feeding the fire with 150,000 ancient books. It was said that the glow of the resulting inferno could be seen across the desert in Bukhara.

They crossed yet another desert, this one even thirstier than those they had seen in Syria, just frozen waves of sand dotted with clumps of dry saxaul bushes. At night they saw a glow on the horizon to the north-east, which Juchi said came from a fire lit in the tower of the Kalyan minaret in Bukhara. It was the tallest building in the whole world, he told him, and it had a brick lantern with sixteen arches at the very top that served as a beacon for merchant caravans in the desert at night.

Josseran dismissed the claim as the typically florid exaggeration of the Mohammedans, but when they finally arrived at the great city he found it was true.

The Kalyan minaret was a finger of baked and banded terracotta brickwork that soared giddyingly into the heavens. Just below the scalloped corbels of the muezzin's gallery there was a necklace of glazed blue tiles in flowing Kufic script. 'It is known also as the Tower of Death,' Juchi said. 'The Uzbek rulers who once reigned here used to toss their prisoners from the top of the minaret down there into the *Registan*.'

It was an astonishing building. Even Chinggis Khan was impressed by it, Juchi said, for it was the only building in Bukhara that he spared, that and the Friday mosque, and even that had scorch marks on the walls.

✛

The rest of the city had been built since the time of Chinggis. It still possessed a desolate air, as if Chinggis and his murdering hordes had passed through just days before. It had a stench like Paris or Rome and the water in the canals was stagnant and green. The houses were drab, chalk-pale, built from whitewashed clay, with crooked door frames. There were few Persian faces; the population here had dark skins and almond eyes: Tatars and Kirghiz and Uzbeks.

The land outside the ruined walls was still desolate. Just an hour's ride from the *Registan* they came upon a pyramid built from human skulls, now bleached by the sun and picked clean by scavengers.

'Dear God,' Josseran murmured.

They had hired an Arab guide for this part of the journey and he looked over his shoulder, to ensure Juchi and his soldiers were not within hearing. 'Before the Tatars, everywhere you looked, there was green. Now everything is dying. Everything!'

The plain was hung with a mournful stillness. It was as if the massacres had happened only yesterday, and the corpses were still rotting in the fields.

'The Tatars did all this?'

He nodded. 'The *qanats*,' he said, using the Persian word for the underground wells that fed the desert, 'were maintained by poor farmers. The Tatars butchered them all, as if they were sheep. Now there is no one to dig out the silt from the wells and so the land has been murdered, too.'

'They killed everyone?'

'No. The poets, the artisans, the physicians, these they took back with them to Qaraqorum. But everyone else.' He shrugged and nodded toward the pyramid of bones. 'They even killed the animals.'

Who are these people? Josseran thought. They have no mercy for anyone. The further we travel, the more futile our embassy seems. If I could return to Thomas Bérard now, what should I tell him? No one in Acre or Rome could imagine a kingdom like this. It stretched to the end of the world and far beyond. In France he might ride from Troyes to Marseille in two weeks. Here two weeks did not even get you out of the desert.

'We shall save these people for Christ,' William said.

'We shall be lucky to save ourselves' Josseran muttered and turned his horse from the grisly monolith.

XX

✞

THEY CROSSED A great plain and villages of whitewashed clay. Occasionally they saw the ruins of a mosque or the solitary arch of a caravanserai, testament to the bloody passing of Chinggis Khan fifty years before. But finally the deserts were behind them. They followed a green river basin towards Samarkand.

The caravan city was circled by snow-lit mountains. The ribbed domes of Mohammedan churches slept under silver poplars, the *Registan* a riot of bazaars within the dun walls of merchant warehouses and travellers' inns. This city, too, had been rebuilt after the ravages of the Tatars, the sun-baked bricks of the madrassahs and mosques newly decorated with a faience of peacock blue and vivid turquoise that sparkled in the winter sun.

Josseran stood on the roof of their *han,* watching the dawn slip its dirty yellow fingers over the multi-domed roofs of the bazaar and into the warren of arcades. The tiled dome of a mosque glittered like ice, the black needle of a minaret was silhouetted against a single cold star. The muezzin climbed to the roof of the tower and began the *azan,* the call to prayer. It echoed across the roofs of the city.

'*Auzbillahi mina shaitani rajim, bismillah rahmani rahim . . .*'

'Listen to them. They warble like a man having his teeth pulled,' William said.

Josseran turned around. The friar emerged from the shadows, like a ghost. He finished tying the cord of his cowled robe.

'It is a hymn very much like our own plainsong,' Josseran said. 'It rises and falls and is just as melodious.'

'Like one of *ours?*' William growled.

'You think it barbarous because you do not understand it. I have lived in the Holy Land these five years. It is a hymn they repeat every day at dawn, the same words, the same harmony. They seek their god as we seek ours.'

'They do not have a god, Templar. There is only one God and He is the God of the one and true faith.'

Josseran made out the ungainly shape of a stork, nesting in the roof of a nearby minaret, a sight as familiar to him here as it was in Acre. He would miss the storks if he ever went back to France, he realized. *Perhaps it is true, perhaps I have lived too long among the Saracen and I am infected with their heresies.*

'I only mean to say that they are not godless, as some believe.'

'If they do not love Christ, then how can they be anything but godless?'

Josseran did not answer.

'We are a long way from Acre here,' William went on, 'but we shall return soon enough and I shall be forced to report on what you say. You would be wise to guard your tongue.'

A pox on all priests, Josseran thought. *And the thought occurred to him: perhaps I shall not go back, if God is kind. But then, when in all my years have I ever seen a merciful God?*

XXI

✛

THE COLOUR OF the lake changed from violet to black. The dark silhouette of the mountains in front of them faded against a leaden sky shot through with shafts of gold.

He shivered inside his furs. Since they had started their climb out of the plains of Samarkand he had taken to dressing in the manner of the Tatars, in a thick fur jacket and felt trousers tucked into his boots. But he was still cold.

His companions were unsaddling their horses. He turned away from his contemplation of the lake and joined them. He stroked Kismet's muzzle, murmuring words of encouragement. Poor girl, he could see the outline of her ribs through her flanks.

He turned to Juchi. 'We have to cross those mountains?'

'You must cross many more mountains and many more deserts before you reach the Centre of the World.' He seemed to take a perverse delight in their discomfort. He himself seemed inured to all suffering. He must have buttocks as hard as cured leather, Josseran thought.

'Your shaman,' Juchi said, using the Tatar word for holy man, 'will not survive the journey.'

'*Deus le volt*,' Josseran whispered, in French. God wills it.

'You would like to see his blood run.'

'He is too niggardly to bleed.'

Juchi looked over his shoulder. 'It is getting dark. Where is he?'

'Is he not with his horse?'

But William was not with his horse, nor was he inside the tent. They searched the camp but there was no sign of him.

Josseran found him by the river, the top half of his cloak stripped down, holding a switch he had torn from a poplar tree. His back was livid and striped with red weals. Josseran watched from Kismet's saddle as the friar flailed the branch over his shoulder.

As he worked the scourge he was chanting, in time with the strokes, although Josseran could not make out the words.

'I would have thought the rigours of our journey are chastisement enough, even for a man of God,' Josseran said.

William turned, startled. He was shivering with cold. 'It is the flesh that causes us to sin. It is right that the flesh should suffer for it.'

'And what sins have you committed this day? You have spent the whole time in the saddle of a horse.'

William threw down the stripling and struggled back into his robe. 'The body is our enemy.'

'Our enemy? If that is so, it would seem to me yours has suffered enough from carrying you around these last few months.'

William finished dressing himself. He had so far spurned the felt boots of the Tatars and his sandalled feet were almost black with cold.

'Is this day's journey not torment enough for you?'

The friar struggled up the bank. 'Do they say how much further we must travel?'

'It may be that by the time we return to the Holy Land our beards will be white and even the Saracens will be too old to mount their horses and chase us.'

William trembled in the bitter upland wind, his blood staining the back of his robe. Josseran felt both awe and revulsion in equal parts. There was something almost carnal in this passion for pain.

'Are you not afraid of what is beyond the mountains, Templar?' William said.

'I am afraid of God and I am afraid of his judgement. Besides that, I do not fear anything on this earth, or any man.'

'But I am not talking of men. Some say that in the land of Cathay there are creatures with heads like dogs who bark and speak at the same time. Others say there are ants as big as cattle. They burrow in the earth for gold and tear anyone who comes across them to pieces with their pincers.'

'I have heard these same stories but I have never met any man who has been to this Cathay and seen such things with his own eyes.' He shrugged his shoulders. 'In Samarkand you said to me that we would soon be returned to Acre. Lately, I must confess, I think we shall never return at all.'

'Then we fly straight to the arms of the Lord.'

'Well, I hope he has a fire warming,' Josseran muttered under his breath, 'for I have never been as cold in my life.'

XXII

☩

THEIR NEW ESCORT appeared from a world of cloud and ice.

There was a squadron of perhaps twenty riders. They wore fur caps with earflaps, some of them with dome-shaped helmets over the top. Their long felt coats hung down their horses' flanks almost to their boots. Arrows bristled in the wooden quivers on their backs; a triangular pennant hung limp from the point of a lance.

Steam rose from the horses; snow drifted slowly from a sky the colour of steel.

Their officer spurred forward. He had a purple silk scarf wrapped around his hair and face to protect him from the cold. With one movement he pulled the scarf aside.

Josseran was startled. It was not a man.

Her lips parted in a smile that lacked kindness and she turned to Juchi. 'So these are the barbarians,' she said, in her own language, thinking he could not understand. Her almond-shaped eyes had been darkened with kohl but there was nothing alluring about them. They were the hard eyes of a horse trader looking over stock for sale in the bazaar.

It was her bearing and the way she rode her horse that made him think her a man, he realized, for she did not dress like a Tatar warrior. Under her fur jacket she wore a wine-coloured robe, long-skirted and high-collared, slit to the waist so as not to interfere with her riding. A wide silk sash was wound tightly around her narrow waist and a single jet braid fell down her back almost to her hips.

'These two barbarians were sent here by our khan, Hülegü,' Juchi said to her. 'They wish an audience with the Great Khan in Qaraqorum. He asks that they be delivered safe to Besh Balik so they may be escorted on the final part of their journey to the Centre of the World.'

The girl turned to one of her companions. 'The thin one will die of cold before we are halfway across the mountains. The other one looks fit enough. But he is as ugly as his horse and his nose is twice as big.'

The Tatars laughed.

'I have no quarrel with you for my own account,' Josseran said in her own language, 'but I object to you calling my horse ugly.'

Her grin fell away and her companions fell silent in astonishment. 'Well,' she said finally. 'The barbarian speaks.'

'But you are right about him,' Josseran added, nodding towards William. 'We might as well bury him here.'

It was Juchi's turn to smile. 'He has learned the language of a Person since we have been journeying. He has a ready mind. He is entertaining for a barbarian.'

'I cannot see how a civilized person might find a barbarian entertaining,' she said. She turned back to Josseran. 'I am Khutelun. My father's name is Qaidu. He is the greatest Tatar chieftain here at the Roof of the World. I am to take you to him. I advise you to watch your manners.'

And she turned her horse away and led the way through the pass to the Fergana Valley.

XXIII

✠

A NOMAD CITY was sprawled across the valley floor, the black beehive domes of the Tatar yurts framed against the snow-dusted steppe and lowering sky. Wagons had been drawn up in a circle around the perimeter, and warriors stood sentry on their horses. Camels, horses and sheep foraged on the open plain.

As they rode into the camp, people came out to stare. They had dark almond-shaped eyes and wind-blackened faces, the men in fur caps and heavy brown coats, the women with their hair coiled on either side of their heads, like ram's horns. The children had shaved heads and long forelocks.

They stopped before the khan's audience tent. By the entrance a banner made from yak tails whipped in a cool, upland wind.

The audience tent was long enough and wide enough to fit perhaps ten thousand people; it was made entirely of silk, was stitched on the outside with leopard skins, and dyed red and white and black. It was supported by stout, lacquered poles.

'Take care, Barbarian,' Khutelun said as they dismounted their horses. 'You or your companion must not tread on the threshold of the khan's yurt. It would bring bad luck on the clan. Then they would have to kill you, and slowly.'

'I should hesitate to put them to such inconvenience,' Josseran answered and passed the warning to William. Such superstition! Josseran thought. They have terrorized half the known world and yet they live in fear of their own shadows.

They followed Khutelun inside.

✠

The great tent was lined with furs of ermine and sable and smelled of wood smoke. It was blessedly warm. As his eyes grew accustomed to the gloom Josseran made out two rows of Tatars, men on one side and women on the other, and, at the far end of the great pavilion, a stern and grizzled figure reclining on a bed of bear and fox furs.

Two fires of briar and wormwood roots were alight in the centre of the yurt. 'You must walk between the fires, Barbarian,' Khutelun said. 'The flames will purge your spirit of evil intentions.'

As an added precaution against evil intentions, Qaidu's guards searched them thoroughly for knives and Josseran was made to hand over the damascened sword. Only then were they allowed to approach the khan's throne.

Josseran noticed a small shrine to one side, with incense burning in small silver pots before the image of a man made from felt.

'You must bow,' she whispered. 'It is the shrine of Chinggis Khan, Qaidu's grandfather.'

Josseran turned to William. 'We must make obeisance before their god,' he whispered.

'I shall not bow down to graven images.'

'Give unto Caesar.'

'It is an abomination!'

'Do it,' Josseran hissed, 'or we die right here. Where will our Pope be without his holy emissary?'

He felt a thousand eyes watching them.

To Josseran's relief William submitted, appreciating the wisdom of compliance. He genuflected, scowling, in front of the shrine; Josseran did the same. Then they approached Qaidu's throne and bent their knee again, three times, as Khutelun had done.

Qaidu, khan of the high steppes, studied them in silence. His robe of silver fur was indistinguishable from his grizzled beard. He wore a gold domed helmet over his fur cap. His eyes were golden, like a hawk's.

He was attended on his right by what Josseran assumed to be his chief courtiers and perhaps also his sons. There was a falconer and some wild-eyed holy men; on his left were the women of his household, their hair in the same crescent-shaped frames he had noticed as they rode into the camp, but these women had silver ornaments dangling from the braided ends.

'So,' Qaidu growled. 'This is what a barbarian looks like.'

Josseran said nothing.

'Which of you can speak the language of men?'

Josseran looked up. 'I can, my lord.'

'I am told that you wish to speak with the Khan of Khans in Qaraqorum.'

'It was the wish of the lord Hülegü, whom it was my honour to meet in Aleppo. I brought him a message of friendship from my master in Acre, which is in Outremer, far to the west of here.'

'The Khan of Khans is dead,' Qaidu said. 'A new Khaghan is to be elected. No doubt he will accept your obeisance when the time is right.'

Josseran was stunned. Their chieftain was dead? He wondered why no one had thought to tell him this before. Would the succession be disputed, as it so often was in Europe? Their own Jerusalem had been in a state of war for years over the crown. If there was a delay in the succession, did it mean they must return to Acre? Or would they be made to spend months, years even, in these lonely mountains while any dispute was settled? He thought about Gérard and Yusuf mouldering in Aleppo.

It seemed to him they would all be old men before this was over.

'You have brought gifts for me?' Qaidu asked him.

'We have gifts for the Great Khan in Qaraqorum. It was a long journey and we could carry only very little.'

Qaidu seemed displeased with this response.

'What did he say?' William said.

'He wants to know if we have gifts for him,' Josseran answered.

'We do have a gift for him. The gift of religion.'

'I do not think it is quite the treasure he was hoping for. I think he would rather have something that is negotiable in the bazaar.'

Qaidu pointed at William. 'Who is your companion?'

'He is a holy man.'

'A Christian?'

'Yes, my lord.'

'Can he do magic?'

'I fear he cannot.' Unless you call turning any sweetly reasonable man into a foul-tempered madman within the space of hours, he thought.

'Then what good is he?'

Indeed!

'He has a message for your Khan of Khans from our Pope, the leader of our Christian world.'

'Pope,' Qaidu said, repeating this strange and cumbersome word several times. 'Does he also wish to gaze on our Khan of Khans?'

'He does, my lord. Is the Great Khan's palace many days' ride from here?'

Laughter from around the court. Qaidu silenced the gathering with a raised hand. 'To reach Qaraqorum, first you must cross the Roof of the World. But it is yet winter and the passes are closed. You will wait here until the snows melt. Perhaps another moon.'

'What is this Roof of the World?'

'It is as it says. They are the highest mountains on the earth, and they are only passable in the summer.'

'What is he saying now?' William said.

'He says the mountains are yet unpassable. We may have to stay here until the spring.'

'Next spring? By the time I arrive we may have a new Pope!'

No, Josseran thought. By the time we arrive Christ Himself may have returned a second time.

'Tell him we must not delay our journey another second!' William said.

'What is this babble coming from the mouth of your holy man?' Qaidu asked.

'He says he will be honoured to be your guest until it is time to move on,' Josseran said. 'Only he is much concerned by the news that your Khan of Khans is dead. He asks if a new Great Khan has been anointed.'

'That is of no concern to a barbarian,' Qaidu said and lifted a hand languidly in the air, to indicate that the audience was over. 'See that they have food and lodging,' he said to one of his aides.

As they left the pavilion Josseran saw the girl among the crowd of faces by the door of the yurt. A longing, as yet formless and nameless, moved in the shadows of his mind. He brushed it aside, as a man might brush aside an importunate beggar. Yet from that moment it dogged him and would not leave him alone.

XXIV

✠

A BAND OF sunset was framed against a pale sky in the doorway of the yurt. Fur-clad figures hurried in and out, carrying broiled sheep or horsemeat for their dinner.

Josseran stared into the cooking fire. The thin blue flame charred the outside of the meat, without really cooking it. He put some of the mutton in his mouth. It was still raw and bloody.

'Look at the fire,' William said. 'It hardly burns. A mark of the Devil.'

Josseran spat a piece of gristle into the coals. 'If there is one thing the Devil can do, it is make a fire burn well.'

'Then how do you account for this magic?'

'The woman Khutelun says it is because we have climbed so high up the valley. It takes the strength from the flames.'

William grunted his disbelief.

They had been brought to the yurt of Tekudai, Qaidu's eldest son. It was unlike any dwelling Josseran had seen so far on their journey. It was a circular, domed tent with a collapsible lattice framework of bamboo or willow poles. The frame had been covered with sheets of heavy felt and the whole structure lashed down with ropes of horse-hair. He supposed it was perfectly suited to the nomad's way of life, for Tekudai said it could be erected or dismantled in a few hours and the whole structure transported on the back of two or three camels when the Tatars moved from the summer pastures down to the winter lowlands.

Even the larger yurts, such as that belonging to the khan and his family, could be carried intact on the back of a wagon.

But the interiors all conformed to the same established Tatar design: in the centre was a fire pit, covered with smoke-blackened pots. Magenta and blue garment chests and rolls of bedding were stored around the walls, along with saddles and riding harnesses and huge earthenware water jars. The beaten-earth floor was covered with rugs. Spiders and scorpions, Tekudai told him, would not set foot on a felt carpet, so they served a dual purpose, keeping the yurt warm and dry as well as deterring insects. The entrance, which faced the south, as they all did, had a heavy flap, brightly painted with pictures of birds.

Either side of the entrance hung two felt figures, one with the udders of a cow, the other with the teats of a mare. The cow hung on the left side, the east, for that was the woman's side of the yurt. The mare hung on the man's side, on the west, for women were not allowed to milk the mares; that was man's work. It was from mare's milk that they fermented their koumiss, the staple of the Tatar diet.

It still astonished him the amount of mare's milk these Tatars could drink at a single sitting. Sometimes it seemed that it was all that they lived on.

Tekudai, as master of the *ordu*, sat on a raised couch behind the fire. Above his head hung another idol which the Tatars called 'the master's brother'. Above his wife's head hung another called 'the mistress's brother'. The Tatars called these idols *ongot*, and there were several in every yurt.

Only Qaidu, as khan, was allowed to keep the hallowed image of Chinggis Khan.

Josseran watched the Tatars as they ate. First they took some of the fat from the meat to graze the mouth of Natigay, another of their gods, then they tore off great chunks of the parboiled mutton and held them close to their faces with one hand, while slicing off mouthfuls of meat with a knife held in the other.

'Look at them, how they eat!' William said. 'They are not men at all. The earth opened up and these creatures swarmed out of Hell itself. Even the woman. She is a she-devil, a witch.'

Josseran said nothing. He did not think her a devil at all.

☩

'Somewhere this way is Prester John. If we can get a message to him, we can save ourselves from these devils.'

Prester John! Josseran thought. As much a superstition as the giant ants!

'You do not believe?' William asked.

'I believe if there ever was a Prester John he is with God now.'

'But surely his descendants live on.'

'The Mohammedans have commerce with the East; some claim they have even been as far as Persia itself and they have never heard of such a king.'

'You believe the word of a Saracen?'

'You believe the word of men who have never been further east than Venice? If this legend is true, where is this Prester John?'

'The Tatars may have forced him south.'

'If he runs from the Tatars like everyone else, what use is he to us?'

'He is this way somewhere. We must listen for word of him. He is our salvation.'

Josseran grew irritable, as he always did when talking to this friar, and returned his attention to the food. Khutelun, sitting just across the fire from him, watched his efforts to eat in the Tatar way and said: 'Perhaps you should eat in your own manner. You have such a big nose you may cut off the end of it.'

Josseran stared at her. 'Among my own people my nose is not considered so large.'

Khutelun relayed this knowledge to her companions, who all laughed. 'Then you must all be descended from your horses.'

Damn her, he thought. He continued using the knife in the Tatar way. He had learned from his many years in Outremer that it was wiser to imitate local customs than to continue with old habits. And besides, he would not give up and let her have the satisfaction.

Some of the men had finished eating and were now supping bowl after bowl of black koumiss. Tekudai's brother Gerel was already drunk and lay on his back, snoring. His companions sang raucously while another played a single-string fiddle.

Josseran watched Khutelun from the corner of his eye. She was beautiful but not in the way of a Frankish woman. Her face was oval, with the high cheekbones of the Tatars, polished like the bronze of a statue that had been much regarded and admired. Her movements reminded him of a cat, sinuous and graceful. But it was something in her manner, her spirit, that attracted him, the way she looked at him.

Though, of course, it was absurd to even contemplate such a union. 'I have never seen hair of such colour,' she said to him, suddenly. He realized that as he had been secretly been watching her, she had been watching him.

Josseran kept his head short-cropped in Acre, as was the rule inside the Order, but since they had been travelling there had been no barbers to attend him and now he was conscious of the length of it. He brushed it away from his face with his fingers.

'It is the colour of fire,' she said.

For a moment their eyes locked.

'So,' she said, finally. 'You have come to make peace with us.'

'An alliance,' he corrected her. 'We have a common enemy.'

She laughed. 'The Tatars do not have enemies. Only kingdoms we have not yet conquered.

'You have seen for yourself. Our empire extends from the rising of the sun in the east to its setting place We have never been defeated in battle. And you say you want to make peace! Of course you do!' He still did not contest with her and she seemed frustrated by his passivity. 'You should have brought tribute for my father.'

'We had not expected to have the honour of gazing on your father. However, we bring words of friendship.'

'I think my father would rather have gold.' The men around her laughed again. Josseran noticed how they deferred to her. In France a woman would never be allowed to talk so freely unless she was a whore and would not be treated with such respect unless she was a queen. It was evident the Tatar customs concerning women were very different to their own.

'Who is your friend?' she asked him.

'He is not my friend. He is a holy man. I am commissioned to escort him to Qaraqorum.'

'He is the colour of a corpse. Does he know how ugly he is?'

'Do you wish me to tell him?'

'What is she saying?' William asked. He had some of the boiled mutton in his fingers and was pulling at the tough meat with his teeth.

'She finds you pleasing to her eye and wishes me to pass on her admiration.'

William's response was startling. It was as if she had slapped him. 'Remind her she is a woman and has no place speaking to a friar in such a manner. Is she a whore?'

'I think she is a princess.'

'She does not behave like any princess I have ever known.'

'Their customs are different perhaps.'

When Josseran turned back to Khutelun, the mocking expression on her face had disappeared. She was looking at the priest with a wild and strange look in her eyes. The Tatars around her had fallen silent.

'Tell him he must go back,' she said.

'What?'

'He must go back. If he crosses the Roof of the World he will never find rest in his soul again.'

'He cannot go back. He has his duty, as I have.'

There was a dangerous silence. The Tatars, both the men and the women, were watching Khutelun; even the lute player had set aside his instrument and the drunkards had stopped singing. She was staring at William; not at him, through him, somehow.

'What is happening?' William said.

'I do not know.'

'Why do they stare? Have we done something to incite them?'

Khutelun spoke again. 'Tell your shaman that if he will not go back, he must learn to suffer.'

'Suffering is something he enjoys.'

'He does not even begin to understand what suffering is,' Khutelun said, and then the look was gone from her eyes and she returned her attention to the mutton.

The moment passed. The talk and laughter resumed. The drinkers attacked the black koumiss with renewed vigour. But Josseran was shaken. He felt a chill along his spine as if the devil himself had stepped on his grave.

XXV

✛

JOSSERAN AND WILLIAM were given their own yurt near the centre of the great encampment, close to Qaidu's *ordu*. Their Tatar hosts had lit a silver bowl of incense by the shrine of Natigay, and though William had quickly snuffed it out, its aroma lingered in the air. Josseran crawled under his blankets of animal skins and lay on his back staring at the sky through the smoke hole in the roof.

Josseran saw William on his knees silhouetted by the glowing coals in the fire. He murmured a prayer for their deliverance.

Josseran huddled further under the furs. He wished William would just shut up and sleep. His nerves were frayed and he needed rest. France, even Outremer, seemed such a very long way away tonight. It was as if they had arrived at some underworld. He had laughed at William's superstition of giant ants and other beasts but now he, too, was afraid. At night it was harder to scoff at tales of men with tails and feet growing from their heads.

They were so far from Christ's mercy. Few survived journeys such as this. Most were swallowed up in the fastnesses of these mountains, lost to Christendom forever, and were never seen again.

William was the only vestige of the familiar that remained to Josseran, his only anchor to the Christian world. What sad irony.

In Acre Thomas would be wondering why he had not returned with Hülegü's response to their entreaties. Gérard and Yusuf would be growing beards down to their knees while they sat in some barred cell in Aleppo. Everyone else would have forgotten about them. Even the Pope, he suspected.

'Do you wish to make your confession?' William asked in the darkness.

'My confession?'

'We have been travelling these many weeks and you have not made confession.'

'I have spent all my time in the saddle of a horse. It has not given me great opportunity to sin.'

'How long since your last confession, Templar?'

More than ten years, he thought. It would be pointless to enumerate my small sins when there is an unwashable stain on my very soul that I cannot, or will not, speak aloud, especially to a priest. 'In the Order we have our own chaplains who serve us.'

'If that is so, then you know you should make penance regularly.'

'When I feel the need for penance, Brother William, I shall advise you.'

Josseran rolled on his side and tried to sleep.

'Why do I feel you carry a great burden with you?' William said.

'I do carry a great burden. He is a Dominican friar and his name is William.'

'I know your opinion of me, Templar. But do not make the mistake of thinking me dull in the wits. I know when a man is greatly troubled. War may be your province. The vagaries of the spirit are mine.'

'I thank you for your concern. Now go to sleep.'

Josseran closed his eyes but sleep would not come. He thought about this Khutelun, and of the black void that had come to her eyes when she looked at William and the way the Tatars had fallen silent around her. It was as if she could see inside his soul. Can she see inside mine as well? He hoped she could not, for it was not the monsters lurking beyond the Roof of the World that he feared most, but those hiding within himself.

XXVI

✠

KHUTELUN HAD HAD the gift for as long as she could remember. It had begun as an energy in her body she could not contain. She had never been able to stay still, even as a child; she had always found it difficult to sleep and several times she had wandered off in the night.

Her brothers would be sent out into the teeth of the wind to search for her in the darkness. Sometimes they could not find her. When she reappeared at the camp the next morning, frozen and wild-eyed, her mother would already be weeping for her, mourning her death.

Khutelun was always filled with remorse afterwards. But there was nothing she could do to stop. The gift would not allow it.

The strange urgings of her soul quieted after her first bleeding, but did not stop. Once she walked her horse to the lip of a cliff and imagined spurring over the ledge into space and the silence of the everlasting Blue Sky. She had thought how she might spread her arms and they would become the great, tawny wings of a falcon.

She could fly.

Fly.

It was her brother, Tekudai, who found her, grabbed the reins and pulled her pony back from the edge.

Soon afterwards Tekudai became ill. Her father called for the shamans and they said their prayers over him, and on their advice three Kerait prisoners were cut open and their blood sprinkled on Tekudai's body as he lay convulsing on his bed of furs. But still he became weaker.

Only the shamans ever entered a yurt when there was sickness for evil spirits could leap from one body to another and it was perilous for an ordinary person to come too close. But one morning Qaidu peered through the flap of the yurt and found Khutelun curled up beside her brother, fast asleep. He rushed in and carried her out, wailing in despair, thinking that now he would lose a daughter as well as a son. But Khutelun did not fall sick.

Instead, Tekudai began to get well.

It was after this that she began to have visions. One day she went to her father and told him not to hunt that day because she had dreamed of a monster eating him. He had laughed away her protests. But that same afternoon, while he was retrieving his arrows from a fallen ibex, he was attacked by a bear. It ripped four great slashes in his chest and when they brought him home there was scarcely breath in him.

Khutelun stayed with him all through that night, sucking the clotted blood from his wounds. When her father survived, the other shamans came to her and told her she had the gift.

An old woman, Changelay, and a man, Magui, taught her the sacred rites and from that moment on Qaidu always consulted her whenever there were important decisions to be made.

But for Khutelun the gift was sometimes a burden. There were occasions when her knowing tormented her, as when she dreamed that one of the men of the tribe was bulling another man's wife. She kept her silence, but was haunted by it until the man was killed in a battle with the Kermids.

She did not want this gift. She wanted to be free, like her brothers, to ride the steppes and gallop with her father.

But in the smoky dark of the night the spirits would talk to her and transport her across the steppe. At first these visions lasted no longer than a splinter of lightning in the mountains at night. But as she grew older she stayed longer and longer in the Otherworld, could sometimes glimpse to the very horizon of time. When the spirit was strong in her she could fly through the whole valley and see into everyone. But it was a dizzying experience and it left her exhausted.

Tonight she streaked across the Roof of the World with the barbarian with the fire-blond beard, twisting the shifting axis of the hours to see what lay ahead for her and for him. It was a terrible prescience, for the future that lay below her in the panorama of the seasons was too frightening to contemplate.

XXVII

✝

JOSSERAN WOKE TO the sound of a commotion outside. He got up and pushed aside the heavy flap at the entrance. A crowd had gathered on the plain, just beyond the first line of wagons. It was clear something of import was about to happen.

'Some viciousness, no doubt,' William said behind him.

Josseran threw on his furs and boots and set off. William hurried after him. The ground was hard, and dusted with snow.

Hundreds of Tatars, men, women and children, had gathered in a circle. The mood was festive. He had seen such flushed expressions before, at public executions in Orléans and Paris.

A woman stood in the centre of the circle, holding a plaited leather horsewhip in her right hand. She was young and sturdy, and there was a knife thrust into her belt.

A young man rode out from the camp and the crowd parted for him. His trousers were tucked into his leather boots, in the fashion of the people of these mountains, but his chest and back were bare.

'What are they doing?' William whispered.

'I don't know.' Josseran turned, saw Khutelun standing a few yards away, her eyes bright with excitement.

The man rode slowly, circling the woman, who hefted the whip in her right fist, testing its weight. What was happening? Was this some sort of tribal punishment? If it was, the victim seemed cheerful enough.

'He is going to let her whip him,' William said, with sudden realization.

Josseran nodded. And then he added mischievously: 'It is not too late for me to find you a horse. Perhaps you could join in.'

He left him and went to join Khutelun. As he turned his back he heard the whip crack.

There was such a look of savagery on her face. Not a woman at all, as I have known them, he thought. She is a primitive. A true lady does not take her pleasure in such spectacles.

'What are they doing?' he asked.

'She is testing him.'

'Testing him?'

'He has asked her to marry him. It is now her right to discover if he would be suitable as a husband. He has to prove himself. What use is a weak husband? A woman cannot feed her children with kisses and endearments.'

The whip cracked again. Josseran turned around. The young man was still upright in the saddle, riding steadily. But already there were two bloody stripes across his back.

'How long does this go on?'

'Until she is satisfied.'

'And if she does not want him for a husband?'

'Then he must decide how long he can endure the whip. If he falls from the saddle he loses any claim to her. She is not expected to marry a man with no courage or strength.'

The whip cracked again and again. The young boy allowed no outward sign of pain to show. But the blood ran freely down his back now, staining his trousers. The girl wielded the whip once more.

The crowd cheered with each slap of the whip. The young man had slumped a little in the saddle, Josseran noticed. His back was a lather of blood. But he kept the horse settled, and did not try to swerve out of range.

The girl waited, watching the rider as he made a complete lap. Then she yelled aloud and put all her weight behind another blow. The boy flinched, but kept his balance in the saddle. Flecks of blood sprayed along the horse's flank.

'If she loves him she will stop now,' Khutelun said. 'He has proved himself.'

'And if she does not love him?'

'Then it would be better if he is not too brave.'

But as Khutelun predicted, the girl tucked the whip back into her belt and raised her arms, her ululating cry rippling through the wild mountains. The watching family members rushed in and gathered around the pony to congratulate its rider, who grinned back and accepted their plaudits, although the smile was really no more than a grimace.

'As a woman, I would expect any man to do as much for me,' Khutelun said. 'As a princess I would expect much more.'

He felt as if she was issuing a challenge.

'In your country are you considered a brave man?' she asked him.

'What does a man have if he does not have honour and valour?'

'Are you a good horseman also?'

'One of the finest.'

'How many horses do you own?'

The Tatars took twenty horses with them on a campaign, more horses than any knight could ever hope for, more than many rich lords possessed; and he himself was anything but rich. How could he explain to her that he had sold much of what he owned to travel to the Holy Land? How might he describe the circumstances of his service to the Order of the Temple?

'I have three horses,' he said, which was only partly true, for though he rode them in battle they in fact belonged to the Temple.

'And how many wives?'

'A man can only have one wife, by God's law.'

'One wife if he has no appetite. As a man will drink just one bowl of koumiss if he is not thirsty.' And she laughed.

Josseran could not believe his ears. It was as well that William could not understand what was being said.

She was close enough that he could smell her scent, a savage alchemy of leather and curds and female musk. He felt himself stir.

'What are your women like?' she said. 'Are they great horse-women?'

'None of them compare to you.'

'Then what can they do?'

'A noble maid is supposed to be beautiful and gentle, with a soft and mellifluous voice.'

'This is what you look for in a wife?'

'She should also be versed in music and tapestry making. The paragon is Our Lord's mother, Mary.'

'I agree that a woman should be able to sew and cook. The yurt and the children are her province. But in times of war or misfortune she should also be able to fight and hunt.'

'Fight?'

'Of course. What else do you Christians look for in a wife?'

'Modesty,' he said, using the Tatar word for correctness, politeness.

Khutelun frowned.

'She must be . . . unbroken . . .' he added, trying to explain it to her as delicately as was in his power.

'You mean she must have the blood veil?'

'Yes,' he answered, astounded at her forthrightness.

'I lost my blood veil a long time ago,' she said. 'Like every good Tatar woman, I gave it to my horse.'

And she turned away from him and strode back to the camp.

XXVIII

✠

JOSSERAN AND WILLIAM became objects of curiosity about the camp. Children dogged their heels, laughing and shouting, one occasionally accepting a dare from his fellows to run up and touch the hem of their jackets before rushing off again. The adults, too, stared at them with undisguised curiosity, would sometimes approach and demand Josseran's knife, or William's silver cross. They did it shamelessly, not as beggars, but with the attitude of lords who took whatever they wanted as a matter of right. Several times Josseran, goaded beyond endurance, was on the point of reaching for his sword.

It was Tekudai, Khutelun's brother, who saved the situation. He adopted them as his personal charges and escorted them wherever they went. The demands and the begging stopped abruptly.

Tekudai was endlessly curious about them, about their religion, their methods of warfare, their castles. He wanted to know if Christian – the Tatars thought their religion was the name of their country – had endless pastures where a man might graze horses; what the punishment was for adultery; what they used to make arrows. Josseran realized that Tekudai was more than simply curious, and that Qaidu had probably ordered him to spy on them, and so he was always cautious in his replies.

If Tekudai was Qaidu's spy he was not a good choice, for he liked to talk as much as he liked to listen, and Josseran gradually drew him out.

'What is your religion?' Josseran asked him. He realized he did not know the word for God, or even if the Tatars had such a word. So he tried to say, as best he could: 'What do you believe in?'

'The world and everything in it comes from the Spirit of the Blue Sky,' Tekudai said, as if he was astonished that Josseran should ask such an obvious question.

'Does he give you your laws?'

'The khan makes the laws.'

'The khan, your father?'

'He makes laws for our tribe here in the valley. But there is a khan who is higher than him in Bukhara, and then there is the Khan of Khans in Qaraqorum.' Tekudai explained that the last Khaghan, Möngke, had just died, so a council would be held in Qaraqorum to choose a new Khan of Khans. This was known as the *khuriltai*, and by the time Josseran and William arrived at the Centre of the World they all expected Mongke's son, Ariq Böke, would be elected.

'And he makes laws for everyone?'

'Of course.'

'The Spirit of the Blue Sky does not give you laws?'

He laughed. 'The Spirit just is.'

'But if the Spirit does not give you laws, how do you know if you are living a good life?'

'Because I will be victorious over my enemies and have many children with my wives.'

'Wives? So you have more than one wife? Like the Mohammedans?'

'Of course. We can have four wives if we can afford them. After that, only concubines.'

This was godless, of course. But for a man, it was also intriguing. He asked Tekudai the same question he asked certain Mohammedans that he knew in Acre. 'But don't they all fight with each other? Is there not jealousy?'

'No, why should they be jealous? They are all looked after just the same. My father, for instance. He even sleeps with the old, ugly ones now and then, just the same as the new ones. He is a good man, my father.'

'But what about when he dies? What happens to his wives?'

'Well they will come to my *ordu*, my household. I will look after them. There is one of them, she has eyes like a deer. When my father dies, I can't wait. She will be first into my bed.'

'You will sleep with all your father's women when he dies?'

'Not my mother, obviously.'

'So a woman is never . . .' He realized there was no word for widow: '. . . she is never left unprotected.'

'Of course not. What do you think we are? Barbarians?' Tekudai then asked him what happened to women in Christian. Josseran tried to explain to him that a man might only have one wife. But when he also tried to explain about widowhood, about old or barren women being sent to live in monasteries, and about men disowning children borne by women other than their wives, Tekudai shook his head in disgust and astonishment.

'And a woman cannot even own her own goat?'

'All possessions belong to the husband.'

Tekudai pointed to Khutelun, who had just emerged from Qaidu's yurt and leaped on to her horse. 'I do not think she would make a very good wife in Christian,' he said. 'You try and tell that one she cannot have her own goat. Try and tell her anything and she will whip you all the way to Bukhara.'

Josseran pointed to the silk belt she wore around her waist.

'What does that mean?' he asked, trying to appear as artless as he could.

'When a woman has a silk sash like that it means she is unmarried.'

Unmarried.

Josseran pushed the absurd thought from his mind. May God forgive him; his duty lay with God, not in the loins of some Tatar savage from the steppes.

As if such a thing were possible, anyway.

✠

He watched the Tatars as they went about their daily lives; the women milking cows, or sitting in groups outside sewing skins or making felt, scolding children or chopping up meat for the pots; the men shaping bows or filing arrowheads, or shouting and whooping as they trained their horses. Others poured mare's milk into leather bags, which they then suspended from wooden frames and beat with long sticks. They would do this for hours on end, to separate the whey from the curds. Tekudai told him they were making koumiss.

The more he saw of the Tatars, the more he was impressed with their fighting ability. 'Show me how you use this bow,' he said to Tekudai when he found him practising at the butts.

It was double-curved and made from bamboo and yak horn, bound together with silk and resin. To release the string, Tekudai used a leather thumb ring. Josseran had never seen one before.

'How do you use this?' he asked him.

'Try it,' Tekudai said. Josseran had never thought of himself as a great bowman, but using the ring he was able to release the string with a better snap than he ever managed with his bare fingers, and hit the centre of a target from over two hundred paces.

Tekudai laughed and slapped him on the back. 'If you weren't so big and ugly, you would make a fine Tatar warrior!' he said.

He showed him the arrows he used, one for fighting at distance, another with a larger blade for fighting close in. He also showed him a blunt signal arrow. The arrowhead was not pointed but instead had a round iron ball, drilled with small holes, affixed to the shaft. It made a whistling noise as it flew, he said, and they used it for communicating with each other in a battle.

'These Tatars are the most extraordinary warriors I have ever seen,' he said to William later that afternoon. 'Their discipline and organization is greater than anything we have at the Temple. In battle they form themselves into fighting groups, ten men part of a hundred who are part of a thousand. They each coordinate with each other with flags and arrows. There is not one of them who is not an expert bowman and horseman by the time they are ten years old. They are virtually unbeatable.'

'But we have God on our side.'

'We would need more than that,' Josseran muttered, under his breath.

But until now he had only been allowed mere glimpses of the Tatar's martial capabilities. If he had been impressed thus far, he was struck with awe when, a week after their arrival, Qaidu allowed him to ride with them on a hunt.

XXIX

✠

IT WAS STILL dark when Khutelun's *mingan* – a Tatar army of one thousand riders – left the camp. Josseran woke during the night to the thunder of the hooves as they rode out on to the steppe.

Soon afterwards, Tekudai came to fetch them. 'You must come,' he said. 'The hunt has begun.'

It was bitterly cold; Josseran threw on his *del* and boots. William followed him out of the yurt. Even he had now succumbed to Tatar ways; he had surrendered his sandals for stubby, felt boots and wore a thick Tatar robe over his black cloak.

They saddled their horses and followed Tekudai to the hill overlooking the camp. Qaidu was waiting for them, surrounded by his bodyguard, and hunched inside a great ermine coat. He wore all the trappings of a khan; his leather cuirass was richly studded with silver and there were carmine trappings on his horse and his wooden saddle was studded with jade.

'We honour you,' Qaidu said to Josseran as they rode up. 'No barbarian has ever seen this.' I have been on hunts before, Josseran thought. He imagined returning that evening with a few boar, perhaps some antelope. He had not the faintest idea of the slaughter that he was about to witness.

They rode hard for several hours, in the Tatar way, without a break. Kismet kept up the pace; she was in better condition for the rest at Qaidu's camp and fattened by the feed she had found on the plain. Josseran was relieved; he had feared that he might lose her.

They reached the crest of a low hill. The blue-white peaks of the mountains surrounded them, like the rim of some giant bowl.

In the dawn light he made out a dark line of Tatar horsemen spread across the valley. These must be the cavalry he had heard leaving the camp. Suddenly the line broke, the flanks galloping forward in two separate horns across the steppe.

A herd of antelope darted ahead, more than a hundred score of them, caught between the advancing wings of the cavalry. He heard their queer, quacking bleats as they stampeded across the frozen tundra. Some of them leaped high into the air above the backs of the herd, like fish jumping out of the sea. William gasped and pointed to the right where a pack of wolves were also running; they were joined by two snow leopards, panicked and howling, padding over the ice on the flank of the charge.

Now a herd of goats darted ahead, corralled by the horsemen.

'In the name of God,' Josseran breathed.

He had hunted stag and boar in the forests of Burgundy but he had never seen a hunt on a scale such as this. It was performed with startling precision. In France they used beaters and hounds to chase down their prey; when a quarry was sighted it was up to the lord or the knight to hunt it down and kill it. Compared to this, such sport was child's play.

Here the Tatars used their entire army, acting in unison.

The horns of the Tatar advance were about to close, encircling the animals on the plain below.

'This is how we drill our soldiers,' Tekudai said. He had to shout to make himself heard above the drumming of hooves on the frost-hard ground. The riders themselves made no sound, wheeling and turning in total silence, their movements coordinated by the messengers who streaked between the commanders on their ponies, by signal flags, and by the occasional singing flight of an arrow.

'Nothing may be killed until the khan himself gives the signal. If a single hare is lost from inattention that man is put in the cangue and given a hundred strokes of the cane.'

Josseran had been raised to believe that battle was a series of individual combats. Personal courage and skill was everything. It was only when he joined the Templars that he was trained to charge and wheel and turn about in unison with the rest of the cavalry. It was this iron discipline that had set the Templars and Hospitallers apart from all others as a fighting force in the Holy Land.

But it was nothing compared to what he witnessed now. When you fought the Tatar, he realized, you fought the entire horde *at once*. The lightness of their armour and their weapons was in stark contrast to the heavy chain mail and broadsword of himself and his fellow Templars. Individually, these wild horsemen would be no match for a Frankish knight; but fighting and moving as a unit, as these men were doing now, they would carry all before them.

If he did not somehow return to Outremer with a truce, he could envisage the whole of the Holy Land being swallowed up by these devils.

Qaidu nodded to the lieutenant who attended him. The man took an arrow from his quiver. It was one of the signal arrows that Tekudai had showed him. The man fired it into the air and it whistled as it fell towards the warriors on the plain below.

It was the signal for the killing to begin.

One of the figures in that great circle of riders leaped from the saddle. Even at this distance he knew it was her by the flash of her purple scarf. Qaidu smiled wolfishly at him.

'My daughter,' he said. 'I have given orders. No one is to kill until she has fired the first arrow.'

She left her weapons on her horse, even her quivers, and strode across the plain armed only with her bow.

'She is allowed one arrow,' Tekudai said. 'She must kill with a single shot.'

There were thousands of beasts milling on the plain, wide-eyed with panic. Khutelun strode among them, apparently unafraid, holding just the slender bow.

A pack of wolves had detached themselves from the howling press of animals and now veered towards her, baying and scampering. She held the bow loosely in her right hand and waited.

'She'll be killed,' Josseran murmured.

He looked around. Beside him, Khutelun's father and brother watched, their faces like flint. Josseran returned his attention to the drama playing out below him. The wolves were closing on her. He felt an unexpected rush of fear. Why should I care what happens to some Tatar savage? he asked himself. What is it to me?

But his heart thundered.

Still she waited, letting the wolves come closer, the bow still at her side.

She has no nerves at all . . .

She raised the bow in one fluid movement and took aim. She is too late, he thought. The pack must overtake her now, before she has to time to loose her arrow.

Suddenly one of the wolves fell, pitching head over tail on the frosted ground, the arrow embedded in its throat. Immediately there was a singing of arrows from the riders behind Khutelun and a dozen more fell in a tangle of legs and bloody fur. But it was not enough to save her. She went down under the rush of the remaining beasts. Her companions rode in, firing one arrow after another into the pack.

Josseran looked at Qaidu.

Nothing. No expression at all.

He held his breath and waited. Khutelun lay face down in the ice.

✠

Finally, a movement, and she stirred and rose slowly to her feet. One of her fellows held her horse's rein and she limped towards him. Impossible to tell how badly she was hurt.

Qaidu grinned. 'Ah, what a son she would have been! But a fine mother of khans!'

The killing continued for another hour. Then another singing arrow was fired into the sky, the signal for the slaughter to end. The iron ring of cavalry broke and the remaining animals were allowed to escape to the northern wastes.

The soldiers set to work, gathering the feast.

✠

'So,' William murmured at his shoulder. 'We shall not be eating mutton tonight at least.'

'Have you ever seen anything as like?'

'Savages at the hunt.'

Khutelun rode up the slope to greet her father. There was blood on the sleeve of her coat and on her trousers, but nothing in the way she held herself indicated that she was wounded. As she came closer he could feel her black eyes watching him out of her sun-coppered face.

He wondered what damage the wolves had done, what wounds were hidden by her thick robes. How could he be so affected by a savage? She smiled hawkishly at him as she rode past, perhaps reading his thoughts. 'Father,' she shouted to Qaidu.

'How are your wounds, daughter?'

'Scratches,' she said. She swayed a little in the saddle but recovered.

'A satisfactory hunt.'

'Thank you, Father.'

'Congratulate your *mingan*. Tell them I am pleased.'

Khutelun grinned again, then she turned her horse to rejoin the soldiers on the killing ground below.

Josseran turned to Tekudai. 'Will she be all right?' he asked him.

'She is a Tatar,' he grunted, as if that were explanation enough, and said nothing more on the long ride back to the camp.

But on their return Josseran saw another side to his new friends.

✛

William and Josseran had been invited to Tekudai's yurt to drink koumiss and celebrate the hunt. A sudden crack of thunder overhead shook the ground under them. Gerel stampeded for the corner, burrowing under a pile of skins, while Tekudai's wives and children screamed and cowered, the youngest taking refuge beneath their mother's skirts.

Tekudai jumped to his feet, a loop of saliva dangling from his chin. He grabbed William by the shoulders and threw him across the yurt, kicking him out through the flap at the entrance.

He turned on Josseran. 'Out! Outside!'

Josseran stared at him, astonished.

'You have brought the anger of the gods down on all of us!' Tekudai shouted.

'It is just a storm,' Josseran shouted over the hiss of the rain.

'Outside!' Tekudai dragged him to the entrance and pushed him into the rain-slashed mud.

William stared at the rolling black clouds, his hair stringy with rain. 'What is wrong with them?'

Josseran shook his head. He picked William up by the arm and dragged him away, back to their yurt. They huddled together by the small fire, still soaking wet, steam rising from their sodden coats.

How to make sense of such people? Scourge of half the world, conquerors of Baghdad and Moscow and Kiev and Bukhara, and here they were, burrowing under their blankets, scared of thunder, like children.

A strange people indeed.

XXX

✠

THERE WAS ONE thing that continued to trouble him, gnawing at him every day, something he had to know. Why should this be of any consequence? he thought. But he had to have an answer.

It was a morning about a week after the storm; the skies were ice blue, the sun bouncing off the snows at the Roof of the World. He was riding with Tekudai on the hill above the camp. Tekudai carried a noose of rope on the end of a long pole, which he used to catch the horses they would take with them on their upcoming journey through the mountains. It required a great deal of skill and strength to snare the animals this way, for they were allowed to run half-wild across the steppe until they were needed and fought madly against capture. Across the valley other horsemen were performing the same task, their whooping cries and the hammer of horses' hooves echoing from the valley walls.

Josseran took a deep breath, knowing this was his opportunity to discover the truth, as unpalatable as it might be. 'Tekudai, tell me something. When you decide to take a wife – must she be . . .?' He stumbled for the right word in the Tatar language, but realized he did not know it.

Tekudai frowned. 'Must she be – what?'

Josseran pointed to his groin. 'What if she does not bleed a little. On the night of the wedding?'

'Are you asking if a wife must have her blood veil intact?' Tekudai said.

'Yes, that is what I mean.'

'Of course she does not. It would be too shameful. Would you have such a woman as your wife?'

'Such a condition is highly prized in my country.'

'Perhaps that is why you cannot defeat the Saracen!'

Josseran wanted to slap him off his horse. Just a boy and he was taunting him!

'I have heard,' Josseran pressed on, 'that your women lose their maidenhood to their horses.'

Tekudai reined in his horse and twisted in the saddle. He seemed confused. 'How else would they lose it?'

'This does not bother you?'

'To have the blood veil is the sign of a woman who has spent little time on horseback. She cannot therefore be a good rider and so she would be a burden to her husband.'

Josseran stared at him. 'They lose their maidenhood riding in the saddle.' He said it slowly, comprehension dawning.

'Yes,' Tekudai said, 'of course.' He stared in bewilderment at this barbarian who needed to be told simple facts three or four times before he understood them. And Juchi had told them he had a quick wit and a lively mind!

'They lose their maidenhood riding in the saddle,' Josseran said a second time, and then he smiled. 'Good. Let's ride on.' Then, for no reason comprehensible to his companion, he threw back his head and started to laugh.

XXXI

✠

HE DID NOT recognize her at first. She wore a red and purple robe and a loose-fitting cap with a long flap that extended down her neck. A coarse black fringe covered her forehead. She held a tambourine in her right hand and a rag flail in her left. She entered the great pavilion backwards, mumbling a long, low chant. She shuffled into the centre of the great tent, between the two fires, and fell to her knees.

She reached behind her and one of the women passed her a tobacco pipe. She inhaled deeply.

'Hashish,' Josseran murmured under his breath. He knew of hashish from the Outremer where certain sects of the Saracens – the Hashishim, the Assassins – used the drug to calm their nerves before an assignment.

After several deep inhalations Khutelun went to each corner of the yurt in turn, falling to her knees and sprinkling mare's milk from a small pitcher on to the ground as libation for the spirits. Then she returned to the centre of the pavilion and sprinkled more koumiss on to the fire for the spirits of the hearth. Finally she went outside and made another offering to the Spirit of the Blue Sky.

When she returned she fell on to the ground and lay there, her limbs in tremor. Her eyes rolled back in her head.

'The Devil has possession of her,' William hissed. 'I told you. She is a witch.'

Like every good Christian Josseran feared the Devil's works, for the Church had warned him many times of the power of Beelzebub. He felt the blood drain from his face.

The yurt was dark and heavy with the incense they had sprinkled on the fire and the sweet, cloying smell of the hashish. Josseran looked around at the gathering of Tatars, their faces as pale and frightened as his own. Even Qaidu, sitting there at the head of the fire, was trembling.

There was a long silence.

Finally she stirred and rose slowly to her feet. She went to the fire and took out the blackened shank of a sheep. She examined it carefully, studying the charred bone for cracks and fissures.

'She summons the Beast,' William whispered.

'It is knavery. No more.'

William fell to his knees, clutching the silver cross at his breast. He held it in front of him and started to loudly intone a prayer of exorcism.

'Get him out of here,' Qaidu snarled and two of his soldiers grabbed William under the arms and dragged him outside.

Everyone in the yurt returned their attention to Khutelun.

'What is the judgement of the spirits?' Qaidu asked her.

'The spirits say it is a good time for the journey,' she said.

Qaidu turned to Josseran. 'You hear that, Barbarian? Tomorrow you leave for Qaraqorum!'

Josseran hardly heard him. He was still staring at Khutelun, who had fallen back to the ground. Her whole body was shuddering as if she was possessed.

By the holy balls of Saint Joseph, he thought. I lust for a witch!

✠

Her scarf whipped like a banner in the wind. Khutelun sat motionless in the saddle, around her the escort of twenty riders who would accompany them on their journey across the Roof of the World. Qaidu and Tekudai were there also, to see them on their way.

'Who is to lead us?' Josseran said.

Qaidu nodded in the direction of his daughter. 'Khutelun will see that you arrive safely at the Centre of the World.'

Josseran felt William's pony nudge alongside his own. 'The witch is to guide us?' he hissed.

'So it seems.'

'Then we are doomed. Demand that they provide us with another guide.'

'We are in no position to demand anything.'

'Do it!' William snapped.

Josseran rounded on him. 'Listen, priest, I bend my knee only to the Grand Master at Acre and to no one else. So do not presume to order me to do anything!'

William reached for the silver cross at his breast and held it in front of his face. He began to recite the paternoster.

'What is he doing?' Qaidu asked.

'It is a prayer for a safe passage,' Josseran lied.

'We have our own way of ensuring a safe journey,' Qaidu said and he nodded to Khutelun.

She dismounted and gave a signal to one of the women in the throng around the horses. The woman stepped forward carrying a wooden pail of mare's milk. Khutelun thrust a wooden dipper into the pail, knelt on the grass and sprinkled some of the milk on to the ground as an offering to the spirits. Then she went to each of the riders in turn and sprinkled milk on to the poll, the stirrups and then the rump of their mounts.

'More witchcraft,' William muttered.

They rode out of the camp, heading north. The sun was a cold copper coin, risen now over the Roof of the World; the air was frigid, searing the lungs. Khutelun turned them to the right, the lucky direction, and then they headed east, towards the sun. From here, Josseran knew, they entered a world where few men, not even the Mohammedan traders, had ever journeyed. They were travelling beyond darkness, and fear settled in his belly like lead.

XXXII

✠

THEY SET OFF across the plain at a hard gallop. He had almost forgotten how much he had suffered riding from Aleppo. After a few hours, Josseran felt as if his spine had been jarred through the top of his head. He looked over at William and could see that the good friar was suffering far more. The Tatar saddles were very narrow, upswept at front and rear, and made of wood painted in bright colours. They were beautiful to look at but like riding on stone.

Khutelun rode ahead of him. Her own saddle was covered in rich red velvet, the pommel studded with jewels. There were silver studs at the level of her thighs. He wondered how she could ride in such a device. It must be an agony. Or perhaps the silk of her thighs was as tough as leather. Well, he thought grimly, that is one mystery I will never learn the answer to.

They rode in the shadow of the snow-capped mountains, through valleys budded with poplars and cypress, fields yet to green after the long winter. Here the people did not live in yurts; they were Kazaks and Uzbeks who lived in square, flat-roofed houses. The houses were made of stone, the cracks in the walls stuffed with straw, the roofs made of branches, grass and dried mud.

The towering grey and white ramparts ahead of them seemed an impossible barrier: Was there really a way over these walls of rock and ice?

After two days of hard riding they wound their way into the foothills, through forests of walnut and juniper, into the high pastures, dotted with the black beehive yurts of the Kirghiz shepherds. Some of the herdsmen had already migrated to the high valley pastures with their flocks.

The sheep grazing on the slopes were not like the sheep of

Provence. They had huge, curling horns, some of them the length of a fully grown man. They were, in appearance, more like goats except that they had curious fat tails, like griddle pans made of wool. Josseran saw fearsome cattle with great coats and massive horns that the Tatars called yaks.

They saw wispy smoke rising through the pines, and stopped at a lonely yurt. There was goat cheese drying outside on bamboo mats. They hobbled their horses, and Khutelun pushed aside the tent flap as if it was her own. They all sat down inside the yurt and the Kirghiz shepherd and his wife brought them goat's milk and some dried mutton. Then, just as abruptly, Khutelun got them to their feet, and with a few murmured words of thanks, they remounted their horses and rode on.

✛

The Christian holy man had collapsed. He lay on his back on the grass, mumbling his incantations into the growth of beard on his face. The barbarian knelt beside him, trying to dribble koumiss from his saddlebag into his mouth. Two more ill-suited companions she had never seen.

'What is wrong with him?' she snapped.

'He is exhausted.'

'We have ridden barely a week.'

'He is not accustomed to it.'

'This Pope of yours selects his ambassadors poorly.'

'He chose him, I suspect, for his piety, not for his ability on a horse.'

'That much is obvious.' She fidgeted in the saddle. Her father had honoured her, of course, by making her escort to these ambassadors, but in truth it was an honour she would have forgone. She was afraid of this man of fire and his crow. She had flown into the future in her dreams and there were dark histories written there concerning these two.

'We must ride on.'

'We have been riding all morning,' Josseran protested.

'If we keep stopping like this we will never get there. This shaman of yours is a weakling.'

William struggled to sit up. 'Must we leave now?' There was resignation rather than protest in his voice.

Josseran nodded. 'It appears there is no time to rest.'

'Then God will give us the strength to do what we must.' He gripped Josseran's arm and stumbled to his feet. Their ponies had been tethered to a nearby pistachio tree. William's horse stamped its hooves, still suspicious of the strange smell of this foreigner; and when it felt the slap of William's hand on its rump it reared in terror, and jerked its rein so hard that it snapped. It galloped away, hammering William into the ground.

Khutelun shouted a warning and set off in pursuit across the meadow. She caught the frightened horse within thirty rods and Josseran saw her lean nimbly from the saddle to grasp its halter and rein it in.

When she returned William was still sitting on the ground, pale with shock and clutching at his shoulder. The other Tatars stood around, laughing. They thought it a wonderful joke.

Khutelun felt only irritation. They would laugh now but later he might do something not quite as amusing. 'Is he all right?'

'There are no bones broken,' Josseran said.

'He is fortunate. Please remind him again that he should mount only from the left side, as I instructed him. The horse will stand still if approached from the near side.'

'I think he will remember better now.'

'I hope so. He cannot ride, he does not speak like a Person, he has no more strength than a child. One day he will bring us bad luck, Barbarian!'

'He is a holy man, not a knight!' Josseran answered, finding himself rushing unexpectedly to the friar's defence. 'And do not call me Barbarian! My name is Josseran!'

So, she had finally baited him to anger. Wonderful. She felt her mood lighten. 'Joss-ran the Barbarian,' she said laughing and wheeled her horse away.

William settled himself into his saddle.

'Do not die on me, priest,' Josseran said, between gritted teeth. 'You are under my protection.'

'God guides and protects me each day. Do not fear for me.'

'I do not fear for you. I just do not like to fail in my duty.'

'Nor I in mine, Templar.'

Josseran watched the friar wearily spur his horse forward. He sits in the saddle like dough on a griddle, he thought. His heart belongs to the Pope, but surely his buttocks belong to the Beast.

XXXIII

✠

THEY SLEPT THAT first night in the yurt of a Kazak shepherd. Although it was spring, the nights were still bitter and Josseran and William huddled under a mountain of furs while the Tatars lay on the carpets with only their felt coats to keep them warm. The sleeves of their jackets could unfold well beyond their fingertips, and this was how they kept their fingers from freezing on even the coldest night.

They were the most self-sufficient people he had ever known, for though they were conquerors of half the world they were still nomads. Everything they needed for survival they carried with them: a fish hook and line; two leather bottles, one for water, one for koumiss; a fur helmet and sheepskin coat; and a file for sharpening arrows. Two of Khutelun's horsemen also carried a small silk tent and a thin animal hide to serve as a ground sheet should they need to make their own shelter for the night.

They climbed the emerald pastures of the valleys, picking their way between boulders and rock falls along a path that snaked between valley torrents and cliffs. Once they even negotiated a waterfall that frothed down the blue-grey of the mountain face.

Spring had swollen the rivers to a silty torrent the colour of blood, and the Tatars used their saddlebags, which were made from cows' stomachs, as floats to ford the raging streams. Sometimes they were forced to cross the same river many times as it twisted down through the valleys.

Josseran stared at the frozen wastes around them. Just a few patches of rock and lichen were beginning to appear from beneath the wind-scattered snow. 'You call this your spring?' he said to Khutelun.

'You cannot even imagine winter on the Roof of the World. We must press hard every day with our journey if we are to see Qaraqorum in time for you to return. The snow comes like a fist over these passes and when its fingers close nothing ever comes out.'

✛

The old man placed his right hand on his left shoulder and murmured: 'Rahamesh.'

The woman of the house clapped both hands in front of her and bowed. Like her husband, she wore a padded maroon tunic over baggy trousers and leather boots with upturned toes. There was a silk headscarf around her head and trailing over her shoulder.

Her husband was the *manap*, the headman, of the tiny village they had found in this lost valley. He waved them inside his house. There was no furniture, only earth mounds covered with richly patterned rugs of scarlet and blue. There were more thick felt rugs on the floors and the walls.

Two young girls entered with bowls of sour milk and thick rounds of unleavened bread. The Tatars tore off pieces of the bread, dipped them into the sour milk and started to eat. Khutelun indicated to Josseran and William that they should do the same.

William ate just a little of the bread. Hunched by the fire, shivering, he was an unprepossessing sight. His nose was red from the cold and wet, like a dog's. When the main dish arrived, still steaming, the *manap*, perhaps feeling sorry for him, placed a huge hunk of boiled mutton in his bowl and dropped a dumpling the size of a large orange on top.

He motioned for him to eat.

The rest of the Tatars did not wait on invitation. They took out their knives and started to tear at the meat. Josseran did the same. William just sat staring at the bowl.

'Your holy man should eat or he will offend the *manap*,' Khutelun said.

How do I explain to her about Lent? Josseran thought. He tore hungrily at his own piece of mutton with his teeth. How could this insufferable priest endure so much without sustenance? 'It is a holy time,' Josseran said. 'Like Ramadan. He is only allowed bread and a little water.'

Khutelun shook her head. 'I do not care if he dies, but it is not fair or just that we should make this long journey into the mountains only to bury him in the valley on the other side.'

'There is nothing I can say that will deter him. He does not listen to me.'

She studied Josseran over the rim of her bowl as she drank down some warm goat's milk. 'We revere our shamans. Yet you treat him with contempt.'

'I am pledged to protect him. I do not have to like him.'

'That is plain.'

William looked up from his miserable contemplation of the fire. 'What are you saying to that witch?'

'She is curious why you do not eat.'

'You should not speak with her. You endanger your very soul.'

'She may be a witch, as you say, but she still has our lives in her care. It would be churlish not to talk with her, do you not think so?'

'Our lives are in the care of the Lord.'

'I doubt if even He knows his way through these mountains,' Josseran murmured, but William did not hear him.

Khutelun watched this exchange, her head to one side. 'You are of his religion?'

Josseran touched the cross at his throat, and thought of his friend Simon. 'I put my trust in Jesus Christ.'

'Do you put your trust in him also?' She indicated William.

Josseran did not answer her.

'There are followers of this Jesus at Qaraqorum,' she said.

He stared at her in astonishment. So, was it really true, the rumours that had filtered back to Acre about Christians among the Tatars? 'They know of the Lord Jesus at the court of the Great Khan?'

'All religions are known to the Khan of Khans. Only barbarians know of one single God.'

Josseran ignored this deliberate barb. 'Are there many who know of Our Lord?'

'When you arrive at the Centre of the World you will see for yourself.'

Josseran wondered how far this savage princess could be believed. Was she merely taunting him, or was there substance to her claims?

'My father says your holy man does not perform magic,' Khutelun said.

Josseran shook his head.

'Then what use is he as a shaman?'

'He does not need to perform magic. He is anointed as God's instrument on earth. If I wished, I could tell him my sins and he would bring me God's forgiveness.'

'Forgiveness, for what?'

'For things I have done wrong.'

'Mistakes, you mean. You need your God to tell you that it is all right to make a mistake?'

'He also interprets for us the mind of God.'

Khutelun seemed surprised at that. 'It is a simple matter to understand the mind of the gods. They stand with those who are victorious.'

It was irrefutable logic, he supposed. Even the Pope said that it was God who gave them their victories and that it was their sins that were to blame for their defeats. Perhaps they were not so unalike after all. 'You are shaman to your people,' he said. 'So can you do magic?'

'Sometimes I see portents of the future. It is a gift that few others have. Among our people I am reckoned the best.'

'Is that why you were chosen to lead us across these mountains?'

'No. My father ordered it because I am a good leader and I am skilled with horses.'

'Why did he not choose Tekudai?'

'You do not trust me because I am a woman?' When he hesitated to reply, she said: 'It was not my wish to lead you. I was commanded. Why should I crave the company of barbarians?'

It seemed he had offended her. She turned away from him to talk instead to her companions; ribald talk, uncomplimentary comparisons between William and his horse.

After the food had been taken away the *manap* brought out a flute, made from the hollowed wing bone of an eagle. He started to play. Another of the men joined in, playing something that looked like a lute; it was a beautiful instrument, the bulbous soundbox had been carved from a piece of rosewood and inlaid with ivory. Khutelun clapped her hands, laughing and singing along, the fire-light throwing her profile into shadow.

As he watched her Josseran wondered, not for the first time, what it might be like to lie with a Tatar woman. He knew for a certainty that she would not be indifferent to him, like the whores in Genoa and Venice. He wondered why he tormented himself with such thoughts. After all, it could never happen.

That night Josseran and William slept together with the Tatars in the yurt of the *manap*, the quilts wrapped around them, their feet towards the fire. Knowing Khutelun was curled up just a few feet away from him tortured his rest, and, fatigued as he was, he found it difficult to sleep. His conscience and his passions went to war inside him.

He argued with himself for his honour. Yet my honour is already stained with blood and with lust, he thought. I have no honour left! Now I want to sully myself even further and find a way to couple myself with a Tatar savage?

By the Rule of the Temple I have sworn myself to obedience and chastity; and I have been entrusted with a sacred commission that may save the Holy Land from the Saracens. Yet all I can think of is bedding a Tatar?

You are almost beyond salvation, Josseran Sarrazini. Or perhaps being beyond salvation means being beyond damnation as well. The Lord God has pursued you these last five years and out here on the steppe I no longer feel his hot breath on my neck. If it was not for this priest, I would perhaps at last be free of him.

XXXIV

✠

THE CLOUDS PLUNGED from the high summits, rolling and broiling like smoke, and the earth under their feet turned to shale. All colour was leeched from the world.

Occasionally, through breaks in the cloud, they saw barbicans of white appear for just a moment before disappearing again. Eagles watched them from the crags, or rode on the freezing winds that were channelled through the cols.

Their ponies' hooves slipped on the loose scree, the rocks tumbling hundreds of feet and they never heard their fall. The horses gasped and fought for breath, and as soon as they reached the crest of a ridge they would have to dismount and lead the beasts clattering and slipping down to the valley on the other side.

They climbed higher and higher.

One evening they reached a high col and for a moment the clouds parted. Josseran looked back and saw the lonely tablelands of the Kazak shepherds far behind them. Then the grey clouds and soft snow closed around them once more, like a curtain, leaving them alone with the clink of horses' hooves on shale, the sound of William's voice as he shouted his prayers to the echoing mountain passes, the distant baying of a wolf. Beside the track the bones of a long-dead horse crumbled into the snow.

The Roof of the World was still far above them, cold and terrible.

✠

When they climbed above the tree line there was nowhere to tie off the reins of the horses. Instead Khutelun showed Josseran and William how to fix their lead reins around the front legs of their horse as a hobble, then showed them the special quick-release knot the Tatars used. The horses seemed accustomed to this treatment. Josseran never once saw a Tatar pony protest at having its legs handled.

Josseran was surprised at the relationship between the Tatars and their horses. Although they were without exception the best horsemen he had ever seen, they did not forge any bond with their mounts, as Christian or Saracen knights did. They would not treat a stubborn horse with cruelty nor would they treat a good horse with any particular affection. They did not talk to them or stroke them or give them any encouragement at all. At the end of a day's ride they would simply give their mount a brisk curry with a wooden blade to scrape away the dried sweat and then the horses were immediately hobbled and turned loose to forage for themselves, for the Tatars did not find feed for their ponies, even in the snows.

Josseran himself worried endlessly over Kismet. He did not think she would survive long up here.

They were in the high valleys now, where not even the hardy Tajiks or Kirghiz would venture. For the last few nights they had huddled under makeshift canvas tents. They stacked saddlebags as low ramparts against the encroaching wind and snow. Tonight, as the sun sank below the Roof of the World, Kismet stood miserable and shivering. She was starving, a parody of a horse, her bones visible beneath her skin. She twitched in the last of the sunlight as the shadows of the cliffs crept towards her and whimpered when Josseran stroked her scrawny neck.

He whispered a few words of comfort into her ear, knowing that unless they came down off these mountains soon, he would lose her.

'Not far, my brave Kismet. You must keep your courage. Soon there will be rich grasses to eat and the sun will warm your flanks again. Be brave.'

'What are you doing?'

He looked around. It was Khutelun.

'She is suffering.'

'She is a horse.'

'Kismet has been with me for five years. I have had her ever since I first arrived in Outremer.'

'Kismet?'

'It is the name I gave her,' he said, stroking the horse's muzzle. 'It is a Mohammedan name. It means "fate".'

'Her name?'

'Yes, her name.'

Khutelun gave him a look one might give an idiot found playing with his own excrement.

'You do not give your horses names?' he asked her.

'Do you give names to the clouds?'

'A horse is different.'

'A horse is a horse. Do you talk to your sheep and your cattle as well?'

She was mocking him, perhaps, but she was also trying to understand. She was the only one of the Tatars who was genuinely curious about him. Although he had taught himself their language, and he could communicate with them easily now, they did not ask him questions about himself or his country, as Khutelun did. They accepted his presence with brute passivity.

'You despise your own holy men, yet you love your horses. You are a difficult people to understand.' She turned and looked back towards their camp: strips of canvas whipping in the mountain wind, their scrap of shelter for the night. She watched William struggle with his saddlebag, leaning into the wind as he staggered towards the tent.

'What is in the bag that is so precious to him?'

'It is a gift for your Great Khan.'

'Gold?'

'No, not gold.' He had learned that the friar had brought with him an illuminated Bible and Psalter, together with the essential regalia of his profession: a missal and surplice and silver censer. He guarded them as if they were the greatest treasure on earth; the Bible especially, for no one outside the church was allowed to have in their possession either an Old or a New Testament. Josseran himself possessed only a breviary and a Book of Hours.

'Why does he guard them like that? If we were going to murder you for your trinkets we would have done it in more comfort a moon ago.'

'I don't know,' Josseran said. 'The only valuable thing he has is a censer made of silver.'

She nodded, thoughtfully. 'I doubt if our new khan will be much impressed. After the *khuriltai*, he will have mountains of silver and gold.'

'William hopes to impress your khan with our religion.'

'Without magic?' She seemed incredulous. She turned around in time to see him stagger and fall on the ice. 'He is not even going to impress the street sweepers. That is, if he gets to Qaraqorum, which I cannot imagine.'

'You underestimate him. He enjoys his sufferings as much as you enjoy your mare's milk. It spurs him on. He will get there.'

'May I see this Bible?' she asked suddenly.

'You must ask Brother William.'

'And he will refuse. But not if you were to ask him for me.'

'Me? He thinks I am a devil. He won't give it to me. He is very jealous of it.'

'Tell him it is his opportunity to impress a Tatar princess with his religion.'

Josseran wondered how much weight this argument might carry when William considered her not a Tatar princess but a Tatar witch. 'I will do what I can.'

He stared at her, unashamedly. So much of her beauty, or her beauty as he imagined it, was hidden under her furs. Or was it? He was curious about her body but it was her eyes that kept him transfixed. When he looked at her, it was as if he could look into her soul.

'Can you really see the future?' he asked her.

'I see many things, sometimes in the present, sometimes things still to come. It is not something I wish for. I have no control over this gift.'

Gift! Josseran thought. In France, the priests would not call it a gift. They would put you to the rack and then have you burned!

The sudden dark descended, leaving them alone with the mournful howl of the wind.

'It is late. I must check the guards. I shall leave you to finish your conversation with your horse. Perhaps later you will share its thoughts with us.'

And she laughed and walked away.

XXXV

✠

SUMMER CAME TO the Roof of the World for just a few weeks and this early in the spring nothing grew. There was just a restless, snow-bitter wind that moaned and murmured hour after hour, rasping the nerves.

At times they pulled their horses through snowdrifts into the teeth of a gale, following a series of finger ridges that snaked ever upwards into a sheer spine of rock. The air was thin here and William seemed on the point of collapse. His face was tinged with blue and his breath wheezed in his chest.

The wind was a constant, tireless enemy. Josseran found he could not speak or even think because of it. It buffeted them with invisible fists, trying to drive them back, raging at them day after day.

One afternoon, the clouds vanished for an instant, and they saw on the other side of the valley the scars of shale and liver-coloured earth that had been carved into the blue-white massifs of the glaciers. An ochre river, coiled like a vein between the mudslides of shale and ice, twisted down to a patchwork of shadowed green valleys, perhaps a full league below them.

It was like looking over the earth from heaven.

Khutelun turned in the saddle, her scarf whipping in the wind. 'You see,' she shouted. 'The Roof of the World!'

Josseran had never felt so small. Here were the dimensions of God, he thought, the length and breadth of Him. This was raw religion.

Up here I am a long way from the man I thought I was. Every day I feel another piece of me is stripped away and I become a stranger to myself. No longer subject to the Rule, or in the thrall of the Church, I have such wild and blasphemous thoughts. It is a savage freedom this journey has afforded me.

He looked at William, slumped over his horse, the hood of his cowl pulled over his face. 'We are far from Christ here!' he shouted at him.

'No man is ever far from Christ, Templar!' William shouted over the roar of the gale. 'The hand of God guides and protects us, even here!'

You are wrong, Josseran thought. The god that lives here has no dominion over me.

✠

The corpse had turned black in the frost. The eyes were gone, torn out by birds, the entrails opened by animals. It appeared above them for a moment through the mist. It had been placed on a crag above the track, an arm hanging stiff over the lip of the rock. It was impossible to tell if it was male or female.

'By the balls of St Joseph, what is that?' Josseran muttered.

'It is the custom,' Khutelun said. 'In the valleys we consign our dead to the worms. In the high passes they leave theirs for their gods.'

William made the sign of the cross. 'Heathen,' he spat.

They saw two other corpses, in various stages of disrepair. And the next day, as they were passing through a narrow defile under a fist of black frost-cracked rock, Josseran heard something fall and he cried out an alarm, thinking it was a rock. Behind him, something landed on William's shoulder in a shower of small stones. It looked for all the world like a giant black spider. William shrieked and his pony shied, loosening the scree under its feet, and almost threw him.

It was Josseran, closest to him, who turned Kismet on the narrow trail and grabbed the reins of William's mount and calmed her.

William stared at the rotted thing that had tumbled on to him from the unseen corpse twenty feet above.

'There you are, Brother William,' Josseran said. 'The hand of God.'

The roar of his laughter echoed through the lonely mountain trails.

XXXVI

☩

JOSSERAN TURNED HIS face towards a cool sun. The ruins loomed above them in dark relief. The fortress had crumbled away over the centuries, and now there remained just a few tumbledown walls of mud brick high on the cliff, testament to some long-ago purpose. Josseran wondered at the lonely men who had soldiered here.

Khutelun reined in her horse beside him.

'What is that place?' he asked her.

'It is called the Sun Tower,' she said.

She walked her horse through the defile. Josseran followed. The path vanished into the black shadow of the cliff. 'The legend says that many years ago a great khan arranged for his daughter to marry a prince who lived on the other side of these mountains. But there were bandits hiding here and the way was uncertain. So she was brought here to the tower, with her retinue of handmaidens. Mounted guards were posted at each end of the defile while they waited for the prince to arrive with an escort to take her the rest of the way. But when he finally came to claim her he discovered she was with child.'

'The guards?' Josseran said.

'Perhaps.'

'What happened to her?'

'The handmaidens were brought before the khan and swore to him that the princess had not been touched by any man, that every day at noon a god came riding from the sky on horseback to lie with her. They said the child belonged to the Sun.'

'And did the khan believe this story?'

'Do you not believe that a god can lie with a woman and give her his seed?'

Josseran laughed. 'There is only one way that I know that a babe can be made.'

And then he thought of his own faith and his laughter died in his throat. Do I myself not believe such a legend, he thought, and is it not the cornerstone of my faith? He glanced uneasily back at the tower and then at William.

The further I travel through these barbarian lands, the further I forget myself. I could be lost here and never find my way back to Christendom again.

And perhaps never wish to.

✠

That night the black mountains froze under a silver moon. The wind whipped the canvas of their tent in a sudden flurry and he felt a droplet of snow trickle down his neck under the hood of his robe.

William shivered beside him.

'Khutelun says there are Christians on the other side of these mountains,' Josseran said.

'When did she tell you this?'

'A few days ago.'

'Why did you not tell me this before?'

'I am telling you now.'

'Is it Prester John?'

'I do not know. She just said that they know already of our religion in Qaraqorum and that there are even those in the court who practise it.'

William took time to frame his response; the cold was slowing his thoughts. 'I told you God would guide us, Templar.'

'We also discussed the tenets of our faith and she expressed a desire to see the Gospels,' Josseran said.

'You told the witch about the Holy Bible I have in my keeping? For what purpose?'

'She is curious about our religion.'

'She is not to touch it! She will defile it!'

Through a hole in the tent Josseran saw a star fall down the sky, leaving a trail of mercury. 'Perhaps you will make your first convert,' he said.

'She is a witch and beyond redemption.'

'She is no witch.'

'So now you are an expert in these matters?'

'She is simply curious about our Holy Book,' Josseran said, feeling his temper rise. 'Surely the word of God brings only good to those who see it?'

'You are enamoured of her!'

Josseran felt this truth like a physical blow. 'Damn you,' he said.

He turned his back and huddled under the furs. As he closed his eyes he thought of Khutelun, as he did every night in the darkness. William was right. He had left France to find redemption in Outremer, and now he was, as William said, enamoured of a witch. Perhaps there is no redemption, he thought, not for men like me. I shall be thrown into Hell. But when it is as cold as this, it makes it harder to fear the fire.

XXXVII

✛

THE CLOUDS WERE below them today. A cold sun hovered in a sky of washed blue. It was as if they were already in heaven.

They had ascended to a world of massive boulders, the playground of giants. Around them were the serrated citadels of the mountains and the great ice flows of the glaciers. Even the rocks here had split from the cold. Khutelun told him this was the highest place in the world; indeed, they had journeyed for days now without seeing habitation or a single other soul, although Josseran once looked up and saw a pair of snow leopards watching him from a ledge, their slow hazel eyes unblinking.

Their only other companions were the wolves, rarely seen, their lonely and mournful cries splitting the night.

They subsisted on the curd the Tatars had brought with them. Khutelun had explained to him how it was made; they boiled mare's milk, then skimmed off the cream until it formed a paste, and then left this residue in the sun to dry. After a few days it hardened to the colour and consistency of pumice. When going on a long expedition the Tatars took ten pounds of this curd in their saddlebags. When local provisions were doubtful they put half a pound in the leather bottle they kept on their saddles and by the end of the day the hammering motion of the ride produced a sort of gruel, which they ate.

It was never enough. Once, at the end of a day's hard climb, he saw Khutelun take her knife and slit the vein at her horse's neck. She held her mouth to the stream of blood and drank it down. When she had finished she held her hands over the wound again until the blood had clotted.

She wiped the blood from her mouth with her sleeve and grinned at him. 'You have a weak stomach, Barbarian.'

He shook his head, revolted.

'A little does not weaken the horse. And it keeps us alive.'

William also saw what Khutelun had done. 'You still think she is not a witch?' he hissed.

'Leave me alone.'

'She drinks the blood of animals! She belongs to Satan!'

'Just get away from me.'

'She is a witch! Do you hear me, Templar? A witch!'

✝

They wrapped fur hides around their legs and hauled their ponies into the teeth of a blizzard. They would have quickly become lost if not for the markers, made of the bones and horns of dead sheep, that had been left to guide travellers through the snows.

Late one afternoon they reached a cairn much larger than any other they had seen, this one made not of bones but of rock. The Tatars called it an *obo*. One after another, they walked their horses around it. Then Khutelun climbed off her horse and added another stone to the pile.

'What are you doing?' Josseran asked her.

'It is for the remission of our sins,' she said. 'According to the holy men who live in these mountains it brings us a better incarnation the next time we are born.'

Josseran had never heard such nonsense. 'A man is only born once,' he protested.

'Here they say that when a man dies his spirit enters another body, and this incarnation is more or less fortunate depending on his deeds during this lifetime. And so he progresses through a thousand lives until he is one with God.'

'Surely you do not believe this?'

'It does no harm. If the holy men are wrong I have wasted just a few footsteps and one stone. If they are right I have made my next life a better one.'

Her pragmatism irritated him. To his mind, faith was faith; you did not temper it according to geography. Yet there was a curious logic to what she said.

'You should do it also,' she told him.

'I have no time for such superstition.'

'Do you wish to bring bad luck on all our heads during this journey?'

He felt the other Tatars watching him. 'I shall do it for the sake of diplomacy then,' he said. He walked his horse slowly round the stones. After all, as Khutelun had said, what harm could it do?

'What is this strange ceremony?' William asked him.

'It is for the remission of sin,' Josseran answered. 'They wish us to follow their example.'

'Confession followed by absolution, administered by an ordained priest of the Holy Church, is the only way sins may be forgiven.'

'All you have to do is walk your horse around the stones, Brother William. You do not have to believe in it.'

'It would be a betrayal of faith.'

'It would take you no more than a few seconds.'

But William wheeled his horse away. 'I will not dance with the Devil!'

The Tatars shook their heads. A shadow raced across the valley towards them. Josseran looked up. It was a griffon, circling on the currents high overhead, scanning the ground for carrion.

Perhaps an omen. He hoped not.

XXXVIII

✠

THEIR CARAVAN TRACKED down once more into the clouds, as a storm rumbled through the passes ahead of them. They saw a valley far below them, where the stone houses of some Tajik shepherds clung perilously to the cliffs above a rushing river. The path crumbled under their feet and a chill, amorphous mist enveloped them, cloaking them in cold and silence.

Their horses snorted in protest as their unshod hooves slipped on the lichen-covered shale, scrabbled for purchase on rocks riven with deep cracks from the bitter cold. They sent small avalanches of loose rock down the slope.

Flurries of wind threw sharp ice in their faces.

They reached a narrow ledge skirting a ravine. The way had narrowed to a path no wider than the shoulders of a horse. One slip would mean both mount and rider would fall to their death.

William watched Khutelun and her companions pick their way across, the vanguard disappearing into the grey mist. He pulled on the reins of his horse, hesitating.

'Put your trust in these ponies, Brother William,' Josseran called behind him. He had to shout to make himself heard over the rush of the river below.

'I should rather put my trust in God,' William called back. He started across, singing a hymn in Latin, *Credo in Unum Deum*.

Josseran started the slow crossing behind him.

They were perhaps halfway along the rock face when William's mount, perhaps disturbed by the nervous jitterings of its rider, lost its footing on the shale.

William felt the pony stumble. It tried to regain its balance, its rump jerking as it attempted to correct its mistake. William lurched sideways in the saddle, throwing the beast further off balance.

'William!'

He heard the warning shout from Josseran. He slid from the saddle and with his back against the rock face he dragged on the reins, in a futile attempt to pull the horse back on to the path. Both the animal's rear hooves were over the lip now.

'Help me!' William shouted at Josseran. 'Everything is in there! Everything!'

The leather bag on the saddle contained the illuminated Bible, the Psalter, the vestments, the silver censer. William released the reins and reached for the saddlebag. He caught a giddying glimpse of bottomless grey clouds and frost-cracked granite walls.

He consigned his soul to God, his fingers refusing to release their grip on the precious Bible and Psalter. He screamed, even as he committed himself to death.

Strong arms closed round his waist, hauling him back from the edge.

'Let go of it!' Josseran screamed in his ear. 'Let go!'

It was a moment that seemed to go on forever. No, William decided, after an age of soul-searching that took but the blink of an eye; no, I will not release my hold. I will die if I must. But I cannot forfeit the Bible and Psalter. Otherwise the journey here will be of no consequence and I will have failed the Lord.

He saw the horse fall, sliding down the rock slope, kicking desperately at the air. Then it was gone and he waited to follow it down into the chasm. Instead he lay on his back on the rock and ice, the Tatar witch standing over him, her face drawn in a grimace of frustration.

She shouted something at him in her heathen tongue. He clutched the precious leather bag to his chest, felt the reassuring weight and bulk of the Bible and censer inside it. Knowing that it was safe, he rolled on to his knees and shouted a prayer of thanks to the merciful God who had saved him for His higher purposes.

☩

Khutelun stared at the Christian holy man, the pathetic bundle clutched to his chest. The barbarian lay beside him, unmoving. She knelt down and pulled back the hood of his cloak. When she took her hand away there was dark blood smeared across her fingers. He had smashed the back of his head on the rocks saving this madman.

'What is so precious in the package that the crow is willing to die for it?' one of her escort growled. The crow: the name the Tatars had given the Christian shaman.

'I don't know,' Khutelun answered.

The barbarian's eyes had rolled back in his head. Perhaps he was dead. 'Joss-ran,' she whispered.

Inexplicably, a fist closed around her heart.

XXXIX

☩

'I AM GOING to give you the unction,' William whispered. He
kissed the precious purple stole for which he had risked his life
and placed it around his neck. He murmured the words of the last
sacrament, putting his fingers to his lips, eyes, ears and forehead
as he repeated the familiar Latin benediction:

In nomine Patris, et Filii, et Spiritus Sancti . . .

They were in the lonely dwelling of a Tajik shepherd. Outside the
wind growled and rushed, like the moaning of the Devil himself.

'Now you will make your confession,' William whispered, 'so that
you may be received straight away into heaven.'

Josseran blinked, but found it difficult to focus his eyes. The
friar's face was thrown into shadow by the orange glow of the fire. 'I
am not . . . going . . . to die.'

'Make your confession now, Templar. If you die unshriven you
will have to face Satan.'

Josseran tried to sit up but the pain pierced his brain like a knife
and he cried aloud.

'I shall make it easy for you. I shall make your confession on your
behalf. Repeat my words. "Forgive me, Father, for I am a sinner. I
have sinned in my heart, for I have harboured unholy thoughts
about the witch, Khutelun. In the night I have abused myself while
thinking of her and spilled my seed as I did so." Say it.'

'Damn you, priest,' Josseran grunted.

'You have lusted for her. It is a mortal sin, for she is a
Mohammedan and a witch. You must be absolved!'

Josseran closed his eyes.

'Say it! "I have spoken against His Holiness the Pope and against
William, his vicar. I have uttered blasphemies."'

'I am not . . . going to die . . . and I do not need . . . your absolution.'

'Open your eyes, Templar!' Josseran felt the priest's fetid breath on his face. 'Before this night is ended you will come before your Father in heaven!'

My father, Josseran wondered, or God the Father? He did not know which meeting he feared the most.

'You will come before the judgement and you will be cast down into the pit of hell.' William raised his right hand, holding it in front of Josseran's eyes. 'Unless I absolve you with this hand! With this hand!'

Do it, Josseran thought. Why this stubborn resistance to the confessional?

✠

He had waited until his father had been called away to a parlay in Paris. King Louis had called for another armed pilgrimage to the Holy Land to free Jerusalem from the Saracens. As a knight and liegeman of the Count of Burgundy his father was obliged to answer the call to arms.

That very night Josseran went to her in her chamber. And may God forgive me, he thought. Four times he had her that night, rutting like a dog, she panting underneath him, their sweat and seed spilling on to his father's bed. Each time he coupled with her he heard the Devil laughing as he dragged him down into hell.

What could he have been thinking?

The next night he went again. The deeper he fell into his offence the less it seemed to matter to him. Sometimes, it seemed, the only way to ease the pain of the guilt is by sinning again.

He drowned his conscience in her hot, moist flesh. Was there also a trace of pride in taking that which belonged to his father, youthful arrogance persuading him that now he was the greater man?

✠

'Tonight you shall see Christ or you shall see Satan. What do you say?'

'I have not . . . sinned with her,' Josseran croaked.

'You have sinned with her in your heart! It is the same thing!'

Josseran winced. 'I am sure God lies awake in his heaven

worrying about my desperate and lonely pleasure in the darkness. Your God is worse than any mother-in-law!'

He heard the hiss of breath as William took in this latest blasphemy.

'You must confess!'

Yes, confess, Josseran thought. Let him have his way. What difference did it make now?

✠

The friar had removed the barbarian's robes. His face was flushed but the skin of his shoulders and arms was like polished ivory. His chest and belly were covered with a fine matt of hair that shone like bronze in the firelight. His muscles were hard like corded rope.

The strangeness of him made her suck in her breath. Naked, he appeared terrifying, yet in some strange way, exciting too.

She could not think why the death of one barbarian offended her so. Her concern was surely just for her father's anger should she fail to deliver her charges safely to Qaraqorum, as she had been ordered to do.

Whatever the reason, she could not let him die.

✠

William heard a sound behind him and turned his head. 'You!'

She walked in backwards, as she had done in Qaidu's *ordu*. She sang a low, rhythmic chant in the infernal language of the Tatars. Three of her soldiers followed her in, their faces grim. Khutelun shuffled to the centre of the tent and knelt beside the fire, clutching her rag flail and tambourine, the Devil's devices.

Her eyes rolled in her head.

He tried to cover Josseran's naked body. 'Get out of here!' he shouted and grabbed her by the shoulders to eject her. Immediately her Tatar escort took him by the arms and dragged him outside. They tied his wrists with thongs and threw him on the cold ground to scream his protests to the lonely night.

William sobbed with frustration. The Devil was about to drag another soul down to hell.

XL

✠

JOSSERAN OPENED HIS eyes. Wood smoke drifted lazily through the roof; weak yellow sunshine angled across the carpets. The entrance flap had been pulled aside to reveal a high, green meadow. He heard the neighing of horses.

William sat by the fire, watching him.

'It is well for you that you did not die, Templar. Your soul is steeped in sin.' William lifted his head and brought a wooden bowl of fermented mare's milk to his lips.

'How long have I . . . slept?'

'Just a night.'

'Khutelun . . .'

'The witch is outside.'

Josseran put his fingers gingerly to his scalp. The dried blood had matted his hair and there was a gaping wound beneath. 'I thought I should die.'

'It was not God's will.'

'She was here. I remember now. She was here.'

'She tried to enslave you with her devilment.'

A shadow fell across the entrance. Khutelun stood there, her hands on her hips. Josseran thought he saw a measure of relief in her eyes when she saw him awake but the look was gone as quickly as it had come.

'You seem to have recovered your strength,' she said.

'Thank you,' Josseran mumbled.

'For what?'

'For . . . your prayers.'

'I would have done the same for any of our party who was sick.' She held a bowl of steaming boiled meat. 'Here. You should eat.'

I wish I knew what you were thinking, Josseran thought.

'I am glad you are recovered. My father would have been angry if you had perished. He was charged with your safe delivery to the Centre of the World.' She left the food and gave him an enigmatic smile that made his heart leap. Then she left.

William clutched his crucifix to his breast. 'What did she say? Doubtless the witch claims credit for your recovery.'

'You were ready to . . . bury me. Why should I not give her my thanks?'

'You suffered no more than a knock to the head. It was not serious.'

'You were about to administer . . . the rites.'

'Just a stratagem to have you confess and unburden your stinking soul.'

Josseran stared at the breakfast she had brought him. 'More boiled mutton?'

'Not mutton,' William said. 'This morning we enjoy a variety to our diet.' There was a look on his face Josseran could not decipher. 'One of the horses died during the night.'

'Which horse?' But he already knew.

William did not answer. At least the friar had the decency to appear abashed.

'Kismet,' Josseran said.

'The witch said that we should not leave her for the vultures while we ourselves starve.' William got to his feet. 'In His wisdom He chose to take your horse's soul instead of yours. He perhaps found more value in it.'

'Then He is not just. He should have been more merciful to my horse. I chose this journey. She did not.'

'It was just a beast of burden! Praise God that you yet live!'

William stormed out.

Kismet! Josseran thought. William was right; why grieve over a horse? But although she was, as the friar had said, merely a beast of burden, it did not ease his shame or his sorrow. He had watched her starve by inches over these last months. She had carried him to her last breath. Her suffering was on his head.

Another weight added his load. Well, so be it. He remembered how the priest had carped at him last night to give up his burden and confess. Lay down these sins, he had said. Why had he not taken the opportunity? Why was he so stubborn?

Perhaps it was because he was the harsher judge. Even if God could forgive Josseran Sarrazini, Josseran Sarrazini could not forgive himself.

XLI

✠

THE NEXT DAY Josseran was well enough to travel. William bandaged his head with some strips of cloth and they prepared to resume their journey. They saddled their horses under a perfect sky. The reflection of the sunlight on the snowfields above them hurt their eyes.

He overheard several of the Tatars muttering to each other about William. The crow has brought us bad luck, they said. It is because he would not ride around the *obo*. Now we have lost two horses and a day's ride. Worse will follow.

'Something is amiss with these Tatars,' William said to him, tightening the girth on his saddle. Khutelun had replaced William's mount with one of her own horses, a straw-yellow mare with a milk eye and bad-tempered disposition. Josseran also had a new mount, a stallion of dirty colour with shoulders like a woodcutter.

'I have noticed nothing unusual.'

'They are all scowling at us.'

'They do not scowl at *us*, Brother William.'

The churchman looked bewildered.

'Their ill disposition is directed entirely at *you*,' Josseran said, as if explaining something to a small child.

'At me?'

'They blame you for what has happened.'

'I am not to blame if my horse loses its footing on the rocks!'

'But it was you who refused to pay homage to their cairn of stones.'

'That was just their foolish superstition!'

'They said it was bad luck not to do so and now we have had bad luck. You see what you have done in your pride? You have reinforced for them their belief in the sanctity of the *obo* and now they

146

believe our religion cannot be as strong as theirs, for it did not protect you. So in trying to prove how great we are, you have succeeded only in lessening our esteem in their eyes.'

'I will not demean my faith by allowing their witchcraft.'

'You may be a pious man, Brother William, but you are not a wise one.' Josseran climbed on to his new mount. After Kismet it felt as if he was astride a child's pony.

William jerked the reins, transmitting his ill temper to his horse, which turned her head and tried to bite him.

'See? You even antagonize the horses.'

'It is just a beast!'

'If you say so. By the way, our witch still wishes to see the Bible and Psalter.'

'Never! She will defile it!'

'God's bones!' Josseran swore and spurred away from this damned priest and set off down the trail.

XLII

✛

THE WHITE PEAKS at the Roof of the World were behind them now. They had disappeared into an overcast of lead-grey cloud. The air turned suddenly warmer.

On the fourth day they followed a track down a dune of loose sand to a salt marsh. Their approach startled a flock of wild geese. A boulder-strewn valley led to yet another gorge and then a broad plain of hard-baked sand and black gravel.

A dusty road led to an avenue of murmuring poplars and an oasis town of mud-brick houses, with straw and manure drying in the sun on the flat roofs. They saw donkey carts, piled high with melons and cabbages and carrots, entire families perched on the running boards. Startled faces stared at them from the fields and houses.

Khutelun rode up beside him. Her scarf was coiled around her face and all he could see were her dark, liquid eyes. 'This place is called Kashgar,' she said.

'Then we survived the Roof of the World?'

She pulled the scarf away. 'You had a guardian, Christian.'

Christian? So he was no longer a barbarian.

He looked around, saw the friar slumped over the milk-eyed pony behind them. 'Guardian? I would rather trust my life to a dog.'

'I do not mean your shaman. You have a man riding with you.'

He felt the small hairs on the back of his neck start to rise. 'What man?'

'He has long yellow hair going to grey, and a beard much like yours. He wears a white coat with a red cross painted here, on the left shoulder. I have seen him often, riding behind you.'

The man she was describing was his father.

✛

He had said not a word to him before he left for the king's court but he knew. Josseran could see it in his eyes. When he returned from Paris he told him that he had excused himself from service on King Louis's armed pilgrimage because of his age, but within days of his return he announced a change of heart. He discovered a sudden and uncharacteristic zeal to assist in the liberation of the Holy Land from the Saracen.

But Josseran knew the real reason he took up arms for the King.

They said that when the king's ships landed at Damietta there were scores of Mohammedan horsemen waiting for them. The Frankish knights collected on the beach, braced their lances and pointed shields into the sand and waited for the charge.

His father pulled his horse through the surf to join them on the strand and jumped into the saddle. He did not even stop to put on his coat of mail. He charged past the startled defenders and hurled himself among the Saracen, killing three of them before he himself was brought down by a sword thrust to his belly. They carried him back to the ship, still living. They said it took him four days to die.

Why would he do such a thing?

Josseran could find only one reason for his father's impetuosity.

'Christian?' Khutelun said, jolting him back from his reverie.

'The man you describe is my father. But he is dead these many years and he would never ride with me.'

'I know what I see.'

More sorcery! As if there was not enough to trouble a man's soul. This journey began as a straightforward escort mission. It should have taken no more than a few weeks. Instead I am dragged on an odyssey beyond the limits of the world, and every belief I hold dear to me, my chastity and my duty and my faith, are challenged at every turn.

What is happening to me?

PART III

Caravanserai

*Kashgar to Kumul
the Year of the Monkey*

XLIII

✠

THEY HAD CROSSED the Roof of the World looking for Prester John and the Magi of the Gospels but all they found beyond the watch-tower walls of Kashgar were the Mohammedans. It was not as Josseran had imagined the fabled land of Cathay but seemed only like another town of Outremer, with its *hans* and bazaars, arched porticoes and mosaic domes.

The people called themselves Uighurs. They did not have the almond-eyed and flat-nosed appearance of their Tatar escort. In fact they looked like Greeks and their language was very similar to the Turkic he had learned in Outremer. The Tatars, too, spoke it fluently, bastardized with a mixture of their own expressions.

They made their way to the bazaar, Khutelun and her soldiers clearing a path through the jostle of the streets behind the mosque where old men in embroidered prayer caps sat on the steps of the *iwan* and bare-legged children played in the trickle of a canal. The air was full of dust and tiny flies. Sweat ran down his spine and lathered his face.

Warren-like alleys spread out in every direction, the shadowy lanes shot through with bolts of yellow sun. Crippled beggars moaned and stretched out gnarled claws for alms. Barbers shaved the skulls of customers with long knives, smithies and bakers sweated in black-walled caves, the chink of metal and the cries of the hawkers mingled with the warm smells of baking bread and the taint of offal and excrement.

Josseran had seen many Arab markets in Outremer, but nothing like this. They were hemmed in by crowds on every side. He saw every colour of skin, from fair to nugget brown and every kind of costume: leather-skinned hawkers in turbans like Saracens; sand-blasted horsemen in fur-lined hats, sheepskins flapping against their high boots; Tajiks in tall black hats. The Uighurs were distinctive for their knee-length black coats, while their women either wore colourful silk scarves or were hidden under thick brown shawls so long and shapeless that it was impossible to tell which way they were facing when they were standing still.

The wooden two-storey houses of the city crowded in on every side. Occasionally he looked up and saw a veiled face staring at him from behind an ornate window shutter, only to quickly disappear. Josseran gawped like a peasant at a fair. There were bolts of silk taller than a man, bulging sacks of hashish and huge calico sacks of spices, orange and green and pepper-red; hand-made ornamental knives glittered with jade and rubies; boiled goats' heads stared smoke-eyed from crumbling walls and fatty sheep lungs boiled in vats. On the fretted wooden balconies of the teahouses whitebeards in long gowns sipped green tea and smoked bubbling tobacco pipes.

The market was a bedlam of animals: camels, the fearsome-looking horned cattle they called yaks, donkeys, horses and goats. The smell was overpowering; their droppings were everywhere. A camel roared close by, deafening him; a donkey shrieked through its brown teeth as it swayed and buckled under a monstrous load. They were forced against the wall by a cart, piled high with melons and cabbages and beans, the driver screaming, 'Borsh! Borsh!' as he tried to clear a path through the crowds.

Bearded Kirghiz horsemen galloped and wheeled across the maidan, churning up thick clouds of dust, while others haggled with the horse traders. A crowd had gathered for a cockfight, fierce hawk-eyed men shouting and shoving each other in the cockpit.

Khutelun strode ahead of them, leading her horse, unperturbed. She cut an exotic figure even among this Saracen throng in her purple del, her long silk scarf wrapped tightly around her head. Only the long braid of hair that straggled at her shoulder identified her as a woman. When she finally reached the animal pens, she got involved in a furious debate with a one-eyed camel trader.

'What is she doing?' William asked.

'She says we must trade our horses for camels. After here we cross a great desert to arrive at Qaraqorum.'

'A desert now? How much further will they lead us?'

'Since it is far too late to turn back perhaps it is better that we do not know.'

Josseran felt eyes watching them from every corner of the bazaar. He imagined they were an unlikely spectacle in their makeshift Tatar robes. A beggar pawed at William's sleeve; the friar shouted an oath at him and he recoiled. One of the Tatars rounded on the cripple and slashed at him with his whip.

Meanwhile Khutelun had grabbed the camel man's robe in her fist. 'You are trying to rob us!' she growled at him. 'May your private member grow cankers and rot like meat in the sun!'

'It is a good price,' the one-eyed man protested, still grinning like a lunatic, 'you can ask anyone! I am an honest man!'

'If you are an honest man, there is rice growing in the desert and my horse can recite suras from the Q'ran!'

And so it went on, Khutelun shouting insults and the camel man throwing up his hands in horror every time Khutelun offered him a lower price. If Josseran had not seen such commerce a thousand times in the medinas at Acre and Tyre he might have thought that Khutelun and the camel merchant were about to come to blows. Khutelun spat in the dust and shook her fist in the camel man's face, while he raised his hands towards heaven and beseeched his god to intercede on his behalf before he was made destitute.

But there was no violence and no lives ruined that day in the bazaar. Instead, an hour later, Khutelun and her Tatars left Kashgar with a string of camels in place of their horses and the grinning one-eyed trader as their guide.

XLIV

✠

THE KASHGAR OASIS was spread a day's ride across the plain, through avenues of poplar trees and fields of sunflowers and green wheat. Behind them, the ragged peaks at the Roof of the World were barely visible through the heat haze. Just a dream now.

They spent that night in a drab caravanserai, a fortified inn that provided safe haven from bandits in the lonely deserts. This one had stark mud walls devoid of windows, just slit holes for firing arrows. The only entrance was a barred gate of wood and iron. Animals were sheltered in a central courtyard; there was also a well for water and a mosque. Beside it was a cavernous hall with a high, vaulted roof and beaten-earth floor where travellers ate and slept together. The rules of the caravanserai were immutable, Khutelun told Josseran; it was a sanctuary from all violence. Even sworn blood enemies would not feud while they were inside the walls.

They ate a meal of mutton and rice and spices. Tiny grains of sand had inevitably found their way into the rice and crunched between their teeth. That would be the way of it from now on, Khutelun warned him. The desert would insinuate its way into everything.

Like the Devil, William answered, when Josseran translated what she had said.

'If everything that is said becomes an opportunity for a sermon,' Josseran answered, 'then I shall leave you as a deaf mute for the rest of the journey.'

Just on sunset a rider appeared at the gates of the caravanserai. Josseran recognized him as one of Qaidu's bodyguard. He had ridden hard from the west, and his horse was exhausted, its flanks streaked with froth. He whispered a message to Khutelun and she stalked away, white-lipped.

But whatever had happened, it seemed no one was of a mind to tell the barbarian.

✝

They were the only travellers that night and spread themselves around the vast hall. Even down from the mountains the night was yet cold. Josseran shivered under a huddle of furs on the hard ground.

Shadows lit by the dying fire danced around the walls. The Tatars were subdued; they feared the desert more than they feared the Roof of the World.

He stared at the blackened beams of the roof and wondered how many other travellers had passed through this great vault over the centuries, merchants going east to Cathay or west to Persia, with their silks and spices and ivory and Roman coins. There must have been very few Christian men like himself. He had heard of Venetian traders who were supposed to have come this way, but if they had, they never returned to tell of it.

'When will you make your confession to me?' the friar whispered in the darkness.

'I fear you are growing tiresome.'

'Your soul is in danger.'

'Let me worry for my soul.'

'I have seen the way you look at the witch. Did you not take a vow of chastity when you joined your Order?'

'My vow was not of lifelong obedience. I pledged five years to the Temple as penance. Those five years are almost done.'

William fell silent. Josseran thought he had fallen asleep.

'So you are not a true knight of the Temple?'

'I have faithfully fulfilled my pledge of service to the Order. When it is done I shall return to France. I have a manor house and a few poor fields that have doubtless been stolen by my neighbours in my absence.'

'You abandoned your estate to come to Outremer? What sin required such a penance?' When Josseran did not answer, William said: 'Something must weigh heavily on your conscience.'

'My service to the Order grants me remission from my earthly sins.'

'You say the words but you do not believe them. I can see into your heart, Templar.'

'I shall enumerate my sins to my confessor at the Temple on my return.'

'Be sure I shall enumerate them also.'

'I do not doubt it.'

'Mend your ways if you wish to see France once more,' William said, and then he rolled over and went to sleep.

✝

Mend your ways if you wish to see France once more.

He expected the good friar would accuse him of all manner of blasphemy and disservice before the Council on their return to Outremer. He knew what these Dominicans were like. He could drag this ingrate from the fires of Hell with his bare hands but if he winked at a harlot on the way out, he would report him to the bishop.

He tried to imagine being back in France again. He would have to find himself a wife, he supposed, talk to some of his neighbours about their daughters. He had left a bailie in charge of his affairs and he did not doubt that the man had robbed him blind in his absence and let the fields and the manor house fall into disrepair. He imagined arriving home in the middle of winter with no fresh meat in the larder, filthy rushes on the floor and half the servants asleep or run off.

He had forgotten most of their names. He wondered if even one of them would remember him either. So many memories slipping away from him. If it were not for William he wondered if he would remember France at all.

XLV

✠

THE CAMELS KHUTELUN had bought in the Kashgar bazaar were different from the beasts Josseran had seen in Outremer. These were shaggy Bactrians, with two humps instead of the single-humped camels the Mohammedans used in the Holy Land. They were ugly brutes with spindly legs and cleft lips, and they grew thick tufts of fur on the dome of each of their humps and around their hocks. With the approach of summer they were shedding some of their hair and each day they looked ever more bedraggled.

'These very good camels,' their guide told them. 'Best in all Kashgar. See how their humps stand up? If they all go flip-flop means they are too worn out, too hungry. But I sell you good camels. I am an honest man. Ask anyone.'

As a physical specimen the one-eyed camel man was scarcely better than his camels. His left eye had a milky covering which, taken together with his brown and mossy teeth, gave him the look of one of the beggars in the Kashgar bazaars. Like his beasts, he appeared to be shedding his winter coat, for his beard grew in dark and uneven clumps; and one shoulder was curiously hunched, so that he, too, possessed a sort of hump. Despite his unprepossessing appearance he was expert with the camels and knew this desert, he said, better than any man alive.

One-Eye gave Josseran and William instruction in how to ride their camels.

'First you must make him get up,' he said. He showed them how a cord was attached to a peg that pierced the septum of the camel's nose. He walked towards the herd. The nearest started spitting and snarling. Undeterred he picked up its nose cord and gave it a sharp tug. The camel roared out in protest but grudgingly got to its feet, raising its spindly back legs first.

As it did so, One-Eye placed his left foot on the animal's long neck and scrambled on top of the load on its back. Then, as it rose on its forelegs, he was thrown violently backwards.

'Now what?' Josseran shouted up at him.

'Now you hold on!' One-Eye shouted and grabbed at the load to steady himself.

The animal lurched forward. One-Eye thrust his feet straight out in front, along its back. The camel lurched forward and One-Eye rode it around them in a wide circle. The dismount was simple but crude; he clambered down the animal's neck, released his hold on the load and threw himself clear.

He grinned at them with his bad teeth. 'You see,' he said to Josseran in Turkic, 'very easy. Like mounting a woman. Once you have decided to do it, you must be firm, quick and not be discouraged if they try to bite you.'

'What did he say?' William asked.

Josseran shook his head. 'He said it's easy if you practise,' Josseran said.

✝

The next day they rode out into the desert. The Tatars exchanged their heavy felt jackets and boots for the cotton robes of the Uighurs. Now they imitated Khutelun and wrapped silk scarves around their heads, to protect their faces from the worst of the sun and the whirlwinds of grit and dust.

It was a wasteland not of dunes and soft, butter-yellow sand, but an endless plain of grey salt flats and root hummocks with a few dry, thorny desert plants. They rode into the teeth of a hot wind; the horizon dissolved to a yellow dust haze, and the poplar trees at the rim of the oasis bent and swayed as their caravan wound its way towards the great deserts at the centre of the Earth.

XLVI

✠

RIDING A CAMEL was a different torture from riding a Tatar pony. The Bactrians moved with a long, swaying motion very much like the rocking of a boat and for the first few days Josseran was overcome with something very much like seasickness until he learned to sway forward and back in rhythm with the camel's movements.

His Tatar companions were almost as expert with camels as they were with their horses. They could mount and dismount with such ease that they did not even have to stop the caravan. Khutelun might one moment be walking beside her camel, the next she would pull down hard on the nose cord and, as the beast lowered its neck, she would have already grabbed the load on its back and pulled herself on to the saddle. The secret, it seemed, was to release the nose cord slowly afterwards so that the camel did not jerk its head back up again too quickly and throw you off its shoulder.

Which was what happened to Josseran when he first attempted this manoeuvre, much to the amusement of One-Eye and the Tatars.

William's camel was called Leila by One-Eye but the friar had rechristened her Satan. For reasons of their own the Tatars had given him the most bad-tempered of all the string. She was an intimidating beast, her head topped with a wiry knot of wool, her forefeet as large as footstools. Each time the priest tried to mount her, Satan would turn her head to bite his rump as he climbed up the pack.

At the end of every day, the packs were unloaded and the string was turned loose to forage. One evening, instead of looking for pasture, Satan approached William from behind, put her mouth close to his shoulder and screamed in his ear. William jumped into the air as if he had been struck by the flat of a broadsword.

The Tatars stood back and roared.

Khutelun laughed along with the others. It was the first time she had smiled since that evening in Kashgar when her father's messenger had arrived at the caravanserai.

✠

The message from her father had worried her. Events in Qaraqorum and Shang-tu had moved faster than anyone had expected.

The *khuriltai* to choose the new Khan of Khans had already been gathered in Qaraqorum; and the dead Khaghan's brother, Ariq Böke, had already been elected as the supreme Tatar.

But not everyone had agreed with the choice. His younger brother, Khubilai, conducting the war against the Chin in distant Cathay, had not attended. Instead he had summoned his own *khuriltai* in Shang-tu, his capital, and had his generals elect *him* Khaghan. It was unthinkable that a *khuriltai* of the Tatars should be called anywhere but in the capital at Qaraqorum. It signified nothing less than rebellion and would bring on a civil war for the first time since the days of Chinggis Khan.

The wives and sons of the late Khan of Khans, Möngke, were siding with Ariq Böke. The Golden Clan, the descendants of Chinggis, had also pledged their loyalty, as had Ariq Böke's brother, Batu, of the Golden Horde. Only Hülegü had allied himself with Khubilai.

Khubilai should have been isolated by this lack of support. But he had a large and well-supplied army and a strong power base in Cathay. He posed a potent threat to the whole Tatar empire.

Qaidu's message had ended with a warning: the closer they travelled to the borders of Cathay, the more caution she should exercise. Their caravan might even be vulnerable to soldiers loyal to Khubilai.

The desert was not the only danger they would face during the first summer moon.

XLVII

☩

THEY STOPPED THAT night in the middle of a vast gravel plain. The camels, their forelegs hobbled, grazed on a few brittle salt reeds and dry thorn bushes.

William knelt beneath a wind-blackened willow, the crucifix at his throat clutched in his fist, his lips moving silently in prayer. The Tatars watched him, contemptuous and afraid of this benighted creature in their trust. He had brought them bad luck once. They were convinced he would bring them bad luck again.

Josseran sat down next to the friar and turned up the cowl of his robe as protection against the hot, gritty wind. 'For what do you pray, Brother William?'

William finished his words of supplication and dropped his hands to his sides. 'That we shall serve God's will by our sufferings here.'

'And what do you think is God's will in this?'

'That is not for poor creatures such as ourselves to know.'

'But you know the contents of the Bull his Vicar has entrusted to you. And the Pontiff knows God's will, does he not?' Ever since they left Acre he had been wondering about William's embassy. Did the Pope want a truce with the Tatars, just as the Templars did?

'The Bull is secret. I will read it only to the Tatar king, as I was charged to do.'

'Does he want to make peace with them?'

'He wishes to bring them the word of God.'

'It seems to me they are only interested in loot. They wish for kingdoms here on earth, not in heaven.'

'God will open their hearts and minds.' William rose from his knees and groaned aloud.

'What is wrong?'

'It is just the rheumatics. Do not concern yourself on my account.'

Josseran shrugged. 'Be assured that I won't. But it is my duty to deliver you safely back to Acre'

'I shall try not to disappoint you.'

'Thank you.'

In fact, though he did not wish the Templar to know it, he was suffering terribly. There were swellings at the opening of his bowels that resembled small bunches of grapes and the jerking movements of his camel made each moment on its back an agony. But if he suffered, he suffered for his Saviour and each step across this terrible desert purified his soul and brought him closer to his God.

✠

Khutelun saw the crow get up and walk off to one side to make his water. His camel was grazing nearby and it raised its ugly head and watched him. She could almost see its thoughts written in its vapid brown eyes. It helped itself to the spiny thorns of a tamarisk, chewing slowly, contemplating its tormentor in his black-cowled robe, listened to the splatter of his water on the *gebi* stones. It wandered closer, to the limit of its rope, until it was almost at his shoulder.

Then it regurgitated a bellyful of green slimy curd over his back.

William staggered forward, his water spraying over his robe as he groped one-handed behind his back to discover what had befallen him. One-Eye, who had also seen what had happened, collapsed on the ground, helpless with laughter. William attempted to wipe the foul slime from his robe while still clutching his member in the other hand. He saw Khutelun watching him and tottered away, his face crimson.

Only Josseran did not laugh. She wondered why, for she knew he had no great love for his companion.

'The beast does not like him overmuch,' she said.

'That much is plain.'

'Tell him to wait till the sun dries it,' she said, 'then he may flake it off. Else he will just make it worse.'

'I will tell him,' Josseran said.

William was shrieking as if the regurgitated cud were molten lead. If he were typical of all the barbarian shamans, she thought, they had nothing to learn from them or their religion. Yet this warrior, this . . . Joss-ran . . . was different. He had proved himself strong and brave, and ever since he was injured on the mountain she had sensed a certain kinship with him.

Though why that should be she had no idea.

✛

They were in the lands of the Uighurs, Khutelun told him.

The people here, she said, were vassals of the khan in Bukhara, and had been since the days of Chinggis, to whom they had made their submission to prevent the destruction of their fields and their cities. The nomad Tatars imposed taxes on the people through local governors, who ruled with their sanction. There was an annual tribute, the *tamga*, paid by merchants and craftsmen in the cities, and the *kalan* or land tax imposed on the farmers. Even local nomads paid taxes with a portion of their herds. This was called the *kopchur*. And there was also a 5 per cent levy on all merchants passing through the khanate. It was in this way that the Tatars kept a stranglehold on the lucrative Silk Road.

For nomads, it seemed to Josseran, they had a firm grasp of the principles of empire.

✛

A week later they reached Aksu, the Uighur capital. The ruins of ancient beacon towers rose from what Josseran at first thought to be mist. But as they came closer he saw that this mist was actually a dust storm. The ancient town lay just beyond, a huddle of white buildings sheltering under swaying poplar trees, nestled against the base of yellow loess cliffs. The green strip of the oasis clung to the banks of a river.

Suddenly they were riding through poplar-shaded lanes between green fields planted with tomatoes and aubergines. Water sparkled in the irrigation canals. A young girl veiled her face at the sight of these infidels, while little boys, bathing naked in the streams, stared at them with huge blueberry eyes. People ran into the streets in their skullcaps, old whitebeards pushing and shoving along with the rest to get a better view of these strange barbarians the Tatars had brought with them.

That night they did not stay at a caravanserai but lodged in the house of the local *darughachi*, the Tatar-appointed governor. There was a meal of mutton and rice and spices, and servants with platters of fruit and pots of aromatic green teas and a real bed with silk coverlets.

It was almost like being alive again.

But when Khutelun leaped on to her camel the next morning she shouted a warning to Josseran. 'I hope you have enjoyed your rest! From here we enter the worst desert in the world. Soon you will long to be back at the Roof of the World!'

XLVIII

✛

THE SPEED WITH which night fell in the desert surprised Josseran. It was like being thrown into a windowless dungeon and having the iron door slam shut.

Late some afternoons they might see a lonely caravanserai in the distance, and Khutelun would make them quicken their pace to arrive before sunset, find shelter behind its dun-yellow walls. They would sprawl exhausted among the packs and fibre ropes, the kettles spitting over their fires, grateful for the shelter from the unremitting desert wind.

But other nights they were forced to make their camp in the open desert, huddled by a meagre fire built from camel droppings dried by the sun. The Tatars called this *argol* and in that barren wilderness it was their only source of fuel. At least there was always plenty of it as the route they took was the one all caravans followed; it was marked by a cairn of stones every quarter of a league. One-Eye collected baskets of dung during their daily march and when they stopped to camp the Tatars would collect handfuls more while the fires were lit.

Then they would eat the thin gruel of mare's curd that had become their staple before falling into black, exhausted sleep on the hard ground, curling into their sheepskins.

Then it was the turn of the lice to start feasting.

✛

One night Josseran stayed huddled by the cold fire, long after the other Tatars had curled up to sleep inside their *dels*. Khutelun delayed also; he wondered if she had begun to look for his company as much as he now craved hers.

William stayed awake as long as he could, beggar at the feast, but fatigue finally overtook him. Alone now, Josseran and Khutelun watched the fire die, listening to the rumbling snores of the Tatars. In the darkness One-Eye babbled at the demons who infested his sleep. The camels snuffled and barked.

'Tell me about yourself, Christian,' Khutelun said softly.

'What is it you wish to know?'

'Tell me about this place you talk of. This Outremer. Is this where you were born?'

'No, I was born near a place called Troyes, in Burgundy, a province of a country called France. I have not seen it these five years or more. My home ever since has been a place called Acre, which is a great city and fortress next to the sea.'

'What is it like to live inside a fortress? Do you not sometimes feel that you are in a prison?'

'I have lived all my life inside stone walls. I am accustomed to it. It is these wide spaces that make me afraid.'

'I could never live behind a wall. A civilized person must have the grass beneath their feet and a horse saddled to ride.'

He looked up at the sky. It was like a piece of black velvet, strewn with diamonds. It was beautiful, but it left him feeling naked. 'Once, when I was a child, I decided to find out how many stars there were. I crept out of the castle one night and lay down in the field and started to count.'

'How many are there?'

'I don't know. I fell asleep. My father found me under a big oak tree, almost frozen, and had to carry me back home. I woke up on a fur beside a big log fire. I have never wished to know the night so well again. Neither have I been so cold. Until the Roof of the World.'

He remembered his father's arms around him, warming him, how his beard tickled his cheek. It should have been a pleasant memory, but it was tainted with sorrow like so many of his remembrances.

Perhaps he should have left me there under that oak tree, Josseran thought.

'My father carried me home many times,' Khutelun said. 'I was always running away at night. I wanted to fly, to touch the stars with the tips of my fingers.' She reached out her hand towards the night sky. 'In Christian, do you have names for the stars?'

'That one is the Pole Star,' he said, pointing to the north, 'but we also have names for the gatherings of the stars.' He pointed above his head 'For instance, we call that one the Great Bear. If you look long enough, you can imagine the outline of a bear.'

'Then you have a wonderful imagination,' she said, and he laughed. 'For us it is the Seven Giants. You see that star, there. That is the Golden Nail. It is where the gods tie their horses.'

'You believe in more than one god?'

'I believe there might be. Who can tell?'

'But there is only one God, who made us, and who made all things.'

'How do you know there is only one god? Have you been to the Blue Sky to see for yourself?'

'It is my faith.'

'Faith,' she repeated. 'I have faith that my horse will take me to the end of my journey. The rest I must know for myself.'

They fell silent for a while. 'Have you children, Christian?' she asked him suddenly.

'Once. I had a daughter.'

'What happened to her?'

'She died.'

'What of your wife?'

He hesitated. How much should he tell this woman of his past? And even if he did tell her, how much could she understand of it, when her own ways were so different? 'She is far away, in France.'

'Do you love her?'

'I loved her body.'

'How long since you have seen her?'

'It is many years now. I dare say she has forgotten what I look like.'

'Why do you not return to her?'

'Because she is not, in truth, my wife. She belongs to another. It is a sin on my head.'

Khutelun nodded. Taking another man's wife was a crime among the Tatars as well. She wrapped her scarf tighter around her cheeks against the cold. He could only see her eyes and the glow of the fire reflected in them.

'I will tell you this frankly,' he said. 'I have never thought of any woman as anything more than a pillow, something soft to lie with at night. Do I speak too freely for you?'

'No, of course not. My own father has many wives that he keeps for the pleasures of the body. But he has only one favourite wife, and now he is older and his blood has cooled he spends most of his days with her. They talk much.'

'It is wrong to have more than one wife.'

'Why?'

'A man should control his base desires. They are an affront to God.'

'Is that what your holy man would have you believe?'

'I may not love him overmuch but I believe he understands the mind of God better than I.'

'How can a man understand the mind of the gods? So much in life is uncertain.'

'God's law is immutable. It is for men to keep it.'

'I was taught as a child to obey no law but that of Chinggis, our Great Khan, because that is what makes our empire strong. But as for the gods, we try and listen to the spirits of the Blue Sky as best we can. But nothing is certain.'

'Did your Chinggis teach you that it was right for a man to have as many wives as he wished?'

'A woman is not just a warm place for your desires, Christian. She is also a hungry mouth and she possesses a womb with which to grow children. It is not a man's appetite that constrains his desire for women, it is his wealth. Chinggis says that, by law, a man may not take another man's wife for his pleasure; for that is indeed a crime. But that is only because it endangers the peace of the clan, not because it offends the Spirit of the Blue Sky.'

Josseran had never imagined he might talk so frankly with a woman about such matters. Yet out here, beneath the cold vault of stars and amidst the loneliness of the desert, he felt free from the constraints of his society and the tyranny of his God. But God was the god of all men, surely, and not just the god of the Franks?

'Tell me,' she asked him, 'this confession you talk about, this thing you do with your shamans. What is it you tell them?'

'We tell them our sins.'

'Your sins?'

'Lusting after women. Fornication.'

'Is it only the things you do with women, then, that you must tell them?'

'Not just that. Our falsehoods, our violence to others. Also our impure thoughts.'

'Your thoughts?'

'If we are envious. Or if we are too proud.'

'You are ashamed, then, of those things that make you a man and not a god.' She sounded puzzled. 'Does this stop you sinning? Do you feel better when you do this?'

'Sometimes. I still live in fear of being punished for eternity.'

'You have a god who makes you weak, then punishes you for your weakness. Do you not find that strange?'

He did not know how to answer her. Once again he had failed his faith. He could not even defend his religion in debate with a Tatar woman! Instead he said: 'You said you saw an old man riding with me in the mountains.'

'You do not believe me.'

'It is hard for me to believe it. Yet I am curious.'

'The old man is there whether you believe it or not. He is there if you are curious or not.'

'If it were true, I think I know who that man is.'

'I tell you what I see. I do not wish for your explanation of it. It is not necessary.'

'You describe my father.'

'Your father is dead?' When he nodded, she said: 'Why is that strange to you, Christian? Our ancestors are with us always. We must honour them or they will bring us bad luck.'

'Do you believe the ghost of my father would follow me here to protect me?'

'Of course. Why else would he be there, riding behind you?'

'Why else? As a curse.'

'If he curses you, why did he not throw you off the mountain when you went to save your shaman?'

Josseran could not answer her. He wanted desperately to believe her. He also wanted to hold her. He felt his heart hammering against his ribs and there was an oily warmth in his groin and belly. 'I have never known a woman like you,' he murmured.

For one wild moment he imagined reaching for her and placing a kiss on her lips. He even hoped that she might reach for him first, that they might bundle together under this great blanket of stars even with their companions asleep just a few feet away.

But instead she said: 'I am tired now. I am going to sleep.'

After she had slipped away into the dark he huddled on the ground, confused, exhausted, and unable to rest. His mind and his heart were in turmoil. He put his head in his hands. 'Forgive me,' he whispered into his cupped fingers.

The moon rose over the desert. He listened for his father's voice.

XLIX

✠

THEY SET OFF once again, heading east. Ranged to their left were the
mountains that the Tatars called the Tien Shan, the Celestial
Mountains. Ice caps glittered against an indigo sky, while below
them the spurs of the foothills were gouged with steep gullies, giving
them the appearance of the paws of some crouching beast. Day after
day they rode, watching the mountains change with the passage of
the sun, from the soft pinks of dawn to the coppers and metal greys
of midday, the violets and maroons of twilight.

Everywhere on the plain they saw bones, the bleaching skeletons
of horses and camels and donkeys, occasionally even the grinning
skull of a man.

They were skirting the great desert of the Taklimakan, One-Eye
said. Translated from the language of the Uighurs, it meant 'go in
and you will never come out'. But they would not venture near the
maw of the Taklimakan, One-Eye assured him. Oases ringed the
dead heart like strings of pearls on the neck of a princess. 'Unless
there is a bad storm and we become lost, we will stay well away.'

'How many times a year are there such storms?' Josseran asked
him.

'All the time,' One-Eye answered and broke into his peculiar
cackling laugh.

The desert was a drab plain of gravel and flat stones that the
Tatars called *gebi*. But when Josseran stopped to examine one of
these stones he found they actually contained brilliant colours, both
red and aubergine. But soon the *gebi* plains gave way to a salt pan of
heat-cracked mud with a friable white crust, which in turn surrendered to a wasteland of grey hard sand. It seemed to merge into the
heat haze so that there was no longer a horizon between the land
and the sky. As they left the mountains behind it seemed that they

were not travelling anywhere at all, but trudging the same mile over and over again, day after endless day.

Once, another caravan passed them, heading west to Kashgar. The camels' backs were draped with large oval blankets under their wooden saddle frames, each animal bearing two great bolts of silk on either side. The shouts of the camel driver and the jangle of the camel bells carried to them on the hot wind.

'Do you know where that silk is going?' he shouted to William. 'Venice.'

'How do you know that?' William shouted back, bouncing on the back of his camel.

'This is the Silk Road! Have you not heard of it? The Mohammedans travel along it every year to barter for those silks in the bazaars at Bukhara and Tabriz and Baghdad. But none of them have ever been further along it than Persia. But now Josseran Sarrazini has seen where the great road starts!'

'I don't see any road,' William said.

'Because there is no road. Yet traders have been coming this way with cargos of silks since the days of our Holy Book.'

'You mean that camel man will drive his camels all the way to Baghdad?'

'No, he'll sell his load in Kashgar. The Silk Road is like a chain. He'll trade for coriander or jade in the bazaar. Someone else will take his silk over the mountains and exchange it for dates and glass. And so it goes, until some bishop in Rome buys it for his mistress!'

'Did you tell this story just to bait me, Templar?'

'Indeed no. I thought it might interest you. Are you telling me that none of the bishops you know keep mistresses?'

'They will answer for their sins when the day comes. As you will answer for yours.'

'At least I shall be in good company.'

As he watched the caravan disappear into the rippling mirage of the Taklimakan, Josseran felt himself caught in the sweep of history. For centuries these camels had been trudging across this desert with their precious cloth, and only these last few years had anyone finally discovered how it was made. Incredibly they cultivated the cocoon of a certain kind of *moth*! William might call these people savage. To him they were an endless source of fascination.

L

✠

EACH DAY BEGAN at dawn with One-Eye rising silently and spreading his prayer mat in the direction of Mecca. He then performed his prayer ritual, kneeling, bowing and prostrating himself on the ground, his palms held upwards in supplication to Allah.

Afterwards he drove the camels to their loads. With a jerk of their nose strings he brought them on to their knees one by one so the Tatars could heave their baggage over the wooden pack saddles that straddled their humps. The hemp cords that secured them were then tied under the beasts' chests, despite their roars of protest, to which he paid not the slightest attention. Then, with the eastern sky a dusky orange and the last freezing stars yet in the sky, they rode once more into the desert sunrise.

For the desert crossing One-Eye had tied the nose cord of one camel to the pack saddle of the one behind so that all the camels were in a string. The last camel in the line had a bell at its neck. One-Eye knew that if he could not hear the bell then one or more of the camels had broken free. Josseran soon became accustomed to the soft tinkling sound it made, together with the rhythmic thudding of the camel pads on the hard sand, the somnolent creaking of the ropes, and the whispered 'sook-sook' of their camel man as he walked ahead, leading the way.

The hot wind sucked them dry. Josseran could no longer feel his lips, which were swollen with a hard crust of cracked and parched skin. There was no water to wash but it was of no consequence because the desiccated air stopped any perspiration from collecting on the skin. Even William had lost his stink.

The thorny tamarisk bushes were the only vegetation that survived here. The wind had weathered the ground around them, leaving them exposed in purplish clumps. But even in the most desolate places herds of wild goats grazed on them, somehow drawing sustenance from this Devil's land.

Their meagre diet had left him weak. He feared he was going mad; the endless sky and the grey, featureless desert melted into one another and even time itself became featureless. The heat rising from the desert floor created ghosts on the horizon, the phantoms of trees and castles, and in the afternoons, when his eyes were fatigued and his throat parched, he would see mountains in the distance only to realize a few moments later that they were merely a handful of stones. Or he would see vast lakes and when he looked again they had gone.

To keep himself sane, he tried to recall the songs of the *jongleurs* in the marketplaces at Troyes and Paris, or recite his psalms and paternosters. But the heat and exhaustion had somehow robbed him of his ability to engage in even such simple tasks. His thoughts wheeled erratically and sometimes he forgot where he was.

He was tormented constantly by thirst. Occasionally they came across a shallow basin of baked mud and reeds, and with it a few pools of brackish water. Insects skated across the suds on the surface. The Tatars would cheerfully replenish their water bottles from this richly flavoured soup.

Out in the desert dust storms danced and whirled like wraiths.

Khutelun saw him staring at them one evening as they made camp on the *gebi* plain. 'Ghost spirits,' she said.

'There is always a pair,' he murmured, 'spinning in opposite directions.'

'The Uighurs say they are the spirits of two lovers from different clans who were not allowed to marry, because of a feud between their tribes. Unable to bear the thought of living apart they ran off into the desert to be together and perished in the sands. Now they spend their days dancing and running through the hills.'

'So now they are free?'

'Yes,' she said, 'if you believe the legend. Now they are free.'

✠

The oasis towns would appear dramatically from a grey skyline. Suddenly there would be a thin, green border to the horizon, they would see trees gathered beside a rippling lake, but then within minutes they would disappear again into the haze.

Through a long afternoon they would occasionally glimpse this tantalizing spectre. Finally the lake would transform into mirage, created by dust storms or by the rippling heat, but the trees were real enough, slender poplars that were gold and green in the light of the evening. Just before dusk they would find themselves riding along a shaded avenue, past whitebeards on donkey carts and fields of wheat and watermelons, past walled gardens and dark courtyards dotted with mulberry and ash.

Everyone in the town would come out of their houses to witness their arrival: grey-bearded farmers; women with infants swaddled and slung on their backs; naked children screaming and running through the muddy ditches.

There would always be a Mohammedan church with blue and jade mosaics glittering in the sun. But at a town called Kuqa they discovered an entirely new religion.

They had crossed a gravel plain studded with mounds and clay sarcophagi. Suddenly two gigantic stone idols reared up, standing sentinel either side of the road. These gods had the same benign smiles, and each had his right hand raised in benediction. Erosion by the sand and wind had lent gentle curves to their broad cheeks.

The camels passed under the shadows of the great statues and Josseran suppressed a shudder. He wondered what new devilment lay beyond.

✠

'His name is Borcan,' Khutelun told Josseran that night as they sat by the fire in the courtyard of the caravanserai.

'Is he a god?'

'Very like one. In some places he is revered as a prophet as great as Mohammed himself.'

'I do not understand. You are the masters here yet you allow these people to build their idols in plain view?'

'Of course.'

'But these lands belong to the Tatars. Yet you let them flaunt their religion this way?'

'Of course. This Borcan is a lesser god. If he was stronger than Tengri, the Spirit of the Blue Sky, we could not have defeated them in wars. So we let them keep their gods. It is better for us that way. It keeps them weak.'

Josseran was astonished at this line of reasoning. Unthinkable that Rome would allow any religion to flourish where they held dominion. Pope Innocent III had even ordered a crusade against the Cathars in the Languedoc because they had refused to recognize the authority of the Pope or the liturgy of Rome. Many of the cities were still rubble forty or fifty years later, and Cathar fields still lay fallow beside ruined hamlets.

Yet these Tatar devils – as William would have it – let those under their dominion do as they wished as long as they paid their taxes. It seems to me, he thought, that we Christian gentlemen can learn a lot from these barbarians.

But there were other beliefs he found harder to accept.

✝

Josseran saw one of the camels at the head of the string stagger and slump to its knees. Its head drew back so that it was touching its front hump, its mouth gaping to the sky. The noises it made in its death agonies curdled his guts.

'It was a snake,' Khutelun shouted. 'I saw it strike!'

Josseran drew his sword.

'What are you doing?' One-Eye shouted, running towards him, his robe flapping behind him.

'I am going to put it out of its misery.'

'You cannot!' Khutelun said, joining the camel man.

'But it is a mercy!'

'You cannot throw a camel away! Its soul will bring us bad luck. We must wait and see if it dies.'

'Of course it will die. Look at it! Is there any cure for a viper bite?'

'Nevertheless,' she said, 'we must wait.'

So he waited with Khutelun and the camel man. It took long

minutes but finally the camel emitted one last bellow and toppled on to its side. Its legs kicked convulsively and then it was still.

'You see,' Josseran said to her. 'We could have spared the beast its misery.'

'It would have been bad luck to kill it,' Khutelun repeated and walked away.

Josseran sheathed his sword. 'Superstition!' he hissed.

'No, Barbarian!' One-Eye said. 'She is right. Its spirit would have returned and dogged us for the rest of our journey.' He sighed, aggrieved at the loss of one of his precious string.

Josseran shook his head. Who could ever understand such a people who freely tolerated other religions within their domains and thought that even a beast of burden possessed a soul? What was a Christian knight to make of it?

L I

+

THE DIVIDE BETWEEN the barren and the sown was dramatic. There was no gradual transformation of the landscape; it was like diving from the land into the sea. One moment they were trudging beside their camels, their eyes screwed tight against the glare and the grit, the next they were riding through patchwork fields of rice and hemp and barley. Bright clear water gurgled through the irrigation channels.

Josseran knelt to wash his face. It seemed impossible that there should be so much water in the middle of the desert. It seemed to appear from the mouth of a cave on the other side of the field. Above the cave the earth had been formed into a mound, and beyond this mound was another, and yet another, forming an unbroken line that vanished in the haze in the direction of the violet mountains, perhaps some ten leagues distant.

'They are the *karezes*,' Khutelun said, from his shoulder. She pushed aside her scarf and knelt beside him, cupping the cold water in her hands. 'All of the oases of the Taklimakan get their water this way. Come, I will show you.'

She led him towards the cave. But as they came closer he saw that it was not a cave at all, but the mouth of a tunnel. They were built centuries ago, she said, and had their origins beneath the glaciers in the distant Tien Shan. They were large enough inside for a man to walk upright, and had been artfully designed so that the slopes of the channels were slightly less than the gradient of the great depression of the desert. In this way the water reached the surface close to ground level where it could be used to irrigate the crops.

The mounds they could see were the wells that had been dug to provide access to the tunnels, so they did not become silted or blocked with rubble. She led him over the baked sand to one of these wells. He peered over the mud-brick wall, tossed in a pebble, heard the splash as it hit the stream gurgling below.

'The *karezes*,' Khutelun told him, 'were built by the Tatars.'

Josseran remembered the irrigation systems he had seen near Samarkand and Merv and wondered if they had not really been built by the Persians. Hard to imagine nomads would see the need for irrigation. But he said nothing. These Tatars liked to believe nothing in the world existed before them.

They returned to their caravan and rode along the long avenues of Gaochang. Sunflowers peered down at them over the mud-brick walls; veiled women looked out from darkened doorways. The hawk-nosed men looked very much like the Arabs of the Outremer. Everything so strange, yet so familiar.

They rode through the double walls of the west gate, past a monastery with painted niches above its gates where statues of this Borcan smiled down at them. A great park surrounded the government palace. 'We will accept the *darughachi*'s hospitality tonight,' Khutelun said, and then she added: 'I think you will enjoy Gaochang.'

'Why?'

'You will see, Christian. You will see.'

LII

✠

THE MAN STOOD by the camel pens, his head bowed, deep in conversation with Khutelun. One-Eye and several of the Tatars stood around him, grinning like idiots. Josseran went over, William dogging his footsteps.

'You wanted to see me?' he said to Khutelun.

'This man wishes to talk with you.'

'What does he want?'

'He thinks because you are journeying to visit the Khan of Khans you must be a rich man.'

'Does he want money?'

'He has invited you to spend the night at his house.'

'The quarters here are comfortable enough.'

'That is not quite what he means. He is inviting you to take over his home, with all that it implies. He will move out and you can be the master of his house for the night. He says he has a wife and two beautiful daughters and they are yours to do with as you please.' There was no expression on her face, nothing in her eyes to give him any clue what she was thinking. 'He expects to be paid for this service, of course.'

Josseran stared at her, then at the man.

'What is the matter, Christian? Have you never mated with anything other than your hand?' One-Eye asked him.

The Tatars roared at this.

'Is this seemly?' Josseran said.

'They regard it as an honour here,' Khutelun answered. 'To provide such hospitality draws down a blessing from their gods.'

'What is going on?' William shouted, beside himself with frustration at being unable to understand a word of this argument.

'I am being offered . . . a woman . . . for the night.'

'A whore?' William shouted.

'No, not a whore. She is this man's wife.'

'His wife is a whore?'

Josseran was about to say: 'Yes, and his daughters, too,' but thought better of it. William looked as if he was about to have a fit of apoplexy.

'You have refused, of course.'

But Josseran had not yet decided to refuse. Five years without a woman, he was thinking; five years of penance and chastity has done nothing for my soul. He tried to calculate the month. It must be close to the Feast of the Pentecost. By this reckoning his five years of service were now complete and he had fulfilled his vow to the Temple and was a free man once more. His freedom before God was perhaps another matter, but he was already steeped in sin, so what of another?

I can always confess tomorrow to the priest.

'You will refuse,' William hissed at him. 'We are on a holy mission from the Pope himself. I shall not tolerate this!'

It was this that made up his mind. '*You* are on a holy mission from the Pope. I am just a man, flesh and blood, that is all.' He turned back to the Uighur, who was waiting patiently for an answer. Josseran studied him carefully. His sashed coat was torn and his teeth were bad. There were wisps of hair on his chin that might have been a beard on a youth. Not promising stock.

'*Es salaam aleikum,*' the man said in Arabic and was delighted when Josseran responded, as he had learned in Outremer, with: '*Wa aleikum es salaam.*'

'You would like to be my guest, sir?'

Josseran hesitated. 'Your wife,' he asked. 'She is beautiful?'

The man bobbed his head. 'As God wills.'

An honest answer, at least.

William drew back his shoulders. 'You must stay here at the palace. I forbid this!'

'You may not forbid me anything! I shall stay where it pleases me to stay!'

'Then may God have mercy on your soul!' William said in a tone that implied he hoped He would not. He stalked away.

One-Eye looked quizzically at Josseran. 'He does not like women?'

Josseran shook his head. 'He abstains from all flesh.'

'Not even, you know, the occasional sheep?'

Josseran wondered in what dangerous pursuit their camel man had lost his eye. 'You will not spurn this man's hospitality?' One-Eye persisted. 'He is eager to earn favour with his gods.'

Josseran hesitated, glancing at Khutelun, who pointedly looked the other way. Damn her. Should he pauper himself waiting for riches he would never see?

✠

Well, he is after all just a man, Khutelun thought as she made her way back to her quarters. What of it? Her own father had his private harem, the Great Khan in Qaraqorum had a hundred women at his disposal, or so she had heard. Besides, this Joss-ran was just a messenger from a barbarian country, why should she care where he spent his nights or what mares he mounted?

And yet this man troubled her. Before he came to the steppes her destiny was clear; she might stay the hour as long as she could, but one day she knew she must marry a strong and suitable prince from another clan and have children by him. That would be her life.

Before now she was resigned to it.

So why did her heart now rebel at the prospect? Surely she could not love a barbarian? The very thought was repugnant. Her life was on the steppe, with a Tatar chief like herself, where she would raise her children with the wind in their hair and the grass of the steppe under their feet.

And yet she cursed the Uighur and all his family. She hoped his wife had the face of a camel and his daughters all smelled like goats.

That night the *darughachi* had arranged a feast in honour of his guests but Khutelun failed to appear. When one of her officers went to fetch her from her quarters she sent him scurrying from the room with a well-aimed kick. As he slammed the door shut behind him he heard her knife slap into the wood a few inches from his face. He fled.

Alone, in a foul temper, she watched the shadows creep across the floor. She drank three bowls of black koumiss and passed out in a dead sleep on the floor.

LIII

☩

LIKE ALL THE houses in Gaochang, the man's home was built of mud brick. There was a *khang* in the centre of the room, for baking bread and roasting meat. Rugs hung from the walls, butter yellow and ruby red. An arched doorway led to a courtyard at the rear, which was shaded by a trellis with trailing vines.

His wife stood in the middle of the room, in a robe of home-spun silk. She wore heavy brown stockings and her hair was covered with a brown veil. Even after five years of abstinence I could as well mount my horse as mount her, Josseran thought grimly. Her daughters stared at him wide-eyed. They both wore velvet caps, what the local people called *dopas*, traced with gold thread. They wore pretty blue glass necklaces and their hair was braided in plaits as far as their hips. Only their kohl-darkened eyes were visible behind their veils.

His hostess poured water from a ewer and washed her hands three times, as etiquette required. She indicated that he should do the same. Then she bade him enter.

'Allah send down from heaven a legion of angels for our protection,' she murmured to her daughters. 'Look at the size of him! If his feet are any guide we must pray to merciful God to strike his member with a withering disease or we are all dead! And look at that nose! He is as ugly as a dead dog and I wager he has the manners of a pig!'

Josseran blinked and wondered what to do. He did not want to humiliate his hostess. 'What did you say?' Josseran asked her with sudden inspiration. 'A thousand apologies. I was wounded once about the head and since then my hearing is not what it was.'

'You speak Uighur?' the woman said, appalled.

'I have a few words.'

'My mother complimented you on your fine beard and fire-coloured hair,' one of the girls giggled.

Josseran grinned back at her. 'Thank you. I am honoured to be invited into a home where three such beautiful women abide.'

The wife smiled and bobbed her head, her face betraying fear as well as relief. 'The lord is very kind,' she said. 'Tonight our home is yours and we are honoured to have such a master!'

They took *dastarkan,* a formal supper. A cloth was placed on the floor and the women brought fruit and the flat bread they called *nan.* Josseran sat with his palms uppermost, then passed them over his face in a downwards motion, as if he was washing his face, bringing thanks to Allah for the food and a blessing on the family. The three women watched him, amazed that this barbarian knew the ways of a civilized person.

Afterwards they served him sweet white wine and something they called – and he translated as two words – *ice cream.* They served this delicacy to him in a terracotta jug and watched, giggling, while he scooped the delicious sweet into his mouth and asked for more.

He asked them how this wonder was prepared and the wife told him it was made from a mixture of butter and milk to which they added vanilla as flavour. This concoction was then stored underground in the cellar, and kept cold by packing it in ice which was hacked from the distant glaciers and transported across the plain in the winter months.

After his third bowl he sat back, replete. The silence grew.

By now the daughters had removed their veils. He noted that they were not displeasing to the eye. They were round-faced and cheerful, with pretty smiles and playful eyes. They were as curious about him as he was about them, it seemed. They kept staring at his boots. He knew what they were thinking: women in the East thought they could judge the size of a man's member by the size of his feet.

✛

The wife finally stood up and indicated that he was to follow her. She led him across the courtyard into a separate house; the girls followed, still giggling into their hands. He found himself in a large room, with a cistern of dark, tepid water at its centre. The mother stood there and waited.

'What is it you want?' he asked her.

'Take off your clothes, please, lord,' she said.

Another outbreak of giggling.

Josseran shook his head. Stripping in front of three women?

But the wife was insistent. She tugged at his tunic. After almost a month in the desert it was stiff with dirt and dust. 'I will wash it for you, lord. First we shall give you your bath.'

Josseran was not afraid to bathe, as some of his countrymen were. In Outremer he bathed often, as the Mohammedans did. But he performed his toilet privately. 'I would rather bathe alone,' he said.

'You are the lord tonight,' the wife said. 'It is our duty to give you your bath.'

Josseran relented. 'If that is your wish.'

He removed his tunic and hose and the three women gasped. He gave them an abashed smile. 'Among my own it is not considered a lance of any great length or girth. But I am flattered that you think it so.'

They made him stand on the tiles while they drew water from the cistern with wooden bowls. They washed the dust from his hair and his body, clucking and giggling like hens, pulling at the forest of hairs on his chest and belly, prodding the various parts of him as if he were a camel at the bazaar. They seemed both repulsed and fascinated in equal measure.

Afterwards they dried him and then the wife gave him the long robe that belonged to her husband.

By the time they returned to the house it was sunset. The wife lit an oil lamp. 'This way,' she said and led him to their sleeping quarters. The two daughters sat next to him on the bed and for the longest time no one spoke or moved.

'Do you all intend to stay?' he wondered aloud.

'You are the lord,' the wife said. 'It is for you to say.'

Josseran hesitated. Perhaps the wife read the expression in his eyes, for she nimbly got to her feet, placing the lamp in a niche in the wall. 'I shall bid you good night,' she said. 'May you rest well.'

And she went out, drawing a curtain across the doorway.

Josseran looked at the two daughters. They were not giggling any more.

One of them, the youngest, stood up and took off her gown. He stared at her in wonderment. In the soft yellow light of the lamp she appeared as fragile as porcelain. She had no hair anywhere on her body except on her head. He had heard that Mohammedan women shaved their bodies with sharpened scallop shells.

Her sister was the same, except a little plumper. He felt himself stirring. He heard Catherine's voice whisper to him from the shadows: *Forget everything, Josseran, forget everything tonight except me.*

The two girls lay down on the bed either side of him. They both looked a little frightened.

The older girl took it upon herself to open his robe. 'The lord is mighty,' she whispered.

He reached out a hand. 'You have nothing to fear. I shall be gentle.'

Suddenly the curtain was thrown aside and the lady of the house romped into the room, chortling. She was naked. She threw herself on him with an abandon that would have shocked him had he not spent so much time in the brothels of Genoa on the way from France.

She wrapped her thighs around him and rolled him on top of her. They joined violently. He supposed she must have done this sort of thing before.

The two younger women watched. To his eternal shame he found that their presence spoiled his performance not at all.

✠

The dim-lit saints and their attendant angels mounted the pillars of the great church, drawn in thick brushstrokes of black and gold. Icons of the Virgin flickered in the glow of candles while an old woman with a brown and toothless face poured oil into the lamps that were set in niches around the mud-brick walls.

The choir of young boys in the balcony had begun a falsetto chant while acolytes in vestments of pale violet attended the altar. Incense rose from brass censers while a black-bearded priest opened his arms in prayer.

Nestorians, William hissed from the shadows at the rear of the church.

Nestorius had been Archbishop of Constantinople eight hundred years before. His heretical views – among other false beliefs, he had refused to accept the Pope as his spiritual leader – had isolated him and his followers from the rest of the Christian world and his sect had been forced to flee into Persia. They still survived there, on good terms with the Mohammedans, it was said.

It seemed they had spread their filthy heresies much further east than anyone in Rome had supposed. These must be the Christians that Rubruck had reported seeing among the Tatars. At least it meant some of these savages were not unfamiliar with the word of Christ. All that was needed was to bring these renegade Nestorian priests to the Pope's dominion and they would have a foothold among these devil hordes. If he succeeded, it would make him as great an apostle as Paul.

The priest kissed the gold-embossed cover of the Gospel and read the liturgy in a language William did not recognize; it seemed to be neither Tatar nor Arab. He placed a scarlet cloth around the chalice and dipped the silver Eucharist spoon into the wine to administer the blood of Christ to his congregation.

William's hands balled into fists at his sides. To see such heresy and be powerless to stop it rankled in his very soul. How could a man offer up the body and blood of Christ without sanction from the Pope? It was a corruption of all that was sacred.

And yet the presence of this church so far within Tatary was cause for hope, if not rejoicing. While the Templar was busy fornicating, he, William, had at least found a purpose in their quest. The Silk Road was the path to his destiny.

He slipped silently away.

LIV

✠

JOSSERAN ROSE EARLY and stole silently from the bed. The three women were curled around each other, asleep. Guilt came, as it always does, with the morning. I shall seek absolution from Brother William, he thought. I shall go to him this very morning.

And yet, he thought, compared to my other sins, this is really of no account. This man came to me openly and offered me his women; he considers it a thing of merit. Why should I be in sin for taking what was freely offered?

The sun had not yet risen. The green-tiled dome of a Mohammedan church appeared through a damp and swirling fog. Men in white-laced skullcaps moved silent as wraiths through the streets. A veiled woman scurried from sight behind a wooden, nail-studded door.

It was a nether world, as alien to him as if he had stepped through the crust of the earth. Here, beyond all Christian laws, he was cast adrift with his own uncertainties. Removed from the strictures of the Rule and the suffocating dictates of his Church he saw himself more clearly than he had ever done in his life.

His freshly laundered clothes dried quickly in the dry air. He made his way through the waking town to the *darughachi*'s palace. One-Eye had already saddled and loaded the camels. When he saw Josseran he made an obscene gesture with the finger of one hand and the thumb and first finger of the other. He cackled and hawked cheerfully in the dust.

William was standing by the pens, his hands folded before him like a penitent. 'I shall hear your confession whenever you wish.'

'Damn you, priest.'

'I would have thought damnation a subject you would wish to avoid.'

Josseran sighed. 'I will come to you at sunset. You will hear me then.'

'May God be praised. I was beginning to fear you had no shame.'

'There are many things I am ashamed of.'

He raised his right hand in the air: 'Confess everything to me tonight that I may free you from all your sins with this hand.'

Josseran shook his head. 'I shall accuse myself of what took place last night, but that is all you will get from me.'

'Do you wish to suffer the Devil's torments in the flames?' William hissed at him.

Josseran nodded. 'Perhaps that is exactly what I want.'

✠

Khutelun did not speak to him, would not even meet his eye. An hour after dawn they rode out in caravan, across the misted fields, into the drab grey shale of the desert.

Later that morning they stopped at the far borders of the oasis to replenish their water from the last of the wells. Already there was sand in his clothes, in the tiny crevices of his eyes, in his beard. The desert was quick to reclaim its ground.

She crouched beside one of the muddy ditches, refilling her leather water bag.

'Are we far from our destination?' he asked her.

'Why? Would you rather we stayed in Gaochang?'

Something in her tone pleased him. 'I found Gaochang an oasis of delights.'

'Where we are going,' she snapped, 'there is only desert.' She pushed past him. Josseran stared after her. In a Christian woman he would have said this was very like jealousy. The idea that Khutelun was afflicted with such an emotion on his account put an extra spring into his step. That morning he vaulted easily on to his camel and right through the long hot day he could not stop smiling.

L V

✚

IT WAS THREE weeks since they had left Kashgar. They were travelling perhaps seven or eight leagues every day, spending their nights in one of the oasis towns or behind the walls of a caravanserai. But one afternoon Khutelun stopped the caravan near a stand of gnarled poplars and ordered the Tatars to make camp for the night in the open desert. She gave no explanation for her command.

'Leave your camel saddled,' she said to Josseran. 'I want you to come with me.'

His camel bellowed at this injustice as Josseran forced her back to her feet. He followed Khutelun north across the desert.

They rode through a narrow defile, following a dry stream bed. Red cliffs rose hundreds of feet into the air on each side of them. Khutelun's soft *souk-souk* as she urged her camel on echoed from the rock walls. The heat was intense.

Then Josseran looked up and what he saw made him catch his breath. The cliff face was honeycombed with caves, and at the mouth of each cave idols had been gouged out of the sheer rock. They were like the idols of Borcan that he had seen at Kuqa and some were the height of three men. Delicate stone robes, weathered by centuries, billowed in the windless silence of the canyon.

'By the holy blood of all the saints,' he murmured.

Khutelun halted her camel 'Is it not a wonder?'

'Is this what you wished me to see?'

'There is more,' she said. She jumped down and hobbled her camel's front legs. Josseran did the same.

'What is this place?'

'It is the valley of a thousand Buddhas. A monk named Lo Tsun came here and had a vision of countless Buddhas rising to the sky in a cloud of glory. He spent the rest of his life making his vision true.'

'One man could not have made all these idols.'

'There used to be a monastery at the far end of the valley. The monks who lived there dedicated their lives to making these statues.'

'But how did they get them up there? There is no way up.'

'There is a way, but it is steep. Come.'

Josseran followed her as she sprang up the rocks. He felt like a bear lumbering after a gazelle. Khutelun did not pause for breath. He could not catch her.

She waited for him at a ledge high up the cliff face. A patina of sweat on her forehead was the only outward sign of her exertions. He slumped to his knees, gasping for breath. When he was recovered he looked up at her and saw a slow, mocking smile on her lips.

By all the saints, he thought. Her mother must have been a mountain goat.

He looked around. It was a dizzying panorama, the red cliffs of the gorge, the white peaks of the Celestial Mountains far behind, thrusting through the heat haze of the afternoon.

Around and above him were the statues of the idolaters, some carved from wood, others of stone. Some lay recumbent, their heads supported on their hands like houris at a bath. They were much bigger than he had imagined looking up at them from the valley. He guessed some of them were perhaps a dozen paces long.

When he returned to Acre no one would believe he had seen such things.

He stumbled to his feet.

'This way,' she said, and led him into the mouth of the cave.

It was blessedly cooler inside the mountain and every sound was magnified. He sniffed the must of centuries.

As his eyes adjusted to the gloom he saw there were many tunnels leading from the entrance, honeycombed into the rock. Some led to vaults barely large enough for one man, others were the size of a church, carved square out of the rock with truncated and vaulted roofs.

Opposite the entrance was a rectangular platform that bore a giant terracotta statue of this Borcan, seated with his right hand raised, illuminated by a chevron of light from the entrance. His earlobes were unnaturally long, reaching almost to his shoulders, and his heavy-lidded eyes were lowered demurely like a maiden's. He wore a toga-like robe, and had been elaborately painted in ochres and aquamarines.

His acolytes were ranged in the niches in the rock around him, terracotta statues the height of a man, and so lifelike in the darkness that Josseran was almost ready to reach for his sword.

'They are only clay,' Khutelun murmured and led him into one of the smaller caverns leading from the main chamber.

It was even gloomier in there and it took him some moments to make out the shapes on the ceilings and walls. He gasped. Every part of the wall had been filled with paintings, mostly of this Borcan and his acolytes, with their satyr smiles. But there was a myriad of other figures, his worshippers and angels, as well as portraits of kings and queens in elaborate palaces, soldiers at war, farmers in their fields, hellish musicians with lutes and pipes. They were all elaborately painted in tempera on coatings of plaster, a fantastic nether world of mountain landscapes and fortified castles, skies like marbled paper teeming with thunder demons and monsters and naked houris, all executed with the finest brushwork in blacks and creams and jades.

'It is . . . hellish,' he whispered.

'You do not understand.'

'Borcan's monks glory in such things?'

'The pictures are not for glory but to show the futility of the world,' she said. 'Borcan's real name was Siddhartha. He was born a great prince but one day he gave up his life of ease to become a monk. He taught that everything is transient, that happiness and youth can never last, that all life is suffering, and we are trapped by an endless cycle of birth and rebirth. If you have a good life, your next life will be better. If you do bad things, you will return next as a beggar, or a beast of burden perhaps. But only by giving up all desire can you escape the endless wheel and reach heaven.'

'Give up desire?'

'All suffering is the result of our desire for pleasure, or power. Look.' She ran a finger along the wall. 'This is Mara, the god of illusion. He attacks Borcan with flaming rocks and tempests, and tempts him with gold and crowns and beautiful women. But Borcan knows all these things are phantoms and he will not yield his godhead.'

'So Borcan is not a god?'

'He is a man who has found his way to the source of God. He understands the Spirit of the Blue Sky.'

Josseran shook his head. 'I do not know what to make of all this,' he said. He turned back to her. 'Why did you bring me here?'

'I do not know. I myself have been here only once before. I was still a girl then, I was accompanying my father to Qaraqorum. He showed me this. I remembered it as we rode and I thought somehow . . . somehow you would understand it.'

'But you do not believe in this idol . . . this Borcan?'

'There are many religions and each has its own truths. No, I am not a follower of Borcan. But is it not beautiful here?'

She thinks I will understand. Like him, then, she felt some bond between them, some indefinable sympathy. I am a Christian knight and a Templar; she is a savage, a Tatar, who knows none of the gentleness and modesty of a Christian woman. And yet, yes, she is right, we do understand each other somehow.

'This way,' she whispered.

In the next cave the images danced and joined. Josseran almost reeled back. The walls were covered with the tempera couplings of a man and a woman. The erect phallus of the male had been delicately and faithfully reproduced; his joinings with the maid were joyous and acrobatic. The sunlight here was filtered through the narrow passages, it threw a golden aura on the frieze, bringing the shadowy lovemaking of the idols to shimmering life.

'What is wrong?' she whispered.

'The Devil's work!'

'The artist only portrays a likeness similar to your recent encounters with that woman and her two daughters.'

'It is sinful.'

'You tell me it is sinful yet two nights ago you abandoned yourself to those women with little hesitation. Surely I do not understand what it is to be a Christian.' He could not see her face in the twilight of the cavern but he heard the reproof in her voice.

'William says sex is the Devil's tool. What I did was wrong.'

'What you did was natural. It was only wrong if the woman's husband did not know what you did.' She turned back to the frieze. 'Look at this picture here. Do you see? The god so shamelessly employing the Devil's tool is Shiva, the god of personal destiny. We each of us have a destiny, Borcan says, yet we also have choice.' She ran a finger lightly across the tempera surface. 'Have you not thought of us joined together in this way, as Shiva is joined with his wife? Have you not sometimes thought of this as your destiny? And as mine?'

His voice caught in his throat. 'You know I have.'

'And yet I am not given to you in marriage, can never be. Is that not also a sin for you, Christian?'

'Why do you taunt me?'

She stood closer to the painting, where the lord she called Shiva mounted his wife like a mare. 'This hunger. It destroys our rest but we cannot rid ourselves of it. You and your shaman say you know the path better than we Tatars and yet you are maddened by your natures as a man lost in the desert is tormented by his thirst.'

He could not deny that.

She laid her hand on his shoulder. 'We must go now.'

He was angry. Women should be modest, championed, protected. This savage lady was none of those things. So why was he so drawn to her? First she made him doubt his religion, now she made him doubt even his own heart. And yet, in truth, she only gave voice to every doubt, every rebellious thought he had ever had and never had the courage to speak. She was the siren call to the part of his soul he had kept hidden all his life. He was overwhelmed by blasphemous thoughts and heretical notions and a desperate longing for something that was beyond his reach.

'We must go,' she repeated.

He did not move. His hands hung at his sides.

'Christian?'

'I left Acre to bring the friar to your prince Hülegü. I thought I should be returned inside the walls within the month. I had not wanted any of this.'

'When we begin any journey, we cannot know where that road may lead us. Obstacles fall across the way and force us to other paths. It is the way of things. Come. We must go. It will be dark soon.'

He followed her out of the cave. Outside, the sun was a copper ball and the valley was in shadow. A ghost moon hovered in a sky of exquisite colour. He reached out his hand towards it, felt as if it was close enough to touch.

He followed Khutelun down the trail, leaving the idols to keep their lonely vigil on the mountain for another night.

LVI

✠

ONE-EYE POINTED to the north. 'The Flaming Mountains,' he said.

A range of red hills stretched towards the horizon as far as he could see. Gullies were scoured into their face by countless rivers, making flame patterns in the red clay. Through the haze of the afternoon the mountains indeed appeared like a wall of fire.

And still the worst of the desert was before them.

Josseran walked in the shade of his camel's flank rather than endure the constant jarring of the hard wooden saddle and the torture of the sun. He heard William panting behind him.

'A pleasant day for a walk, Brother William.'

'I am in agony.'

'A condition much prized before God. One day you will be canonized. It will all seem of no account then.'

'Do not mock me, Templar.'

Josseran almost pitied him. The friar's face was blistered from the sun, his beard was matted and the flesh had wasted off his face, heat and exhaustion and piety had taken a terrible toll. 'I had not meant to mock you.'

'I fear I was wrong to entrust my life to you.'

'You are still alive, are you not? Do not forget who it was that saved you in those accursed mountains. Though I have yet to receive a word of thanks for it.'

'It was God's will that I lived. Perhaps He means me to be the instrument of your salvation. Though I see you resist it at every turn. You broke your word to me. You said you would confess your sins to me last night.'

'My sins will keep.'

'Where did you go with the Tatar witch?'

'She wished to show me some cave paintings these followers of Borcan had left in a cave.'

'You fornicated with her, I know it! Stay away from her, Templar! Woman is the gate of the Devil, the path of wickedness, the sting of the serpent.'

'Then why did the Lord create Eve, churchman?'

'She was put on the earth to preserve our species and look after our children and our homes. She was also created as temptress to test our holiness. All evil comes to the world through Woman.'

'Is that what you think, Brother William? Because it seems to me that it comes to us through men. I have not seen women butcher children and violate other women but I have seen men do it. Even men with crosses sewn on to their surcoats.'

'If these women and children you speak of were Saracen, then you will know that the Pope has given a special dispensation to those who rid the world of unbelievers. It is called *malecide*, the killing of evil ones. Therefore it is not sinful. But we are not talking of the sin of violence. We are talking of the sin of lust.'

'Lust does not seem such a terrible thing to me when you have seen men with their entrails out. Does it not say in the Bible "Thou shalt not kill"?'

'You wish to debate theology with me, Templar? I tell you, a man may not always be mild. Did the Lord not cast the moneychangers out of the Temple? It is not a sin to rid the world of sin.'

'I know a sin when I see one. I know when a man butchers another and sells his children to slavers, then that is a sin, whether his victims are Franks or Saracens. And how can a babe be evil? It was God's will that it was born to a Mohammedan, was it not? And what of the Christian knight who chops off the head of that infant after raping the babe's mother and disembowelling her? Does he then go straight to heaven? Is that the justice and truth of God?'

Josseran pulled hard on the camel's nose string and scrambled on its neck. He pulled himself up and settled himself on the hard wooden saddle, preferring the torment of the sun and the jarring of the camel's back to the opinions of the pious.

LVII

✛

THE PLAIN WAS pure ochre now, soft rolling dunes made up of fine grains of sand that found their way into the ears and the eyes, and left filmy, glistening layers on the clothing and skin. The great wilderness yawned before them, and they were swallowed by a heart-breaking silence.

✛

Sunset threw black pools of shadow across the dunes. The camels knelt in the sand, roaring and snapping, while One-Eye removed the loads. The ropes had rubbed sores under the animals' chests, and the wounds ran with pus and some were infested with maggots. No wonder they were so ill-tempered, Josseran thought.

Josseran and William went off to collect *argol* for the fires. Josseran heard a groan, and when he looked around he saw William staring at his hands in disgust. The *argol* he had found had not been sun-dried. In fact it was very fresh indeed.

One of the Tatars saw his mistake and laughed. The others joined in.

William smeared the excrement off his hands and on to Satan's tattered hide. The camel roared its protest at this rough handling and tried to bite him. William stalked away. But there was nowhere for dignified retreat, no tree or rock for concealment, and so he just kept walking.

'Bring him back,' Khutelun said to Josseran. 'Soon it will be night. He will lose himself in the desert.'

Josseran went after him. But William's sense of self-preservation was better developed than she had given him credit for. He had stopped, still in sight of the camels. He was on his knees, his head bowed. 'God asks too much of me,' he said as Josseran approached.

'It is only a little digested cud, Brother William.'

'It is not the filth on my hands. My back feels as if it has been racked, my nether parts are on fire, every bone in my body is weary. How can you endure this?'

'I am a knight and a soldier. It is expected of me.'

'You shame me,' he murmured.

'Also,' Josseran added, 'I had a woman the other night. It is good for the spirits.'

It was all the medicine William needed. 'May God forgive you,' William croaked and jumped back to his feet. 'You are without shame, Templar! You fornicate and you blaspheme and you shall answer for your heretical opinions when we return to Acre!' He brushed past Josseran with a crazed look in his eye. 'All right, you heathens!' he shouted as he stamped back towards the caravan, 'I shall come and pick up more shit for you!' He waved his hands above his head like a madman. 'We shall all bury ourselves in shit!'

✝

It was only a drab, wattle-and-daub town, but a paradise on earth to all those who had spent the last few weeks travelling the borderlands of the Taklimakan. The pens of the *han* were full; camels rested on their bellies, their forelegs tucked beneath them, gazing down their long noses in disdain at their human tormentors as they unstrapped the loads. There were also a few asses, and perhaps a dozen horses, part of a large Mohammedan caravan heading west with a cargo of silks and tea from Cathay.

After she had ensured that their own camels were properly bedded down for the night, Khutelun headed away from the pens towards the canvas awnings of the village bazaar, following the aromas of spices and roasting meats.

Joss-ran called to her and ran over. She experienced a moment's hesitation. She knew the others were whispering among themselves about the amount of time she spent with him. She was a princess after all, and a shaman, and they resented her playful and friendly attitude to this barbarian.

In the cave Joss-ran had confessed that he wanted to possess her, and she did not find his desire displeasing. But having him as her husband was a prospect so fantastic that the only wonder was that she entertained it at all, even in her imagination. Here was a man so estranged from his own nature and so torn in his own soul that it seemed impossible to her that he would ever find peace. How could any woman love such a man, even if it were allowed?

As he came closer she saw that he was holding something beneath his cloak. 'You asked to see one of our books,' he said.

'Your holy book? You have it with you?'

He produced the Psalter from beneath his cloak. It had a thick black binding of hardened leather with embossed gold script. He held it open for her. 'It is written in a language called Latin. These verses are songs to the praise of God.'

She had seen such treasures before; her father owned several illuminated Q'rans of the Mohammedans. They were a rare treasure for only a few still remained on the steppe. Chinggis Khan, it was said, had made the night turn to day when he lit a fire with them outside Bukhara.

The Psalter was coated with dust from the journey but was otherwise undamaged. She opened it at random and ran a finger across the pages. Some of the letters were illuminated in vermilion and royal blue, the calligraphy very precise, like the Kufic script on the mosques in Samarkand, but without its fluid aspect. There were beautiful pictures, wonderfully executed, that reminded her of the cave paintings in the desert, though these images did not have the same energy or joy.

'You will give this to the Great Khan?' she asked him.

'William hopes to reveal to him the mysteries of our religion.'

'He cannot even reveal them to *you*.'

✝

She thumbed the pages of the sacred book he had given her, and then handed it back to him. 'Thank you. Now we have both shown each other our cave.'

'I would show you much more, if I could. There are many things in my own lands that you would wonder at.'

'I wonder at the steppes and the mountains and the rivers. For all else, I am merely curious.'

'And yet . . .' he began, but was not able to finish. Their conversation was interrupted by a commotion from the camel pens. William had thrown One-Eye to the ground, and had him by the throat. One-Eye cursed him back in Turkic while he fumbled for his knife. Josseran hurried over. 'William? What is wrong?'

'This thief has stolen my Psalter!'

'No one has stolen it,' Josseran said. He held up the psalm book.

William stared at him in bewilderment. He rolled off the camel man, who got to his feet, dusted off his robes and spat in William's face for good measure, before stalking away.

William looked over Josseran's shoulder at Khutelun. 'You let the witch desecrate it?'

'She did not desecrate it. She wished to understand more of the mysteries of our faith. Who knows? Perhaps you will have a convert there.'

William snatched the book from his hands. 'I would as like baptize the Devil!' He waved a gnarled finger in his face. 'You have gone too far!' William shot a look of pure loathing in Khutelun's direction and stalked away.

One-Eye watched him depart. 'May you grow boils in your ears the size of watermelons,' he shouted after him, 'and may your stalk turn into a chicken and eat your testicles a peck at a time!'

Josseran turned back to Khutelun. 'It seems I have greatly offended him. He thinks you have desecrated his holy book.'

'It is not the Psalter that offends him,' she answered. 'Your shaman has a great fear of women. I can see his weakness and he knows it.'

'He does not fear women. He merely despises them.' He smiled. 'There is a difference.'

'Is that what you really think?' she said and smiled sadly, and turned away.

✝

Oh, but you are wrong, Khutelun thought, as she walked away. Your holy man fears me, as he fears all women. She had sensed the fracture in the priest's soul that first night in Tekudai's yurt and even though she could not see how it would be done, she knew that one day his weakness would divide along its fault and break him.

LVIII

✠

THE LAKE FORMED a perfect crescent between the dunes, the flat, black water enclosed by sedge and reeds. A fat yellow moon hung over the ruins of a temple at the shoreline. Josseran made out the faint glow of an oil lamp, smelled incense burning in pots by the altar.

Khutelun stood at the lake's edge, the wind trailing the silken scarf at her face. 'Do you hear that, Joss-ran?'

He cocked his head to listen.

It was the sound of riders, their horses' hooves drumming on the sand. Instinctively his hand went to his sword.

'Do not alarm yourself. It is just the Singing Sands.'

'They are all around us!' he shouted.

'There is nothing out there. Just phantoms. The spirits of the desert.'

He sheathed his sword, listened again. She was right. The sound was gone.

'The Singing Sands?' he repeated.

'Some say it is just the sound of the wind blowing across the sand. But the Uighurs believe there are cities out here that were buried long ago by the advance of the desert. They say the sounds you hear are the souls of the dead, crying from beneath the dunes.'

He shuddered and put a hand to the cross he wore at his throat.

'The spirits are lonely,' Khutelun said. 'They are looking for more souls to join them.'

'Join them?'

'They prey on the caravans that cross the desert. A traveller falls behind his party and he hears the sound of the hooves and rushes across the dunes in their direction to try and keep up. But the more he hurries the further away the sounds appear, luring him even deeper into the wilderness. By the time he realizes it is just the sand spirits he is hopelessly lost and the desert claims him.'

The wind shivered on the surface of the water.

Josseran heard it again, the drumming so close this time he imagined an army must suddenly appear at the crest of the nearest dune. But then it abruptly vanished on the wind.

'I have seen and heard such things on this journey as no one will ever believe when I return.'

'There are still many wonders yet, Joss-ran.'

'We still have far to travel?'

'Not far now. Before the moon is full you will gaze on the face of the Khan of Khans.'

'That is all the time that is left?'

'Is this journey not long enough for you? The mountains were not high enough, this desert too small?'

He did not answer her.

'At Kumul we will trade the camels for horses and ride north towards Qaraqorum. You will pay your fealty to the Great Khan and then you will go back to Christian.'

'I am not here to pay fealty to your khan.'

'No, but you will.'

The Singing Sands returned, a sound very like voices now, high-pitched, like the plainsong in a church. He could understand how a man might be drawn to follow it.

'Are you not eager to return to your own?' she asked him.

'There is a part of me that does not wish this journey to end.'

'All journeys end. Only the wind and the waters never change.' She sighed. 'They say the sand is blown here every day by the wind yet the lake never fills and it never changes its shape. You dream of your conquest of the Saracens; in Qaraqorum other men dream of being Khan of Khans. But the days move on, the wind blows, men die, empires fall. And still the lake is here, the same as it has always been, like the desert, the steppes, the mountains. The wind blows across the surface and the sand whispers. And all men are forgotten.'

'So we are fools if we do not seize every moment that is granted to us.'

She stood at the lake's edge, silhouetted by the moon. How old are you? he wondered. Eighteen summers, twenty? You have the brazenness of a Marseille whore, the arrogance of a queen, and the mind of a philosopher. I have never known a woman like you. I wonder what your body is like, and what passions you are saving for your husband? I wonder if I could lose myself in you, if you might be the heart where all my passions at last find their rest?

'Why do you stare at me like that?' she said, suddenly.

'I was thinking how beautiful you are.'

In truth, he could not see her in the darkness. Her beauty was preserved in his mind; her exotic almond-shaped eyes; a wisp of jet hair loosed by the wind; her skin burned to bronze by the wind. 'Are you courting me?'

'I would if I could.'

'Because you think me beautiful? But what does beauty do for the woman? She abandons her freedom for her husband's yurt and a brood of children. The stallion mounts his mare and is satisfied. He is still free. The beautiful mare is held captive by her young. I do not understand why the loveliness you see in me is such a wonderful gift.'

'If a woman is not to be a wife, why did God give her milk?'

Khutelun came close. For one wild moment he thought this exotic creature might be about to kiss him. 'If only I had my whip,' she whispered.

'What would you do with it? Beat me? Or test me for your husband?'

'You would fall in the dust after three strokes,' she said and turned on her heel, leaving him to the siren calls of the sands.

LIX

✚

DAYS, WEEKS; FORMLESS, endless, the monotony of the journey broken only by almost imperceptible changes in the desert surface and the vagaries of the weather. One morning broke warm and blue, but by noon the sky was leaden with clouds and the winds turned the horizon to an impenetrable yellow haze. The storm lasted an hour. By the afternoon the sky had cleared and the desert was once more a furnace.

The next morning they woke with ice in their beards.

Flat *gebi* stones gave way to sand, which flowed like breakers on a big sea and changed shape in the wind even as they watched. The dunes stretched as far as they could see, some as high as the walls of Antioch.

There were no birds, or lizards, or shrubs. The way ahead now was marked only by occasional clumps of crumbling *argol* and the bones of long-dead animals, bleaching under a relentless sun.

They spent two weeks in that howling wilderness, which One-Eye called the Storehouse of the Wind. It blasted them, day after day, the landscape constantly shifting and changing. When they camped at night One-Eye would tie an arrow to a long stick and plant it in the sand to indicate the direction they should take the next morning. Then they would huddle together under the cold stars, listening to the susurration of the sand, and in the mornings when they woke their surroundings had changed utterly and if it were not for their camel man's stratagems they would have become hopelessly lost.

Once they came across the ruins of a large city. Josseran was walking beside his camel, One-Eye in front of him at the head of the string, Khutelun behind.

As they reached the crest of another great dune the camel man stopped in his tracks. Below them lay all that remained of a forest, the gnarled fingers of the petrified trunks reaching from the ground like the fingers of a half-buried corpse. Beyond them the roofs of an ancient city protruded from the sand. In some places Josseran could make out the outlines of streets and laneways, in others there were just shapeless piles of rubble.

'What is this place?' Josseran asked.

'I do not know the name of it,' One-Eye answered, his voice dropping to a whisper, 'perhaps it is the Golden City of the legend.'

'What golden city?'

'There is a story of a great king who built his capital here in the Storehouse of the Wind. The city had fabulous wealth, for this place was not desert then, there was an oasis here, larger even than Gaochang or Aksu. Stories of the riches that this lord possessed spread far and wide and a tribe came down from the steppes to attack him. After he had invested the town, the chief of the tribe sent a messenger to the king saying that if he gave him ten chests of gold he would leave in peace. But the old king refused. Every day the chief sent a messenger to the walls with his offer, but always the king sent him away with words of defiance. After a long siege the city fell and the king was taken prisoner and brought before the chieftain. Again he made the same offer, ten chests of gold and he would let the king have his life and he would leave the city and all the people in peace. But still the king refused. You see, the king loved the treasure more than his own life.'

'What happened to him?'

'The chieftain told him that if he loved his gold so much, then he should have it with him always, even in death. So he had him executed by pouring molten gold into his ears and eyes.'

Josseran shuddered. 'And his city?'

'The chieftain's soldiers ransacked it but they did not find the gold they believed was hidden there. So before they returned to the north, they poisoned all the wells. Without fresh water the people died, the crops withered, the city crumbled away and was forgotten. But legend says the gold is still here somewhere, hidden underneath the sand.'

'It sounds like a story a minstrel would tell around a camp fire.'

'Perhaps you are right,' One-Eye answered, and shrugged his shoulders.

Josseran watched the wind lift feathery grains of sand from the dunes and send them whispering through the crumbling walls. He remembered what Khutelun had said that night by the crescent lake: the days move on, the wind blows, men die, empires fall. What this city had once been, or how it had come to ruin, they would never know.

The wind howled again, sent grit whipping into their faces. Josseran heard again the strange rumbling of the sands, like the tramping hooves of some invisible army.

What if some marauders were to sweep down on us? Josseran thought. We would never suspect until it was too late.

✠

That night Khutelun was visited in her dreams by the Spirit of the everlasting Blue Sky.

She dreamed she was shut inside the walls of a great palace and from her window she could see the grass of the steppe blowing in the wind. It looked like the ripples on a lake. She ran to find her horse but there were no doors and the window had a grille of iron bars.

She ran up some winding stone steps to the tower and reached out for the grasslands, so close and yet so far away. If only she could fly. *The only way out was to fly.* She woke calling out her father's name in fear.

After the dream, she lay awake the rest of the night, unable to sleep. Her thoughts wandered inevitably to the Christian and his foul-smelling crow and their stories of palaces and churches and forts.

William could not sleep either. The closer they came to Qaraqorum, the easier his journey became. He realized now that God had been testing him, and he knew he had proved himself worthy. The Tatars were his destiny. The Papal despatch was merely God's way of getting him beyond the known world.

He was to be an apostle of the new age.

At some future time, he would be spoken of in the same breath as the Church's greatest disciples, his journey to Tatary compared to Peter taking the Gospel to Rome. *Saint William, the preacher who brought God to the ungodly.* The agonies of this journey would all have been worth it. He could not wait for the morning, to ride atop of Satan to a new dawn. The heathen souls of half the world were in his hands.

LX

✠

IT CAME OUT of a blue sky, sweeping down from the north.

The camels sensed it first. They began to fidget and growl long before the first clouds appeared on the northern horizon. Then Josseran saw a dirty yellow haze creep quickly up the sky. Dust devils leaped and danced all over the plain, vanguards of the terrible onslaught to come.

It was still afternoon when darkness fell on the desert. The sun disappeared behind the thunderheads, and lightning flickered in sheets along the borders of the desert.

A cold wind whipped sand into their faces, as if flung at them from a giant fist.

The camels shrieked and pulled on the ropes. One-Eye shouted for everyone to dismount.

'The *karaburan*,' Khutelun shouted. The black hurricane.

A dun-coloured veil of dust rolled towards them across the desert, herded by the storm. It came on them quickly, like a wave rising from a calm sea. There was nowhere to shelter, nowhere to run.

There was a clap of thunder and the younger camels screamed and stamped their hooves. The older beasts knew what was happening and had already dropped to their knees and begun to bury their mouths and noses in the soft sand. One-Eye ran up and down the string, jerking on the nose cords of the younger animals to drag them to their knees, forcing their muzzles close to the ground.

'Help me!' he shouted to Josseran. 'Otherwise they will suffocate!'

When the work was done, Josseran took the only shelter there was, crouched in the lee of his camel's flank. The first sheets of rain swept towards them. A few minutes before they had been blistering in the sun. Now they shivered under a barrage of driving sleet.

He looked up, saw Khutelun, her face transformed by the storm-light, eyes wide. There was no mistaking the look on her face: the ice princess of the Tatars was afraid. Her companions, too, were jibbering like fools, shrieking and ducking with each peal of thunder.

'It is a signal from Tengri,' Khutelun shouted. 'The Spirit of the Blue Sky is angry with us!'

It is only a storm, Josseran thought. Some rain and some thunder. How bad can it be?

✛

Only a storm.

A storm, yes, but unlike any storm he had ever known. The wind howled like a banshee. Away to their left a massive dune had started to avalanche, the sands drumming down from the crest like the breaking of a golden wave.

And then the driving sleet turned to hail.

Khutelun huddled against the flanks of her camel. She was no more than a dozen paces away from him but was now almost invisible through the sheets of icy rain and wind-blown sand. Josseran stumbled over and threw himself down beside her.

'Pull your hood over your mouth and nose!' she shouted at him. 'Or you will die!'

He did as she told him to do. She was right. There was sand in his eyes, his mouth, even his nose. Already it was almost impossible to breathe.

There was a terrible groaning, as if the ground itself was creaking open. Josseran pulled the hood of his robe further over his face, choking on grit.

Even in his terror he was aware of the closeness of her. He put an arm around her shoulders, a gesture of possession and protection, and he felt her inch closer to him. Now their bodies were touching. He even felt himself stirring, despite the upwelling of fear, or perhaps because of it.

He felt her arm close around his waist.

If it should end now, he thought, in this storm, if our bodies are buried entwined in the sand and never found, it would be a fitting ending. Then I will never have to suffer the agony of leaving her, as I surely must. We will become dust devils, and dance forever on the Taklimakan.

☩

They lay there for what seemed like an eternity, clinging to each other with the same urgency as they clung to life, surrounded by roaring, choking darkness. No words were spoken; none were possible. Yet Josseran knew that a pact had been joined.

The ice-wind whipped and tore at their clothes, sand and stones thrown into the air around them clashed in a maelstrom of noise, as if the Devil himself were cursing and shrieking at finding them in their embrace.

Josseran shuddered with cold, but with the warmth of her body pressed against him, like the heat of a raging fire, he was not afraid.

☩

It went on for hours, and departed as abruptly as it had come. The noise stopped. The sun broke through a leaden sky, like a second dawn; Josseran felt its heat again on his back. He stirred, cautiously, slowly raising his head from the sand. Khutelun's camel, which had been their shelter through the storm, staggered to her feet, coughing and braying.

The orange dust-tail of the storm hastened down the sky.

Their robes were soaked with ice and rain, and they steamed in the heat of the sun. Khutelun tore the scarf from her face, and lay gasping and coughing on her back. Finally the spasm passed and she sat up.

They looked at each other. Neither of them spoke.

The dunes around them were covered with tiny, misshapen hummocks. One by one these hummocks rose and were transformed into the shapes of men and camels who had been half-buried by the storm. The Tatars stumbled around like drunks tumbling from an inn, laughing and patting each other on the shoulders, congratulating each other on their survival.

Then Josseran heard William's groans. A hillock of sand, no more than ten paces away from him, crumbled and moved, and

William sat up, sand clinging to his cheeks and lips and eyelids, like some long-buried turtle.

He was trying to breathe.

Josseran cradled William's head in his hands and held his leather water bottle to his lips. The friar coughed violently, vomiting most of the water back into the sand, and then lay on his side, gasping like a stranded fish. Josseran pulled him clear of his sandy tomb. Wind-blown gravel had shredded his cloak.

'It is over,' Josseran told him. 'The tempest has passed.'

He felt Khutelun's eyes on him. When he turned back to her she had on her face a look such as he had never seen before on any woman – well, perhaps Catherine that first night. Her eyes could have melted candle wax.

He was wrong. It was not over. The tempest had not passed.

LXI

✠

AFTER A FEW days the sand gave way to a plain of hard quartz pebbles that crunched under the hooves of the camels. The distant, snow-capped peaks of the Tien Shan finally dropped below the horizon.

With the passing of the storm the Taklimakan had blossomed, if only for a few days. Tiny yellow trumpet flowers bloomed on brown thorny shrubs and pale yellow lupins pushed their way to the surface. A miracle of the desert. Some seeds, One-Eye told him, might lie dormant for decades, waiting for just one day of rain.

They were on the borders of Cathay now, One-Eye announced. Soon we will be in Kumul. Khutelun and the other Tatars appeared nervous. Some of them had even taken to wearing their leather armour, despite the heat. Josseran buckled on the damascened sword meant for their Khaghan. If there was fighting to be done then he would be ready.

Khutelun had not spoken to him since the storm. What am I going to do? Josseran wondered. A man should act, he thought, else he is carried along with the way of the world and his decisions are made for him by fate. But what can I do? Do I really imagine myself staying here with her, living like a savage on these plains at the edge of the world? Can I spend the rest of my days milking the mares and drinking koumiss with her ripe and barbaric brothers?

Would she, the daughter of a Tatar khan, give up her own people to return with me to Christendom and life in a small and draughty castle in Burgundy? He could hardly imagine her sitting on a stool in his manor house, weaving a tapestry with needle and thread.

What, then, was the answer?

The answer was that there was no answer. If the Lord were kind he would have buried them in the storm, locked in each other's arms. It was the only way they could ever have forever.

Soon they would arrive at Qaraqorum and their torment would be over.

☩

They pushed on through a wasteland of clinkers and scorched stones, a black plain devoid of life as if some marauding army had passed this way, putting even the ground itself to the torch. Brother William prayed almost constantly, even in the saddle. He believed they had almost reached the end of the world. Strangely, he seemed almost cheerful about it, had even stopped his complaining and sermonizing.

He would never fathom him out.

Khutelun called a halt in the middle of the afternoon for a rare moment of rest. There were no trees so they sat in small groups in the dismal shade of their camels, regathering their strength. In the east the oasis of Nan-hu appeared as a green island floating on the plain. They would be there by nightfall, One-Eye told them, but no one among them seemed encouraged by the prospect. This endless desert had even tired the Tatars.

The raiders appeared like ghosts rising out of the very ground itself. The trap had been carefully laid, Josseran realized later, the horsemen waiting for them in a slight depression to the east, their presence masked by the glare of the sun.

They heard only the sudden rumble of hooves. Khutelun shouted a warning. The Tatars jumped to their feet but they were too late. They came out of a white sun; he had to shield his eyes even to see them. There were perhaps threescore riders, he guessed, riding broad-shouldered Tatar ponies.

The camels shrieked in their hobbles; several of them were hit in the flanks and shoulders by the first volley of arrows. One-Eye screamed and ran up and down the string sobbing. The camels were his life and his livelihood. It was as if each arrow had pierced his own flesh.

Their attackers rode straight at them, firing from the saddle. Josseran drew his sword and instinctively ran out to meet them.

'Stay back!' Khutelun shouted at him.

He saw three of the Tatars stagger and fall, hit by the second wave of arrows. Without his war horse and his suit of chain mail, he was all but defenceless. He readied himself to die. He wished he had had time to better prepare. Perhaps I should have made my confession after all, he thought.

The horses thundered into them; he heard more of his companions go down screaming under the hooves.

Perhaps as many as a dozen of the riders detached themselves from the main force and rode towards him. But they did not run him down, as he expected them to do. At the last moment they veered away, encircling him. It must mean they wished him alive, for some reason. It gave him the advantage.

Josseran held his sword two-handed and waited for them to come. They were Tatars, he saw, but they wore heavier armour than any he had yet seen: iron lamellar sewn on to leather cuirasses, giving them a fearsome aspect, like massive brown beetles. Their helmets were winged and decorated with gold, and some of them had leopard-skin furs around their shoulders and brilliant red blankets on their horses. More than just bandits. But there was no time to speculate on who they might be and why they had laid this trap.

He saw William, perhaps twenty paces away, darting among the horses and camels in his flapping black robe, clutching the leather saddle with the Bible and missal. One of the horsemen ran him down and clubbed him on the back of the head with the flat of his sword. The friar went down, face first, and lay still. This time he could not protect him.

Josseran tightened his grip on the hilt of the sword. The jewels in the hilt glittered in the sun. The riders kept circling. He decided to make the first move.

He ran at the nearest horseman, slashing double-handed with his sword. The man parried the blow with his own weapon, but made no attempt to strike back at him. Josseran swung again and the man panicked and rode away a dozen paces. He was no swordsman.

He heard the other riders closing in behind him and he wheeled around and slashed again, forcing them back. Josseran grinned wolfishly. If this was the best they could do he could keep this up all day.

Their leader shouted an order and they all spurred in at once. He brought two from the saddle but then they crowded in, their horses perfectly disciplined. He did not even see the blow across the skull that finally sent him crashing to the ground.

PART IV

Cathay

Kumul to Shang-tu & Qaraqorum
late spring, in the year of the Incarnation
of Our Lord 1260

LXII

✠

LIKE CRAWLING OUT of the grave.

Josseran struggled towards the light, his head throbbing with pain. He did not know how long he had been unconscious. He lay for a long time without speaking, staring at the bewildering passage of the stars spinning across the sky like comets. Finally he rolled on to his side and vomited. He heard men's laughter. He tried to say the word: 'Khutelun,' but no sound came.

Someone was leaning over him splashing water on his face.

Remembrance came slowly: the sudden appearance of the Tatar horsemen in their curious beetle-like armour; the deadly singing of the arrows; the riders surrounding him; the sickening blow to the back of his head. They must have hit him with the hilt or the flat of a sword, or he would be dead.

They had clearly meant to capture him, but his hands were not tied, and there was no one standing over him with a sword. Why?

A face swirled into his vision, a sparse black beard and a drooping moustache: a young Tatar with a thin mouth and eyes liquid and brown like a leopard.

'Barbarian, wake up!' He felt a boot in his ribs. 'You want to sleep forever?'

Josseran sat up and groaned as the nausea gripped him again.

The Tatar squatted down beside him. 'A little tap on the head and you swoon like a woman!'

Josseran aimed a blow at the Tatar's face but the man jumped back, laughing. Josseran found himself once again face down in the gravel.

The other Tatars were laughing too. 'So, you have some spirit left!' the young man shouted. 'That's good!'

'Do not antagonize them! I fear they mean to take our lives.' It was William's voice, for the love of God.

So. They had taken the friar also.

William was huddled miserably by a camp fire, his face pale as chalk, and there was blood caked into the hair at the back of his head. Josseran wondered if they had taken any of the others, but there was no sign of them.

'If they wanted . . . our lives . . .' Josseran began. If they wanted our lives, they would have killed us by now. He gave up. What was the point of explaining such things to a churchman?

Josseran stared at his tormentors. They crowded around, jostling each other for a good look at their prize. Grinning like wolves.

'Did they . . .' Josseran turned back to William. It was an effort to talk, his tongue felt twice its normal size. 'Did they kill . . . our escort?'

'I don't know,' William said, irritably. 'I was half-dead when they dragged me off. What does it matter? Find out what these bandits want with us. Tell them I have an urgent commission for their khan from the Pope.'

'I am sure . . . they will . . . be greatly impressed.'

One of the Tatars nudged him with his boot, as if he were something he had found dead on the ground. 'He's big.'

'Ugly, too,' their young leader said. 'And look at his nose!'

'The next one . . . of you flat-faced bandits who . . . speaks ill of my nose I shall run through with . . . my sword.'

The young Tatar grinned. 'So! You are the one who speaks like a civilized person. We heard this but we did not believe it.'

Spies had been watching them at the caravanserais then, Josseran thought. But whose spies? 'Who are you? What is it you want . . . with us?'

'My name is Sartaq. I and my brothers here are soldiers in the service of Khubilai, Lord of Heaven, Emperor of the Middle Kingdom, Khan of the Whole Earth. And we want nothing of you. It is you who wants to parlay with the Emperor. We have been sent here to escort you to him.'

'But we had an . . . escort. You murdered them. We were on our way to parlay . . . with the Khaghan . . . when you kidnapped us.'

Sartaq spat angrily on the sand. 'Your escort are traitors. They were taking you to Qaraqorum. All you will find there is the Emperor's brother, Ariq Böke, a usurper and by appearance no lovelier or more gracious than the hind parts of a horse. If you want to see the true Khan of Khans you must come with us to Shang-tu, to Khubilai, Emperor of Heaven.'

'What are they saying?' William asked.

'It seems we have stumbled into a . . . civil war. He says there are two kings and that this Ariq Böke, in Qaraqorum, is a usurper.'

'But what do they wish with us?'

They were caught up in Tatar politics now, Josseran realized. If this Khubilai believed himself the rightful khan, he would want to treat with all foreign ambassadors himself, to give himself legitimacy. 'They wish to take us to see the one they call the true king . . . they call him Khubilai, and his capital is Shang-tu.'

'So they do not intend to murder us?'

'No, Brother William. We are safe from the glory of heaven for now.'

'The good Lord looks over us still! He guides our steps. We should have more faith.' Josseran saw that William had had the presence of mind to sling the leather satchel over his neck before they were captured. 'We still have the Psalter and the Bible,' he said, beaming.

Josseran was indifferent to the contents of the satchel. All he could think of was Khutelun. She had been beside him when the skirmish began. What had happened to her? Had she survived the assault?

Sartaq squatted down beside him. 'I am sorry about the blow to your head; we were merely defending ourselves. You fight like a lion. You wounded two of my men.'

'I prefer the company of the others.'

Sartaq stared into the night. 'If you wish to find them, they are out there in the desert somewhere. But you will have to run like the wind for they are many miles away now. Our horses are swift and they have only camels.'

'Then you did not kill them all?'

'My orders were only to capture you and your companion.'

'Some of them are still alive?'

Sartaq cocked his head to one side. 'You care about this?'

'The woman? The woman who led our party? Is she dead?'

A murmur among the Tatars. Sartaq appeared shaken. 'There was a woman with you?'

'What happened to her?'

'We saw no woman. Just Tatar renegades. Bandits from the steppe.'

You must have seen her! Josseran thought. And yet . . . perhaps this Sartaq was telling the truth. When she wore her scarf around her head like the other men, how would they know? He supposed he would never know if she had survived. His torment was over, at least. He would do his duty now by the Grand Master of the Templars and by his God. He would relay the Pope's messenger to Khubilai and try to forget he had ever contemplated betraying his religion and his warrior brothers for a savage and a witch.

LXIII

✠

THEY SPED ACROSS the *gebi* plain at full tilt, leaping the gullies at breakneck speed. Josseran consigned himself again to the tender mercies of the Tatar ponies. Exhausted from months of travel and ill from the wound to his head this time he did not even attempt to stand in the stirrups as they did, but resigned himself to a pounding, slumped in the saddle, league after spine-jarring league.

His new companions, he had learned, were cavalry from Khubilai's own imperial guard. Sartaq was the only one he knew by name; two others, who appeared to be his lieutenants, he christened Angry Man and Drunken Man. Angry Man scowled and spat on the ground every time Josseran came close; Drunken Man got his name the first night they stopped at a caravanserai and he soused himself with black koumiss and staggered around the courtyard singing at the top of his voice.

Sartaq was an engaging fellow and Josseran found it hard to dislike him, despite the circumstances. He squatted next to him in the firelight and gave him a detailed account of their civil war, telling him that Ariq Böke and his supporters in Qaraqorum were all idlers and fools and confidently predicting their slaughter.

Josseran did not care which of their khans prevailed but it posed a dilemma for him and William; even if they made an accommodation with this Khubilai, what purpose would it serve without the agreement of the other? And how might they return to Acre with Qaidu and his followers standing astride the Silk Road, barring their way? As soldiers, these men were better equipped than Qaidu's troopers. As well as a bow and three wooden quivers of arrows, each man carried an iron mace or battleaxe on his hip and a dagger strapped to his left arm.

'What is this for?' Josseran asked him, pointing to the silk undershirt Sartaq wore underneath his lamellar armour. 'Where I come from only women and emperors wear silk.'

'It is protection,' Sartaq said. 'Silk is strong.' He pulled at the edge of the material. 'It will not tear, so even if an arrow pierces my armour it will bind itself to the arrowhead and wind tightly around it. It makes it easier to withdraw the arrow without damaging too much flesh.'

'I shall have to get one,' Josseran said.

'I will see what I can do for you, Barbarian. If you ever fight against us, you will need a whole bale of silk!'

LXIV

✠

'THE JADE GATE,' Sartaq announced. On one side the green gables of the fort were set against the snow-capped backdrop of the Qilian Mountains. Triangular emerald and white flags snapped from the pennants on the walls. On the other rose a series of black hills that their companions called the Horse's Mane.

Drunken Man pointed out the ruins of a wall the Chin had built between their land and the steppes as protection against Chinggis Khan's ancestors.

'You may judge for yourself how well it served them,' he said, laughing.

In the distance they glimpsed a patchwork of fields and stands of poplar. 'From here,' Sartaq said, 'the plain narrows to the valley that runs between the Qilian Shan and the Horse's Mane. Here we say goodbye to the Taklimakan.' And he spat in the sand.

Josseran translated what he had said for William.

'Then we have survived, by the grace of God,' the friar responded.

Josseran nodded.

'So where does he say we are now?'

'He calls this place the Middle Kingdom. I believe we are headed for Cathay, where the Silk Road begins.'

William had recovered from the battering he had taken when they were kidnapped and seemed quite undeterred by their change of fortune. He pointed to the dun-coloured temples and drum towers of the idolaters that rose above the squat and dreary town below.

'We have much work to do here,' William said. 'With your help I shall bring these people the word of God. I admonish you to help me in this. We are part of a grand design.'

'I shall do my duty as I see fit,' Josseran said and spurred his horse down the slope after Sartaq and their Tatar captors.

Paper offerings burned in a copper bowl. An almond-eyed god, his black beard flowing down his gilt armour, snarled at them from a corner of the chamber. Offerings of fruit and flowers lay at his feet.

The altar soared almost to the ceiling between two vermilion pillars. In the tabernacle a great-bellied bronze god with earlobes that hung like dewlaps to his shoulders sat cross-legged and surveyed them with a merry grin. Josseran recognized him as the god Khutelun called Borcan. He was coated with gold leaf, which was dulled with centuries of incense. Other depictions of the god, carved from bronze and wood, were ranged around the temple, on plinths, or set in niches in the walls.

There was silence, save for the gentle tinkling of a brass bell.

A monk knelt before the shrine, a book of mantras and a brass prayer bell at his knees. His head was shaved and gleamed like polished steel in the gloom. He heard them enter and rose to greet them. His face registered neither surprise nor fear.

'Who is he?' William asked Josseran.

Josseran spoke to the man in the Tatar language. 'He is the abbot,' Josseran translated.

'He heard of our approach and was expecting us. He says we are welcome here.'

'Expecting us? How could he be expecting us?'

'I do not know. But that is what he says.'

The abbot spoke again, nodding his head towards William.

'He asks to know how old you are,' Josseran said.

'Tell him I have three and thirty years. The same as Our Lord when he died for us on the Cross.'

Josseran passed this information to the abbot. There was another brief exchange and Josseran laughed bawdily and the abbot's face split into a gap-toothed smile.

'What now?' William said.

'He said you look a lot older. Then he asked if you have led a very dissolute life.'

'And what did you answer him?'

'I told him you were a notorious whoremonger.'

A hissing of breath. William had lost all patience with his

Templar compatriot. All the way from Acre he had been subjected to a tirade of ridicule and blasphemy. He had always suspected that the Pope's trust in the Order of the Temple was misplaced. These men were all heretics and recalcitrants and this particular knight showed no piety at all. One day, he promised himself, there would be an accounting. God's truth would be served.

The abbot was watching him intently from rheumy eyes. He was dressed, like many of the idolaters in these lands, in saffron robes, but wore no other ornamentation. He was very old. His smooth skin was stretched tight across his skull but hung in dewlaps under his jaw, and his high cheekbones and wispy beard gave him the appearance of a sad and curious monkey.

'Tell him I have come to bring him the good news of Our Lord,' William said.

Another whispered conversation in the strange tongue.

'He says he always welcomes good news.'

'Say that I have come from the Pope, God's mortal representative on this earth, with word of the one and true faith. Tell him he must cease his idolatrous practices immediately and worship God, whose son Lord Jesus Christ came to this earth to die for men's sins. If he does not do this he will fall into hell and suffer eternal punishments at the hands of Beelzebub.'

'He is an old man, Brother William. That might be a lot for him to take in at once.'

'Just do as I ask.'

A long conversation. William watched the old monk's face for sign that he understood the import of what he was being told. Finally William grew impatient. 'How does he respond?'

'He asked me a lot of questions about hell. I tried to explain it to him as best I could.'

William clenched his jaw. Now the Templar believed himself to be a theologian! 'It would be better if you would direct all such questions to me. You are not qualified to speak of hell with any authority. Not yet, at least,' he added, with a sour smile.

'I qualified my opinions, Brother William.'

'What was it that he asked you?'

'He seemed very interested in hell as a place and wanted to know if it was anywhere near the Taklimakan.'

'Tell him it is not of this world. It is a place reserved for the souls of the damned.'

Josseran made a face. 'This is what I said. But he answered that he already believes in hell.'

William felt a surge of hope.

'He thinks this world forms the greater part of such a place,' Josseran went on. 'He watched his own father die in agony of the plague, saw his mother raped and disembowelled by Chinggis Khan's soldiers, then was forced to stand by while all his brothers and sisters had their throats cut. He is curious to know what you think your Devil can do to frighten him.'

'You must tell him his immortal soul is at stake. He should not be frivolous.'

'I assure you, he was not being frivolous.'

'Tell him that the Devil is ten times worse than Chinggis Khan.'

Again Josseran entered into conversation with the old man. William dearly wished that he had the facility for language that God, in his wisdom, had given to the Templar.

Josseran turned back to him at last. 'He says if you think the Devil is worse than Chinggis Khan, you did not know Chinggis Khan.'

'But does he not wish for eternity?' William said.

Josseran posed the question. 'He thinks not,' Josseran said.

William could not believe his ears.

'He says he has suffered from gout for many years, which is a pain like no other. The physicians tell him death is the only cure. He also says he has pain in the joints of both his knees and the only way he can endure it is by reminding himself he will not have to suffer it much longer.' Josseran hesitated. 'He is also curious why you yourself wish to live forever when you have bad skin and such a foul smell.'

William felt the blood drain from his face. Now these barbarians insulted him. And he was there to bring them their salvation! For a moment outrage left him speechless.

Meanwhile the old man leaned forward and whispered something else.

'What does he say now? More insults?'

'He asserts that there is no god that can grant immortality to flesh. Look around you, he says. The snow melts, the leaves fall from the trees, flowers die; everything has its time. Heaven cannot grant permanence to anything so why do we seek it? Empires are built and will crumble; even Chinggis Khan did not live forever.'

'You must tell him the story of Our Lord Jesus . . .'

Josseran shook his head. 'No, Brother William. I am tired of this. He is an old man and I think in many ways he is wiser than you. I think we should leave here now.'

'Are you refusing to assist me on my holy mission?'

'I fought the Saracens for the Pope. Isn't that enough?'

He walked away. The old *bonze* regarded him from rheumy eyes, immobile, mute. William felt the frustration of his position and wanted to weep. So many souls to be saved, and all he had to assist him was one obdurate knight with a heart as black as a bear. What was he to do? Where was he to find his inspiration, where was he to find God in this wicked land?

LXV

✠

LATE ONE AFTERNOON, they stopped at a remote post house and were unsaddling their horses when he saw a horseman approaching from the north. Josseran heard the plaintive whine of a post horn. As the rider galloped into the *yam*, a groom appeared from the pens leading a fresh horse, already saddled, resplendent in scarlet halter and saddle blanket. Without a word the rider leaped from one mount on to the other and rode on.

Josseran caught just a glimpse of him; his torso was strapped with leather belts, his head wrapped in swathes of cloth. There was a large gold medallion around his neck. Then he was gone, leaving the groom holding the reins of the steaming and exhausted horse. Within minutes he was a distant speck on the plain, heading west, the way they had come.

'Who was he?' Josseran asked Angry Man.

He spat on the ground and walked away.

Sartaq overheard his question and walked over and slapped him on the shoulder. 'That was an arrow rider. One of the Emperor's messengers.'

'What is an arrow rider?'

'They carry urgent despatches to and from the imperial court. They are expected to ride at full gallop for the entire day. That way they can travel perhaps eighty leagues a day, changing horses at every post house. If it is an emergency they may even travel at night, and footmen will run in front with torches.

'Every hamlet, every town must provide horses for the *yams*, so it costs the Emperor nothing. He provides horses only for those stations on the steppes or in the desert where no one lives.'

'Why was he wearing all those belts?'

'They help keep him upright in the saddle. The scarves around his head protect him against the wind and the flying stones.'

'And the gold medallion?'

'It is a *paizah*, the seal of the Emperor himself. If his horse goes lame he can empower any man to give up his own horse for him, on pain of death. You look surprised, Barbarian. Do you not have anything like this where you come from?'

Josseran did not know how to answer him. I have never seen anything like this, he thought. But how much should I tell these Tatars about us? They already call us barbarians.

✛

He estimated that there was a *yam* around every eight leagues or so. They were like a Mohammedan caravanserai, but far more luxurious than any he had seen in the desert. Most were surrounded by green meadows, with hundreds of horses at pasture, others waiting in the stables ready to be saddled at a moment's notice.

An imperial official was always waiting for them on their arrival and Josseran and William were each furnished with an apartment with wooden beds to sleep on and sometimes even silk coverlets. There were even servants to bring them refreshments.

The privations of the Taklimakan seemed a distant memory already.

LXVI

✠

THEY FOLLOWED A great river between high green gorges. The villages here were so close to each other that on leaving one hamlet they could already see the walls of the next. Everywhere there was rich pastureland dotted with walled farms; mud houses with straw-thatched roofs crouched below sparse groves of poplars; men with stringy muscles tilled fields with ox-drawn ploughs or fished in the shallows of the river.

Josseran saw ruins of watchtowers and fortresses everywhere, gateways and barbicans crumbling into disrepair. What was it the old monk had said? *Empires are built and will crumble; even Chinggis Khan did not live forever.*

The river flowed like a yellow vein into the heart of Cathay. The gorges above it were scalloped with rice fields, and the yellow loess cliffs beehived with row upon row of caves. The people winnowed grain in the sun, retreating inside the mountain at nights, as they had done for thousands of years.

Everything seemed strange and frightening and compelling at once: the demonic clash of cymbals and doleful beating of a gong from the temples; the rhythmic chanting of priests; the massive statues of Borcan reclining beside the road, painted with stupen-dous colours. Once he saw a statue the height of ten men, hewn from bare rock in the cliff face.

The Silk Road was no longer a lonely place, it was crowded with creaking carts, or peasants treading their way to market with baskets of fruit and vegetables balanced across their shoulders on bamboo yokes. Small caravans of a few mules or camels brought silks and teas from the south. Occasionally Josseran heard an imperial postman run past with his great belt of bells. They saw countless orchards of mulberry trees, where they harvested the moths for their precious silk cocoons.

The villages they passed were mostly poor, the huts made of mud and straw and thatch. Pigs and geese waddled through muddy alleys; bare-bottomed children squatted to defecate in the ditches.

Once they passed a funeral cortège. The boarded coffin was covered in dazzling silk coverlets, and the mourners were laughing and singing as if it were a feast day. A troupe of musicians followed behind, trumpets wailing. Josseran had never known any funeral that was not an occasion for mournful silence and seeing people celebrate a death left him astonished.

'They are happy for the dead,' Sartaq said. 'They do not have to worry about the cares of the world any more. The loud noises keep away the evil spirits.' He leaned closer. 'I must be an evil spirit because I hate the sound of those trumpets too!' And he laughed.

The people of the Middle Kingdom found them just as curious, and perhaps even more terrifying. Plump, moon-faced children, squatting under roofed gateways, would run inside as they passed, pointing at them and screaming in fright. Old whitebeards set aside their long pipes and stared open-mouthed; old women in quilted vests and trousers, with toothless mouths and impossibly small and slippered feet, hurried inside their hovels, wailing like the small children.

Late one afternoon they came in sight of one of the greatest cities Josseran had ever seen, larger even than Constantinople or Venice or Rome. The walls, he estimated, were seven or eight leagues around, disappearing into the mist on either side. Drum towers and pagodas rose in astonishing profusion.

Its name, Sartaq said, was Kenzan Fu, and it was where the Silk Road began. More than a million people lived there, he said.

'This is where we shall meet Khubilai?' Josseran asked him.

'No, Barbarian,' he laughed. 'We go to a finer city than this!'

At the time Josseran thought this an idle boast.

But they did not stop at Kenzan Fu. Instead they followed the Yellow River north. It was swollen with rain and thick with mud, not yellow now but reddish-brown. They passed another great city which the Tatars called Tai Yuan and very late one afternoon came upon a sight that left Josseran open-mouthed in disbelief.

Ahead of them was a wall of beaten earth and mud brick. It stretched away for mile after mile across the hills, sinuous as a snake, before finally disappearing into the mist. It was the height of two or three men. Watchtowers had been built along its length in both directions.

'By the balls of St Joseph,' Josseran said.

Sartaq dismounted below the wall. They followed him, leading their horses up a causeway to the battlements where they again remounted, and started riding along the carriageway at the summit. They continued along these battlements not for hours, but for several days. They passed endless guardhouses. The soldiers who manned the walls were armoured like their escort, and carried the same green and white pennants.

They never reached the end of this astonishing structure. Long before then, they came to Shang-tu.

LXVII

✠

PERHAPS IT IS well the gods intervened, Khutelun thought. Who knows what madness I might have undertaken if they had not?

I am a princess, a Tatar, the daughter of a great chieftain; he was a barbarian, and an ugly one at that. Yet he made my heart jump whenever I looked at him. I have never felt that way before when I was with a man of my own tribe, and now I ache to feel that way again.

Already I miss him. At night when I fly with the spirits of the everlasting Blue Sky, I shall seek him out again. I shall never forget him.

✠

The anvil of a grey thunderhead drifted across the mountains. The summer rains had begun, and the whole countryside shimmered with water. The grass ocean of the steppe was carpeted in wild flowers, yellow, purple, carmine and violet, and the sheep grazing in the valley were already so fat they waddled like geese. In every yurt in every valley the leather bladders that hung inside the doorways were bloated, bulging with koumiss.

Faces appeared at doorways of the yurts dotted across the plain, hands shielding eyes from the glare of the sun, watching these strangers gallop past. The shepherds' dogs would rush out at them, howling, running with them for a time before peeling away again and heading home.

A flock of wild geese flew across the sun. The desert was just a dream.

But such a dream! A dream that had cost the lives of sixteen of her brothers, as well as One-Eye, their camel man, his throat torn out by a cavalryman's lance. A dozen had been butchered there on the plain, by Khubilai's horsemen, four more had died from their wounds on the long journey back across the Taklimakan.

After the ambush by Khubilai's soldiers she had considered returning immediately to her father at Fergana. She had postponed that unpleasant prospect, deciding instead that Khubilai's betrayal should first be brought to the attention of the Khan of Khans, Ariq Böke, in person.

She exchanged their surviving camels for horses in Kashgar and led the survivors of her party racing across the northern steppe. After the death of so many of her comrades she found it a comfort just to ride, to forget what had happened in the desert. It made it easier to forget, too, what Joss-ran had said to her by the crescent lake and how he had held her so tightly in the storm.

Such memories should now belong to another Khutelun.

✠

One day they reined in their horses on a high ridge and looked down on Qaraqorum, the City of the Black Sands, capital of the Blue Mongol. On the lush pasture below, thousands upon thousands of felt yurts were spread over the plain. At the centre of this vast encampment the curlicued roofs of a handful of wooden pagodas glittered jade and yellow in the late afternoon sun. The *stupas* of a dozen temples pushed into the blue sky, the dome of a single Mohammedan church nestled among them. Beyond the city, the white necklace of the mountains was reflected in the flooded pasture.

And the desert was just a dream, she reminded herself again as she led the ragged remains of her escort down the hills towards Qaraqorum. Just a dream.

✠

The defences of the city were a token, for the Great Khan of the Mongol Horde was unchallenged as the lord of all Asia. The earthen walls around the city rose to barely the height of a man, the moat scarcely as deep as that.

The entrance to the city was guarded by two stone tortoises. The imperial edicts of the Great Khan, the *yassaq* of Chinggis, were placed here, inscribed on stone tablets the height of two men, with dragons carved into the crown of the stele. They were written in the flowing Uighur script that the Tatars had borrowed from one of their vassal peoples.

By the strength of Eternal Heaven, and by order of the Universal Ruler of the Empire of the Mongol . . .

Khutelun had journeyed here just once, with her father, for the *khuriltai* that had elected Möngke Khan of Khans. She had been just a child then, and her memories of the city were vague, its wonders magnified by her child's innocence. It had seemed impossibly huge then.

In fact there were just a handful of buildings at its heart, the wooden pagodas of the palace and some granaries and stables of rough-hewn stone. There was also a cramped quarter of mud brick and thatch, home to the Cathay saddle smiths who plied their trade in the muddy streets.

As they entered the city they were swallowed up in the milling chaos of the sheep market. They walked their horses through thick, stinking mud, heard the babble of a dozen different languages, the deafening bleating of animals slaughtered or sold.

They passed a great house with swooping red roofs, the lintels adorned with golden dragons. Ahead of them were the walls of the palace. She heard the chanting of monks, the rattle of a shaman's drums.

They came to two massive wooden gates, studded with nails. The imperial guards stepped forward and asked for their weapons and they were questioned as to their business. Her identity established, Khutelun and her companions were escorted by the officer of the guard to the customs house, a long and narrow building supported on thick wooden pillars. There was a brick stove in the centre of the room where the guards warmed their hands. They eyed Khutelun and her companions with cold suspicion.

Finally they were given permission to pass through another gateway and into the silent heart of Qaraqorum.

✝

The palace of the Khan of Khans rose above the marsh on a mound of beaten earth. Its design had been borrowed from the Cathays. Dragons writhed up the colonnades, its tiered roof ended in curlicues of lacquered tiles in vermilion, jade and gold.

Storehouses and treasuries and the private apartments of the Golden Clan clustered around it; the lesser palaces where the court secretaries attended to the business of the Khaghan's empire were connected to it on raised pathways, like the spokes of a wheel.

She glimpsed another mound at the far end of the royal enclosure, on which large yurts of white felt had been constructed. By day the Khan of Khans and his princes might now receive their visitors in this grand palace, but at least they still slept with a smoke hole above their heads at night like true Tatars.

✢

To the Cathays it was known as the Palace of a Myriad Tranquillities; the Tatars themselves called it simply Qarshi, the Palace.

The entrance hall was supported on thick, lacquered poles, and there was a vaulted roof, raging with gilt dragons. Khutelun and her escort stopped before three massive doors, glittering with gold leaf, guarded on either side by the figures of a bear and a lion.

The keepers of the palace, members of the Great Khan's own bodyguard, again searched them for weapons, then a chamberlain came to escort them inside. They entered at the southern end of the hall, taking great care not to step upon the threshold, and were ushered into the presence of the Power of God upon the Earth, Master of Thrones, Ruler of Rulers, the Great Khan of the Blue Mongol.

LXVIII

✠

It was the most breath-taking sight she had ever seen.

The glazed aquamarine tiles beneath her feet seemed to shimmer, as if she were walking on the surface of a lake. The colonnades on their granite bases were painted crimson and lacquered to a sheen. Golden-scaled dragons slithered upwards to the great vaulted ceiling, their talons extended, green wings spread.

The palace had been built in the shape of a cross. There was a nave running north to south, and along the transepts golden shafts of light pierced the mullioned windows. Six rows of colonnades, three on each side of the nave, led to the dais at the northern end of the hall, focusing the attention of all who entered on the figure reclining there at the head of two flights of marble steps.

The Khan of Khans reposed on a couch of solid ebony. His throne was inlaid with gold and pearl and jade, and enfolded by a tent of purple silk. Despite the magnificence of these surroundings, Khutelun noted that the court was arranged in the traditional manner of a Tatar yurt; below the Khaghan and to his right was another dais where his sons and his brothers attended him. To the left there was a similar platform for his wives and daughters.

There were elevated seats along the walls for other members of the Golden Clan. Khutelun was aware of the rich furs and brocades, the visceral glimmer of rubies.

A fire of briars and wormwood roots burned in the centre of the room.

There was a feast in progress for Qaraqorum was still celebrating Ariq Böke's elevation to the title of Great Khan. Steam rose from cauldrons of boiling mutton. The men were drinking koumiss from silver bowls and at each toast white-robed shamans sprinkled a little of the mare's milk in the four corners of the hall to appease the spirits of the Blue Sky.

'You should wait until the feasting is done,' the chamberlain whispered to her. 'The Khaghan will hear you then.'

But by the time the gathering had finished their carousing, most of the courtiers on the men's side of the hall were lolling on the carpets in a stupor. The jugglers and acrobats and fire-eaters were brought on to entertain those who were still upright.

Finally a snow leopard was led into the pavilion at the end of a long silver chain. Its attendant released it from its collar and it padded, docile, up the steps of the throne and dropped, as if in obeisance, at the Great Khan's feet.

A mean trick, Khutelun thought. She would rather have her Khaghan prove his worth by confronting a wild leopard with a single arrow in his bowstring.

The chamberlain turned to her and ushered her forward to bring her news to the Khan of Khans.

Ariq Böke lolled on the divan, bleary from drink and food. Khutelun glimpsed a corona of fur around a thin beard and a cruel mouth. He watched her with a savage indifference. Rubies glistened on his fingers like old blood.

She greeted him on her knees, as was the custom, and relayed her story. There were angry oaths around the hall when she told him of what had become of the Christian ambassadors. The raiders who took them, she announced, had made no effort to disguise their identity. They were warriors of Khubilai's own imperial guard.

When she finished her tale there was a long silence. The Khan of Khans gazed around the room, his eyebrows beetling with displeasure. He was assuredly blurry from drink, but when he spoke, his voice was clear enough.

'My brother covets the throne of Chinggis Khan, which is mine, by proper election in *khuriltai*! He has disobeyed the *yassaq* that our grandfather, Chinggis Khan, gave to us, and he should fear the retribution of the Mongol horde!'

There were growls of assent from his generals. Those who were still sober, anyway.

'We all know that he has become that which every Mongol despises,' Ariq Böke shouted. 'A Chin, our age-old enemy! He knows that you, his own people, do not love him so now he turns those we conquered against us! He calls himself Chung t'ung, like a Chinese emperor. He governs like a Chinese, with secretariats and courtiers and clerks! He even calls himself the Son of Heaven! He fawns to the Chin as if they were the victors and we the vanquished!'

More angry murmurs.

Khutelun, still on her knees, realized that Ariq Böke might have already heard her news. His speech sounded as if it had been carefully rehearsed.

'He has a Shang-tu Construction and Protection Office! He has a Court of the Imperial Stud, a Court of the Imperial Tack, a Directorate of Animal Feeds. A Directorate of Animal Feeds! Why should a grandson of Chinggis Khan need such a thing? A good Tatar pony needs only to be let loose in a field and it will find its own food in ten feet of driven snow! He has forced the Chinese generals and bureaucrats to crown him Emperor of China because he knows we Mongols will never crown him Khan of Khans!'

The gathering shouted and cheered him. The leopard sat up, pricking its ears.

'Khubilai went to Cathay as a lion and they have made him a lamb. My brother has forgotten how to ride!' he shouted, the worst insult a Tatar could say of another. 'We shall march on Shang-tu with an army of our best horsemen and we will reduce his city to rubble!'

Uproar.

The firestorm had to come, Khutelun thought, as the courtiers around her bayed for Khubilai's blood.

And it seems Joss-ran is the lightning that will set the spark.

LXIX

✠

For Khutelun, Qaraqorum was both a wonder and a disappointment. She wondered if Chinggis Khan would have approved of his
ancestors building themselves palaces such as the ones he had spent
a lifetime tearing down.

A canal had been dug across the plain from the Orkhon River, to
power a waterwheel for the city's blacksmiths. But these foundries
were not only forging arrowheads and swords and wheels for siege
engines, but picks and ploughs, mattocks and sickles also.

They were cultivating the plain, she realized with a sickening
lurch. The Tatars were becoming farmers, that which they had
always despised.

Ariq Böke might revile his brother Khubilai, but it was clear he
himself was no Chinggis Khan either. The comforts at his palace
both astonished and dismayed her. In the cellar was a brick furnace
that carried heated air throughout the building in stone flues. In this
way every room of the palace was kept warm at night. It was an
impressive accomplishment, but was this the way for a Tatar
horseman to live?

And then there was the silver tree.

Chinggis and the Khaghans that had succeeded him had taken
captive craftsmen and artisans from the cities they had conquered in
Persia, Cathay and even Europe. Among them was a master gold-
smith, who had been brought back from a raid on a distant land called
Hungary two decades before. He had been commissioned to design
and build a tree of silver for use at the Great Khan's feasts. It had been
artfully designed, with four silver serpents entwined around the
branches. From each of the serpents' mouths came a different
beverage; from one, rice wine; from another, black koumiss; from
another, honey mead; the last spouted red wine made from grapes.

Underneath this tree was a crypt in which a man was hidden; a pipe led from the crypt to a silver angel, holding a trumpet, perched at the very top of the tree. When one of the beverages ran low the man blew on the pipe, and the angel's trumpet gave a blast that alerted the servants in the kitchen. They then hurried to pour more beverages into the vats hidden below the tree.

In this way there was never an excuse for any man to be sober at one of the Khan of Khan's feasts.

In itself it was assuredly a wonder and Khutelun had no objection to a man getting good and drunk. Men had always intoxicated themselves; they probably always would. But drinking from silver trees? Was this the way they had been taught to live? A Tatar's strength came from the steppe, from the cold wind and the wide valleys and living day by day on milk curd and snow. On the Roof of the World there were no palaces heated with furnaces and no silver trees to feed their gluttony.

This Ariq Böke might have the blood of Chinggis in his veins, but he did not have his heart. She was, at least, relieved to find that the Great Khan's soldiers shunned the palace and disdainfully pitched their yurts on the plain. But this practice also meant that there was now a divide between the Great Khan and his people. She wondered what Chinggis Khan would have thought of that.

☩

Ariq Böke sat on his ebony throne. At his feet, fish-eyed and bloody, was the corpse of a prisoner. He had recently been disembowelled and steam still rose from his body cavity. The Great Khan had his left foot inside the gaping wound.

The day after their arrival Khutelun was escorted back into the palace by a chamberlain for private audience with Ariq Böke. She knelt down at the foot of the dais.

'So, Khutelun.'

She waited, her eyes fixed on the corpse.

'We have heard much about you.' He grunted and shifted his weight. 'And how is my cousin, Qaidu?'

'Great Khan, my father rides like a youth and wrestles men half his age.'

'We hear many reports of his strength and wisdom.' She wondered what it was he wanted with her. Surely their business was concluded. 'He did you great honour to entrust the barbarian ambassadors to your care.'

But I failed in my duty, Khutelun thought. Is that why I am here? Am I to be punished?

'Tell me about them.'

'The barbarians, Great Khan? One was a holy man, sickly looking and with no magic. The other was a warrior, a giant with hair like fire. He was clever as well as strong. He had even learned to talk like a Person.' She nodded to the khan's chamberlain, who stepped forward with the gifts she had salvaged from Joss-ran's horse after the ambush.

Ariq Böke studied them carefully in turn; first the mailed helmet, the leather gauntlets, the ebony inkstand and then the rubies, which he discarded on the marble floor as casually as a man might toss aside a few grains of rice.

Finally he examined the damascened sword she had found lying on the grass after the fight. She still felt a sickening lurch in her stomach as she looked at it now. She prayed they had not harmed him when they took it from him.

'They were Christians?'

She understood the nature of the question. She had heard that Ariq Böke favoured the Nestorians. 'They prayed to Jesus and the Christian saints. They held Mary in great esteem. But they spoke also of someone they called the Pope, whom they said was their God's chosen upon the Earth and to whom they gave their obeisance.'

'This Pope is their Khaghan?'

'I do not think so. From what I understood, this Pope is not a warrior. It seemed he was more like a priest.'

Ariq Böke grunted, no doubt remembering how even Chinggis himself had to execute a holy man in order to gain supremacy over his own tribe. Perhaps the barbarian princes had not been as wise and had lost control of their clans to the shamans.

'I would have liked to talk with these barbarians. There is doubtless much to learn from them. It is no doubt why my brother thought to snatch them from you.' He shifted again. It was evident now that he was in pain. 'You know that I am to ride against Khubilai?'

'Yes, Great Khan.'

'When I move against my brother, can I count on your father's support to protect my flank?'

Khutelun's heart beat faster. Qaidu had instructed her to give Ariq Böke his support at the *khuriltai*, but he had not empowered her to make military treaties, least of all with the Khan of Khans. 'I am sure he will protect his right to live as a Tatar by whatever means he can.'

The Khan gave a low laugh. 'A careful response. But it does not answer my question.'

'I cannot know the mind of my father, Great Khan.'

'I think you know it well enough. Tell me then how you think a Tatar should live.'

Khutelun felt her heart beating hard, almost painfully, in her chest. 'In the saddle of a horse and by the *yassaq* of Chinggis Khan.'

'And my brother Khubilai? Does your father think he lives like a true Tatar?'

'As I have said, Great Khan, I do not know my father's mind. But I know he is pledged to obey the true Khan of Khans here in Qaraqorum.' Well, up to a point.

Ariq Böke sighed. He stared at the body at his feet. 'It is for the gout,' he said, though she had not remarked upon his present situation, nor would she have imagined doing so. 'My shamans say I have to leave my foot there until the body cools.'

Since she had not been invited to speak, she did not do so.

'I had to wait for the full moon. They have said their prayers over me and they tell me it will cure it.' When she still said nothing he said: 'They say you are a healer and soothsayer.'

'Yes, Great Khan. They say I have the gift.'

'And what do you think of my shamans' remedies?'

There is danger here, Khutelun thought. If I denigrate them, they have the Khan's ear and I will surely lose one of mine for criticizing them. 'If a remedy proves effective, then it is a good one.'

Ariq Böke gave another laugh, as compliment to her shrewdness. 'Indeed. And should it not work, can you think of a better way?'

'Should it fail to provide you with relief, Great Khan, I may perhaps try. But I fear my poor shaman's tricks may not be as spec-tacular.'

'And what poor shaman's tricks do you employ?'

'Some say that they feel better after I have made sacrifice to Tengri and laid my hand on them. For myself I profess no qualities of healing. I only repeat what others tell me.'

He stood up, gasping with pain as he did so, and kicked the corpse over the edge of the dais. It rolled down the steps and finally came to rest, sprawled horribly on the carpets at the foot of the throne. 'Then may you place your hand on my left foot here! Because for the last three moons I have had my foot inside men's guts and the only relief I have had is knowing they were my brother's soldiers!'

She noticed the shamans creep from the room like shadows.

'I must rid myself of this gout if I am to ride against my brother.'

'Great Khan, I will do what I can,' she said. 'But first I must meet the spirits.'

'And what do you need for that?'

'My drums and my flail. And then hemp smoke or strong mare's milk.'

The Khan slumped down on his throne. 'Do what you will. But take this Devil from my toes!'

LXX

✠

AN IMPRESSIVE GATHERING, Khutelun thought. She recognized many members of the Golden Clan, as well as the previous Khan's most powerful generals, fearsome in their lamellar armour and winged helmets. Ranged behind them were khans from all the great clans north of the Gobi, their silk pavilions spread across the plain, a riot of colour against a lowering sky.

Ariq Böke was carried out of the city on a litter, resplendent in a gown of pure white, decorated with gold. He was surrounded by an honour guard of his best soldiers. Drummers, mounted on camels, followed the procession, beating the dirge. Silken flags of red and gold and white snapped in the wind.

As he passed her Ariq Böke saw Khutelun and held up his hand to order the procession to halt.

'Khutelun!' he barked.

She dismounted and bent the knee three times, as was demanded by custom.

'You are returning to the Fergana steppe?'

'Yes, Great Khan.'

'We are sorry to see you go.' He stamped his left foot hard on the wooden floor of the litter. 'You took the fire from our foot. We can ride again! We would have you as our own shaman if you will stay in Qaraqorum.'

Khutelun gave another slight bow of her head. 'You honour me, Great Khan. But my father awaits my return.' *And your shamans would have me poisoned in a week should I decide otherwise.*

'We are sorry to lose you.' He leaned on the rail of the litter. 'When you return to Fergana tell your father that I ride to find Khubilai and that the Golden Clan rides at my back!'

'I will, Great Khan.'

'I shall return with my brother in chains!' he shouted and gave the order to move on.

She watched the procession make its way across the plain, the army of the Great Khan of the Mongols on its way east once more, to again make war on the eternal enemy, the Chin.

But now, for the first time, the Tatars would be fighting one of their own.

PART V

Xanadu

Shang-tu
from the time of the third summer moon to the
first autumn moon in the Year of the Monkey

LXXI

☩

'THERE,' SARTAQ MURMURED.

Shang-tu, capital of the Son of Heaven, Celestial Ruler of the Whole Earth, lay spread before them, beside a lake the colour of rippled steel. It was surrounded on all sides by truncated mountains that reminded Josseran of the humps of camels. The skyline was, to a Christian eye, an impossible collision of faiths inside a single city wall; the *stupas* of the idolaters and the minarets of the Mohammedans needled into the sky above the dun-coloured lamaseries of the Tanguts and the painted pavilions of the Cathays.

Beyond the walls mud-brick houses crowded together along twisted and muddy lanes, except to the north where the tiered roofs of the imperial palace glistened in the sun, among the green and shaded pathways of the royal parks.

William shouted a prayer of thanks to God, startling their Tatar escort. 'The Lord has guided and protected us through our long journey! May He be praised and thanked!' Angry Man stared at him as if he had gone mad.

'You are being a little premature,' Josseran grunted.

'Have we not reached our destination, ingrate?'

'It is true we have journeyed this six months, and endured hardships such as I did not believe I could bear. But it is well not to forget that we are still only halfway there.' He turned back to gaze on the spectacular vista before him. 'We still have to go back. Remember that.'

An earth embankment formed a defensive perimeter around the city. The city lay beyond, green banners fluttering from the stone walls, armoured sentries gazing down at them from the watch-towers.

They entered through an arch in the South Gate and were immediately assailed by the stench. In this at least, Josseran thought, Shang-tu was little different from Saint-Denis or Rome. They made their way through the press of crowds and cramped wooden houses. Josseran noticed how the noise subsided the closer they came to the palace. When they reached the palace walls themselves no one in the street raised their voice above a whisper.

They stopped in front of two huge, iron-studded gates.

The guards in the tower recognized the uniform of the imperial guard and the gates swung open.

Inside, the silence was complete. After the squalor of the streets this was a sanctuary; there were flagged courts and soaring pagodas with upturned eaves and tiles of lacquered bamboo of peacock blue and jade green, all glazed so that they shone like glass in the sun. Sentries with the same golden helmets and leopard-skin cloaks as their escort presided over the silence. The Pavilion of Great Harmony loomed before them on a vast earthen platform, perhaps ten rods wide and as much as thirty rods long. It was stupefying in its symmetry and its size. Lacquered vermilion pillars supported the triple roof. Golden dragons and serpents coiled up the pillars and writhed along the eaves high above; the scudding white clouds made it appear that the dragons themselves were in motion, their golden-scaled wings bearing them aloft.

The palace was surrounded by a huge terrace, skirted with balustrades, all made of pure white marble. There were bronze cauldrons each holding hundreds of incense candles, so that the air was sickly sweet with their fragrance. Below them was a tiled court, silent and empty, shaded by ancient pines and cypresses.

At Sartaq's command they left their horses and climbed the marble steps to its summit.

Two enormous stone lions, each the size of a Tatar pony, guarded the entrance. There was a brass-studded door and two smaller doors on either side.

Their arrival had been anticipated. A chamberlain, dressed in a pillbox hat and robe of crimson silk, was on hand to escort them through the portals to the Hall of Audience.

Josseran and William were ordered to remove their boots. The chamberlain held out the white leather buskins they were to put on their feet so that they did not soil the silk and golden carpets within.

'Remember, do not step on the threshold,' Sartaq whispered. It was in fact to the height of his knees so he would have to clamber over it. 'It is considered the most terrible omen and anyone who does so is subject to the harshest penalty.'

'Even the ambassador of the Christians?' Josseran asked him.

The expression on Sartaq's face was answer to that. William prepared himself for this momentous occasion. He opened his leather satchel, put on the white surplice and purple stole that he had carried with him all the way from Rome. In one hand he held the illuminated Bible and Psalter, in the other he had a missal and silver censer. He slipped a silver crucifix around his neck.

Josseran thought of the gifts he had brought from Acre: the damascened sword, the rubies, the leather gauntlets, all lost in Sartaq's raid. He thought, too, of the white mantle with the red cross pattée of the Order of the Temple. He had intended to wear it for his audience with the Great Khan but instead he would appear dressed like any other Tatar. He felt like a beggar.

'Are you ready, Templar?' William sniffed.

'As ready as I shall ever be.'

'Let us confront the heathen, then.'

Josseran drew a deep breath. William went ahead of him; he entered the great court of Khubilai Khan singing *Salve Regina*.

LXXII

✠

A RIOT OF COLOUR, a scene of impossible splendour to stir the soul and dazzle the eyes.

Everywhere there was silk and brocade, furs and gold; Josseran saw Cathays in iron pot helmets and crimson gowns; Tangut lamas with shaven heads and saffron robes; courtiers with thin and drooping moustaches in the garb of the Uighurs wearing orange robes with high silk hats, tied with a bow. There were scribes in the flowing robes of Mohammedans alongside Tatar holy men, almost naked, with tangled beards and wild hair.

Above their heads the green and white triangular flags of the Emperor hung from the walls, among pillars of vermilion and gilt. This entire fresco was captured again in the mirror sheen of the marble floors.

Khubilai, the Power of God upon the Earth, Master of Thrones, Ruler of Rulers, sat on a high throne of gold and ivory, with gilt dragons coiling along its arms. He wore a robe of golden brocade and a bowl-shaped helmet with a neck-piece of leopard skin. There was a buckle of pure gold on his sash belt.

He was a short, stocky man, Josseran noted, well into his middle years. His hair was looped in two braids at the back of his head in the manner of a Tatar. He had gold-hooped rings in his ears and a thin, drooping moustache. His face was unusually pale, though his cheeks were rose-pink. Josseran realized with shock that this effect had been achieved with the aid of powdered rouge.

His throne faced south, in the Tatar way, away from the north wind. The Empress sat beside him, on his left. On his right hand were his sons, seated at a smaller dais and at such a height that their heads were level with his feet. Opposite them were his daughters. Other princes of the court sat below them, in descending order of privilege, the men to the west, the women to the east.

The lesser court attendants were ranged along the wings of the hall; Khubilai's ministers in curious brimmed helmets; Chinese women in hooded gowns, long hair fastened on their heads with elaborate designs of pins; Tatar princesses in elaborate plumed headdresses; and, ever present, the imperial guard, with gold winged helmets, leather cuirasses, and leopard-skin cloaks.

But even among this exotic throng, the most fantastic sight to his western eyes were the Confucian scholars in their black silk turbans, two braids sticking out behind like stiff ears. Some had let their fingernails grow almost to the length of their fingers, like the talons of a predatory bird. He could not stop staring at them. This fashion, he later learned, was intended not to intimidate, but as a means of setting themselves apart from the common people, to demonstrate that they did not earn their living by manual labour.

Josseran noted that there were fewer women than there had been in Qaidu's court in Fergana. The only females present appeared to be ladies of very high rank and they were greatly outnumbered by the men.

Beside Khubilai, on the dais, was a man in the *del* of a Tatar, but with the shaven skull of a Tangut. 'Phags-pa,' Sartaq whispered to him. 'A lama, despite his dress, the Imperial Preceptor, the Emperor's chief adviser and wizard.'

Their entrance was largely ignored for a great feast was in progress. The court chamberlains led them to the back of the great hall and they were invited to sit. Only the greatest sat at table, it seemed; most of the court sat on the bright silken carpets that were strewn around the floors.

Attendants brought them platters of boiled mutton, borne in beautiful glazed dishes in olive and cinnamon colours.

William was affronted. He squatted uncomfortably in his surplice, clutching the sacred relics he had brought with him to his chest. 'This is insufferable,' he hissed at Josseran. 'We have travelled the length of the world to present ourselves and he makes us wait at the very back of the chamber!'

Josseran shrugged his shoulders. 'It behoves us to be patient.'

'But I am the emissary of the Pope himself!'

'I don't think he would care if you were Saint Peter. He seems hungry.'

More dishes arrived in ceramic bowls; eggs, a beer made from millet, some raw vegetables seasoned with saffron and wrapped in pancakes and some platters of roasted partridge. Sartaq told them the fruit and partridges had arrived fresh that morning from Cathay on the *yam*.

Josseran put his fingers into a bowl of rice and scooped a handful into his mouth, the same way he had eaten with the Tatars throughout the entire journey. Sartaq knocked his hand away and shouted at him. For a moment he thought he might even draw his knife.

'What are you doing, Barbarian?'

'I am hungry.'

'Even if you are dying of starvation, you should still eat like a Person when you are in the Palace.' Sartaq picked up two pointed sticks inlaid with ivory and holding them with his index finger and thumb picked a morsel of chicken from one of bowls, and brought it to his mouth. 'Like this, you see?'

Josseran picked up the ivory sticks and tried to hold them in the same way that Sartaq had done. He dropped them into a bowl of soup.

Sartaq shook his head in despair.

Meanwhile William sat and fumed, ignoring the food. It was clear that everyone around them was intent on getting drunk.

In the centre of the hall was a wooden coffer, perhaps three paces across, covered in gold leaf and bearing elaborate carvings of dragons and bears. There were gold spigots on each side and from these the stewards poured koumiss into golden jars, each jar enough to quench the thirst of ten men. One of these was placed between every man and his neighbour. He and William were possibly the only sober men left in the room.

Two stairways led to the dais where the Emperor supped. Full goblets were carried ceremoniously up one stairway, empty ones down the other, and there seemed to be a brisk traffic. Chinese musicians in violet caps and gowns, partly hidden behind a painted screen, began to play their doleful gongs and violins. The Emperor raised his chalice to his lips, and everyone in the hall fell on to their knees and bowed their heads.

'You must do the same,' Sartaq hissed.

Josseran complied. William sat obdurate, his face pale with anger.

'Do it!' Josseran breathed.

'I shall not.'

'You will, or I shall break your neck and save the Tatars the trouble!'

William looked startled.

'You will not put my life in danger as well as yours!'

William fell, reluctantly, to his knees. 'So now we pay obeisance to the Devil's capacity for drunkenness? May God forgive me! Next we will light candles before the barbarian's virile member and say vespers while he deflowers one of his virgins!'

'If necessary,' Josseran grunted. 'It is all in the name of courtly diplomacy.'

The Emperor upended his goblet and the koumiss squirted over his beard and ran down his neck. When he had finished his draught the music stopped, a signal for the attending court to resume their own gluttony.

✠

At last one of the chamberlains came over and ushered Josseran and William to their feet.

'You are to present yourselves to the Emperor now,' Sartaq whispered.

'Now?' William protested. He had imagined a grand entrance. If not that, then at least he had expected the King of the Tatars to be middling sober.

Instead he was herded unceremoniously towards the centre of the hall. He and Josseran were practically thrown to their knees in front of the great throne, like prisoners.

The chamberlain announced them and the hall fell silent.

The Emperor had been dozing after the big meal. He came reluctantly awake. Phags-pa lama stood beside him, his face like flint.

They were all waiting.

Josseran took a deep breath. 'My name is Josseran Sarrazini,' he began. 'I have been sent by my lord, Thomas Bérard, Grand Master of the Knights of the Temple, in Acre, to bring you words of friendship.'

Khubilai did not appear to be listening. He had turned to Phags-pa lama and was whispering something in his ear.

The Tangut cleared his throat. 'The Son of Heaven wishes to know why you have such a big nose.'

From the corner of his eye Josseran saw Sartaq stifle a grin. He was doubtless wondering if he intended to make good on his threat to disembowel the next Tatar who remarked on this prominent feature. 'Tell him among my own people it is not considered so large.'

Another whispered exchange.

'Then the Son of Heaven thinks you must be a very big-nosed people. Do you have gifts to present?'

Josseran nodded to William who understood that this was his cue. He reverently held out the missal and Psalter. 'Tell him these are gifts to help him with a new and glorious life in Christ,' he said to Josseran. The chamberlains bore the sacred volumes to the throne where Khubilai examined them with the delicacy of a pig examining a pine cone. He opened the Psalter. It was prefaced by a twenty-four-page illumination of the life of Jesus Christ. He turned several of the pages and it seemed to entertain him for a few moments. Then he picked up the missal, which was illustrated with depictions of the saints and a seated Virgin and Child, etched in royal blue and gold. He stabbed his finger at one of the illustrations and made some remark to his wizard. And then he tossed both books aside as casually as if they were chicken bones. They landed with a thud on the marble floor.

Josseran heard William gasp.

It was clear that neither their appearance nor their offerings had made a deep impression on the great lord. He would have to salvage what he could from their situation.

'You are the one to whom God has given great power in the world,' he said. 'We regret we have little gold and silver to give you. The journey from the west was long and arduous and we could bring few gifts. Alas, we lost our other presents . . .' He was about to say: *when we were kidnapped by your soldiers*, and corrected himself. '. . . we lost our other presents along the way.'

Khubilai was ready to go back to sleep. He leaned across and murmured something to the Tangut standing at his right hand. Josseran understood this accoutrement of power; a king did not demean his person by talking directly with supplicants, even if they were ambassadors from another realm.

'Even as the sun scatters its rays so does the Lord of Heaven's power extend everywhere,' Phags-pa lama answered, 'therefore we have no need of your gold and silver. The Son of Heaven thanks you for your poor gifts and wishes to know the name of your companion. He also asks what business brings you to the Centre of the World.'

'What is he saying now?' William hissed, at his shoulder.

'He asks who we are and why we are here.'

'Tell him that I am in possession of a papal Bull. It is to introduce me, William of Augsburg, prelate to His Holiness Pope Alexander the Fourth, to his court. It empowers me to establish the Holy Roman Church in his empire and bring him and all his subjects into the fold of Jesus Christ, under the authority of the Holy Father.'

Josseran translated what William had said, but omitted to mention that William was to establish the Pope's authority in Shang-tu. A little premature, he decided.

He looked around at the bodies of courtiers piled on the floor like corpses, some of them with wine leaking from their mouths. Somewhere one of the sleeping Tatars broke their wind. Another began to snore.

'Tell him that he must listen very closely to what I have to say,' William was saying, 'so that he can follow my salutary instructions from the Pope himself, who is God's emissary on earth, and so come to acknowledge Jesus Christ and worship His glorious name.'

Josseran stared at him. 'Have you lost your mind?'

William kept his eyes on Khubilai. 'Tell him.'

You are a madman, Josseran thought. It is lucky I am here to protect you. 'We thank God for our safe arrival,' Josseran said to Khubilai, 'and we pray to Our Lord, whose name is Christ, that he grants the Emperor a long and happy life.'

William went on, for it had not occurred to him that Josseran might do otherwise than translate for him exactly as he had been instructed. 'Now tell him we demand an immediate end to the devastation of Christian lands and advise him that if he does not wish to fall into eternal damnation he should repent immediately and prostrate himself before Jesus Christ.'

He turned back to Khubilai. 'Great Lord, we have been sent by our king to suggest to you an alliance.'

For the first time the Emperor seemed to raise himself from his stupor. His eyes blinked open and he whispered something to his preceptor.

'The Son of Heaven wishes to know more about this alliance of which you speak,' Phags-pa lama said. 'An alliance against whom?'

'Against the Saracens of the west. Your great prince Hülegü finds them common enemy with us. My own lord bid me come here and offer that we join our forces against them.'

The Emperor considered this proposal. My timing may be propitious, Josseran thought. If he is indeed in dispute for his throne, it will be in his interest to make his western borders secure before he sends this Hülegü against the threat within.

He waited long minutes for the Emperor's considered response. Then he heard a loud snore. The Ruler of Rulers had fallen asleep.

'The Son of Heaven hears your words,' Phags-pa lama said. 'He says he will think on them and speak with you again.'

And they were summarily dismissed.

☩

As they left the Hall of Audience Josseran noted that the rule of which Sartaq had so ominously warned them, that of stepping on the threshold, was not enforced by the guards – perhaps because almost the entire throng were incapable of observing it. A number of the courtly gathering not only stepped upon it but several of them actually fell directly across it, flat on their faces, dead drunk.

LXXIII

✛

'He is a slattern and a drunkard,' William hissed, when they were outside the chamber. 'See how he disports himself! They are a godless rabble!'

'Yet it is we who travelled six months across deserts and mountains to speak with him.'

'What was his response to my words? You must tell me everything he said.'

'His last words before he fell to his slumbers were that the chamberlains should be sure to send a virgin to my bedchamber tonight together with a dozen pitchers of koumiss.'

'I should expect no better of you should you accept such a gift,' William sneered. 'Did he make mention of me?'

'He did.'

'And?'

'When I told him you were a friar of St Dominic he ordered you flayed alive and your hide hung on his yurt.'

Josseran turned and walked away. They had travelled to the end of the world, risked their lives in countless ways, and it seemed that it had been for nothing. He wanted no more of this business. Damn William. Damn the Pope. And damn Khubilai Khan as well.

✛

William wandered out of the gates, his heart and mind in turmoil. He had promised himself nothing less than the salvation of Christendom and the conversion of the Tatar horde. Instead he had been treated with ignominy, and this Templar who was supposed to help him in his sacred mission had turned out to be no better than a heretic himself. But he would find a way. God had chosen him, and he would not fail.

The inner city was the preserve of the Emperor and his court, but away from the golden curlicues, the city of Shang-tu itself was crowded and squalid, like every other great city William had seen, be it in Christendom, in Outremer, or here in Cathay. The houses were narrow, hovels of boards or mud brick, the timber joists of one resting on its neighbour so that the houses formed one long façade along the lanes. The windows were covered with torn strips of hemp.

Unlike the courtiers he had seen in the palace, the poor people of Shang-tu wore simple blouses and trousers of hemp cloth, with little cloth turbans on their heads and wooden sandals on their feet. Most were clean-shaven though a few had long side whiskers or a sparse goatee beard.

The alleyways were a seething mass of people and animals. Heavily laden mules were prodded along with bamboo sticks, ox carts rumbled past piled with bulging sacks of rice. A great lady swayed through the mass on an embroidered litter, jade pins in her glossy black hair, jewelled earrings swinging against her cheeks. Sugarcane sellers attracted customers by beating on a piece of hollow bamboo; the pedlars on the street corners and the hawkers at the canvas-covered stalls tried to outdo each other in screeching out their wares. Porters with wicker baskets and earthenware jars suspended on poles buffeted him as they hurried past.

By the hump-backed bridges, where the congestion was worst, entertainers gathered to ply their business with the crowds. There were acrobats, men juggling large earthenware jugs, a sword swallower, a one-armed man with a performing bear.

There was even a puppeteer, the man's legs protruding ludicrously from beneath a curtain-covered box, and some actors performing burlesques for the crowd. William could not understand a word of what was said, but the Chin, laughing uproariously, seemed to enjoy the performance. The entertainment stopped abruptly when a troop of the Emperor's soldiers appeared on the bridge. The actors scurried away.

He passed a window, saw a huddle of ancient whitebeards, heard the chanting of a Q'ran. It plunged him deeper into despair. Was there no place here for the one true God?

He wandered into a small courtyard with a covered arcade and stumbled on to a teahouse, apparently the haunt of wealthy merchants and courtiers. The windows were open to the street. Lanterns of vermilion and gilt hung from the eaves; the walls covered with watercolours and fine calligraphy. A knot of singing girls leaned on the painted balustrade, inviting the passing trade to join them inside for tea and plum-flower wine. Giggling, they beckoned to William, who turned and fled. He came upon a dry earth wall with one small door opening on to the street. There was a crude wooden cross on the tiered roof. He caught his breath. Not even daring to hope, he ventured inside.

It was dark, the air heavy with dust and incense. An oil lamp burned on the altar, which was laid with a gold cloth embroidered with images of the Blessed Virgin, and beside her, John the Baptist. He gasped and made the sign of the cross. 'God is here,' he murmured. 'Even here in the heart of so much darkness!'

He saw a silver crucifix set with jade and turquoise. Beside it was a small silver statue of Mary and a heavy silver box similar to the ones he had used in Augsburg to hold the sacrament. It was a miracle, the sign that he had been asking for. He cursed himself for his doubts.

He fell to his knees and whispered a prayer of thanks. As he began to recite the words of the paternoster a figure emerged from the gloom at the back of the church.

William rose to his feet. 'My name is William,' he said, in Latin. 'I have been sent here by the Pope, who is the Vicar of Christ on earth, to bring you the benediction of the one true faith and lead you to the protection of the Holy Father.'

'I am Mar Salah,' the priest answered, in Turkic, 'I am the Metropolitan of Shang-tu. I have heard all about you and I do not want you in my church. Now get out!'

LXXIV

✠

William hurried back through the streets of Shang-tu to the palace, both excited and disturbed by what he had discovered. He had been unable to communicate directly with the priest; he would need the Templar for that. But there was no doubt the man was a heretic, infected with the blasphemies of Nestorius. He had all but thrown William out of the door.

But this did not trouble him overmuch for it was now clear that these Nestorians had been energetic in bringing word of Jesus here to Cathay. It would make his job so much easier. All that was required was to bring this rebellious church to heel and they would have their foothold among the Tatar.

It was the task God had chosen for him. And he was ready.

✠

'The Lord is here,' William said.

Josseran stared at him. What was wrong with this damned priest now? His face was flushed and shining and there was a strange light in his eyes.

'There is a house in the town,' William went on. 'It has a cross above the door and inside there is an altar and images of the holy saints. The priests are plainly heretics but it proves that the people here know of Christ. You see? The word of the Lord has reached even here. Is it not a miracle?'

Josseran grudgingly admitted that it was. 'Do they have many converts?' he said. He wondered what this might mean for them and for their expedition.

'There were but a handful of people inside. But it scarce matters. It means Christ has a foothold here.'

'They may not care much for the Pope, though.'

William ignored him. 'We need only to bring these followers of the Nestorian heresy back to the fold of Rome, and we can build a strong church here. Once we have properly brought the word of God to these Tatars we can together banish the Mohammedans not just from the Holy Land, but perhaps even from the face of the earth!'

Unlikely, Josseran thought, since so many Tatars were also followers of Mohammed. But if there was a Christian church here in Shang-tu it still promised much for the future.

'You must come with me straight away and speak to their priest!'

Josseran shook his head. 'It behoves us to be a little more circum-spect. Do not forget, their founder was hounded from Constantinople by Roman priests. They are not likely to love us.'

William nodded. 'You are right, Templar. My love of God makes me reckless.'

'We should learn more of the Tatars and their king before we make our move.'

'Yes. Yes, I must learn to be patient.' He took Josseran by the shoulders and for a terrible moment Josseran thought he might embrace him. 'I feel we are destined to do good works here! I shall go now and be at my prayers. I should thank God for this sign and listen in the silence for His word.'

He turned and left the room.

Josseran sighed and went to the window. It was late and night had fallen over the city. He felt desperately tired. William's words echoed around his head. *I feel we are destined to do good works here.* Well, that would be unexpected. All he had ever thought to do until now, was to do the best he could.

☩

Their lodgings in the palace were sumptuous. Josseran's quarters were hung with curtains of ermine and silk. His bed was like no bed he had ever seen; it had a carved frame and was closed on three sides with white satin partitions, painted with delicate watercolours of waterfalls and bamboo groves. The bed covers were lined with floss silk.

There were several low tables about the room, all made of polished black lacquer, and some exquisite jade ornaments in the shapes of elephants and dragons. But the most curious object was a porcelain cat with an oil lamp cunningly concealed inside its head. At night, when the lamp was lit, the cat's eyes appeared to glow in the darkness.

The whole room was redolent with incense and sandalwood. A long way, he thought, from the bare brick walls and hard wooden bed of his monk's cell in Acre.

This whole city was as a dream. Should I ever return to Troyes, and tell my cousin barons the things I have seen, they will all call me a liar.

He fell exhausted on to the bed and slept.

LXXV

✠

SARTAQ ROUSED HIM from his sleep the next morning. He told him he had been assigned to Josseran as his escort while he was in Shang-tu, and his first duty was to accompany him to Khubilai's treasurer, Ahmad.

'The Great Khan wishes another audience this afternoon,' Sartaq told him as they made their way along the terrace.

'I hope this time he will not fall asleep during our interview.'

Sartaq grinned. 'I hope not, also. Perhaps you should try and tell him something to interest him.'

I had expected that he would hang on our every word anyway, Josseran thought. It had never occurred to me that an emissary who had travelled six months for an audience might also need to entertain him. 'Tell me something, Sartaq. What is your religion?'

He shrugged. 'I am a Mohammedan.'

'I did not understand. How can this be? I walk around this city I see Mohammedans everywhere. They have their own bazaar, their own hospital, their own church. Yet everywhere on our journey I saw with my own eyes how you have fought with them and laid waste their towns and their cities. The khan whose troops were to escort me to Qaraqorum was Mohammedan. And now you tell me you yourself follow their religion.'

'The war has nothing to do with the gods. There are many gods. But if someone will not bow their knee to our Great Khan they must be made to submit.'

'So all these people you have conquered are your slaves?'

Sartaq looked genuinely bewildered. 'Slaves? The people pay us taxes, but it is the right of every ruler to collect taxes from his subjects. But we Tatars are warriors not clerks. So we collect the wisest and the best from everywhere to help us rule. So we have Confucian scribes,

Tibetan holy men, Nestorians, Uighurs, from all over our empire. They are not slaves. Some of them are indeed very rich.'

'So you do not make war on the Mohammedans because they are Mohammedans?'

'Of course not. They make good accountants. They understand the silk trade.' Sartaq slapped him on the shoulder and laughed. 'You are a very strange man, Barbarian. I swear I shall never understand you!'

Josseran began to see the futility of William's plans, and his own. When they set out from Acre he and his fellow Latins had believed the presence of Christians among the Tatars meant that their cause would find special favour with their khan. It was now clear to him that no religion had particular favour among the Tatars. Hülegü's cruelty to the Saracens in Aleppo and Baghdad was not typical, just tactical.

But how could he explain this to William?

The treasury was in one of the great palaces on the other side of the great court; it was a large chamber, dark with cherry wood, open to the gardens on one side. Ahmad himself was a white-robed Mohammedan with a grizzled beard. He sat cross-legged on a rich carpet of burgundy and peacock blue, surrounded by his minions, and there were scrolls wound on wooden spindles, an abacus and piles of mulberry-coloured paper lying on the carpets around him.

Josseran was handed, without ceremony, some of the mulberry paper. These, Ahmad explained, were in exchange for William's silver censer and silver cross, which were to be handed over at once. They were now the property of the Emperor.

And he was cursorily dismissed.

✝

'These Tatars, I do not understand,' Josseran said to William. 'They are conquerors of every land we have travelled these six months and yet they allow the Mohammedans and the idolaters to freely practise their religions. Indeed, they even adopt their gods among themselves. They say Khubilai's favourite wife is an idolater, and worships this Borcan. In Fergana, Qaidu was an avowed Mohammedan. And by all reports Hülegü's wife is Nestorian.'

'It is a weakness among them,' William answered. 'A weakness we should exploit.'

'Or is it rather their strength? Some would call such tolerance a virtue.'

'A true faith does not abide tolerance! It is an offence to the one and true God! These Tatars have no abiding god so they search for another. That is why the Lord has brought us here. To show them the one and true way.'

Perhaps, Josseran thought. Yet things might have gone better for us all in the Holy Land had we employed some of their forbearance.

William read his expression. 'You are a man of heretical thought, Templar. If it were not for the protection of your Order, you might have found yourself before an Inquisitor long ago.'

'All I know is that these Tatars have conquered half the world, while we scarcely retain our few castles in Outremer. Perhaps we have something to learn from them.'

'Learn from them?'

'These Tatars never fight wars for their religion. They let men decide for themselves what god they choose. They do not blunt a single idea. They absorb something from everyone and it makes them stronger, not weaker.'

William stared at him in horror. He is no doubt wishing for his thumbscrew and a handy bonfire, Josseran thought. 'A good Christian defends his faith against all unbelievers. To do less is to crucify our Lord all over again.'

'You are a priest,' Josseran said, 'so I am sure you must be right.' He decided to say no more; he had already said far too much. He held out the mulberry-coloured paper notes that Ahmad had given him and thrust them in his hand.

'What is this?' William said.

'It is for the censer and the silver cross,' he said.

'The censer?'

'And the silver cross. The Emperor has taken possession of them.'

'You gave them to him? But they were not brought as gifts!'

'It seems not to matter. Sartaq tells me that all gold and silver objects in the realm are, by law, taken by the Emperor for the treasury. It is an offence for any but Khubilai himself to possess such metals. But in exchange he gives you this.'

William stared at the pieces of paper in his hand. They had been made from mulberry bark and were struck with the vermilion chop of the Emperor's seal. They bore writing on both sides in Uighur script. 'Paper? Is this a further insult?'

'They call it paper money. You can exchange these for goods as if they were coin.'

'They play you for a fool.'

'On the contrary, Brother William. I went with Sartaq to the bazaar and bought these plums with one of these notes. The hawkers took my paper without murmur and gave me these strings of cash into the bargain.' He held up the chain of coins, each with a hollow centre, threaded on a thin string of twine.

William stared at him. Paper money! Who had ever heard of such a thing? He turned to the window. A golden dragon snarled back at him from the eaves of the split-bamboo roof. 'I shall protest to the Emperor directly. When are we to have our next audience? There is much to discuss.'

'We have an audience this afternoon.'

'Let us hope this time he is not drunk.'

'Let us also hope that this time you speak to him as befits a ruler and not as a pauper in your church come for confession.'

'Do not lecture me on how to conduct the Church's business!'

'I really do not understand why the Pope chose you for his emissary. Did he tell you nothing about obeying the polite forms when you are speaking to the prince of a foreign kingdom?'

'All men are equal before God.'

'We are not before God. We are before the king of the Tatars. A good ambassador must learn to bow and scrape. So why did the Pope send you? Was he hoping to get rid of you?'

'What do you mean?'

'I mean that if I had translated everything you said, we would both have had our heads cut off in Aleppo and a dozen times since.'

'I was chosen for my zeal, and for my love of Christ, not because I am artful with words. God guides me in all I do.'

'Or was it because no one else was mad enough to do it?'

'How dare you speak to me that way!'

'Yes, I think that must be it. You are expendable. And no one else close to the Pope thought it was the right thing to do.' He tossed the rest of the Emperor's paper at him as he left. 'Here,' he said, 'buy yourself some plums.'

LXXVI

✠

FOR THEIR SECOND encounter they did not meet with the Emperor inside the great Hall of Audience, but were instead escorted through a pair of roofed gates into the sanctum of a park behind the palace. This court, Sartaq told Josseran, was set aside for Khubilai's personal pleasure.

It was the most beautiful garden Josseran had ever seen. Green-tiled pavilions nestled among stands of willows and bamboo and the sun rippled like mercury on the still waters of a great lake. Long-life fishes – as the Chin called them – swam lazily in the shadows cast by hump-backed bridges with balustrades of carved stone. Peacocks eyed them with the cold suspicion of kings, white swans swam serenely between the lotus blooms or stretched their long wings in the sun.

They passed along an avenue of willows. Ahead of them Josseran saw the white yurt of the Emperor, a token at best, for its luxurious appointments mocked anything Josseran had seen on the steppe. It was raised on a dais of beaten earth and surrounded by flagged courtyards and weeping willows. Above the trees a yellow paper sun and a blue and orange butterfly floated against the sky, the bright-coloured kites of the courtiers' children.

As they waited to be admitted, Sartaq whispered to Josseran that they must approach the Emperor's throne on their knees. Josseran relayed these instructions to the friar, with predictable result.

'I refuse!' he hissed. 'I have bent the knee enough to these savages! From henceforward I bend my knee only to God!'

'Have we not discussed this? You are not an Inquisitor here, you are the Pope's emissary to a foreign king!'

'It is a blasphemy!'

'Give unto Caesar.'

William hesitated. His face betrayed a dozen conflicting emotions. Finally, he accepted the wisdom of what Josseran had said. When the chamberlain came to fetch them, he fell to his knees alongside Josseran and in that way they again approached the Son of Heaven.

It was warm inside. The courtiers, in their red brocade gowns and curious helmets, were busy with their silk fans. The fans were stiff and round and decorated with watercolour and calligraphy, and fluttered like a thousand brightly painted butterflies. Josseran noticed that many of the nobles also carried small and delicately carved vases in which they would occasionally expectorate; this, so that they should not be obliged to spit on the Emperor's carpets. Tatar musicians played behind a great screen, the two-stringed lutes and gongs and drums creating melodies jarring to Josseran's ears.

The Emperor seemed better disposed to receive them today. Sober, at least. He reclined on a throne of gold and ivory. He had on a rimmed helmet of beaten gold and a robe of crimson silk. His feet were clad in stubby leather boots with upturned toes in the Tatar style. This time he did not have Phags-pa beside him as intermediary. His golden eyes were as watchful and languorous as a cat's.

Josseran and William were required to remain on their knees but one of the attendants at least brought them a silver cup filled with black koumiss.

William refused.

'Does he not like our wine?' the Emperor asked Josseran directly.

'It is forbidden him because of our religion,' Josseran answered.

'He does not drink? That has not been my experience of Christians. Are you also forbidden?'

'I am not a priest.'

'So you like our wine?'

'Very much.'

'And do you like the chalice?'

'It is very fine,' Josseran answered, wondering where this line of enquiry was leading.

'It is called the Wrath of Chinggis Khan.'

Josseran examined it, speculating on why it was so highly valued. It was a large bowl, covered in silver, but very plain and without decoration.

'It is made from the cranium of a chief who defied my grandfather,' Khubilai explained. 'He captured him and had him boiled alive in a cauldron. When he was dead he removed his head with his own sword and had his skull set in silver.' He paused, to allow his guests to digest this information. 'Do you have such vessels in the barbarian lands?'

Aware of the implied threat, Josseran assured him that they did not.

'What is he saying?' William demanded.

'He informs me that this cup was fashioned from the head of one of his grandfather's enemies.'

William made the sign of the cross. 'Savages!'

'What is this other one saying?' Khubilai asked.

Josseran hesitated before replying. 'He is fearful in your presence,' he said, 'and wishes to extend his warm wishes from his master.'

The Emperor grunted, satisfied.

'Tell him I bring him good news of the one and true faith and the promise of life everlasting for him and all his subjects!'

'Be still,' Josseran snapped.

'I am an emissary of the Pope himself! I will not be still! This is the reason I journeyed here. You will translate for me while I read this fellow the papal Bull!'

Josseran turned back to the Emperor. 'We wish to bring you word of the Christian religion, which brings hope and joy to men everywhere.'

'We already have the Luminous Religion in our realm.'

'But it is not the true form of our religion.'

The Emperor gave a soft smile. 'Mar Salah, who is Metropolitan of Shang-tu, says it is you who are not true Christians and that I should not listen to you.'

Josseran absorbed this news without expression. William eagerly awaited his translation. Josseran gave it to him, word for word.

The friar's face suffused purple. 'This savage would take the word of a heretic over that of the Pope himself?'

'We would be best served by acting with dignity in the face of this provocation,' Josseran reminded him.

But William had already produced a parchment from his robes. He broke the metal seal. It must be the Pope's Bull.

It was clear he intended to read it, regardless of Josseran's efforts to stop him. He will antagonize the Emperor and cost us any chance of a fair hearing, Josseran thought. He may perhaps even cost us our lives. God forgive me, but I have no intention of translating the Bull. William is too importunate and the Pope is not here. If we are to return to Outremer with credit, then I shall trust in my own judgement.

'. . . so that you may acknowledge Jesus Christ as the Son of God and worship His name by practising His religion . . .'

William was now on his feet and was reading the Pope's letter at the top of his voice, in Latin, which neither the Emperor or any of his courtiers could understand. Madness. If he continues in this vein the Emperor will have another chalice to add to his collection. The Wrath of Khubilai Emperor.

'. . . that you desist from the persecution of Christians and that after many and such grievous offences you conciliate by fitting penance the wrath of Divine Majesty, which without doubt you have seriously aroused by such provocation . . .'

'What is he saying?' Khubilai wanted to know.

'I fear, great lord, that the journey has greatly fatigued him. Perhaps we may continue our conversation alone and allow my companion the rest he so desperately requires.'

At a nod from the Emperor, two men of the *kesig*, the imperial bodyguard, stepped forward and took William by the arms. He yelped in alarm. Ignoring his struggles, they dragged him bodily from the tent. Josseran could hear his shouts of protests even as they marched him back up the avenue of willows.

LXXVII

✟

'TELL ME, BARBARIAN, who is your khan?'

'My king is named Louis.'

'He sent you here?'

'No, my lord. In Outremer I give my allegiance to the Grand Master of the Knights of the Temple, who put their service at the feet of the Pope, who is the head of the Christian Church.'

Khubilai considered this. I suppose it must seem to him a fantastic and confusing arrangement. 'Where is this Outremer that you speak of?'

'It is far to the west of here, my lord. Its capital is a place called Acre, close to Aleppo, where Prince Hülegü lays siege.'

'The siege is ended. I learned many months ago that Hülegü is now master of Aleppo and another city called Damascus.'

Josseran stared into the Emperor's golden eyes and wondered what else he knew. Had the Tatars also laid siege to any of the castles of Outremer? Had they already routed all of the Saracens and besieged Acre as well? If Khubilai knew the answers to these questions, he was clearly not of a mind to say.

'Where are you from, Barbarian?'

'I am a Frank, great lord. I come from a place called Troyes.'

'And do you have good pastures there? Do you raise many horses?'

'The lands are very different from here.'

'They say the horses you brought with you were large and slow and did not even survive the journey to the Roof of the World.'

'My own horse had served me well through many campaigns.'

'Yet it died on the journey.'

'I did not have the means to feed her.'

'Your horses cannot forage for themselves?'

'No, great lord. That is not in their nature. They are not accustomed to mountains and deserts.'

And so it went on. Khubilai asked endless questions in a similar vein: Did Frankish kings live in palaces as fine as his? What was the punishment for stealing a horse? What was the punishment for putting a knife in the fire – an action, Josseran had learned, that was considered heinous among the Tatars. He wanted to know everything he could about Christendom but did not seem disposed just yet to allow Josseran to ask any questions of his own.

Finally, Khubilai turned his attention to matters of religion. 'Mar Salah is of this Luminous Religion, as you yourself claim to be. He says his God is named Jesus. He also has this one he calls the Father. And this Holy Spirit as well. Do you have these same gods?'

'There is just one God. Christ was his son on earth.'

'Just one god? It seems to me, then, that for all your bluster you do not place great store by religion.'

'On the contrary. We fight wars for our religion. It is why we made armed pilgrimage to Outremer. There is a place we call the Holy Land where the Son of God was born. Men came from all over Christendom to protect it.'

The Emperor studied him for a long time. 'And this is why you wish for alliance with us against the Saracen. So you can possess this place?'

'Indeed.'

Josseran waited, feeling his heart hammer in his chest. Finally they were to talk of the matter for which they had travelled these six long months.

Khubilai's expression was unfathomable. 'I will consider what you propose,' he said, finally. 'Perhaps you will reside here in Shang-tu and enjoy the hospitality of my court while I discuss such a treaty with my ministers. In the meantime, I am curious about this religion of yours, and how it is different from the Jesus which we already have. I would also like to know more of this Pope that you speak of.'

'My companion, who is a priest, and sent by our Pope himself, would be most delighted to instruct you further.'

'Can he do magic?'

'Magic?' Josseran looked at him, mystified.

'Yes, this shaman who accompanies you. Can he do magic?'

'I fear not, lord.'

'Mar Salah claims that this Jesus could raise the dead and turn water into wine. Can this Pope and his priests do likewise?'

'Our Saviour could do this, yes,' Josseran told him. 'But William is just a man.'

Khubilai, Lord of Heaven, seemed disappointed in this answer. He nodded slowly. 'What good is religion without magic?'

Six months before he would not even have understood such a question. But at that moment, Josseran Sarrazini, sinner and knight, felt a certain sympathy with the Great Khan's predicament. 'I should like to speak with your shaman but there are many affairs of state which already occupy my time. However, if it pleases you, there is another who may be interested in what you have to say.' Josseran waited while the Emperor studied him with his deceptively soft brown eyes. 'I shall arrange it.'

✝

There were guards posted outside William's door when Josseran returned to the palace. According to Sartaq they had orders to keep the 'barbarian madman' in his quarters until his ravings had ended.

Josseran took a deep breath and gently eased the door open.

William was standing by the window, his face white with anger. For a long time neither man spoke. 'What was the meaning of your behaviour?' he said finally.

'It was your doing. You put us both in danger.'

'I am the emissary of the Pope! You are my escort, not my master!'

'Did I not warn you to be more circumspect? Did I not encourage you to diplomacy? Why will you not pay heed to me?'

'I know why you were sent here. Your Grand Master, Thomas Bérard, thinks he is more powerful now than the Holy Father. You are here to make a secret treaty with the Tatars, is this not true? Should the Pope hear of your perfidy, he would withdraw his protection from your Order and you would all be destroyed!'

'Threaten me all you want. I have a duty to perform and I intend to see it through. If you want this Khubilai to hear you out, you will have to trust me.'

'Trust you? I would rather trust a serpent!'

'Be that as it may, I have some news for you. The khan, it will please you to hear, wishes you to instruct his daughter in the Christian faith.'

William sat down heavily on his bed, astonished. 'His daughter?'

'Yes. So, regardless of what you think of me or my methods, I would suggest we have both made some progress this day.'

'God be praised.' William fell to his knees and whispered a short prayer of thanks. When he stood up again he seemed somewhat consoled. 'Very well, Templar. I shall trust your devices for now. We are not to know God's mysteries. Perhaps even one such as you may be His instrument.'

'Thank you,' Josseran said with a smile, and left the chamber, seething.

LXXVIII

✠

FROM HIS WINDOW high in the palace, Josseran looked over the darkened streets of Shang-tu. A single mournful note sounded from a wooden drum, followed by the resonant echo of a gong as the watchmen on the bridge tolled the hour of the night.

I have travelled further than a hundred merchants might travel in a lifetime, he thought, further than I had ever hoped or wanted. And I have never felt so lonely.

He thought of Khutelun. He had imagined that the madness would have left him by now. But the thought of her lying dead or bleeding in the desert tormented him constantly. I must believe she survived the skirmish, he thought. Else how will I ever rest? If only there was some way of knowing for certain.

What am I to do? I finally find a renegade spirit to match my own and she is forbidden to me. I grieve when I think her dead; I ache when I tell myself she might still be alive. She has left me broken as a mourner, weak like a boy.

Did she really see my father ride in my shadow?

A visceral pain bent him double. I do not think I will ever be at peace if I never see her again.

LXXIX

✠

WILLIAM WAS IN a towering rage. The news that the Emperor wished him to instruct his own daughter in the Christian faith had mollified him for a few hours, but only as long as it took him to discover that there were Christian artisans in the city, brought as captives from Hungary and Georgia many years before, who had been denied the sacrament by Mar Salah.

Communion had been withheld from them until they consented to being baptized again in the Nestorian church, and repudiated the authority of Rome. Even then, Mar Salah would only perform the liturgy for payment.

This Mar Salah had further corrupted God's law by taking three wives, in the Tatar manner, and benighted his own soul by consuming large quantities of black koumiss every night.

'This man is a blot upon the reputation of clerics everywhere!' William shouted at Josseran.

'On the contrary, Brother William, I would say he is exactly like every cleric I have ever known.'

William nodded, conceding the point. 'Yet it is outrageous that such a man speaks out against me, the Pope's emissary!'

'He doubtless sees you as a threat to his own position.'

'As a priest, to think of oneself before God is unconscionable. We are all servants of Christ!'

'It behoves us to be politic, William. This Mar Salah has some influence at court. If we wish to treat with the Tatars, we should take care what we say about him.'

'We are here to show them the true path to salvation, not treat with them! You speak of them as if they were equals. These Tatars are uncouth, loud-mouthed and foul-smelling!'

'They have said the same of you.'

'I care nothing for their opinions. I care only for the truth! I wish you to come with me now and confront this Mar Salah and remind him of his duty before God.'

Josseran shot him an angry look. He would not take orders from this arrogant churchman. Yet he could not deny him his services as translator.

'As you wish,' he sighed.

LXXX

✛

THE GLOW OF a single oil lamp was reflected in the silver cross on the altar. William fell on his knees, repeating the words of the paternoster. Josseran hesitated, and then did likewise.

'What are you doing here?' Mar Salah said, in Turkic.

Josseran rose to his feet. 'You are Mar Salah?'

'I am.'

'Do you know who we are?'

'You are the barbarians from the west.'

'We are believers in Christ, as you are.'

With his long, angular face and hawk nose Mar Salah looked more like a Greek or a Levantine Jew. He even had a tonsure, like William himself. But his teeth were bad and he had a disease of the scalp that had left raw, red patches on his skull. 'What is it you want?'

'Brother William wishes to speak with you.'

Mar Salah studied them down the length of his nose. 'Tell him he is not welcome here.'

'As I told you, he is not overjoyed to gaze upon us,' Josseran said to William.

'Ask him if it is true that he told the Emperor that we are not true Christians.'

Josseran turned back to Mar Salah. 'He knows what you said to the Emperor about us.'

'He asked me what I thought of you. I told him.'

'What does he say?' William said.

'He dissembles.' Josseran turned back to the Nestorian. 'Brother William is angry because you refused to give the Georgians and the Hungarians the sacrament until they were baptized into your church.'

'Who do you think you are to question me? Get out!'

'What is he saying *now*?' William shouted. If only he had the gift for tongues that this godless knight possessed!

'He says you have no right to question him.'

'No right? When he debauches himself with three different wives? When he shames the name of his church by drinking himself into a stupor every night and takes money from the poor souls that the Tatars hold hostage here, just to perform the liturgy!'

'He says you sin with three wives,' Josseran said to Mar Salah, 'and that you steal money from the Christians for performing your religious services. What have you to say for yourself?'

'I am not answerable to you for what I do here! Or your Pope in the west! The Emperor is not going to listen to you. Now get out!'

Josseran shrugged his shoulders. He had no taste for theological argument between two hot-smelling priests. 'He says he has nothing to say and we are to leave. We serve no good purpose here. Let us do as he says.'

'Tell him he will burn in hellfire! God will know him for what he is and send His avenging angels down on him!'

Josseran was silent.

'Tell him!'

'Curse him in your way if you will. It does not serve us.'

He slammed out of the church. Even from the street, he could hear the two priests still insulting one another inside, each in their own language. They sounded like two tomcats in an alley at night.

LXXXI

✠

THE NEXT DAY they presented themselves at the Palace of Coolness. Miao-yen received them kneeling on a silken carpet. She was a striking creature with almond eyes and bronzed skin. Her long jet hair had been combed back from her forehead, wound in rolls and pinned on top of her head in a chignon. It was decorated with hair-pins and ivory combs and ornaments of golden birds and silver flowers. Her eyebrows had been plucked and replaced with a thin but well-drawn line of kohl, and her fingernails were tinted pink with an ointment made from crushed balsam leaves.

Khubilai's youngest daughter was very different from the woman Josseran had expected. He had anticipated a robust and spirited creature like Khutelun; yet this woman was more like a Christian princess in her manner and refinement. While Khutelun was tall for a Tatar, Miao-yen was petite; while Khutelun was haughty, and quick to temper, Khubilai's daughter had downcast eyes and appeared as fragile as a porcelain doll.

She was likewise dressed, not for the steppe, but for the court. She had on a long gown of pink silk with a white satin collar at the throat, fastened on the left side with little oblong buttons that were tied into loops of cloth. The sleeves were so long that her hands could not be seen. There was a broad girdle at her waist with a jade buckle in the shape of a peacock and on her feet were tiny red satin slippers adored with gold embroidery. She had the look, not of a princess, but of a pretty child.

He remembered Tekudai's admonition: *To have the blood veil is the sign of a woman who has spent little time on horseback. She cannot therefore be a good rider and so she would be a burden to her husband.*

He wondered what he would think of *this* Tatar princess.

They settled themselves on the carpets around the table. Josseran looked around the room. The windows were covered by squared trellis and glazed with oiled paper, and on the floor there were carpets of rich gold and crimson brocade. Watercolours of snow scenes hung from the walls. They are intended to induce a feeling of coolness in the hot weather, Sartaq had told him. It is how the pavilion got its name.

Calligraphy scrolls hung on the walls, brilliant vermilion on a white background. On the low black-lacquered table was a statue of a horse, made from a single piece of jade, and a vase made of agate to which had been added a spray of plum blossom. At the princess's side was a bamboo cage containing a giant green cricket.

In the corner, three young Chinese girls in beautiful gowns played tiny harp-like instruments. Their music drifted across the lake.

'They tell me you have been brought here to educate me in the ways of your religion,' Miao-yen said.

'It was your father's wish,' Josseran answered.

'Is it your wish also?' she asked him.

'I wish for everyone to know of the one true God.'

Miao-yen smiled. Two servant women brought them something she called White Clouds tea. It was served in cups of fine blue and white porcelain from a lacquered tray.

As they sipped the scalding liquid she asked endless questions of him. She was intensely curious and, like her father, wanted to know about Christian – which was how she referred to France – and about Outremer and also about their journey and what they had seen. She listened hungrily to Josseran's descriptions of the Roof of the World and the Caves of a Thousand Buddhas. William pestered him endlessly for translations, requests which he ignored or answered only peremptorily.

Finally William grew impatient. 'Enough of this. It is time we talked to her of Christ.'

Josseran sighed. 'He wishes to begin your instruction now.'

'So you are not my teacher?'

Josseran shook his head. 'I am merely a warrior and a very humble lord.'

'You do not have the eyes of a warrior. Your eyes are gentle. His eyes are very hard for a shaman'

'I wish I were more gentle than I am.'

Miao-yen indicated William. 'Your companion does not speak like a Person?'

'I shall be his tongue and his ears.'

She gave a small, trembling sigh, like wind rustling the leaves of a tree. 'Before we begin I have one last question to ask of you. Do you know the reason my father sent you to me?'

'He says he wishes to know more of the Christian faith.'

'We already have the Luminous Religion here in Shang-tu.'

'But it is not the true form of our religion. The monks who teach it are rebels. They do not recognize the authority of the Pope, who is God's emissary here on earth.'

'And you think to convert my father to your ways?'

'What now?' William said.

'Wait a moment,' Josseran told him, hoping to seize this unexpected opportunity to gain an insight into Khubilai's character. He turned back to Miao-yen. 'You think he toys with us?'

'You have seen our royal court. There are Tanguts and Uighurs and Mohammedans and Chinese and Kazakhs. From everyone he takes something, gathering the wisdom of the world to him like a squirrel storing all it can before the winter comes. He will not buy from you, but he will pick your purse.'

He had not expected such a bald assessment of the Ruler of Rulers from his own daughter. 'The friar here believes that we can convince him that ours is the one and true way,' Josseran said.

She tilted her head, a gesture that could mean many things.

'You do not think so?'

'What I think is that I should not talk so freely with you. Should we not begin my instruction now?'

Josseran reminded himself to be patient, as he had so often counselled William. There would be many other days.

'So what does she say?' William asked him.

'Nothing of consequence. But thank you for your patience, Brother William. She is ready to begin her lessons now.'

LXXXII

✠

WILLIAM WOKE IN the middle of the night, panting as if he had just run from a fire. He rolled on to his side, tucked his knees into his chest, making himself as small as he could. He imagined himself hiding from God.

The fault was not his. The Church warned of demons who came to men and women in their sleep and ravished them while they were in this helpless state. He had battled this she-devil many times, but now she had returned in a new guise, with almond eyes and a willowy body.

He leaped from the bed and removed his friar's robe. He fumbled in the darkness for the switch that he had made himself that morning from cherry-tree branches.

He heard the rustle of silk as his succubus slipped her crimson brocade gown down her shoulders. He saw the pulse of blood at her throat, her ivory breast like a teardrop. He ran her long jet hair through his fingers.

No.

He lashed again and again, but he could not drive her out. She knelt at his feet like a penitent. He smelled her musk and imagined her long and warm fingers reaching beneath his robe. She was so real to him that he did not feel the blood running from his striped back, only the heat of her as he gripped his flesh in his own hand and gave his she-demon his seed.

✠

William blessed the wine and held it aloft.

'The blood of Christ,' he whispered, and raised his eyes to the vault of the incense-blackened roof. His white vestments were ragged and stained after the long journey from Outremer, but they were still the robes of the Holy Mother Church and he imagined they shone as the rays of the sun in this black heathen land.

It was a poignant moment for his secret congregation of Hungarians and Georgians, none of whom had attended a Latin rite since they had been captured in Sübedei's sweep through Europe twenty years before. William had commandeered Mar Salah's own church for this mass, had brought with him his Gospel and the missal and Psalter so carelessly cast aside by Khubilai.

Even in the darkness, he thought, God will shine his light. There is no corner of the earth that He cannot find us. I shall be his angel and emissary.

Suddenly the door to the church boomed open and Mar Salah stood framed in the entrance. His own black-robed priests were ranged behind him. He stormed up the aisle, his face contorted with fury.

'How dare you defile my church!'

William held his ground. But then, in order to display his piety before the congregation, he fell to his knees and began to recite the *Credo*.

They were on him then, kicking and beating him while the exiles looked on, guilty and afraid. Mar Salah's priests dragged him back up the aisle and hurled him outside into the mud, his Psalter and missal tossed into the muck after him.

The heavy door slammed shut.

A few startled townspeople stared as they hurried past on their way to the market. William got slowly to his feet, grimacing at the pain in his ribs. If I should suffer like Christ, he thought, then it only brings me closer to my beautiful reward. They can beat me and revile me but I will never waver. God is with me now and I cannot fail.

LXXXIII

✠

THE LOCAL CUSTOM was to bathe at least three times a week and Josseran found that, as in Outremer, the habit was pleasing both to his body and his mind. In his quarters there was a great earthenware bath with a small bench on which to sit while he bathed. To heat it, a fire was built underneath it using the special black stones that the Chin mined from the mountains. When it was fired it gave off great heat for hours before finally crumbling to grey ash.

On other mornings the attendants they had assigned to him brought him at the very least a jug and a bowl of water for washing his hands and face.

William, by the smell of him, did not avail himself of any of these opportunities.

Josseran also found, as he did in Outremer, that it was more comfortable to dress in the local fashion when possible. He was given a broad robe of golden silk. Its sleeves reached almost to his fingertips and it had a phoenix artfully embroidered on its back. It was tied with a broad sash that had a buckle of horn that came from a country they called Bengal. He was given also a pair of silk sandals with wooden soles.

No one, he noticed, went barefoot or bareheaded except the Buddhist monks. So he took to wearing a turban of black silk as was the custom among the nobles. He also summoned the palace barber and had his face shaved clean. Unlike Outremer, where the Saracens considered it unmanly not to grow a beard, most men in Shang-tu were clean-shaven. The Tatars and the Chinese did not grow beards easily and those he saw tended to be sparse.

Only William remained intransigent, odiferous, hirsute and scowling in his black Dominican's robe.

✝

Shang-tu, which meant Second Capital in the Chin language, was Khubilai's summer residence; his main seat, where he spent the long winters, was the ancient Chin city of Ta-tu, First Capital, further to the east. Shang-tu had only recently been completed, its construction supervised by Khubilai himself, its site chosen on the Chin principles of *feng shui*, the happy conjunction of wind and water.

It had been laid out with mathematical precision, in a grid-work of parallel streets, so that from his window high inside the palace near the northern wall Josseran could see all the way along the city's main thoroughfare right up to the southern gate.

'The Chin say that heaven is round and the earth is square, so that is why Khubilai's engineers designed it this way,' Sartaq told him.

'What about the characters painted over the lintels? Every house has them.'

'It is the law. Every citizen in Cathay has to display his name and the name of everyone in his family, as well as the servants. Even the number of animals. This way Khubilai knows precisely how many people live in his kingdom.'

Josseran was astonished at the order he had imposed on his empire. These restrictions even applied to his own life.

By Tatar custom he possessed four *ordos*, or households, from each of his four wives, who were all Tatars like himself. But he also kept an extensive harem for his personal use. 'Every two years a commission of judges is sent on an expedition to find a new intake of virgins,' Sartaq said. 'I was given the honour of providing an escort last summer. We visited countless villages and they brought out their most beautiful young girls, and they were paraded before the judges. Those selected we brought back here to be assessed.'

'Assessed? Who assesses them?'

'Not me, unfortunately,' Sartaq said, grinning. 'The older women of the harem, that is their job when they are retired from night-time duties. They sleep with the new girls, make sure that their breath and their body odour is sweet, and that they do not snore.'

'And if they are not suitable?'

'I wish they would give them to me! I would not mind if some of these women I saw snored like donkeys! But no, they are employed instead as cooks or seamstresses or dressmakers.'

'And the ones chosen for the Emperor?'

'They are given special training to prepare them for their attendance upon the Son of Heaven. When they are ready, he accepts five of them in his bedchamber each night for three nights. So should we all like to be the Khan of Khans! But Barbarian, you look pale.'

'Five women a night!'

'Do you not have harems in Christian?'

'I know of them from the Mohammedans only. In France a man may have only one wife.'

'Even your king? Just one woman his whole life?'

'Well, if a man is inclined, he sleeps with other men's wives, or the household servants.'

'Does that not cause a lot of problems? Surely it is better our way?'

'Perhaps. Brother William might not agree.'

'Your shaman,' Sartaq said, tapping his forehead with his finger, 'is a good example of what happens to a man when he does not have enough women.'

☩

Every day there was some new wonder. The food prepared in Khubilai's court was beyond comparison to anything he had ever tasted, and quite unlike the unrelenting diet of milk and singed mutton he had become accustomed to during their journey across the steppe. At various times he sampled scented shellfish in rice wine, lotus seed soup, fishes cooked with plums and a goose cooked with apricots. There was also bear's paw, baked owl, the roasted breast of a panther, lotus roots, steamed bamboo shoots and a stew made from a dog. The methods of preparation were more painstaking than any he had ever seen. They would use only wood from a mulberry tree to cook a chicken, claiming that it made the meat more tender; likewise only acacia wood would do for pork, and only pine for boiling water for tea.

Josseran practised every day with the ivory sticks they used for eating and after a time he became reasonably proficient. After the ravenous frenzies which had distinguished his meals among the

Tatars on the steppe, Josseran's repasts in the company of Sartaq and the rest of the courtiers had all the delicacy of needlepoint.

But what astonished him most were the books they possessed. William's Bible was a rare and precious object in the Christian world; but in Shang-tu everyone owned at least one almanac and an edition of the *Pao*, which was used by the idolaters to enumerate the merits and demerits of almost every action in their lives. They were not copied by hand, as they were in Christendom, but reproduced in large numbers using woodcut plates which reproduced their calligraphy on paper.

Sartaq took him to a large shop to see them being made. In one room a scribe copied the book on to thin oilpaper, in another these sheets were pasted on to boards of apple wood. Then another artisan traced each stroke with a special tool, cutting the characters in relief. 'Then they dip this block into ink and stamp it on to a page,' Sartaq said. 'This way we can reproduce each page, each book, very fast, as many as we want.'

Sartaq showed him his copy of a book called the *Tao de-jing*. 'It is a book of magic,' he said. 'It can predict wars and the weather. I also have this.'

'You believe in magic also?'

He showed Josseran the amulet he wore at his neck. 'It is very expensive. It protects me from all danger. Because of this I will live a long and happy life.'

'I don't believe in charms,' Josseran said.

Sartaq laughed and tugged on the cross that Josseran wore at his throat. 'So what is this then?'

Most of the Chin were followers of an ancient sage, Kung Fu-tse. Sartaq called them Confucians. 'Is this the god I see everywhere, the one with all the incense and flower offerings at his feet?'

'Yes, that is Kung Fu-tse but he was not really a god. He was just a man who understood the gods and how life is.'

'Like our Lord Jesus.'

'Yes, that is what Mar Salah says. Only he says his Jesus was more clever and had better magic. But of course, he would say that, wouldn't he?'

'What god do these Confucians believe in then?' Josseran asked him.

'They have many, even I don't remember them all. God of the hearth, god of money. They light joss to their ancestors too, because they are afraid of them. But the god they love most is Rules! They have a rule for everything. They follow a code called the Five Virtues and they say this is their guide to living a good life.'

'Like our Ten Commandments,' Josseran said, thinking aloud.

'I have never heard of this Ten Commandments but if it means you say one thing and do another, then yes, just like that. These Chin are very good at counting and organizing but I wouldn't trust one of them with my back turned. They have one virtue to us, they do what they are told. What good are their gods and their Five Virtues anyway? We are overlords here, not them, so that tells you how much use their religion is.'

✝

The beating William had taken at the hands of the Nestorians had left his face so bruised and swollen that he looked like one of the diseased beggars Josseran had seen in the streets. But it had not dampened his spirits or weakened his resolve. He spent hours every day outside the Metropolitan's church in the poor quarter of the city, shouting out his prayers for divine intervention and attracting crowds of curious Chin who came to stare at this strange-looking and evil-smelling foreigner on his knees in the mud.

Josseran tried to persuade him to desist, but William would not be swayed. He said the Lord would provide a miracle and bring the Nestorians back to God's true Church.

And he was right, because soon afterwards he confounded Josseran and got his miracle, just as he said he would.

LXXXIV

✠

THEY SPENT HOURS every day with Miao-yen in her yellow-tiled pavilion. She proved a good student and could soon recite the pater-noster and Ten Commandments by heart. William also taught her that the Pope was God's divine emissary on earth and that her only way to salvation was through the Holy Church. William was a patient tutor, but tolerated no questions. Her immortal soul was at stake, he reminded her.

He did allow her, once, to look through his missal. She pointed to one of the figures and asked who it was.

'That is Mary, the mother of God,' Josseran told her.

'Mar Salah says that God cannot be a man, so no woman can be the mother of God.'

'Mar Salah is a heretic!' William said, when Josseran translated what she had said. 'Tell her she is not to listen to his foul teachings, or question the mysteries of faith.'

Miao-yen seemed to accept this. She tilted the page to the light so that she might examine it more closely. 'She looks very much like Kuan Yin. Among the Chin she is known as Goddess of Mercy.'

William was exasperated. 'Please tell her she cannot compare the Holy Virgin to any of her heathen idols. It is blasphemous.'

Miao-yen took the rebuke mildly, and never again offered comment on his lessons, which she devoted herself to wholeheart-edly. But despite her apparent enthusiasm for the task Josseran sensed that it was nothing more than an intellectual exercise for her. She remained, in her heart, a Tatar.

After a while even William sensed her recalcitrance and was no longer satisfied with merely giving her instruction in the forms of the Catholic religion. He looked for a sign that his lessons were bearing fruit.

'Tell her,' he said to Josseran one day, after he had told her the story of Jesus's resurrection from the dead, 'tell her that to be godly she should refrain from using perfumes and putting paint on her face.'

Josseran put the request to her as delicately as he could.

'But she says it is required of her both as a Chinese lady and the daughter of the Emperor,' he said.

'She has the look and smell of a whore.'

'You want me to tell her that?'

'Of course not.'

'Then what do you wish me to say?'

'Tell her she should pray to God for guidance. A woman should be virtuous in all things and paint and perfume are the tools of the Devil.'

'What does he say?' Miao-yen asked.

'He compliments you on your beauty,' Josseran said. 'Even without your lotions and perfumes he thinks you would be the most exquisite woman in Shang-tu.'

Miao-yen smiled and bobbed her head, and thanked Josseran for his kind words.

He turned to William. 'She says she will think about it.'

There were some days when, after William had finished his instruction, Josseran would remain behind with her in the pavilion. He hoped to learn more from her about Khubilai and his great empire. He was also fascinated by this strange creature, although not in the same way he had been drawn to Khutelun. He was simply intrigued as to how the daughter of the Emperor could be trapped here in this gilt palace, while Khutelun lived her life from the saddle of a horse. Were they not both the daughters of Tatar khans?

He felt that in turn she enjoyed his companionship. They talked for hours over the fragrant teas brought by her maidservants, for she was endlessly curious about France. 'You are a khan in Christian?' she asked him.

'Yes, a khan I suppose. But not a great khan like your father Khubilai. I am the lord of just a few people.'

'How many wives do you have?'

'I have no wife.'

'No wives? How can this be? A man cannot live without a wife. It is not natural.'

'I have pledged myself to live as a monk for a time.'

'How can a khan be a monk? I do not understand. A man must be one thing or nothing. How do you know who you really are when you are so many things?'

One day they were sitting together watching one of the servant girls feed the goldfishes, when she pointed across the water at a stag that was standing silently under the willows in the Emperor's park. 'Do you hunt in the barbarian lands?' she asked him.

'Indeed. We hunt for food and for sport.'

'Then you would like to hunt in my father's park. It is truly a wonder.'

Josseran thought of Khutelun and how she had brought down a charging wolf with a single arrow. 'Do you not hunt?'

She gave a bitter laugh. 'Sometimes I long to.'

'Then why do you not?'

'It is not the way of the Chin for women to behave as the Tatars do.'

'But you are not Chin. You are Tatar.'

She shook her head. 'No, I am Chin, because that is what my father wishes. My father has in every respect taken on the forms and manners of a Chin. Have you not seen this for yourself?'

'I confess I do not always know what to make of the things I see.'

'Then I will tell you this: my brother, Chen-chin, will be the next Emperor and Khaghan of the Tatar. Do you not find this strange? At his age my grandfather, Chinggis Khan, already rode at the head of his own *touman*, and had conquered half the steppe. Chen-chin spends his days closeted with Confucian courtiers learning Chinese customs and etiquette, reading *The Book of Odes* and *The Analects of Kung Fu-tse* and learning Chinese history. Instead of the smell of a horse, he has the smell of aloe and sandalwood from the censers. Instead of conquest, he has calligraphy.'

'Khubilai does this to win over the people, no doubt.'

'No. My father does this because his soul is barren. He wishes to be all things to everyone. He even wishes to be thought of kindly by those he has crushed.'

It stunned him to hear such a brutal judgement of the Emperor from his own daughter. 'If that is his aim, it would seem to me that he has succeeded,' he murmured.

'It is only "seems". The Chin smile pleasantly at us and do our bidding and fill our courts and pretend to love us. But privately they call us barbarians and mock my father for his inability to speak their language. They make fun of us in their theatres. Their actors make jokes about us; their puppeteers lampoon us. They ridicule us because we want so much to be like them. It makes them despise us all the more. The truth is that we are invaders and they hate us. How could they do otherwise?'

Josseran was shocked. The Son of Heaven, then, was not as omnipotent as appearances would have him believe. He faced both civil war in his homeland and rebellion in his empire. 'But Sartaq tells me that many of Khubilai's soldiers are Chinese.'

'He uses them wisely. All his levies are assigned to provinces far from their own homes so they feel as much like foreigners as their Tatar officers. My father retains his own bodyguard, the *kesig*, and has hand-picked regiments from his own clan stationed all over his empire to crush any rebellion. They have torn down the walls of all the Chinese cities, have even ripped up the paving stones in their streets so they will not obstruct our Tatar ponies should we need to attack them. You see? They do not hate him openly because they do not dare. That is all.' She realized she had said too much and lowered her eyes. 'I speak too freely with you. You are a good spy.'

Silence, save for the murmur of a fountain, the clicking of bamboo.

'It is politic that I live here in this beautiful park with only the birds and long-life fishes for company, for my father wishes me to be a Chinese princess. But it is not only politics. He genuinely loves these Chin whom he has vanquished. Is it not strange in such a man?'

He nodded. 'It is as you say.'

'Strange and unfortunate. For I long to ride on a horse and learn to fire an arrow, like a Tatar. Yet I must sit here every day among the willows with nothing else to pass the hours but to place pins in my hair. Our father gives us life and then becomes our burden. Is that not true, Barbarian?'

'Indeed,' he said, wondering if he might ever set down his own load.

✙

'Where have you been?' William demanded when Josseran returned to the palace later that afternoon.

'I have been talking with the princess Miao-yen.'

'You spend too much time with her. It is not worthy.'

'I learn much about the Emperor and his people through her.'

'You lust for her. I see it in your eyes.'

Josseran was affronted at this accusation, for it was unjust. 'She is a princess and the Emperor's daughter.'

'When has that ever deterred you from your base instincts? The smell of her, the artifices she employs on her face, the silk robes she wears! She has all the Devil's devices. I lavish hours on showing her the path to virtue and to God and you undo all my good works!'

Josseran sighed. 'I do not know what more you wish of me.'

'I wish nothing of you. It is God who wishes you to help me bring these people to the love of Christ.'

'Have I not done all that is in my power?'

William shook his head. 'I do not know,' he said. 'God alone can answer that.'

✙

Khubilai awaited her in the Pavilion of Sweet Flowers. He wore a gown of green silk brocade and an expression of watchful discontent.

The pavilion was open to the gardens on all sides. Urns had been planted with pink-flowering banana and cinnamon, and windmills were artfully placed about the tiled courtyard so that the gentle movement of the spars carried the fragrance of the flowers into the halls. The chatter of birds in the trees that overhung the eaves was almost deafening. An altar stood at the northern end of the pavilion. It contained grass from the steppe, as well as earth brought from the Tatar homeland; ochre mud, yellow sand, black and white pebbles from the Gobi. Although it was ostensibly a Tatar shrine, the Altar of the Soil was a Confucian ideal. It was covered with a mantle of red brocades, with benedictions written on the cloth in the gold characters of the Chin.

So many contradictions here.

She approached on her hands and knees. Then she joined her hands and bowed her head three times on the marble floor before looking up into the silken eyes of her father. The stern faces of his Confucian and Tangut advisers watched from the dais below his throne.

'So, Miao-yen. You do well at your studies?'

'I am diligent, my lord.'

'What do you make of your tutors?'

'They are sincere, my lord,' she answered carefully, wondering what it was her father wished to know.

'And what of this religion they bring with them?'

'It is as you said, Father. It is very like the Luminous Religion of Mar Salah, except they have great esteem for this man they call Pope. They find much fault with the joining of a man and a woman and they also believe in the confession of a person's sins to their shaman, which brings about immediate forgiveness from their god.'

'They find fault with the joining of men and women?' Khubilai said, no doubt thinking of his own extensive harem.

'Yes, my lord.'

He grunted, unimpressed with this philosophy. 'They say that in the barbarian lands all the people bow down to this Pope.'

'It seems he is their Khan of Khans, and has the power to make kings among them, yet he does not himself carry sword or bow, if they are to be believed. It would seem he is a shaman, who has risen to be more powerful even than the greatest of their warriors.

'This almost once happened to us,' he said. She could imagine the direction of his thoughts. He would want no part of any religion that would threaten the supreme position of the Emperor.

'Do they have magic?'

'I have not seen them do magic, my lord. They have taught me prayers that they wish me to say, and told me of this Jesus that they hold so dear, as does Mar Salah and his followers.'

'You like this religion they have?'

She looked into Phags-pa lama's eyes. 'I do not think it as great as that of the Tanguts, my lord, nor as powerful.'

Phags-pa seemed to relax. Her father, too, seemed satisfied with her answer.

'What of the warrior? What do you think of him?'

'He seems an honest man, my lord. Yet this I do not understand; he says he travelled to another land to fight these Saracens, as he calls them, when he has nothing to gain for himself in either loot or women. He claims to do it for the merit of heaven. Yet it also seems they are frightened to leave their forts for fear of these same Saracens they are pledged to destroy.'

Khubilai grunted, her appraisal matching his own. 'I do not believe they will make strong allies. Even Mar Salah preaches against them, and he worships this Jesus, as they do. The Metropolitan says they wish to subject us all to the rule of this Pope, of which they speak overmuch.'

'All I know is this Joss-ran deals kindly with me and seems earnest,' Miao-yen said quickly, for she felt an affinity with this barbarian giant, and wished him no harm.

'And his shaman?'

'For him, I cannot answer,' she said, 'other than that he smells vile.'

'I commend you for your report, daughter. Be diligent. If they tell you something you think I should know, convey it to me yourself, in person.'

She was dismissed. She shuffled from the hall, tottering backwards on tiny feet.

LXXXV

✠

WILLIAM WAS WOKEN by a loud banging on his door. One of the Metropolitan's black-robed priests stood breathless in the corridor, two of the Emperor's *kesig* beside him. He was babbling incomprehensibly in his heathen tongue.

One of the guards went to fetch Josseran from his chamber. The Templar finally appeared, dishevelled and scarcely awake, hastily wrapping a silk robe around him. He listened to what the priest had to say and then explained to William that the man had been sent by Mar Salah. The Metropolitan of Shang-tu wished to see him at once.

He was dying.

The soldiers went ahead with flaming torches and they followed them through the darkened streets of Shang-tu. They came to a great house close to the palace wall. It was surrounded by a high wall, roofed with glazed ceramic tiles in the traditional split-bamboo pattern. The iron-studded door below the roofed gate was flung open and they followed the priest through a courtyard of flagstones, bordered with willows, pine trees and fishponds of golden carp. There was a cloister supported by lacquered pillars. Some servants stood by a doorway at the end of this gallery, wailing.

As they entered the main house Josseran was struck by the richness of the furnishings; he saw a cross made from sandalwood and agate; camphor chests inlaid with pearls; vases of beaten gold and precious blue and white porcelain; carpets of rich brocade; ornaments in jade and silver. Mar Salah lived in the sort of splendour that would not have shamed a Christian bishop, Josseran noted.

Churchmen! They were the same the world over.

The bedroom, too, was sumptuous, with hangings of silk and ermine. In the corner was a huge bronze urn filled with dried flowers. Mar Salah lay on the bed, behind a painted screen. Josseran was shocked at his appearance. He was deathly pale, and there were plum-coloured bruises around his eyes. The flesh had wasted off him. He had been coughing up blood; there was a froth of pink spume at the corners of his mouth.

His three wives were gathered around the bed, keening.

Josseran knew the smell of death; he had encountered it many times before. But he found the wailing of the women unnerving and he had the soldiers usher them from the room.

He looked at William, remembering how he had spent the last weeks in prayer outside Mar Salah's church, inviting the vengeance of the Lord God. He shuddered, feeling the prickling of the small hairs at the back of his neck. *Surely not.*

Mar Salah raised his head from the pillow and raised a clawed finger to indicate that Josseran should come closer. When he spoke, his voice was no more than a whisper.

'He asks what you have done to him,' Josseran said to William.

William's lips were pressed together in a thin line of contempt. 'Tell him I have done nothing. It is God's judgement on him, not mine.'

'He thinks you have cast a spell.'

William threw back the black hood and placed about his shoulders the purple stole he had brought with him from the palace. In his other hand he clutched his Bible. 'Tell him I shall hear his confession if he wishes it. Or else he will burn in hellfire.'

Mar Salah shook his head.

'He says he does not believe in the confession,' Josseran said. 'He claims that there is no mention of it in the sutras of the Gospels.'

'Tell him that he is going to hell for all eternity unless he makes a full confession to me now.'

Mar Salah looked defeated and very afraid. Josseran told him what William had said.

'He is frightened and says he will do it. But you will have to instruct him.'

'Very well,' William said. 'But I shall do this only on the condition that before he dies he summons all his priests to this room and before them recognizes the Pope as the father of all Christians everywhere in the world and agrees to pass the leadership of his church to the authority of the supreme Pontiff in Rome.'

Josseran could not believe his ears. 'You would blackmail a dying man?'

'Is it blackmail to unite our Blessed Church as God intended? Tell him what I say.'

Josseran hesitated, and then bent over the dying priest. His breath was rank. 'Mar Salah, Brother William says that before he can give you absolution, you must pass authority of your church over to our blessed Pope in Rome.'

'. . . never.'

'He insists.'

'No,' Mar Salah croaked.

Josseran turned to William and shook his head. The prospect of dying unshriven was something every Christian feared. He thought of his own sins and wondered again if his resolution to condemn himself to this same fate would falter at his last moments. 'Do you have no pity?' he said to William.

'None, for sinners.'

'He still says he will not do it.'

'Remind him again of the torments of hell. The hot brands applied endlessly to his naked flesh, the pitchforks thrust again and again into his belly, the whips with their metal tips. *Tell him.*'

Josseran shook his head. 'No.'

'You will not defy me in this! The future of the Holy Church here in Cathay is at stake!'

'I will not torture a dying man. That, as you have made abundantly clear, is the Devil's work, and I want none of it.' And over William's outraged protests, he strode from the room.

An hour before dawn, just as the cries of the monks with their alms bowls were heard in the street below, Mar Salah gave up his ghost, and went to the Devil and his exquisite banquet of tortures.

LXXXVI

✠

THE SOLDIERS OF the *kesig* stood guard while the Emperor strode to the water's edge, a fur of leopard skin around his shoulders against the dawn chill. Phags-pa lama was with him. Mist clung to the lake. In the distance a range of black mountains, dark and treeless, folded upon each other like silks on a bed.

Josseran appeared, escorted by Sartaq and one of his troopers. He knelt and bowed his head, awaiting the Emperor's wishes.

'The Metropolitan of Shang-tu is dead,' Khubilai said.

'I fear so, great lord,' Josseran answered.

'Your companion placed a curse on his head.'

'I believe it was an act of God alone.'

'Then you must indeed have a very powerful god. More powerful than Mar Salah's, it would seem.'

So, they too believed it was witchcraft that had ended the Nestorian bishop's life. Khubilai must have been persuaded that William had worked some kind of devilment because of the Metropolitan's opposition to him.

'I am inclined to think there is more to your religion than I first thought,' Khubilai said. 'Each of my advisers says their way is the best and the truest. But now we have another new religion, stronger than Mar Salah's. How shall I decide?'

Josseran knew that this was the opportunity William had dreamed of. They did not have to convert millions, just one man, if that man was Khubilai himself. If William could persuade the Khaghan to convert to Christ, and impose his new religion upon his empire, as all Christian kings were obliged to do, then the whole world would belong to Rome. In Outremer, they could trap the Saracens between themselves and the Tatar and retake the Holy Land. Jerusalem would return once more to Christian hands.

'I have arranged a debate,' Khubilai said.

'A debate, great lord?'

'I will decide for myself which of all the religions is best. Tell your holy man to present himself at the Audience Hall at the seventh hour. There he will meet with the other great shamans of my kingdom and debate with them on the nature of their beliefs. And then I shall decide once and for all which of these gods is most true.'

'We shall be honoured, my lord,' Josseran said, stunned by this dramatic proposal.

Josseran bowed once more, avoiding Phags-pa lama's venomous gaze. Sartaq escorted him back to his apartments. A debate! That should suit Brother William's style. With so much at stake he only hoped he could stop him talking before they all died of old age.

LXXXVII

✛

THE EMPEROR'S SUMMER palace lay just beyond the walls of his hunting park. It was in fact a yurt, built in the Tatar style, but its walls were made of the finest silk instead of the felt used by the Tatars of the high steppe. Hundreds of great silk cords held it braced against the wind. Its roof was made of split and varnished bamboo, decorated with paintings of animals and birds. Coiled serpents were carved into the lacquered vermilion pillars.

'Is it not a wonder?' Sartaq whispered to him. 'It is constructed in such a way that it can be taken down and removed to another more pleasant spot within hours, should the Emperor wish it.'

Josseran agreed that it was indeed a wonder, though he suspected such removal had never been attempted and was simply another legend to bolster the myth of Khubilai as a traditional Tatar chieftain.

The hall was already crowded with the holy men of Khubilai's court; the Emperor's own shaman, his hair and beard wild and unkempt, his skin scaly with filth, eyes staring in hemp-induced trance; the Tanguts with their shaven heads and saffron-coloured garments; the idolaters, in cloaks of orange and purple brocade and black pillbox hats, holding curved wooden prayer boards; the black-robed Nestorians; and the white-bearded Mohammedans in white skullcaps.

Below the throne, to Khubilai's left, was the Empress Chabi, Khubilai's favourite. Josseran had learned from Sartaq that she was an ardent devotee of Borcan. She eyed them with cold suspicion as they entered. To Josseran's further consternation he saw Phags-pa standing at the Emperor's shoulder. It was apparent that he was to be both the convener of the debate and its leading participant.

Khubilai signalled to Phags-pa lama, who announced that the proceedings would now commence. To begin the affair, a spokesman from each faction was to give a brief account of his own religion and afterwards they would debate in open forum.

As the discussions began, Josseran found himself bewildered by the heresies and witchcraft and idolatry to which his ears were subjected. He translated it all faithfully to William. When it was William's turn he stood up, resplendent in his white surplice and purple stole, and gave what he called the true account of history, from the time of the making of the world and the creation of Man and Woman by God.

He then spoke of the miraculous birth of Christ and related the story of His life and sufferings, and finished by enumerating God's laws, as vouchsafed to Man in the Ten Commandments. He then expounded on the special place that the Pope and the Holy Mother Church held in the heart of God.

It was an inspired speech. His eyes burned with his fervour, and his oratory was impressive. Gone was the carping, hateful little friar, replaced by a giant with a voice like thunder. Josseran had never seen this aspect of his character before. At last he understood why the Pope had sent him.

When he had finished, the Emperor, through Phags-pa lama, announced the debate. It soon became obvious that William, as the newcomer, was to be the target of all.

It was Phags-pa lama himself who led the inquisition and Josseran would have enjoyed William's discomfort except that it was vital for the Templar cause that they make a good impression here. And, for all his misgivings, Christianity was yet the religion of his heart.

First, Phags-pa lama asked William about the Ten Commandments of God.

'But our Emperor does not follow your God's precepts and he has trodden all other nations underfoot. Does that not mean that he alone is blessed and your and all other gods are inferior?'

William was unflustered by such argument. 'Tell him a man's worth is not measured by what he owns in this world. Christ Himself told us that the earth shall be inherited by the meek.'

'That has not been my experience,' the Emperor growled when he heard William's reply and some of his generals, listening curiously to this debate, laughed aloud.

'How can a man know the mind of the gods except if what he does earns their favour or displeasure?' Khubilai said, now placing himself inside the debate.

'Tell him it is a matter of faith,' William said when he heard this.

'No, a man is not defined by what he believes,' Phags-pa said, 'but by what he does. A thousand years of wisdom has been condensed into our book of the *Pao*. It allows every person to calculate the merits and demerits of his life.'

'But if a man can earn demerit by his actions,' one of the idolaters interrupted, for the moment deflecting the attention from William, 'surely then the way to serenity is by performing no action. That is the way of the *Tao*.'

And so it went on.

Josseran was dazzled to be present at such a discourse. He had never been exposed to such a diversity of thought and as the arguments raged about him and he breathlessly relayed each word to William, he realized how similar were the arguments of the Mohammedans to their own. Indeed, they also spoke of prophets and the immutability of one God and his laws. Of all of the religious present that afternoon, it seemed to him that the Mohammedans, their bitter enemies in Outremer, were their closest allies.

The Nestorians, for their part, attacked William with the same ferocity as the Tanguts.

Khubilai's own shaman was now saying that words were unimportant, that the rightness of a religion could only be gauged by the efficacy of its magic. The Emperor interrupted him to point out that if that were true, then the Pope had very powerful magic for behold what William's God had done to Mar Salah.

On hearing this William tried to press his advantage by saying that from the day God had created the world all he wished was that all the people of the earth should recognize him and give him due praise and obedience. He would only bring down his vengeance on those who denied him. As he had on Mar Salah.

An old monk in a saffron robe spoke next. 'He says that the world is an illusion,' Josseran translated. 'He says that life will always disappoint us and birth, old age, illness and suffering are inevitable.'

'Tell him that is why Christ came to save us!' William almost shouted, his cheeks flushed with excitement. 'That if we endure our sufferings in a Christian way we can find heaven!'

Josseran conveyed this perspective to the monk, who stared deep into William's face as he made his response. 'Even the peasant in the field endures,' he said. 'Reading sacred texts, abstaining from meat, worshipping the Buddha, giving alms, all these gain merit for the next life. But for release from suffering, what is required is a personal revelation of the emptiness of the world.'

'How can the world be empty?' William shouted. 'It was created by God! Only man is sinful!'

The monk frowned. 'He asks what you mean by sin,' Josseran said.

'Lust. Fornication. Weakness of the flesh.'

When he heard this the monk murmured a response which Josseran seemed unwilling to pass on.

'What was it he said?' William demanded.

'He said – he said that you were right to fear such weakness.'

'What did he mean by that?'

'I do not know, Brother William. He would not explain further.'

'The righteous man fears nothing!' William shouted at him. 'Those who keep God's law will be rewarded in heaven!'

Khubilai held up a hand for silence. He then began to conduct a long and whispered conversation with Phags-pa lama.

As this was happening William turned to Josseran. 'You have not properly translated all that I said!' he hissed.

'Since you do not speak their language, how do you know what I have said?'

'It is obvious by their looks and their expressions. If you had spoken the true words of God, they would have already been persuaded. Should we fail here today it will be your doing and I shall denounce you before the Haute Cour upon our return to Acre.'

'I translated all you said faithfully and without prejudice!'

'It is clear to me that you did not!'

The consultation between the Emperor and his adviser ended abruptly and Phags-pa lama turned to face the assembly. 'The Son of Heaven has listened to all your arguments and believes that each of you spoke eloquently and persuasively. He will think on all he has seen and heard. Now he wishes you all to leave him to his tranquillity. Except the barbarian.' He indicated Josseran.

'I shall stay also,' William said as the others filed from the room. 'I cannot leave you here without instruction.'

Phags-pa lama glared at him. 'Tell him he must leave now.'

Josseran turned to William. 'I fear if you do not leave this moment, they will drag you from the chamber as they did before. It does not leave a good impression.'

William hesitated, red-eyed with exhaustion and fervour and rage, then reluctantly made his obeisance to the Son of Heaven and left the room.

✛

When they were alone in the great pavilion. Khubilai Khan, Son of Heaven, regarded Josseran Sarrazini for a long time. 'We have thought deeply about what we have seen and heard here today,' he said at last.

Josseran waited. The fate of their entire expedition hinged on this very moment. 'I trust you were pleased with our arguments, great lord.'

'We were greatly impressed with all we heard here today and we thank you for making the long and dangerous journey to our court. It has been most instructive. As to the matter of religion, these are the words of my heart . . .'

LXXXVIII

✠

WILLIAM WAITED ON his knees on the flagstones, repeating the words of the paternoster. When he saw Josseran he leaped to his feet.

'What did he say?' he asked, his voice hoarse with strain and excitement.

'He says he has made his considerations and would like us to know that of all the religions he has heard . . . he likes ours the best.'

William could scarcely believe his ears. He dropped back to his knees, shouting his praises to God. All the trials and misfortunes had been worth the price. He had done as God had asked him to do and brought the king of the Tatars into the fold.

Josseran did not join him in his thanksgiving. He left him there, still on his knees, and made his way back to his apartments. He sensed that their celebration was premature. Even after so many months spent travelling the roads of Middle Asia and Cathay, the conversion of the Son of Heaven, Ruler of Rulers, Khan of Khans of all the Tatars, now seemed to him . . .

. . . too simple.

LXXXIX

✠

THE NEXT MORNING they again presented themselves at Miao-yen's apartment. William was hollow-eyed from exhaustion. He had been too overwrought to sleep and had spent that entire night repeating prayers of thanks and supplication. Josseran had not slept either. He felt torn in two. They had seemingly achieved a triumph beyond imagining, yet the arguments he had heard during the debate had cast a shadow over his soul.

Such blasphemies could never be spoken aloud in Christendom; such open debate was impossible. The opinions and philosophies he had heard had shaken his faith more deeply than ever. Could a man really know the mind of God? In the face of so many other theories and opinions how could any man be sure that he had stumbled upon an absolute truth?

Miao-yen awaited them, seated on a silk mat. She bowed her head as they entered. They returned her greeting and sat down, cross-legged. One of her maids brought bowls of plum tea and set them on a black lacquered table between them.

'Tell her today I shall teach her the way we make confession,' William said.

Josseran relayed this, watching the young girl's face, wondering what went on behind her black eyes.

'I am honoured to learn this confession,' Miao-yen told him. 'But first I should congratulate you. I have heard of your triumphant hour in the Emperor's pavilion.'

'Your father seemed well pleased with us,' Josseran said.

A curious smile. 'He was well pleased with everyone.'

'But he assured me that he liked our religion best of all.'

Miao-yen still smiled. 'He said this to you?'

'Indeed.'

314

She turned and gazed dreamily out of the screened windows at the lake. Josseran heard the rasp of a willow broom in the court outside. 'You do not understand my father,' she said finally.

'What is it we do not understand?'

'What does she say?' William wanted to know. 'Must you always frustrate me like this, Templar?'

'I am not sure of her meaning.'

'Do not try and instruct her yourself,' William warned. 'I will not have her infected with your heresies.'

'Very well, I will tell you what she says,' he answered. 'She casts doubt on our victory before the Emperor yesterday.'

'But you heard the verdict from his own lips!'

'She implies that what the Emperor says is not what he means. It would not be the first time a king has dissembled for his own ends.'

Miao-yen turned from the window. 'All think they are victors in the debate. Did you not know?'

Josseran took a breath.

'You did not really believe he would so isolate himself from his allies in the court? The debate was merely a device to set you all against each other. My father is all things to all men; I told you this. It is the core of his strength.'

'But he said he found most reason in our religion.'

'When he is with the Tanguts he follows the ways of Buddha; to the Mohammedans he is the upholder of the Faith. To Mar Salah, he was the protector of your Jesus. He does and says what it is politic to do and say.'

'Tell me what she says!' William almost shouted.

Miao-yen kept her eyes lowered while Josseran translated what she had just told him. William's face turned ashen and the euphoria that had been with him all morning evaporated entirely. 'She makes mischief,' he said. 'I do not believe her.'

'That Khubilai toys with us for reasons of politics makes more sense to me than his sudden conversion.'

'I do not believe it!' William said but Josseran could see that the awful truth had already taken hold.

'You may be right. It is only her opinion.'

'But you believe her?'

Josseran did not answer.

William jumped to his feet. His hands were shaking. 'I am the emissary of the Pope himself!' he shouted. 'He cannot toy with me in this fashion!'

And he marched away.

After he had gone Josseran turned back to Miao-yen. 'I fear there will be no instruction today,' he said.

'A thousand apologies. But it is better that you understand the game my father plays, even if you do not know all the rules.'

'Yes, my lady,' he said, and wondered if the Emperor knew she was telling them this, or if Miao-yen had taken it on herself to tell them the truth.

And so, he thought, our great triumph of yesterday was purely imaginary. Treating with these Tatars was like trying to capture smoke in your fist.

He looked into the doe eyes of the princess and wondered what else he would learn from this strange creature. Does she wish to be our ally or does she merely wish to torment us with our own foolishness?

✠

The pleasure barge floated on a lake of velveteen beauty, as glossy black as coal, and dappled with light from the lanterns of the pagodas along the lake's edge. The night was cool and scented with jasmine. From the cabin of her barge Miao-yen could see the entire city; the lacquered tiles of the palaces and temples glittered under a three-quarter moon.

She lay on her back on the silken carpets, naked except for a pair of small silk slippers on her feet. Her body was the colour of alabaster, aromatic from the perfumed oils from her bath.

A servant woman knelt at her head. With her right thumb she applied pressure at the Place of a Hundred Meetings, easing the tension in her body. Then, using both her thumbs, she concentrated her attentions on the Hall of the Imprint between the eyebrows, before dragging around to the highest yang at the soft temple, where she felt the gentle throbbing of her pulse.

Her expert thumbs went next to the Wind Pond, at the lower margin of the occipital bone, then she pinched the skin at the nape of the neck, kneading down towards both *jian jing* acupoints in the thick muscles of the shoulder well.

The ceiling of the cabin was painted in watercolours with flowers and mountain landscapes, a nether dreamworld of cloud and willow. Miao-yen felt herself drifting among them.

Employing the tips of her thumbs, the masseuse worked along her smooth arms, concentrating the pressure at the Inner Pass, above the soft crease of the wrist, and the Spirit Gate beneath the ulna, pressing hard into the Joining of the Valleys; press-release, press-release, so that the princess groaned aloud, feeling the pressure build between her eyes and then suddenly and wondrously disappear.

She moved to the legs, avoiding the triple yin crossing, for a good masseuse will not excite the sexual longings of a maiden.

Miao-yen rolled languorously on to her stomach. She worked her fingers into the Jumping Circle with the knuckle of the bent middle finger, pressing hard into the silk depression below the right and left buttocks, heard the girl gasp and bite the flesh of her arm with sudden pain.

She finished with a number of two-palm presses along the gently curving spine, using the muscular pads on the heel of her hand. Miao-yen's eyes were closed now, her body relaxed, her lips parted.

The masseuse stood up, her work finished. She examined the girl's body with the critical gaze of an older woman. She envied her taut muscles and fragrant skin. She would be the perfect jewel for some Chin prince, she thought.

And best of all, she had the wonderful secrets of the slipper.

☩

William lay in the darkness of the third hour, listening to the mocking sounds of the city; the cry of the Mohammedan summoning the heathen to their church and the booming of the gongs of the idolaters as they set out through the darkened streets. He was surrounded by unbelievers, a lamb among the dogs of hell. He felt the burden of his charge, this great pact God had made with him, to bring his holy word here to the end of the world.

His eyes ached for sleep but his muscles and his nerves were as taut as bowstrings.

He closed his eyes, remembering the sweet powders and fragrant teas of his new student, heard again the lapping of the waters of the lake around her pavilion, the strange music of the Cathay lutes. The rustle of silk was as ominous and piercing as thunder.

He got out of his bed and knelt on the floor, tried to concentrate his heart with prayer. His hands began to shake.

He tore the robe from his shoulders until it hung about his waist and searched in the darkness for the switch. He found it in its hiding place, beneath the bed. He began to flail at his back with great enthusiasm, for at stake was the greatest triumph of his faith, if he had but the strength.

Or would he, in his way, cause his Lord to suffer again?

X C

✝

THE HUNTING PRESERVE was to the west and north of the city, abutting the city walls, a vast paradise garden of meadowlands, woods and streams, stocked with wild hart, buck and roe deer. There were also herds of white mares, their milk the sole property of the Emperor. The park was enclosed by an earthen wall that snaked sixteen miles around the plain and was surrounded by a deep moat. The only entrance was through the palace itself.

Josseran had seen the park from Miao-yen's pavilion and had thought never to go there. But one day, much to his surprise, he was invited to ride to hunt with the great Khubilai himself.

✝

The howdah was mounted on the backs of two grey elephants. It was sumptuously appointed, the walls and roof draped with leopard skins, the interior rich with cloths of silk brocade and furs. This is not the way Qaidu would ride to hunt, Josseran found himself thinking, and for a moment he saw this great chieftain through the eyes of the true Tatars, like Khutelun, and he understood their bitterness.

The howdah creaked in time with the rolling gait of the great elephant as they set off along the shaded paths. A line of riders followed them, his *kesig* in light armour, some with bows, others with falcons on their gloved arms. The leading officer had a leopard sitting on his horse's croup.

The Emperor himself wore a gold helmet and white quilted armour. He had a gyrfalcon resting on his arm, and he stroked its head as if it were a kitten.

I wonder what he wants of me? Josseran thought.

'They tell me,' Khubilai said, 'that you came here across the Roof of the World.'

'Indeed, my lord.'

'Then doubtless you were the guest for a time of my lord Qaidu. Did he speak of me?'

Josseran felt a thrill of alarm. What was this about? 'He spoke much of Ariq Böke,' he said carefully. He clung to the sides of the howdah, unused to the swaying movement. Like being on a ship during a stormy passage.

'And he gave him great credit, no doubt, for qualities he does not possess. What did you think of my lord Qaidu?'

'He treated kindly with me.'

'A careful answer. But you know the reason that I ask you these questions. Not all Tatars think of Khubilai as their lord.' He did not wait for a reply. 'You know this for you have seen our dispute with your own eyes. But know this also: I am lord of both the Mongol and the Celestial Kingdom, and those who defy me I will grind into dust. Hülegü, in the khanate in the west, acknowledges me and is obedient to my wishes.'

We may yet forge our alliance then, Josseran thought. Or is this another of his games? The gyrfalcons had been released by Khubilai's horsemen, and they shrieked as they swooped on the cranes in the lakes.

'There are some who think we should spend all our lives as our grandfathers did, on the steppes, stealing horses and burning towns. But Qaidu and my brother Ariq Böke live in a time that is gone. Are we to live as Chinggis lived, to conquer the world every winter, only to withdraw again during the summer to tend our horses and sheep? If we are to keep what we have won then we have to change our old ways. The world may be conquered from horseback but it cannot be ruled from it.

'The Mongol Tatar is the best in the world at fighting, but we have much to learn from the Chin in the way of governing. Qaidu and Ariq Böke do not understand that. A sage is needed to unite the world of Cathay and the people of the Blue Sky.' It was clear to Josseran from the way that Khubilai spoke who he thought that sage should be.

Their elephant raised its trunk to the heavens and trumpeted as a boar dashed across their path from the undergrowth and crashed away into the brush. The howdah gave a sickening lurch. Khubilai signalled to the horseman who carried the hunting leopard on his horse's croup. The officer unleashed the beast's chain and immediately it plunged after the boar, its head bobbing, the sinuous spine lengthening with each stride. The boar screamed and twisted and darted as it tried to escape but the leopard brought it down.

'I have decided to agree to this alliance you ask for. When our armies have won our victory we shall let you keep your kingdoms along the coast together with this town of Jerusalem you speak of. In return your Pope must send to me a hundred of his most learned advisers to help me in the administration of my kingdom.'

Josseran was stunned by this sudden offer. But then he realized: Khubilai wants to free Hülegü from the fighting in the west as soon as possible, so that he can support his own claim for the khanate. But a hundred advisers? What did the Emperor hope to gain from a hundred priests? One was enough of a burden.

'Brother William asks that he may be permitted to baptize you into our holy religion,' Josseran ventured.

Khubilai studied him, his eyes cold. 'This I did not promise you.'

'You greatly favoured us with your opinion that you liked our religion better than any other,' Josseran said, caution cast aside now. He would test for himself Miao-yen's charge of her father's duplicity.

'We Mongol believe, as you do, that there is but one God, by whom we live and by whom we die. But just as God gave different fingers to the hand, so he has given different ways to men. This the Emperor accepts. You must understand that the Son of Heaven is not free to choose his religion as others are. I indeed told you that I admired your religion above all others, but you were mistaken if you thought that I could then accept its forms and its customs. Be satisfied with what you have, Barbarian. It is what you came here for.'

The leopard had been retrieved by its handler and the gyrfalcons loosed to enjoy their dinner. As he watched the birds tear at the flesh of the boar, Josseran felt curiously depressed. He had succeeded in the task that the Order had set for him, despite the interference of the friar; but now it was done he only experienced that same dismal sense of shame that always settled over him in the aftermath of a battle.

He had duped the priest, he had used the Emperor's daughter for his spying, and he had been lied to in turn. He wondered if any of this manoeuvring would come to any good. All he knew for now was that the great adventure was almost over.

XCI

✢

MIAO-YEN SAT at the screened window of the pavilion known as the Palace of the Reflecting Moon. It had been constructed in such a way that the view of the moonrise over the mountains could be enjoyed to its best effect. Tonight a blood moon hung low above the bamboo stands, and was reflected in the still waters of the black lake.

It was a rare and breath-taking sight but tonight it pleased her not at all.

On top of her dressing table her cosmetics and jewellery spilled out of a box of red lacquered wood. Next to them lay a mirror of polished bronze. She picked it up and stared at her reflection in the glow of the painted silk lanterns that hung from the ceiling.

The face that stared back at her was that of a Chin princess, hair teased in the manner of a Chin, face powdered and painted in the way of a Chin. But in her heart she was a Tatar, one of the Blue Mongol of Chinggis Khan, and she yearned to ride.

She stared across the lake, at the chimera of the moon in the water. She felt a shiver along her spine, perhaps some clairvoyance of a darker future. In sudden rage she drew back her arm and hurled the mirror away from her. A moment later she heard it drop into the lake.

And then the night was silent again, except for the chirruping song of the crickets.

XCII

✠

THEY WERE USHERED before the Son of Heaven for the last time, while his courtiers, generals, shamans and saffron-robed Tanguts looked on. It was a ceremonial occasion, and this time there would be no informal words between them as there had been on the howdah. This time the Emperor would speak only through Phags-pa lama.

'The barbarians from the West have made petition to the Son of Heaven for clemency and protection,' Phags-pa announced.

Josseran smiled grimly, and wondered what William would say if he heard their treaty thus characterized.

'The Emperor wishes it known that if the barbarians desire to live in peace with us, we will fight the Saracens together as far as their borders and leave to them the rest of the earth to the west until it is our pleasure to take it away from them. In return the barbarians will send one hundred of their shamans to our court here in Shang-tu to serve us.' A courtier stepped forward and handed Josseran a parchment in Uighur script, sealed with the royal chop. 'This is a letter for your king, the Pope, confirming the essence of the treaty,' Phags-pa said.

Another courtier handed Josseran a gold tablet, which he called a *paizah,* similar to the one he had seen worn by the *yam* riders. It was a flat plate of gold engraved with falcons and leopards and imprinted with the seal of the Emperor.

'Place this around your neck and do not take it off. This tablet places you under the Emperor's protection. With this you will receive escort and succour across the entire world, from the Middle Kingdom to the very rim of the earth, which is under the command of the Son of Heaven.'

Josseran took the golden tablet. He read, in the Uighur script which so closely resembled classical Arabic: *By the strength of*

Eternal Heaven! May the name of the Khan of Khans be holy! He who doth not pay him reverence shall be slain and must die!

There were other gifts to be presented; a bolt of finest silk, a watercolour, a scroll of Chin calligraphy, black on red. He was also handed a Tatar bow. 'The Emperor lets it be known that this is his seal on the treaty between us,' Phags-pa announced. 'It is to remind the barbarian Pope, who is king of the Christians in the western lands, that should he ever break his word and fight against us, such bows can reach far and hit hard.'

'What are they saying?' William asked him.

Should I tell him that it is ratification of a secret treaty between the Order of the Temple and the Tatars? Josseran thought. That Hülegü was now bound to fight with the Franks against the Saracens? He does not need to know such details. 'It is a letter of friendship to the Holy Father from the Emperor. He commends his felicity and asks for a hundred priests to journey here to start the work of conversion.'

'A hundred priests? This is indeed good news. We Dominicans shall be at the forefront of such a ministry. And does the Emperor also abase himself before God?'

'I think not, Brother William.'

William seemed on the verge of tears. 'Why not? You must beg him to reconsider! Tell him that if he fears for his mortal soul he must embrace the Lord Jesus Christ!'

'He has said all he will say on the matter.'

William gave a long, shuddering sigh. 'Then I have failed. The woman was right. He is recalcitrant.'

'He has asked for one hundred priests. Surely that gives us cause for hope.'

'If the king will not accept our holy religion, what good is it?'

'Be that as it may, we have done all that we can. The invitation to one hundred priests is not an insignificant achievement.' Josseran moved backwards to the door, never once turning his back on the Emperor, as was the custom. As soon as they were outside William fell to his knees and again prayed for divine intervention.

By the sacred foreskins of all the saints! The man will wear out his knees!

Josseran walked away and left him there.

XCIII

✜

'IT IS CALLED the Garden of the Refreshing Spring,' Miao-yen told him.

A stream murmured into a small pond where golden long-life fishes moved slowly in the dark waters. Ancient, gnarled pines curled over the path; incense burned in a grotto carved into the rock face of a waterfall. The hollows were redolent with the scent of jasmine and orchids.

Miao-yen twirled a parasol of green silk over her shoulder to shield herself from the hot afternoon sun. 'So you are leaving Shang-tu,' she said.

'We are racing the winter to the Roof of the World.'

'So there are to be no more prayers and no more stories about Gesu?'

'No, my lady. And no more paternosters.'

'I shall miss you, Christian. But I shall not miss the odour of your companion's body. How do you endure it? Even the ducks swim to the other side of the lake when he comes here.'

Josseran had only ever met with her before this seated in her pavilion or on her pleasure barge. This was the first time he had seen her walk and he was struck by her strange, waddling gait. The reason for it was immediately obvious. Beneath the long gown he glimpsed a pair of impossibly tiny feet clad in silken slippers. They were so small it was a wonder she could move around at all.

She noticed the direction of his stare. 'My feet please you?'

'It pleased Nature to make them so small?'

'Nature did not do this.'

He looked puzzled.

'My feet were bound when I was a small child. My father ordered it. He thinks one day to marry me to a Chinese prince and he wishes me to embody all that the Chin find beautiful.'

'Your feet are bound up? Does it distress you?'

She gave him a smile of infinite pain. 'How may I answer that?' She stopped walking and looked up at him. 'I was four years old when my mother first wrapped tight bandages around my toes, curling them under my feet. Then she placed large rocks on the instep to crush the bones.'

'God's holy blood,' Josseran breathed.

'It is not something you do but once. The foot, of course, tries to heal itself. So the toes have to be crushed again and again. I cannot remove the bindings. Even now.'

'That is unspeakable,' he managed, finally.

'On the contrary, I have heard men say it is very beautiful. The Chin call them lily feet. For them such dainties are the epitome of womanhood. Perhaps they also think it is beautiful to see a leper or a one-armed man.' She blushed and lowered her face. 'Again, I speak too freely with you. It is because of the part of me that is still Tatar.' She gazed wistfully into the black water. 'My grandmother and my great-grandmother were thought to be very great women. They both ruled as regents of the clan while the men waited for the *khuriltai*. I shall never rule anywhere. A girl with lily feet is no more use than a cripple.'

'I could never imagine you as anything other than fair and wise,' he said to her.

She bobbed her head at the compliment, but did not smile. 'My mother was a concubine from the *ordo* of Tarakhan, my father's third wife. Perhaps if I had been born to Chabi instead, he would have treated me otherwise.'

They stood for a long time, listening to the murmur of the water. Josseran was unable to dispel the image of a young girl constantly tortured beyond pain for the sake of fashion, at her father's whim.

'You must be eager to return to your home,' she said at last.

'I am eager to take back the news of our treaty with the Emperor.'

'And yet there is great sadness in your face. You do not wish to go.'

'This journey has opened my eyes to the vastness of the earth. I have seen things other men only dream of. Now I fear that when I return to my own world its boundaries, even its beliefs, will be too small for me.'

'You fear they will bind your feet.'

'Yes. Yes, I imagine that is what I mean.'

'Is that all that makes you sad?'

How could he explain to her about Khutelun? He knew that when he returned to Acre the dream of her would disappear along with his memories of Shang-tu and the great, shimmering desert of Go-in-and-you-will-never-come-out. His heart ached. Yet what else could he do but make himself forget?

'You know your return will be more dangerous than your first passage here?' she said to him.

'How is that possible?'

'Has my father the Emperor told you there is civil war between him and his brother in Qaraqorum?'

Josseran shook his head. Khubilai had not entrusted him with such information, though he had suspected it. He had seen a vast army of soldiers leave the city a few days before, headed west. 'Ariq Böke also calls himself Khan of Khans, and he has the backing of the Golden Clan, the descendants of Chinggis Khan.'

'Your father, then, is the usurper?'

'Usurper?' She smiled. 'Let me tell you this. Most of my father's soldiers are levies, Chinese or Uighur or Tangut or Burmese, but they have been trained in Mongol tactics by Mongol generals. The infantry are armed with short stabbing spears, not for use against men but to bring down horses. Once the vast numbers of our enemies meant nothing in the face of Tatar cavalry, but now, thanks to my father, the Chin and Uighur soldiers they once so easily defeated are more than a match. Khubilai has lost his home and his legitimacy but in return he has gained an empire. So now it is Ariq Böke who is the usurper. Because as sure as the sun will rise and set, he will not defeat my father on the battlefield and it is power that makes the Khan of Khans, not legitimacy.'

'And what of you?' Josseran whispered.

'Me?' she whispered, not truly understanding his question.

'Which Great Khan do you believe is the usurper?'

'My opinion does not matter. I am neither Mongol nor Chin. I have the blood of Chinggis Khan but the feet of a Chinese princess.

I cannot ride a horse or even walk very far on my own. I am not a Person any more. I am my father's sacrifice to those he has conquered.' She stopped walking. 'I am tired now. You should leave. I hope we shall meet again.'

'I do not think such a happy event is likely. But I wish you the peace of God.'

'To you also. And a thousand blessings on Our-Father-Who-Art-in-Heaven,' she said, using the name she had given to William.

'My lady,' he murmured and bowed.

And there he left her, in the Garden of the Refreshing Spring, the princess with the heart of a Tatar, the body of a doll and the tiny, terrible, lily feet of a child.

☩

They set out on the second moon of the autumn, accompanied by a hundred imperial troops. Sartaq led the vanguard with Drunken Man and Angry Man. They took the road south, towards the teeming villages and towns that stretched along the green plains of Cathay and then to the dusty and meagre trails of the Silk Road to the west.

PART VI

The Singing Sands

*The Taklimakan Desert
from the Feast Day of the Assumption of
Our Lady to the Feast of St Michael*

XCIV

✧

IT HAD BEEN a rainless summer and the spiked haze from winnowed husks mixed with the fine loess dust that had blown in from the northern steppes. It was a world so golden it was difficult to discern tracks from rivers. The fields had been laid with round stones from the riverbeds, to prevent the topsoil from turning to dust and being borne away by the wind. A whole landscape lay honeyed and choking.

Behind this yellow veil lay the evidence of the frenetic summer industry of the farmers: the carefully tended mulberry orchards where the precious silkworms fed; hay stacked into twist-topped beehives; winter grain and vegetables drying on roofs. Here and there a few farmers were yet busy with sickles in their fields, their sinuous brown bodies clad only in loincloths. Mules laden with wicker panniers, stacked high with the last of the harvest, plodded along crumbling tracks on the banks of the Yellow River.

As they travelled west they came across more and more evidence of military activity: imperial cavalry in their lamellar armour; lightly armoured levies marching west with their short lances over their shoulders; squadrons of Uighurs and Tanguts led by Tatar officers in winged helmets.

Josseran thought again of Miao-yen's warning: *You know your return will be more dangerous than your first passage here.* If war began, they might be stranded here in Cathay for years. If that happened, their treaty would mean nothing when . . . indeed, if . . . they reached Acre.

✧

William no longer concerned himself with present or future hazards. His thoughts had turned inward, contemplating his own failure. He had thought he had won a king for Christ; instead he had been played for a fool.

A hundred priests! How might such an expedition be gathered, and if it was, could they really trust this Khubilai? He had dreamed of an apostolic mission of Pauline proportion, bringing all the souls of the East to God. Instead he would return with mumbles and promises.

The realization had come to him that he had failed because God had examined his heart and found him unworthy.

He journeyed in silence, rarely speaking a word to Josseran, the cowl pulled over his face, alone with his misery. He was no longer afraid, or hopeful; he was a different man to the one that had travelled these same roads two months before.

✠

Prayer flags fluttered in the wind; there was the sonorous booming of a gong, an ochre wall flushed pink by a lowering sun, a gate of timber studded with heavy nails. Josseran followed William into the courtyard of the lamasery and looked around. Galleries had been carved from the ancient black timbers on all four sides. Two camels were tethered by their nose cords to the twisted limbs of a pomegranate tree.

They wandered through a cloister alive with brilliant frescoes of scarlets and greens, where snarling devils dismembered unfortunates in a heathen hell. William gave a shout of fear as a bear rose snarling from a doorway.

'It is just a statue,' Josseran grunted.

But it was not an ordinary statue. It was, he saw, the fur and skin of a bear, preserved in its likeness, though there were dark cavities where its eyes had been. Its flanks were sticky with ritually applied butter.

They found another corridor, musky with incense. A row of monks, their shaved domes shining in the glow of the oil lamps, sat in their cross-legged posture on the ground. Their dolorous chanting echoed from the scarlet pillars and dark walls.

'I am cast into shame, Templar,' William said. 'These people love their religion better than I.'

'No one loves religion better than you, William.'

'Look at them. They do not sell their services for money. They do not feast like bishops or fornicate like priests or politic like the clerics in Rome. They have not faith yet they live holy lives.'

'If they have not the redemption of Christ, what good is all their holiness?' Josseran asked, repeating the litany that had been the thorn in his conscience ever since he was a child.

'Everything you have said to me on this journey about my fellow priests is true. I know that many are venal and grasping. Our Order was founded to confound such behaviour and bring holiness back to the Church. It is why I sought my vocation among them. But I am unworthy, Templar. I am an unholy man.' He brought up his hands. 'Pray with me, Templar.'

Josseran prayed with him, not out of piety, but because he felt such pity for the friar at that moment. He put his hands together and raised them to a God that did not inhabit these cloudless blue skies and together they said a score of paternosters for the living and another half-score for the dead. Finally he said another paternoster for himself, that he would find some way back to the living from the forgotten and the lost.

XCV

✆

Fergana Valley

AT THE ROOF of the World the brief summer was almost over. The red poppies were already dying, and the shepherds were preparing to return to the sheltered valleys of the lowlands, leaving the mountains once again to the wolves and the snow leopards and the eagles.

The wedding feast was still in progress when Khutelun rode into the camp.

The bride was younger than she, a broad-faced, bronze-cheeked girl, her features set like stone while around her the men and women of the clan were laughing and shouting and drinking. Her headdress of bronze coins reflected the light of a thousand torches. She was seated beside her husband in the silken pavilion, while vats of mutton bubbled and steamed and men spilled koumiss on the rich carpets and fell over the bodies of their fellows who were already passed out on the floor.

While she had been in Qaraqorum, Qaidu had taken another wife. She was the daughter of a chieftain from west of Lake Balkash, and the union had further entrenched his power on the western borders of the Khaghan's empire. Like Hülegü in the west and Batu in the north, her father was looking to protect himself now that Möngke was gone.

He was slumped on his ebony throne beside his new bride, hard-faced and brooding in the midst of the revelry going on around him. When he saw her, he got to his feet and swept out of the tent, his bodyguard with him. She followed him outside. There was a stone in her throat. Now she must tell him how she had failed.

'Khutelun,' he said. 'Daughter.'

She knelt to receive his blessing in the light of the soldiers' torches. 'Father.' A cool upland wind whipped the silk of the tent.

'I am happy to see you safe returned.'

'A thousand good wishes on this happy day.'

'It is just politics, daughter, you understand that. How was your journey?'

She hesitated. 'I failed you, my khan,' she said, choking on the words.

'Failed me, how?'

'I allowed my *arbans* to be ambushed by Khubilai's soldiers. We lost sixteen of our party. The barbarian ambassadors were kidnapped.' There. It was done, it was told, not couched in a pretty speech.

He grunted. 'Yes, I know of this.'

Of course. News would have reached him from Qaraqorum. He had his own spies at court, like every khan of any influence and worth.

'The fault was not yours,' he said, finally. 'If you thrust your hand in a hornet's nest, it is no surprise that you are stung. I should have sent you by the northern way, around Lake Balkash.'

'I have made sixteen widows.'

'You did not make them. Khubilai made the widows. And soon he will make many more.' He took her by the shoulder and pulled her to her feet. 'You saw Ariq Böke?'

'I gave him your oath of allegiance. He wished to know if you would send armies to support him against Khubilai.'

'And what did you say to that?'

'I said that I could not know the mind of my father. How else was I to answer him?'

He smiled. 'A good answer. For I cannot help him, even if I wished to. I dare not leave myself unprotected here, not now.'

From inside the pavilion she heard the shouts of the dancers and the raucous carousing of the drinkers.

The soldiers' torches crackled in a flurry of wind. 'I have news also. There is a new khan in Bokhara. Organa has been murdered and Alghu has taken the khanate.'

'He has pledged his support to Ariq Böke,' Tekudai said.

'For now, he has,' Qaidu said. 'But men will do whatever suits their purposes best at the time. Alghu is ambitious. He cannot be trusted.'

'What of the other khans?'

'All look to their own lands now, and their own dynasties, and we must look to ours. Möngke was the last of the great Khaghans. Once more our Tatary is not an empire, but a gathering of rivals.' He reached out his right hand and placed it upon her head. 'You did not fail me. Indeed, it pleases my heart to see you safe returned. Now, come inside and enjoy the wedding feast.'

Khutelun followed him into the great pavilion. Gerel was passed out on the rugs, as usual. Her return had not gone as badly as she had feared; indeed he had brushed aside her shame as if it were nothing. Yet she could not enjoy the revelry. She understood her father's stony-faced contemplation of his new bride. This was not a marriage; it was an alliance in preparation for war.

XCVI

✠

the Taklimakan desert, west of Tangut

THEY HAD EXCHANGED their horses for camels at the Jade Gate and
set off once more into the Taklimakan. The heat-racked emptiness
was almost familiar to him now. At times the desert consisted of
hard-packed gravel and the camels made good progress; at others it
was just thin grit with a friable crust that collapsed under the
camel's hooves and made every jarring step a torture for both man
and beast.

The summer had claimed even more victims. They saw the still
drying bones of horses and camels and once the contorted skeleton
of a donkey, mummified by the heat, still with a partial covering of
skin and fur. The ghosts of lakes and rivers rippled among the vastness of grey shale.

The sun flogs us, Josseran thought. Is it possible to hate the sun?
Once was enough. I do not think I can endure this crossing again.

XCVII

✠

THEY LOADED THE camels just before dusk, under a windless sky. They had come once more to the great sand dunes of the Taklimakan and had begun travelling by night to avoid the terrible heat of the day. When the moon rose it made the desert beautiful, for the sands seemed to ripple like fine silk laid upon a flat table.

Their caravan set off, the shadows of the camels monstrous on the undulating sands. Even scrawny patches of tamarisk took on terrible shapes, like the devils that William had spoken of when they set out on their journey.

The hushed silence of the night-time desert threw a pall over their spirits, and the only sound was the creaking of cordage and the soft padding of the camels' hooves in the sand. There were no land-marks here, and when the moon set over the desert they followed a single bright-lit star to the west. By the time the purple staining of dawn appeared on an empty horizon, the camels were coughing with exhaustion and had to be forced along by their ropes.

They stumbled on even as the sun rose up the sky and halted only when it became too hot to continue. Then they collapsed in the lee of their camels and tried to sleep through the furnace of the day, restless in the baking wind. They would wake just before evening, their throats parched and their bodies coated in wind-blown sand. There was time only for some bitter tea and rancid meat and then they would load the camels again and resume their endless journey.

The first hours beyond dawn were the worst time. Crushed with exhaustion, minds and spirits sapped by the rigours of their journey, they were often forced to dismount and haul their protesting camels over the last miles.

One morning, just before light, with the desert yet black and bitter cold, Josseran was walking beside his camel, head down into the nagging wind. He was thinking, as he always did, of Khutelun. There were times when he convinced himself that she might appear over the horizon, on her white Tatar mare, the purple silk of her scarf trailing in the wind behind her.

And he looked up, startled, for at that very moment he heard the sound of riders galloping towards them from just beyond the next line of dunes.

'What is that?' William shouted, from behind him.

They all stopped. Josseran remembered the last time he had heard this same drumming, by the lake of the crescent moon. 'It is the sand spirits,' he said to William. 'They wish to lure us into the desert.'

'What sand spirits?'

'The dead of the desert.'

William made the sign of the cross.

Josseran listened again. The drumming was gone, the sands had returned to silence.

The caravan continued. But from time to time William stopped to listen to the cries of the lonely spirits, and he thought he heard them call his name.

There were endless tracts of salt pan, heat haze rippling off the scorched wastelands, the way ahead marked by crumbling, ancient beacons. Beyond them lay another vast expanse of dunes.

From the saddle of his camel William found it impossible to see even to the head of the string through the yellow haze. Lulled by fatigue and the hammering of the wind, he hid his face in the cowl of his robe and consigned himself instead to the voices of self-recrimination carping inside his head and the jarring lurch of the camel.

Some time during the morning the wind died and he ventured to throw the hood back from his face, hoping to see some change in the monotony of their horizon.

It was then he discovered that he was alone.

There was no way of knowing when the string had broken, whether it was minutes or hours. He stared at the frayed end of rope trailing from the camel's halter in horror and disbelief. He searched the sand around him for tracks but even those left by his own camel were quickly covered by the drifting wind. The dunes stretched away in all directions, like the march of waves across the ocean.

He heard babbling, someone talking too fast and too loud, unintelligible words. He looked desperately around, thinking there must be someone behind him, and then realized that the sounds were coming from his own throat.

XCVIII

✛

Fergana Valley

A sharp wind from the north chased clouds like mare's tails across the sky before the march of a grey thunderhead reached them and a flurry of icy rain stung her face. It was time to drive the herds back down to the valleys.

The sheep were spread across the high pasture. There were thousands of them, waddling like geese, their rumps and tails plump from the rich summer grazing.

Tekudai rode up behind her. They had spoken little since her return from Qaraqorum. He had felt the task of escorting the barbarian ambassadors should have been his, and now he rejoiced in her failure.

'I trust you do not find these poor valleys too dull after the fine courts of Qaraqorum.' When she did not answer him, he went on. 'It is a pity you were not able to deliver the barbarians to the Khaghan. As our father ordered you to do.'

She clenched her jaw and said nothing.

'Though some say the barbarian was kidnapped not a moment too soon.'

'Who says it?' she hissed.

He smiled. 'My sister the stallion is a mare after all.'

She turned away. *I will not give him the satisfaction.*

'They say he mounted you three times.'

She twisted in her saddle, and suddenly her knife was in her fist. He grinned back at her, lifted his chin to expose the soft flesh of his throat. A futile gesture matched by his empty defiance.

She felt the blood pulse in the veins at her temple. 'Who said this of me?' she hissed.

His eyes glittered but he said nothing.

She sheathed the knife, knowing how foolish she had made herself look. 'It is a lie,' she said. She dug her heels into her horse's flanks and galloped away. But she could hear her brother's triumphant laughter ringing in her ears.

XCIX

✛

the Taklimakan

WILLIAM SCRAMBLED OFF his camel and threw himself to his knees. The sand was scorching hot. 'Please, oh Lord . . . dear Lord Jesus, protect me! . . . Save me!'

Precious saliva leaked down his chin. He screamed, throwing handfuls of sand into the air, hardly aware of what he was doing. It was then he heard the hollow drumming of hooves and knew that God had answered him. He shouted thanks to the scorching sky and, staggering back to his feet, stumbled up a gully of crumbling sand in the direction of the returning caravan. When he reached the soft crest he shouted Josseran's name, and fell tumbling down the drift.

Only emptiness.

Yet he could still hear the drumming, just beyond the next dune. He ran down the loose-packed sand, rolling and falling, then, on hands and knees, scrambled up the face of the next crest. His heart hammered against his ribs, feeling as if it would burst.

'No! . . . Please . . . Gracious Lord, hear . . . your servant in his hour . . . Wait for me! Josseran! . . . All praise to you . . . my Redeemer . . . It is William! Wait!'

He reached the top of the ridge, expecting to see the caravan below him, but there was only emptiness. He stared about him in confusion. The desert was silent again save for the whisper of the wind. He remembered what Josseran had told him about the sand spirits, and he knew the devils that lived in this accursed desert had tricked him too.

Snakes of sand licked and whispered around his legs.

He ran blindly back down the ridge, the soft sand sucking the strength from his legs, and finally he collapsed, exhausted. He should find his camel. *His camel with the water bag.* He stood up, whimpering at the cramping pains in the muscles in his thighs and calves.

He stumbled in circles, eyes screwed tight against the white glare of the desert. He searched for his tracks, but already the wind had covered them and he realized he was utterly lost. He looked up to the heavens and screamed.

C

☩

THERE WAS AN instant of bronze twilight before the night fell. Josseran huddled in his cloak. They all sat around a poor fire of *argol.* The camels coughed in the darkness.

'There is nothing we can do,' Sartaq said.

This is my good fortune, Josseran thought. The friar is lost. Now there will be no one to call me heretic and blasphemer when we return to Acre. I have a treaty with the Tatars and the glory will be mine alone.

But he could not bring himself to abandon that cursed priest. It was his duty both as a Templar knight and as a Christian to go back and search for him. There was a chance he might still be alive somewhere in this vast wilderness.

'We have to go back for him.'

Sartaq gave a snort of derision. 'When a man is swallowed by the desert, the Taklimakan never gives him up. It is like looking for a man inside the stomach of a bear. You only ever find the bones.'

'We must go back,' he repeated.

Angry Man spat in the sand. 'The barbarian is crazy.'

'A man cannot survive as much as a day without water in this desert,' Sartaq said. 'Even a seasoned traveller cannot live out here alone. And your companion knows nothing of the Taklimakan. I guarantee that by now he has already wandered away from his camel.'

Josseran knew he was right, and besides, he owed William nothing. You could even call it God's will. William would, if the situation was reversed.

'I shall go and search for him tonight, alone if I must. You must make your own decision, then. But will the Son of Heaven show you favour when he learns that you have lost *both* your ambassadors?'

Angry Man spat again and shouted and cursed at him until Sartaq ordered him to silence. Drunken Man, without the solace of strong mare's milk, started to croon softly into the quickening ashes of the fire while the moon rose over the desert.

It was a Tatar dirge for the dead.

✛

William woke to the moon. He thought about other Christian men like himself looking up at this same sky, safe in their monasteries and presbyteries in Toulouse or Rome or Augsburg. As consciousness filtered back, the terror of his predicament hit him like a physical blow and he began once more to weep. He felt such a longing for his own life that he moaned aloud. The consolations of heaven meant nothing to him now, nothing at all.

The wind had died and the vast sea of the desert was calm. It was then he saw the remains of a tower, thrown into sharp relief by the phosphor glow of the moon. He stared at it for a long time without comprehension. Then he got up and stumbled towards it.

It was only a few stones, perhaps part of a fortress that had once stood in this spot many centuries ago, before the sands reclaimed it. He scrabbled at the sand with his fingers, made a little hollow in the lee of the ruined wall for a bed, and curled into it. Somehow he felt safer here, the boundaries of the stones providing some protection from the terrible void around him.

He lay there for a long time, shivering with cold, listening to the trembling of his own breath. It sounded to him like the panting of a wounded animal. He tried to sleep.

Perhaps he succeeded, for when he opened his eyes again the moon hung almost directly above him, pale and trembling. It was full, a hunter's moon, and drew him to the treasures lying in the sand near his feet, set them glittering like glass.

He crawled towards them on his hands and knees. His breath caught in his throat.

A ruby, a huge one. He turned it in his fingers, letting the moonlight play on every facet of its cut. He tore at the sand with his fingers and found another and another. After a few minutes of digging his fists were bulging with jewels and there were more still only half-covered by the sand. The ransom of a king, buried here in the Taklimakan, as the camel man had told them.

He started to laugh.

One of the great treasures of the world, and vouchsafed to a dead man! He rolled on to his back and howled at the great vault of the skies. It was God's great and last joke on him. When his laughter had spent itself he lay there, his chest heaving.

In this parlous state he imagined a hundred Dominican friars accompanying him back across this desert to the court of the Emperor Khubilai to preach the holy religion and bring countless millions into its fold. With this treasure they would build a hundred churches. This must be what God had always intended

If only he could find his way out alive.

C I

✛

Fergana Valley

THE RIDER APPEARED out of the east, exhausted, fingers black with cold. The man was brought before Qaidu in his *ordu* and given a bowl of boiled mutton and some hot rice wine. After he had relayed his message the khan emerged, stern-faced, and called for his eldest son and most favoured daughter to attend him immediately.

✛

Qaidu sat on a mat of silken carpets behind the cooking fire, his eyes fixed on the mountains framed in the entrance of the yurt. Tekudai and Khutelun were greeted by the wife of Qaidu's second *ordu*, and took their proper places either side of the iron cooking pot. Warm bowls of koumiss were brought.

'I have just learned,' Qaidu said, 'that Khubilai has taken control of the Silk Road all the way from Tangut to Besh Balik. My cousin, Khadan, has pledged him his support and with his help he has cut Ariq Böke's supply route to the south and the east.'

'The whole of the Blue Mongol has risen against Khubilai,' Tekudai said. 'This can only be a temporary setback.'

Qaidu gave him a look of impatience. 'Khubilai has too many friends among the Uighurs and the Tanguts now. The whole of the Blue Mongol may no longer be enough.'

Tekudai fell silent after this rebuke. 'The empire of Chinggis Khan is gone,' Qaidu went on, 'as I prophesied. Hülegü and all the other khans have their own kingdoms now. What the two brothers fight over now is Cathay.'

'The messenger was from Khubilai, then?' Khutelun asked.

Qaidu nodded. 'It is his heart's desire that I brighten his eyes with my presence in Shang-tu next summer.'

'You will go?'

He shook his head. 'I will not bow the knee to Khubilai.'

'We shall fight then?' Tekudai asked. 'We will join Ariq Böke?'

'We must consider what will happen to us if Khubilai proves to be the stronger,' Khutelun said.

'Your sister is right,' Qaidu said and Tekudai glared at her. 'Before Chinggis Khan, men lived on these steppes without a palace at Qaraqorum and without a Khan of Khans to sit in it. The Tatars have lived this way since time began. If we must now return to those days, then this is what we shall do.

'I have made my decision. We shall not rebel, nor shall we co-operate with these mighty lords. We will keep the caravan trails open, but all who wish to cross the Roof of the World must pay tribute now to Qaidu. It will be well for Khubilai to remember that in the Fergana Valley at least, Qaidu is khan of khans!'

CII

✠

the Taklimakan

THE LINE OF camels and horses snaked across the dunes. Sartaq led the way, on foot, leading his camel by its string. Josseran followed. Just before dawn they stopped to rest. No one spoke, but Josseran felt the Tatars' fury. It was Angry Man, predictably, who broke first. He threw an empty leather water bag in the sand. 'We will not find him!' he shouted at Sartaq. 'This barbarian is mad!'

Sartaq looked at Josseran.

'I cannot abandon him,' he said.

Sartaq looked back at Angry Man and shrugged his shoulders.

Josseran went back to his camel and dragged on the nose cord, jerking her back to her feet. He trudged on. The Tatars had no choice but to follow him.

And so they filed across the dunes, back the way they had come, looking for one solitary swimmer in that great ocean of sand.

✠

He had always expected to find peace, perhaps even elation, at the moment of his death. But he had never imagined that he would die unshriven and alone in the wilderness. As the sun rose over the Taklimakan he curled inside his robe and sobbed like an infant, saying the name of Christ over and over again.

The dark angels had gathered already. They swarmed around him, their terrible wings spread, tiny eyes bright and greedy. William raised his head from the sand. 'No!' he shouted.

The spectres ventured closer, ready to bear him down to hell. He could imagine the brands glowing in the braziers, all the instruments of his torment prepared for him. God had no mercy on sinners. As Christ had said, it was not only the actions that a man performed in his lifetime but the longings of his heart that betrayed him in the sight of God.

Even beyond the Taklimakan, an eternity of suffering still awaited him. 'Get away from me!' William shouted. 'God have mercy!'

The griffons fluttered backwards, just a few paces, wary but not deterred. They were the largest vultures he had ever seen, each of them as tall as a man's chest and with a wingspan of perhaps two rods. They knew the carrion was theirs but they would not set to work with their beaks until their prey was still.

'I am saved in Christ!' William shouted again and threw a handful of sand at the nearest bird. Then he collapsed, weeping, on his face.

✠

Josseran watched his hopeless thrashings with the same feelings of pity and disgust he experienced at a bear-baiting or a public execution. The rest of the Tatars were gathered behind him in awed and dreadful silence. They had not expected to find the other barbarian, but it seemed that they were too late anyway. The sun had driven him over the brink of madness.

He had been on the point of abandoning the search, but just after dawn he saw the griffons circling in the sky. William had been saved, in the end, by a flock of vultures.

'You have no claim on me!' William shouted again. He raised his arms to the sky. 'Holy Father, forgive me for my sins and bear me on the arms of angels to heaven!'

Josseran ran down the sand. The vultures craned their ugly heads around at his approach and one by one they fluttered away, reluctantly giving up their prize. But they did not yet take to the sky. They waited at a safe distance, yet hoping for easy pickings.

'William!'

The priest was half-blinded by the sun, his face blistered raw. There was sand stuck to his lips and eyelids.

'William!'

The friar did not recognize him, nor even understand what nature of creature he was. He collapsed on the sand, still raving. Josseran tried to haul him to his feet but could not.

He felt the weight of the priest's robe. 'What in God's name have you got there?' he grunted.

The friar hooked his fingers into Josseran's cloak. His lips were bleeding, and burned skin hung in paper-thin strips from his forehead. 'Protect me,' William croaked, 'and half shall be yours.'

And with that he fainted away.

☩

William was too weak to continue the journey. The Tatars made a makeshift shelter with some poles and strips of canvas, and laid him there in the shade. Josseran dribbled water into his mouth while he shouted and raved. The wind came up again and they huddled together inside the protective ring of the camels and endured as best they could the miserable whipping of the sand.

By evening William was no longer screaming at the phantoms of his delirium and had instead fallen into a deep slumber. Josseran brought him some more water and as he bent over him William's eyes blinked open.

'I had a dream,' he murmured. His tongue was so swollen it was difficult to make out his words. 'I was lost.'

'It was no dream,' Josseran said.

'Not a dream? Then . . . you have rescued . . . the treasure?' Watery blood oozed from his blistered lips.

'What treasure?'

'With it . . . we shall build a church . . . in Shang-tu. A church as fine . . . as the Holy . . . Sepulchre . . . in Jerusalem.'

'William, there was no treasure.'

'The rubies! Did you . . . not find them?'

'Rubies?'

'There were . . .' He held his hand in front of his eyes, as if he still expected to find the gems in his palm. 'I held them . . . in my hand.'

'You dreamed it. Your cloak was weighed down with stones.' Josseran picked up William's cloak, showed him the rent in the cloth. He put his hand inside, scooped out a handful of dust and crumbled brick from the ruined tower. 'Just stones,' he repeated.

William stared at him. 'You . . . you stole them?'

'William, there were so many rocks concealed in your robe, I could barely lift you on to my camel.'

William's head fell back on the sand and he closed his eyes. If there had been moisture in him he would have wept. Instead he grimaced in an agony of despair and the blood from his lips ran into his mouth in place of tears.

CIII

✠

IF QAIDU'S MOUNTAINS were the Roof of the World, then Kharakhoja was its dungeon, a great depression far below the level of the sea. The oasis was just a grey jumble of hovels and dusty fields. Somehow the Uighurs who lived there had coaxed vineyards and fig and peach orchards out of that grey oven of a desert, using the glacial waters of the *karezes*.

Like the other oases of the Taklimakan, it was a village of dusty narrow alleys and mud-walled courtyards. But here many of the dwellings had been built underground as sanctuary from the boiling heat of summer and the incessant, gritty winds. They were roofed over with wooden poles and straw matting and were invisible except for their chimneys, sticking up through the hard grey sand.

The vines were bare now, just broken brown fingers protruding from the earth, and the red mud roads were cracked like paving stones. A solitary donkey stood miserably beneath a dead tree, flicking its tail at the hordes of flies.

Dispirited, they made their way towards the *han*.

'The worst place on earth,' Sartaq growled. 'They say you can boil an egg here by burying it in the sand. If you kill a chicken you do not even have to cook it. The flesh is already white and tender.'

His odd, barking laugh was without humour. They had survived the desert but they were close to the borderlands now and Qaidu and his renegades were out there somewhere, waiting. Sartaq knew the many ways an ambush might be laid. Now the tables had turned on him.

✠

Josseran stood on the roof of the *han* staring into the darkness. He could make out the silhouette of the Celestial Mountains against the night sky. Beyond them, somewhere, was the Roof of the World.

'I did not think to find you here,' William said. 'I thought you would be disporting yourself with the wives of the heathen. It seems our Tatar escort have availed themselves almost to a man of the whoring that passes in these lands as hospitality.'

Josseran had been offered similar comforts but tonight he had no interest in such consolation. But he would not allow William even this small victory, and so he said: 'I fear there were only the ugly women left. Sartaq has offered me use of the camels, should I find . one that is not too displeasing to my eye.'

'Knowing you, you will find one.'

'I see you are recovered from your ordeal.'

'Why did you come back for me?'

'I gave my word that I would protect you on this journey.'

'Many men give their word, few keep it. You are a man of many contradictions, Templar. There have been times when I thought your sole purpose was to confound my every effort to bring Christ to these godless lands. Yet now I owe you my life.'

'It was God's will that we found you.'

'Do not think you have me now in your debt.'

'Oh, I would never think that. I am sure that in the weeks to come I will rebuke myself many times for not letting you die in the desert.'

'Perhaps you should have done.'

Josseran was startled by this admission. He wondered what had prompted it. But William was not about to say more. He turned away and left Josseran there on the rampart, under the cold shelter of the dispassionate stars.

CIV

✠

THE NIGHT WAS a torment. Fleas and mosquitoes and sandflies feasted on Josseran with voracious appetite and there was no escape. Finally, exhausted, he drifted into fitful sleep, only to be rudely woken in the middle of the night when something fell on him from the beams above his head. He sat up, his heart hammering in his chest, and reached for the candle. He saw a spider with a body as large as an egg scuttle away across the earth floor. There was a red-eyed cockroach in its jaws.

After that, sleep was impossible.

✠

He was roused from his bed at dawn by terrible screams. William! His first thought was that the friar had been bitten by a scorpion. Josseran stumbled to his feet.

The friar was sitting with his back against the wall, eyes wide with shock. His face and arms were covered in hard, reddening lumps from the bites of the lice and fleas. Otherwise he appeared unharmed.

Sartaq was standing over him, holding a torch he had snatched from the wall. The other Tatars appeared one by one, stumbling through the shadows, also woken by his screams.

'I heard him shout out,' Sartaq said. 'When I got here there was a giant cockroach sitting on his face.'

'How could you tell?' someone said. It was Drunken Man.

Sartaq and the others roared with laughter.

William curled into a ball, scrabbling at the earthen floor with his fingers, making a soft mewing sound like a wounded animal. The laughter died stillborn in their throats.

'He is possessed by the sand spirits,' Sartaq hissed. 'They crawled into his body while he was lost in the desert.'

'It is all right, I will deal with him,' Josseran said. 'Leave us.'

'He has a bad-luck demon,' Sartaq insisted, and then he and his fellows withdrew. He heard them outside, preparing the caravan, saddling the horses and camels for the day's journey.

Josseran crouched down. 'William?'

'I dreamed of the Devil,' he mumbled.

'It was a roach. That is all.'

'Beelzebub knows how sinful I am. He knows I have failed.'

Perhaps the sun has turned his mind, Josseran thought, just as Sartaq said. 'William, it is morning. We must continue with our journey.'

'I have put my fingers in the wounds of Christ and still I do not believe! I do not have the faith. I am filled with lust and envy. It is why God did not vouchsafe me the souls of the barbarians.'

'The sun will soon be up. We have to leave.'

'I have failed. All my life I have wanted to bring God to men but I have failed.'

Josseran helped him to his feet and led him outside. They were back to travelling by day again. The horses stamped in the dawn chill, and the camels hawed and complained as Sartaq tied them to the string.

He helped William astride his camel, leading him as he might a blind beggar. As a mauve dawn spread along the horizon they set off again, through the gates of the *han*. William kept his eyes fixed on the horizon and the private fancies of his nightmares. He did not speak all that day. The Tatars muttered among themselves and kept their distance.

✛

Another endless day of furnace heat. Midway through the morning the dust haze cleared suddenly and the Celestial Mountains loomed before them. The necklace of snow seemed unbearably close. Far to the west, they could even make out the white ridges at the Roof of the World.

The haze descended again as quickly as it had lifted and the mountains vanished once more behind the yellow mists of the Taklimakan.

✙

They rested that night in the ruins of an abandoned caravanserai.

It was as desolate a place as Josseran had ever seen. The dome of the mosque had collapsed many years ago, and moonlight filtered in through the vault, dappling on the flagged stones of the floor and the broken black beams. There were scorch marks on the walls where it had been fired, perhaps by the soldiers of Chinggis Khan half a century before.

Josseran and William sat apart from the others. The Tatars huddled around their fire, muttering darkly among themselves and casting hostile glances in William's direction. But Josseran was not afraid of them. The Tatars had learned cast-iron discipline in Khubilai's army and they would see them safe to their destination, even though he knew Angry Man for one would have gladly cut both their throats.

Josseran gazed upwards. Through the ruin of the roof he saw a single star appear in the northern sky. *That is the Golden Nail. It is where the gods tie their horses.*

Perhaps it was William's fall from grace that had unnerved him, or that day's first glimpse of the Roof of the World, but tonight the burdens of his life weighed heavier on him than they had ever done. For all his rhetoric, he was yet a Christian, and in his heart he lived in terror of his fearsome God. He regretted his blasphemies tonight, or, rather, he feared their consequence.

William sat hunched against the wall, his face hidden by the hood of his robe. Josseran measured the distance between them; just a few strides, and yet as great a journey for him as their odyssey from Acre to Shang-tu. But it was not God that brought him to his feet and made him kneel in front of the priest. It was rather that he was simply exhausted. He could not carry his father one more step.

'William, hear my confession,' he whispered, and fell to his knees.

William looked up at him, startled. When he spoke, his voice was gentle as a woman's. 'I shall fetch my vestments from the camels,' he said and went to gather the trappings of his vocation and save at least one soul for God.

C V

✠

'MY MOTHER DIED when I was nine years old and my father, the Baron of Montgisors, married the daughter of a nobleman from Troyes. Her name was Catherine. She was much younger than my father, and perhaps only five years older than I. She had eyes as black as sin and when she looked at me it filled me with heat. I was just a boy, seventeen years old, and my loins were as raw and inflamed as an open wound.'

'Go on,' William murmured. He was aware of the Tatars watching them: the mad Christian shaman, the purple stole around his neck; the giant barbarian on his knees before him.

'I sought constantly to catch her eye but she ignored me, and left me in a frenzy of despair. Whenever she walked past me I caught the scent of her. I could not sleep at night; I woke in lathers of sweat and spilled my seed in my hand whenever I thought of her. I even prayed in the chapel that he would die so that I could have her. I was lost in my unholy devotion to her.'

He stopped, ran a hand across his face. Just thinking of her again made him sweat. 'My father was a knight of some renown in Burgundy. Every day he trained me in the use of sword and lance, and how to fight from the back of a horse. And all the time we practised I wanted him to kill me, I was so ashamed.

'One day I took her, when we were out riding together. It was over quickly, before I even realized what I had done. That of itself should have been sin enough for my young bones. I had sated my youthful lust, was it not enough? But no, I hungered for more.'

He took a deep breath, his voice hoarse.

'What happened next was no accident. My father was away in Paris. I went to her chamber, all the while wanting the door to be locked, even hoping she would scream to the servants, shame me in front of the household. Instead, she received me into the heat of her embrace and that night we became lovers.'

He stopped, remembering.

'You cannot know how painful it is to say these things to someone who has forsworn himself from women. Because you see, all the while I loved her, I hated her too, for what she had done to my father and what she had made of me. She had given him the horns, and she had made me despise myself to my very core.

'My father had been called to the court by the King together with a number of other nobles. Louis had hoped to persuade them to join him on holy armed pilgrimage to the Holy Land. But my father was getting old and when he returned from the court he told me that he had begged leave not to go. But a few days later, without explanation, he changed his mind, and made preparations to embark on crusade. I can only imagine that he divined what had taken place in his absence and this had turned his mind.'

He stopped and cleared his throat, for it was becoming more difficult to speak.

'He armed a dozen of the peasants, who were to accompany him on the great pilgrimage, and sold ten hectares of land to finance this venture. Catherine herself sewed the scarlet cross on the shoulder of his surcoat.

'After he had departed I stayed behind in Montgisors as master of the manor and the lands. Now Catherine became brazen. She came to my room every night. But because she feared getting with child she made me take her only in the forbidden way.

'But with my father gone I found that I could not do that which I had so often dreamed of doing. Her response was to laugh at me. She said I was my father's son, mocking him and me in the same breath. Soon she stopped coming to my room and I was left with the memory of my sins and no more.'

He took a deep breath.

'Within a year I had news of my father's death at Damietta.'

He was silent for a long time.

'Despite Catherine's precautions she found she was, after all, with child. I sent her to a convent to bear the infant and when she returned the child was given to the wife of one of my grooms, who lived on the estate. The woman was barren and loved the child like her own. But when he was four years old the girl died of the croup and so my mortal punishments were complete.

'So you see, I have slept with my own stepmother and driven my father to his death. I have lived with this sin for these many years. I continued to manage my father's estates but never again went to his widow. Then some six years ago I took myself to the Holy Land hoping that I would die in battle and that would atone for my sins. I secured a loan from the Templars to finance my crusade, and in return pledged myself to their service for five years. But I did not die, and I have not been redeemed.'

William was silent for a long time. Finally he raised his right hand. 'With this hand I absolve thee of sin,' he said. 'As penance I command you to remain chaste for the rest of your days and give up the remainder of your wealth and all your lands to the Holy Mother Church.'

Josseran felt his breath catch in his throat. He had not anticipated such a penance when he had embarked on his confession. He had deluded himself that William had discovered his humanity in the desert and instead the friar had used the moment's advantage to crush him, as he had with Mar Salah.

Josseran got back to his feet. 'I hold you beneath contempt, as I do all priests of your Order. I shall not fulfil your penance nor shall I expect God's forgiveness. Enough that I shall forgive myself from this moment on. My penance shall be that I will live a better life.' He went back to his corner of the *han* and fell almost directly into a deep and dreamless sleep.

PART VII

Spirit of the Blue Sky

The Roof of the World
autumn, in the year of the Incarnation
of Our Lord 1260

CVI

✛

THE DESERT WAS behind them now, the great crossing made for a second time. At Kashgar they stopped at the fort, manned by soldiers loyal to Khubilai, and exchanged the camels for fast Tatar mounts. They rode out towards the western passes.

Above them, the first snows had dusted the foothills at the Roof of the World.

They followed a steep valley up through the mountains, past rushing streams and massive boulders that had been washed down in the spring floodwaters, between red cliffs that disappeared into the clouds. They emerged from the valley on to a plateau and paused for rest beside a salt lake.

Josseran shifted in the saddle of his Tatar stallion. The green spruce of the forest appeared dismal against the white broiling of clouds. The wind brought with it a mist of chill rain and in moments it had washed the valley clean, leaving it verdant in the yellow sunlight. A rainbow arced across the valley.

They would have to hurry before the ice closed in on the Roof of the World and left them trapped, Sartaq said. Once across those mountains they would be but a few months' ride from Aleppo, and safe returned to their home.

'Home,' he murmured.

What home was there now for Josseran Sarrazini? Perhaps it was the nearness of winter in this wild place, but he felt suddenly the fading of his years. He was over thirty years old, and there was little time left for grand designs. Perhaps fifteen years, if he returned to Provence, less if he chose to stay in Outremer, with its disease and assassins and endless skirmishes and wars.

A man's fate was certain, for we all owe God a death, but now all he wanted was to find either strength enough to die, or reason enough to live.

CVII

✠

SARTAQ ORDERED THEIR tiny column to a halt by a fast-flowing stream. The horses had been hobbled and were foraging for pasture while the Tatars refilled their water bags. Further downstream a family of cranes eyed them with startled suspicion.

The glacier-fed stream was already rimmed with ice and the sedge at the bank crackled with frost. They had climbed high into the mountains and winter was racing them to the passes.

A kite wheeled high overhead, shrieking. It sounded like the cry of an infant. Josseran looked up, startled. They received no other warning.

The man at Josseran's shoulder reeled back suddenly, clutching his throat. An arrow had passed straight through. He fell on to his back in the river, his legs jerking spasmodically, a terrible gurgling sound coming from his mouth as he died. His blood quickly stained the shallows.

Sartaq was first to react, splashing through the stream to his horse and instantly releasing the hobble. Josseran did the same.

He looked over his shoulder, saw a line of horsemen racing towards them from a dry gully just a quarter of a league distant. More arrows rained into them, and Josseran's horse screamed as two found their mark, sinking almost to the flight into its shoulder and flank. Sartaq was screaming orders to his men from the saddle, trying to organize a defence.

Their attackers were close enough now that Josseran could see their faces. They were Tatars like his escort, but not regular soldiers, they were bandits with little armour, light horsemen dressed in furs and armed with bows and crude lances. There were perhaps no more than a score of them but they had the advantage of surprise.

There was another singing of arrows and then they were on them, stabbing with their hooked lances, felling those not quick enough to their horses. Josseran rode into the line, swung wildly with his sword and brought one crashing from his horse, then charged at another, unseating him.

He heard a scream and when he turned around he saw William splashing through the shallows of the river, trying to escape on foot. One of the Tatar bowmen was no more than ten paces behind, following him. He was grinning, enjoying the game. He slowed his horse to a trot, lowered his bow and leisurely drew his sword from his belt. He leaned from the saddle for the killing stroke.

Josseran spurred his horse to a gallop and rode straight at him. The Tatar saw him too late. He looked around in horror, knowing what was about to happen and knowing, too, that he could not stop it. His sword arm was raised, exposing his ribs, and it was there that Josseran plunged his own sword, straight-armed, to the hilt. The man screamed and slipped from the saddle. As he fell the weight of his body wrenched the sword from Josseran's hand.

Josseran wheeled around, looking for William. Another of the Tatar horsemen rode in, grabbed William under the arms and dragged him across his saddle.

'William!'

✝

Already, the skirmish was over. There were perhaps half a dozen bodies lying in the stream, pierced with arrows. More fur-wrapped bodies lay on the grass. The raiders were galloping away.

Sartaq had mustered his men and formed a defence on the other side of the stream. 'Let them go,' Sartaq shouted. 'Let them go!'

'They have William!' Josseran shouted. He jumped from the saddle and retrieved a lance from one of the fallen Tatars. Then he remounted and spurred after the retreating horsemen.

He started his horse up the slope in pursuit, but they had already disappeared beyond the brow of a hill. He reached the crest and started down. William had somehow got free of his captor and was scrambling back up the hill, clutching the hem of his robes like a woman as he ran. Josseran heard hoofbeats behind him and wheeled around. Two of Sartaq's men had followed him down the valley. He recognized one of them, Drunken Man.

'Barbarian! Sartaq orders you to return!' he shouted.

But the warning came too late.

As Josseran turned his pony he realized he had been lured into a trap. As many as a dozen of the Tatar horsemen had circled behind them. They loosed a volley of arrows and Drunken Man and his companion screamed and slid from their horses. Josseran felt an excruciating pain in his left shoulder.

William had almost reached the crest of the hill. Josseran spurred his mount after him. He heard another singing of arrows and his horse staggered and fell. Josseran landed on his back on the wet grass and felt the breath go out of him. The arrow shaft that was embedded in his shoulder snapped as he rolled.

He pulled himself up on to his knees. The pain was sickening. The Tatars were milling around him, shouting to each other, deciding who would have the honour of the kill. One of them dismounted and rushed over, pulling a rusted sword from his belt.

Josseran had dropped his lance when he was thrown from his horse. He fumbled in the grass, and his fingers closed around the shaft. As the swordsman brought down the killing blow he brought up the lance in defence, felt the shaft snap, deflecting the stroke, delaying the coup for a moment.

The Tatar raised his sword a second time.

Josseran rolled to the side, bringing his leg around and kicking the Tatar's legs from under him. The man went down, dropping the sword. Josseran was first to it, rolled on to his feet and jumped back, bringing the sword around in an arc, driving the other Tatars back.

He knew there was no chance, not one against this many. So this is how it will end, he thought. I had always imagined I would die wearing the cross of a crusader, not in some inconsequential skirmish in the mountains, against an enemy I do not even know, dressed in furs and a ragged coat. But I will not die cheap. I will take some of you devils with me to heaven or hell or the Blue Sky, whatever lies beyond. There were black spots in front of his eyes, and he staggered backwards. His vision blurred. There was a roaring in his ears. He heard the Tatars laughing, they knew he was gone.

CVIII

✠

'STOP!'

He knew that voice.

He blinked, saw a pair of black eyes below a purple scarf. 'Khutelun,' he said. The world began to spin faster. He put his hand to his shoulder. It came away sodden with blood. His knees collapsed under him.

And that was the last thing he remembered.

✠

They laid him on his back on the floor of the yurt and stripped off his robe. His skin was chalk-white, his silk undershirt sodden with blood from the shoulder wound. There was another wound above his eye, where he had struck his head after he fell from his horse.

Khutelun stared at him. She had thought never to see him again. How could this have happened? Was this what the spirits had tried to show her? She pushed the others aside. Then she took out her knife and cut away his shirt from around the wound. She felt her breath catch in her throat. Memories came to her unbidden; how she had taken him to the Buddha caves in the Flaming Mountains; that night by the crescent lake when they listened to the Singing Sands and he had said he thought her beautiful; the feel of his hard body pressed against hers during the *karaburan*, how terrified she had been and how his presence had reassured her.

She angrily brushed such thoughts aside. He was her prisoner now. The past meant nothing, nothing at all.

His eyes blinked open. 'You,' he murmured.

'I have to remove the arrowhead,' she said.

He nodded.

She had brought four of her *arban* with her. She assigned one of the barbarian's limbs to each of them and they held him down, leaning their weight on him while she set to work.

Because of the barb on the metal tip, an arrow made a larger wound when it was removed than it had on entry. But his undershirt had bound itself tightly around the arrowhead, and Khutelun was able to use the silk to turn the barb without tearing too much flesh. But the muscles of Josseran's shoulder went into spasm and she had to use a great deal of force. Josseran groaned and bucked as she worked. Finally it came free with a wet, sucking sound and Josseran gasped aloud and fainted again.

She soaked up the blood with a cloth. Just as she had finished she heard the entrance flap behind her thrown aside. Her father stood in the doorway, his hands on his hips.

'Is he going to live?'

She nodded. 'The arrow lodged in the muscle and damaged no vital organs.' She held up the golden tablet she had removed from around his neck. 'He carries the *paizah* of Khubilai.'

'Khubilai's chop means nothing here,' Qaidu growled. He stared at the body of the giant barbarian at his feet. He shoved him with his foot, more from irritation than spite. 'It would have been better if the arrow had pierced his heart.'

'The spirits of the Blue Sky were protecting him.'

'Then I do not understand the ways of the spirits.' Their eyes met. She realized that he knew more of her thoughts and feelings than she supposed. 'This is not as I would have desired.'

'An unfortunate coincidence.'

'Indeed,' he agreed. 'But there is no help for it now. When he recovers bring him to my yurt. I will examine him there.'

☩

Qaidu prowled the carpets, his hands clenched into fists. Before him were his three prisoners; two of Sartaq's escort, both of Khubilai's *kesig*, and the barbarian ambassador. The barbarian shaman had escaped, Khubilai's cavalry had appeared just as Khutelun's men were about to recapture him.

But they had retrieved the barbarian's saddlebag and found the treaty Khubilai had offered to the Christians in Acre. They also found the Khan's gifts.

'What is this you have here?' Qaidu growled. He tore open the bundle and threw the scrolls of fine brushwork on to the floor. 'Is this what Khubilai considers valuable?' He stood on the scrolls in his boots, to show the barbarian what he thought of them.

Josseran swayed on his feet. He had lost a lot of blood. 'In our land, they would be considered . . .' Josseran searched for the Tatar word for art, but he did not remember it, did not know if he had heard such a word. 'People would admire them for their beauty.'

'Beauty!' Qaidu spat. There was a shuffling silence. Josseran was aware of the press of Tatar bodies and the gleam of lance points in the filmy darkness. The smell of sweat and leather and fire smoke was overpowering.

'A true warrior lives in a yurt,' Qaidu was raging. 'He rides his horse each day, he fights, he drinks koumiss, he hunts, he kills. The Chin have sapped Khubilai's strength and he has forgotten how to live like a Person. Look!' He picked up one of the scrolls and held it in his fist. 'What good is this to a man?'

Josseran staggered again. It was difficult to concentrate on these proceedings. He was just a pawn in this civil war now. Qaidu considered him Khubilai's creature and the gold *paizah* that was to ensure his safe passage might instead seal his fate.

'Khubilai has proved he is no Khan of Khans. He is more Chin than the Chinese.'

'Surely it is not wrong to learn a little from others,' Josseran said, finding himself, even now, moved to defend his patron.

'Learn? What is there to learn from those who are not strong enough to defeat us?' Qaidu was working himself into a towering rage. 'We are the masters of the Chin, and yet he builds his palaces in Cathay, and lives at his ease. Now he wants to change even our way of life, the ways that made us masters of the world! He wishes us all to become like the Chin and live in towns and cities. He no longer understands us, his own people! For us, to settle is to perish!'

The Tatars roared their assent, closing in around Josseran and his fellow captives. We are an entertainment now, Josseran thought, and a rallying cry. Qaidu is using our capture for his own purposes. His raging is to impress his soldiers and his allies.

'If Khubilai has his way our children will wear silks, eat greasy food, and spend their days in teahouses. Our sons will forget how to fire an arrow from a galloping horse and they will hide themselves from the wind. And then we will become like the Chin and we will be lost forever. Look at all we have!' He spread his arms to encompass the pavilion, their encampment, the grasslands on which they lived. 'We have a yurt that we move with the seasons. We have our horses and we have our bows and we have the steppe, we have the eternal Blue Sky! With these we have made ourselves Lords of the Earth! That is the Tatar way, the way of Chinggis Khan, the way of Tengri! Khubilai is Khan in Shang-tu perhaps, but he is not my khan. He is more dangerous to the Mongol people than all our enemies!'

'Your dispute is of no import to me,' Josseran shouted over the cheering, fatigue and the pain of his wound making him cast all caution aside. 'I came here seeking an alliance with the khan of the Tatars against the Saracen. The struggle for the throne among you is not of my making. I am merely an emissary from my masters in Outremer.'

'If you wished to treat with us,' Qaidu shouted, 'you should have made your peace at the feet of Ariq Böke in Qaraqorum.'

'I shall gladly make my peace with whoever rightfully holds the throne.'

'The throne belongs to Ariq Böke! But you are right, you are just an ambassador, not like these dogs.' He kicked out at Drunken Man, who cried and thrust his head further into the carpets. 'What I will do with you, Barbarian, is yet to be decided. If we allow you to return to your fellow barbarians, you will tell them that we are in discord. Yet you are an envoy and it behoves us to proceed with caution. Put him in a cangue so he cannot escape and we will think further on this!'

As they led him away Josseran searched the throng for Khutelun but he saw only his old friend Tekudai, his expression as sullen as the rest. It occurred to him for the first time that she might have abandoned him.

CIX

✠

THEY CALLED IT a cangue, a yoke of heavy wood that fitted around the neck and had two smaller holes on each side that held the wrists. Once it was in place it was impossible to lie down, to rest or to sleep. The weight of it on his neck and the cramping it caused in the muscles of his shoulders were doubtless intended to break his spirit.

Blood had crusted over his right eye, which had now swollen shut. From time to time he felt a trickle of watery blood on his cheek. But it was nothing compared to the pain in his shoulder. It burned as if the joint had been opened with a white-hot metal hook.

He felt himself falling towards darkness, a phantom world inhabited by the drums of the shamans and cold, relentless pain.

From what seemed a long way off he heard the mumbles and laughter of men's voices moving about the camp, an eerie keening over the rattle of the drums, then a scream, perhaps imagined, of one of his fellow prisoners.

'Joss-ran,' a voice said.

He looked up. All he could see was the orange glimmer of camp fires through the entrance of the yurt.

'Joss-ran.'

He realized she was here, his beautiful witch Khutelun, her eyes glittering in the dark. She crouched down in front of him. 'You should not have ridden out,' she said.

'It was my duty to protect the priest.'

'You thought to be brave. See where it has left you.'

There it was again, that terrible keening. 'What is that?' he asked her.

'They are grieving for the widows you made today.'

'It was not my intention to make widows; I was fighting for my life. And what of the widows you made?'

She reached up and her fingertips traced the contours of the wound on his forehead. A show of tenderness, at last, he thought. Perhaps she has not forgotten the desert entirely.

'What is to happen to me?'

'My father is angry with me that I brought you back as my prisoner, and he is angry with you that you could not die of your wound. He would have you dead but he does not wish the responsibility for it.'

He tried to move his position but the effort sent another spasm of pain through his shoulder. 'Tell him I regret the inconvenience I have caused him.'

'He has read the missive you brought with you from Khubilai. It has clouded the waters. Some of my father's generals say you are an ambassador and you must be treated with respect. Others say that as you treated with Khubilai, then you should be executed. There are a few who wish to keep you as a hostage. But is your life of any worth to Khubilai?'

He forced a savage grin. 'Tell them the Emperor of Cathay loves me like a brother.'

She did not smile. Something in her expression disturbed him.

'And what is your father's opinion?'

'My father favours execution. He says that dead men eat less food.' She sighed. 'I shall do all I can to sway him. I will find a way to set you free.' She had with her a wooden bowl, filled with water. She soaked a piece of rag in it and used it to wash away the dried blood around his eye. Then she cleaned the arrow wound, tenderly as a lover. Even now, in his desperate condition, he was aware of the warmth of her breast against his silken undershirt.

'I still want you, God help me,' he whispered.

She made no answer.

'Did you hear me, Khutelun?'

'I may wash your wounds. Beyond that, there is nothing I can do for you.'

'I have to know. Do you feel nothing at all for me?'

'You are a barbarian from the west. How can I feel anything for you? I shall marry the son of a khan who will make my own sons princes of the steppe like my father.' She finished her ministrations. It was a kindness, he thought, though it had done nothing for his pain. 'The wound is clean.'

'Why does your father torment me with this collar? Tell him that if I vex him so, then he should do what he will. I am not afraid to die.'

'I will tell him what you said.' She stood up and went to the doorway of the yurt.

'I would give everything to lie with you for just one night before I die.'

'Then you are a fool,' she said and slipped away into the darkness.

CX

✠

JOSSERAN HAD WORN the cangue for just a few hours and already he felt as if he bore the weight of the cathedral at Chartres on his shoulders. Every small movement was agony. Pain and fatigue brought on a reverie that was not quite sleep, for sleep was impossible, but a delirium that transported him from his terrible predicament back to a cave above a narrow defile in the Mountains of the Sun. *'Had you not thought of us joined together in this way, as Shiva is joined with his wife? Have you not sometimes thought of this as your destiny? And as mine?'*

He realized there was someone else in the yurt and when he looked up he saw Qaidu standing over him, watching him. Perhaps this was the pronouncement of his sentence. He would soon know how he was to die.

Qaidu had his hands on his hips, his legs splayed. 'What should I do with you, Barbarian? My generals say I should execute you with the others.'

'The others?'

'Khubilai's dogs. They are traitors to the people of the Blue Mongol and a stain on the legend of Chingghis Khan. I have decreed they are to be boiled alive.'

Even as he spoke Josseran could hear his fellow prisoners going to their deaths. He hoped they had given Drunken Man some of the black koumiss he loved so much to help him through his ordeal. He shifted his position slightly so that he could look into the other man's eyes.

'And what is it that gives you pause on my account?'

The screams of the tortured men echoed through the camp. Ah, they have warmed the pot already. Josseran could not imagine such a death. But I will not beg for my life, he promised himself. If they break me bone by bone, I will not beg. May God give me the strength to resist these devils.

'Perhaps I can offer you another choice,' Josseran said.

A wolf grin. 'What choice could you offer me, Barbarian?'

'Let me marry Khutelun.'

How quickly the smile fell away. Qaidu's hand went to the sword at his belt. Josseran thought he would strike off his head then and there. But instead he contented himself with placing one foot on the cangue, forcing it almost to the ground, bending Josseran's neck down between his knees. 'Do you toy with me?'

Josseran did not, could not, respond. The pain was beyond imagining. With a grunt Qaidu removed his foot and stepped back.

Josseran tried to raise his head. It was like trying to lift his own horse in his arms. My back is broken, he thought.

Unable to straighten up, he collapsed on to his side. He uttered a grunt of pain, his whole weight supported now on his right hip and knee.

'Perhaps I will have you boiled with the others after all,' Qaidu growled.

'I mean . . . what I say.'

'There are many ways a man can die, Barbarian. You are not making it easy for yourself.'

'I propose . . . a test.'

He heard the hesitation in the other man's voice. 'A test?'

'A race, on horseback . . . Khutelun against . . . me. Should I . . . win, I have her . . . in marriage.'

'And what would you do then? Would you take her with you to the barbarian lands?'

'I would . . . stay here.'

'Here?' Qaidu's voice shrill with disbelief. 'Why do you wish to stay here?'

Josseran had no answer to that. Yet why not? What was there to return to? Was there even one soul who would weep for him if he did not return to Acre?

'What would you wager for this?' Qaidu asked.

It is the agony of the cangue making me mad, Josseran thought. May the Lord in heaven forgive me. I am trading everything I possess in body and spirit for the glimmer of a bauble, a whispered promise in a bazaar. Madness.

'Many young men have asked for her before you,' Qaidu persisted. 'Not ragged barbarian envoys, these were fine Tatar princes and each wagered a hundred horses against the promise of her as wife. If Khutelun wins, as she surely must, what have you to offer?'

'My . . . life.'

'Your life is forfeit anyway!'

The screaming began again. How long does it take a man to boil?

'I still have it . . . at this moment. It is all I . . . have since you have not yet . . . made up your mind what my . . . fate will be.'

Qaidu grunted, perhaps in grudging admiration of Josseran's courage. 'And if I told you that I intend to let you go free? Would you still make this wager?'

Josseran did not answer. How does a man make such contracts with his head and arms tortured by the cangue? Qaidu nodded to one of the guards who grabbed the edge of the infernal device and pulled Josseran upright. The weight was returned to a more tolerable position and Josseran uttered a sob of relief. Enough for now to lean the cangue against the frame of the yurt, and take a moment's blessed relief from the crushing weight.

'So will you set me free, my lord Qaidu?'

'Yes.'

'Then I have the means to make the wager. I have a life to barter with, after all. So do we agree?'

'This is all I want from you!' Khubilai's missive to the Templar command was thrust under his nose. He tore it into shreds. 'We shall not let the usurper arm himself with Hülegü!'

'It makes no difference. The messenger and the message are the same. You cannot grasp one without the other. Should I return to Acre I shall inform my masters and the prince Hülegü of all that I have seen and heard. You are better served agreeing to the wager. Either way I shall remain here. It would not be wise to let me go, my lord.'

'You know, of course, that it is Khutelun and Khutelun alone who argues for your life!'

A moment's stillness, a moment to smile. He heard himself say, as if from very far away: 'That is why I do not want my freedom. I want Khutelun.'

'You are a fool.'

'She told me this also. I am sure you are both right.'

Qaidu studied him for a long time. 'You are strange to her, and that fascinates her, because she is a shaman and not like other women. She is drawn to things that those of us who do not have the gift rightly fear. But you are not for her.'

'Let her decide that,' Josseran said.

Qaidu took some time to consider. Josseran could hear his breathing, though he was unable to raise his head to look into the khan's eyes. 'It were better you had died today,' he said finally, and left the yurt. From outside came the beat of the shaman's drums, the inhuman screams of the boiled and not yet dead.

CXI

✠

KHUTELUN SAT ON a knoll above the camp, beyond the corona of the night fires and the protective perimeter of the *kibitkas*. She had come to be alone with the spirits, under the sheltering canopy of the World Tent that was tonight suspended from the bright nub of the Pole Star. Her body was buffeted by a bitter wind.

She could make no sense of the turmoil inside her. She hugged her knees with her arms and pressed her forehead against her fists. She let out a small cry that startled a sentry, dozing on his horse somewhere below her.

For as long as she could remember she had hated her sex and all that it represented. As a child she had preferred her brothers' company to that of her sisters, a fondness that had been tempered by competition. She had learned to best them at hunting, at riding, even at wrestling. As she grew she had done all she could to win her father's favour, though she sensed that he smiled more kindly at her brothers than he did on her. From watching the horses in the pasture she learned the difference between mare and stallion, and she understood that this was the source of the problem.

But a Tatar woman does not sit quietly and compliantly like a Chin with her braided hair and lily feet. She set out to prove to her father that she was tougher and braver and more skilled than any in the clan. She had practised hour after hour, day after day, with bow and arrow. And these last two seasons she had won her reward, for Qaidu had allowed her to ride beside him in the hunt, had even given her command of her own *mingan*.

But she was still a woman and he expected her to marry and bear sons. And if that was how it must be she had promised herself that one day it would be her children, and not any of her brothers' spawn, that would take her father's place as khan of the clan and lord of the Fergana steppes.

But her ambition had been betrayed by a weakness she had never suspected within her. There was simply no advantage to a union with this barbarian and yet she had allowed herself to imagine it.

She could not understand why he harboured this craving for her. When he discovered she was a mare like any other he would be disillusioned, and then she would be powerless, both as a woman and as the man she had tried to become.

So why did she persist with this dangerous game?

Qaidu had told her of the challenge that the barbarian had issued. That he would do such a thing, take such a gamble for her, truly astonished her. But she had told her father that she would accept. He would take the test that all her suitors had taken. If she won, he would die; if he won, she would relinquish her saddle and surrender herself to him as wife to husband.

Which would it be?

Let tomorrow decide.

CXII

✠

THE VALLEY HAD been washed clean and the sky was a pale blue, the blue of Tengri, Lord of the Blue Sky. In the distance the snow-flecked green of the spruce forests swooped down to a cobalt lake.

Khutelun sat astride her white mare, in long *del* and riding boots, her face wrapped in her purple scarf. She did not spare a glance for Josseran. They had given him an unappealing and irritable yellow mare with bad teeth and an ugly disposition. His long legs nearly reached the ground either side of her.

The whole village had gathered to watch the entertainment. There was a carnival atmosphere, for everyone knew the ugly barbarian was certain to lose. Perhaps this evening they would have another boiling to look forward to.

Qaidu emerged from his yurt, went to Khutelun and placed a hand on her horse's poll. He leaned towards her. 'You must not lose,' he whispered.

'I know what I have to do.'

'Do not let your womanly feelings for this barbarian stand in the way of the interests of the clan.'

'I have no womanly feelings for him, Father.'

'I know this is not true. But whatever you feel, do not let me down!'

Her white mare stamped and flicked its tail in its eagerness to begin. 'I have raced and beaten better horsemen than this,' she said. 'I will win.'

Josseran gritted his teeth against the pain in his shoulder. It was a blessed relief to be out of the cangue. But the arrow wound had left him with virtually no power in his left arm, and blood was still soaking his shirt. He would have to ride one-handed.

Khutelun would not meet his eye.

He felt a flicker of unease. She may be my equal on a horse, he thought, and she knows these hills better than I. But she surely understands the nature of the gamble I have taken. This contest is not a test of horsemanship, but a trial of the heart.

I hope I am right about her.

'Whoever brings me the goat has their will,' Qaidu shouted, and as he stepped back he slapped the rump of Khutelun's mare. It leaped away and the race was on, leaving Josseran's horse standing.

☩

He galloped after her, towards the wooded hills at the foot of the ridge. The flat, hammering run of the pony sent shocks of pain through his shoulder. He ignored it. The only thing that mattered now was this race.

Khutelun's horse suddenly veered away, towards the steepest part of the hill, the spur that the Tatars called The Place Where the Ass Was Felled by a Goat. But Josseran had already decided on his own ascent, straight up the broad shoulder of the col.

Although he trailed already by the distance of a crossbow shot, he knew he would win because in his heart he did not believe that Khutelun would let him die.

He reached the shadow of the ridge and looked over his shoulder for Khutelun. Where was she? She had taken what seemed to him the steepest and most circuitous path and he expected now to see her far below him on the trail. But there was no sign of her.

But then a shadow fell across his face and he looked up, startled, and saw her above him, at the very summit. She scooped up one of the carcasses and swung it above her head, in triumph.

He remembered again what William had said. *She is a witch and beyond redemption.*

No! He refused to believe she would trick him.

He spurred his horse up the trail. When he reached the ridge he leaned from his saddle and scooped up the other carcass and laid it across the saddle of his horse. He looked around desperately for Khutelun.

Now he saw the way she had come; there was a narrow defile that traversed the col, all but invisible from below. She was returning down this same trail, the bloodied carcass in her left fist. He spurred his own horse down the slope after her.

He felt a thrill of fear in his belly. Perhaps this was, after all, the real Khutelun; Khutelun the Tatar, Khutelun the vixen who could not countenance defeat by any man, willing to stake his life against her own pride.

He urged his pony over the loose scree, its hooves slipping on the loose rocks. But he knew he had lost. She was a hundred feet below him, her mare picking its way swiftly down the narrow trail as it had done scores of times before. Khutelun rode upright in the stirrups. It would be impossible to close the gap on her now.

It occurred to him that he might turn his pony around and ride back over the mountain, away from Qaidu and the steppes of Fergana. Perhaps that was what Qaidu, even Khutelun also, had intended; this race was merely a diversion that provided him with a fresh horse and put him a safe distance from the camp.

That was it. Qaidu wanted him to escape, and relieve him of the responsibility for his ultimate fate. They would make a show of coming after him, of course, but the khan would ensure that they did not catch him. Khutelun would have her victory and this night they would laugh about the barbarian around their fires, while the mutton grease and koumiss shone on their chins.

He reined in his horse and watched her go. He wondered if she had loved him at all.

He saw her turn in the saddle and look back up the ridge. She raised a hand into the air. In farewell, or in triumph?

And then her horse stumbled.

CXIII

✠

HE WAS SILHOUETTED against the sun, a hundred feet above her. She felt a momentary stab of pain at what she had done. But this way was best. She had saved his life and also acted in the best interests of her father and the clan. As a Tatar princess it was the only choice.

She saw him turn his horse around, abandoning the chase. She twisted further around in her saddle for one last glimpse of him.

It was all that was needed to change everything.

If she had been watching the way ahead she would have seen the loose scree and guided her mare around it. Or perhaps her twisting in the saddle unsettled the pony. But moments later she felt a jolt as her mare lost her footing. Khutelun leaped clear to prevent them both sliding headlong down the slope.

It was the mare's instincts as well as her own agility that saved them. She jumped back to her feet, grabbing for the reins while the pony scrambled to keep its footing on the crumbling shale. Khutelun felt the rocks slip away beneath her boots and she fell hard on to her back. But she held on to the trailing rein, keeping the terrified animal in check. With a final effort the mare scrambled back on to the path.

Khutelun lay there, winded by the fall. She got slowly to her feet, gasped at the pain in her ribs where she had fallen on a jagged rock.

And then he was on top of her.

She heard him galloping along the narrow trail, the fleece of the goat carcass slapping against his pony's flanks. He was going too fast, but somehow he kept himself in the saddle.

Her hand went to her belt and the plaited leather whip appeared in her right hand. It arced through the air with a crack like a falling tree. Josseran's pony shied and bucked and Josseran slid to the ground.

She quickly recovered her own mare and jumped into the saddle.

✝

Josseran scrambled to his feet and watched her ride away down the trail, numb with disbelief. He looked down at his left hand, at the bloody weal left by the whip. It had even shredded the fabric of his coat. His shoulder was on fire again; he could feel fresh blood running down his arm.

His pony was skittering a few yards away, kicking its hind legs, its nerves and its temper not improved by this most recent experience. Josseran ran after him, caught the reins and tried to gentle him. It was still not too late to ride back up the trail and across the ridge. He could still get away, as he was sure they had all intended.

No, damn her.

He remounted swiftly and spurred the pony down the trail.

✝

Khutelun looked over her shoulder yet again, hoping this time he had taken the lifeline she had thrown him. Surely he had abandoned the chase.

She could not believe her eyes.

He was still in pursuit. 'Get away!' she shouted at him in frustration. 'Get away!' Her voice echoed around the mountain, along the defile, through the forest of spruce and fir, across the deep black pool at the foot of the ridge. 'Go back! Go back to Kashgar! Save yourself! Go back!'

He reined in his pony, was silhouetted for a moment on the ledge above her. She waited to see what he would do. Finally he turned away. As she watched him retreat she experienced a flood of relief, mingled with bitter disappointment. He was just a man like any other, after all.

✝

He knew he could not catch her. His little pony was fighting for every step on the loose rock. If he pushed him too hard he would eventually stumble and send them both sliding to their deaths down the side of the mountain.

He had reached a broad ledge, and between the walls of the gorge he could make out the dun-coloured steppe and the black yurts of the Tatar encampment. A stream rushed down the mountain, foaming into a black pool far below. The sedge at the lake's edge was still hardened with the night frost; the surface of the lake was black, afloat with sheets of ice. Patches of hardened snow clung to the hollows of the tarn where the sun could not reach.

He peered over the lip of the cliff, heard the clatter of hooves echoing from the rock face on the trail below him. Khutelun's voice echoed along the valley: 'Get away, Joss-ran! Go back!'

Go back. Go back with the mark of my whip on your face, Joss-ran. Go back without me, wonder about me for the rest of your life.

'Better to drown in that cold black lake than boil in your damned father's pot,' Josseran said, aloud. He dug in his heels and tried to spur the pony towards the ledge. He would not move. So he took his dirk from his boot and slammed it into the pony's rump.

A wild leap into space.

As they tumbled through the air Josseran threw himself from the saddle, still clutching the goat's carcass in his right fist. He thought he saw the shadow of rocks hidden beneath the surface. He hit the water feet first. If death it was, then by some mercy he prayed it would be swift.

✠

There was horror in such spectacle, but wonder as well; wonder at his courage and his pride. One moment she had been staring upwards, shielding her eyes against the glare of the sun, thinking he was gone. Then suddenly there was a great mushrooming of water in the tarn below as the pony disappeared into the black water, and another, smaller splash as Josseran followed.

Khutelun gasped. She had never imagined he might do something like this. The shock waves from where horse and rider had plunged in rushed towards the rocky shallows, where they lapped and foamed.

How could anyone do such a thing?

The pony's head broke the surface first, and it swam desperately for the far bank. It struggled out of the water on tottering legs, blood streaking down its flank from a dagger wound in its rump.

Still no sign of Josseran though. She choked back a cry of grief.

CXIV

✝

AND THEN SHE saw him.

His head bobbed to the surface, streaked with blood. He struck out for the bank with his good arm. He dragged himself from the water and lay gasping on the rocks. He still clutched the goat carcass to his body in the crook of his injured arm. Then he dragged himself back to his feet, reclaimed his horse's reins, and scrambled back into the saddle. The pony, defeated by this madman, shocked and probably in pain, was compliant as a lamb.

Khutelun cursed under her breath. It would have been better for them both if Josseran had died. Now there was no hope for him, or for her.

She could try and swim across the tarn, or she could ride around it; whatever she did he had an unassailable advantage. So instead she just walked her horse along the trail, knowing she could not catch him now.

✝

Josseran was slumped over the poll of his horse, blood streaked down his face from a new laceration on his scalp, fresh blood dripping from the tips of his fingers where the wound on his shoulder had opened again. He was shivering so that his teeth chattered, soaked from the icy waters of the tarn. His horse, too, had blood streaked along its rump, and a mist of steam rose from its flanks.

He walked the pony through the human corridor the Tatars had formed on the plain, directly to the doorway of Qaidu's yurt. The silence was deadly and complete.

Qaidu was pale with shock. His daughter had never been bested before. Now she had been defeated by the one man it was impossible for her to marry. Hers was a tiny figure, still two hundred paces away across the plain.

Josseran threw the goat carcass at Qaidu's feet. 'The race is mine,' he said.

Qaidu nodded to his bodyguards. They dragged Josseran from his horse.

'You cannot marry my daughter,' Qaidu said. He turned to his soldiers. 'Take him away. Put him back in the cangue. Tomorrow he dies.'

And he stormed back inside his yurt.

CXV

✠

'You had the chance to escape. Why did you not take it?'

He did not answer her.

They were alone in the yurt, the wind hurling itself against the walls of felt. His head was bowed by the weight of the cangue. They had betrayed him. They had both betrayed him.

✠

He bears his pain without murmur, Khutelun thought, as a man should. Her whip had laid open the flesh on the back of his left hand and at his temple. He had injured his left leg when he hit the water, and his knee was swollen to the size of a melon. His shoulder, too, had opened again and there was a fresh clot of blood around the wound.

But his trials had won him only an appointment with Qaidu's executioner.

The spirits of the Blue Sky had indeed had their joke at her expense. Finally she had found a man who had proved himself to her, who had bested her on horseback, and now he was to die. She knelt in front of him, cupping a small wooden basin of water in her hands. She dipped a cloth into it and started to clean his wounds. 'Why did you not take the chance to escape?' she repeated.

'Let me ask you this first,' he said. 'Did you know what your father was going to do?'

'I am the daughter of a khan. I cannot marry a barbarian.'

'And so you thought I would run to save my own life rather than stay and fight for you.'

'Any sensible man would have taken his chance when it was given him.'

'A sensible man would not be sitting on this godforsaken plain thousands of leagues from the place where he was born. A sensible man would not have sold his lands to serve five years as a monk and a soldier. A sensible man would not run a fool's errand across half the world.' He blinked slowly, as if waking from a dream. 'But you did not answer my question. I asked you if you knew what your father planned.'

'Of course I knew.'

She slipped the scarf from her face. She ducked her head and put her mouth over the wound on his shoulder and started to suck at the clotted blood.

'What are you doing?' he whispered. He felt her teeth pull at the flesh of the muscle, small trembling tugs like a child at the breast. Her mouth was moist and hot.

'It is to clean the wound.'

'Please don't,' he said, his voice hoarse.

She pulled away again and looked up at him, puzzled. There was a brightness in her eyes that had not been there before. 'But the blood will turn bad.'

'Just leave me.'

'Is it what you wish?'

'No, but leave me anyway.'

There was blood on her lips. The smell of her stirred him, not sweet perfumes and ointments, but blood and leather and sweat.

'You cannot marry a Tatar princess,' she said.

'How does your father intend to kill me?'

'The traditional way for men of high birth and great valour. You will be rolled in a carpet and trampled by horses. That way your blood cannot be spilled on the ground and bring the tribe bad luck.' She unexpectedly reached out a hand and touched him, just below the heart. 'You are too brave. You should have run when you had the chance. That was my plan; my father conspired with me on it. I did not want this.'

He was not listening. Even now all he could think about was her breath, her heat, her eyes and, as he had so often wondered about, her body. The look in his eyes again betrayed his thoughts.

'It cannot happen,' she said.

'Please,' he said.

For a long moment neither of them spoke. Then she stood up and went to the doorway of the yurt. He thought she was about to leave. But instead she turned down the flap of the tent and came back.

CXVI

✝

KHUTELUN REMOVED HER boots and heavy felt trousers. She unfastened her coat and let it fall open.

He held his breath. His mouth was as dry as it had been at any time during their crossing of the desert. If this is to be my last night on earth, he thought, then I do not care any more. This is enough. His desire overwhelmed even the agonies of the cangue, the terrible pain in his shoulder, the dread of dying.

The silk undershirt she wore beneath her *del* reached just below her waist. She lifted it over her head. Her skin was burnished like bronze, the muscles beneath her flesh taut as bowstring from a lifetime standing in the stirrups of a horse. Like all the Uighur women she had no hair anywhere on her body. There were fresh, white scars along her right thigh and her right shinbone. He remembered how she had gone down under the wolf pack the day of the hunt and he guessed these were the results of it.

She knelt down, straddling his legs. He groaned aloud with frustration. He could not touch her, could not even kiss her because of the cangue. She sat that way for a long time, her knees on either side of him, her eyes locked on his.

She lifted his ragged and blood-stained silk undershirt and he felt her fingers stroke the skin of his flanks. She had a small frown of concentration on her face, as if she wished to commit every contour of his body to her memory. Then she bowed her head and kissed his chest, small soft kisses, tugging gently at his skin with her teeth.

She took his face in her hands. 'Is this what you threw your life away for?'

'You are all I care about now.'

'You will be disappointed. When it is over you will wonder why you risked so much. The joining of a stallion and mare is as commonplace as the wind and the rain.'

'You know it is so much more than that. We are the same spirit, you and I.'

She shucked his felt trousers down around his hips. 'My stallion,' she murmured. At last she wet her fingers with her mouth, slowly, one at a time, and stroked him, gently. He gasped aloud.

'I would stay here on these steppes for you,' he murmured. 'There is nothing for me to go back to.'

He felt her body pressed against him. She bowed her head beneath the wooden yoke and put her face against his chest. He thought his shoulders would break with the strain.

'You remember the cave paintings in the desert?' she whispered.

'I remember.'

'Even if we had a thousand nights and we joined in all the different ways like the lord Shiva and his wife, eventually you would grow tired of me and you would want to return to your own land.'

'You are wrong, Khutelun. When you are old and toothless I would still sit by your side.'

'Those are just words.'

'When I said I would ride for you, they were not words. I said I would do anything to win you: they were not words. I jumped from the cliff into the water and I did not know if I should live or die. You had my word that I would stake my life for you and I kept it.'

She wrapped her legs around the small of his back; he felt her belly and her groin pressed against him and he groaned aloud. She kissed his shoulder, leaving the moisture of her mouth on his skin. He could not see her face. The dimensions of their lovemaking were prescribed for him by the sound of her soft breaths, the whip of the wind outside the yurt, the shadows thrown by the fire, the corona of her hair.

His hands clenched into fists.

'How is it with your Christian women?'

'Never like this. Never.'

'I must believe you, if that is what you say. For myself, I have never done this.' She leaned backwards, her hands on the carpets, raising her body and arching her torso. He tried to join with her, but the weight of the cangue prevented him.

'Was this the moment with me for which you risked so much?'

'It was for every moment I have till the end of my life.'

She moved down on him almost imperceptibly. He gasped aloud. 'Dear God and all his saints . . .' he breathed.

When she had taken all of him she wrapped her arms tightly around him. He could feel her breath on his neck, the indescribable softness of her breast against his chest. She stayed that way, barely moving, for what seemed like an eternity.

'Please,' he whispered.

Very gently, very slowly, she rose on to her knees, and he waited for her to move down on him again. But without warning she slipped away and their coupling was over before it had begun.

'What are you doing?' he gasped.

She held her face close to his, her fingers closed around him, stroking him.

'Khutelun!'

She brushed the braids from her face. 'I cannot take your seed. Do you wish me to carry your child when you are gone?' Her fingers moved faster and faster. He groaned, and his body shuddered with unbearable pleasure and wordless grief. 'This is all the gods will allow,' she whispered. She replaced his clothes and got to her feet. There was blood streaked along her thighs. 'You see. I can bleed a little for you, as you bled for me.'

She kissed him one last time. 'I want you to burn for me forever,' she whispered. She dressed quickly, and was gone. In her place came the darkness, and with it the despair of a life without a true ending, an empty hand reaching towards a fathomless sky.

CXVII

✠

His GUARD WAS no more than a boy. He sat in the doorway of the yurt, holding his rusted sword in both hands. He studied Josseran with a look of sullen malevolence, trying to appear older and braver and more belligerent than he really was. Josseran pretended to sleep, watching him from under lidded eyes, biding his time.

Some time during the long night he heard the boy's deep even breathing and saw his head fall on to his chest. This was his moment.

He tried to rise to his haunches but the weight of the cangue had cramped the muscles in his thighs and there was no feeling in his legs. The wound in his shoulder had stiffened too and when he tried to move it was as if someone had thrust a red-hot brand into the joint.

It was long minutes before he was finally able to stretch out his legs and as the circulation returned it felt like needles piercing his flesh. Finally the pain eased. He flexed his leg muscles, testing them again. Once again he tried to get to his feet, but he lost his balance, rocking back on his heels and falling against the bamboo frame of the yurt. He thought the noise would wake the young sentry but the boy snuffled in his sleep like a hog and did not stir.

Josseran staggered to his feet at his third attempt.

He stood motionless for a long time, until the pounding of the blood in his ears had subsided and he was once more sure of his balance. His knee throbbed with pain. He limped across the floor of the yurt in a lop-sided run.

At the last moment the boy woke. His eyes blinked open and he stared up at Josseran, his youthful face framed in the moonlight. Josseran dropped to his knees, at the same time forcing the cangue around in an arc, so that the edge of the great wooden board caught the boy on the side of the temple. There was a terrible crack and he slumped sideways on to the ground. His limbs twitched several times and he was still.

For all his desperation, Josseran hoped he had not killed him.

The effort of swinging the cangue had sent his neck muscles into spasm once more. He felt as if his arm had been ripped off. God's bones! Somehow he staggered upright again. He pushed through the felt entrance flap into the darkness. It was bitingly cold and the ground was frozen hard with frost. He had on just a silk undershirt and felt trousers, not enough to keep him alive on the freezing steppe until morning. But there was nothing he could do about that. It was a choice between freezing or being trampled by Qaidu's horses. Neither prospect held great appeal. At least, he told himself, I can die on my own terms.

He ran blindly into the night, away from the camp. But within minutes he was shivering so badly that he stumbled and fell, the weight of the wooden collar jarring his neck and spine as he hit the ground.

He could not breathe for the pain.

Finally he forced himself back to his feet. He was clear of the camp now. He had wondered at the single guard they had placed at the entrance to the yurt and now he understood the reason for it. Where was there to run to? He had traded a swift Tatar execution for a slow and frozen death in the tundra. In this thin shirt he would not live the hour.

All around him was the dark steppe: no shelter, no food and no allies. He fell back to his knees, trembling with cold, his neck and shoulder racked with agony. He heard the Tatar horses on the plain, stamping their hooves in their hobbles. They had smelled his foreign scent on the wind.

He collapsed in the frozen mud, too cold and too exhausted to continue.

He was beaten.

☩

He felt the thunder of horse's hooves on the hard ground but he no longer had the strength to rise. He saw the blade of a sword flash in the moonlight. He twisted his head, made out the wiry frame of a Tatar horseman standing over him, the vapour of his breath on the wind, the smell of his horse.

Just let it be quick.

CXVIII

✛

THE CANGUE SPLIT under a single downward stroke. The Tatar kicked out savagely, splintering the cangue along its length and breaking the hinge. Josseran shrugged off the terrible device, sobbing with relief. He tried to get to his feet but there was no strength left in him. He lay shivering on the frozen ground, the cold seeping into him like death.

'I thought you were never coming,' she said.

Khutelun?

She threw some furs at him. 'Put these on before you freeze. There is some koumiss and dried mutton in the saddlebag of the horse. Your people are two days' ride from here. Perhaps seven for you.'

He did not move.

'Quickly! Before the whole tribe is awake.' She grabbed him by his shirt, forcing him upright, and pulled the coat around his shoulders. He grunted with pain as she forced his left arm into the *del*. Then she hauled him to his feet and dragged him towards the horse.

'You must hurry!'

He could feel a warm wetness on his chest, knew the shoulder wound had opened yet again. His neck muscles were rigid from the cangue, so that he could barely move his head. He was no longer certain if he had strength left for this. His knee buckled and almost gave way under him.

'Keep the north star behind you,' Khutelun said. 'At daylight you will reach a broad valley. You will see a mountain in the shape of a woman lying on her back. Follow that valley and it will take you to Kashgar. Your friends are there.'

'You are not coming with me?'

'Why would I do that?'

She helped him into the saddle, placed the reins in his right hand.

'I will not see you again,' she said.

'Do not be so sure of that.'

'If you ever come back to these valleys again my father will kill you. Go home now, Joss-ran. Forget about me, forget you were ever here.'

'Come with me,' he repeated.

'Twice now I have saved your life. What else do you want from me? Now quickly, you must hurry!' She grabbed his hair and pulled his face towards her to kiss him. 'I would have liked to have borne you sons,' she said and then she slapped the pony's rump. It spurred away into the blackness, towards the steppes and the dark massif of the mountains to the south.

✠

Qaidu stood at the doorway of his yurt, Khutelun beside him. Nothing moved in that black and terrible cold.

'He made his escape?' Qaidu asked her.

'He has a horse and provisions and furs. And he is a man of many resources.'

'Indeed,' Qaidu murmured. 'What about the guard?'

'He has recovered, though I fear he will bear the scar for the rest of his life as testament to his carelessness.'

'I should punish him, or some will suspect I had a hand in this.'

The vapours of their breath drifted on the wind.

'I shall curse the day he ever found his way to the Fergana Valley,' he said.

The silence was uneasy testament to his daughter's feelings.

'If he had been a Person and not a barbarian, you would have married him?'

'He was a man.'

'I concede he had courage,' Qaidu grunted. 'But then one may find courage in a horse also.'

'I had a dream last night,' Khutelun said.

'What was in your dream?'

'I dreamed that I saw him again.'

'It is impossible.'

'It was my dream.'

Qaidu shook his head. It would not do. He could not have her moon-eyed for a barbarian. 'You did the best thing for the clan,' he said. 'Now you must forget this ever happened.'

As if she ever could.

CXIX

✠

LATE SUMMER IN Kashgar and the streets were filled with dust and flies, black swarms that crawled over the sheep's heads and fatty lungs for sale in the street. Tajiks with beards like fine wire and slant-eyed Kirghiz cracked sunflower seeds between their teeth as they swaggered through the bazaars, or lolled on wooden divans in the *chai-khanas*, sipping green tea spiced with cinnamon from cracked china pots.

The market stalls groaned under the weight of the late harvest: peaches, watermelons and figs, melons, grapes and pomegranates. The alleyways were ankle deep in melon rind. But with the fruits of summer came the harbingers of winter. Donkey carts clattered through the dusty streets, loaded with bundles of twigs and logs, fuel for the fires.

There was snow already in the foothills below the Roof of the World.

✠

Josseran opened his eyes. He was aware of a pulsing ache in his shoulder, a searing pain in his skull. His mouth was gummy and dry. As he came awake his nostrils twitched at the aromas filtering into the room: fresh-baked flat bread, charcoal, roasting meats; all the familiar smells of the bazaar.

'So,' a voice said, 'you are alive.'

A face swam into his vision. William. He tried to speak but no sound came. William raised his head and brought a cup of water to his lips. It was ice cold and tasted to Josseran as delicious as wine.

'Where . . . am I?'

'You are not in heaven, if that is what you were expecting.'

'When I saw you . . . I knew assuredly it was not heaven.' He was lying on a thick bed of carpets. It was a *khang*, a raised brick platform heated from below by a fire, and soothingly warm on his back.

'Where am I?'

'We are in the fort at Kashgar. You were brought here three days ago by Tajik tribesmen. They found you half-delirious and wandering in the mountains on a Tatar horse. You have two wounds to your head and an arrow wound in your shoulder that was greatly inflamed. However, it is now mending, no thanks to these Tatars. They wanted to send in their filthy shamans to practise their sorcery on you but I dissuaded them. I said prayers for your benighted soul and I bled you. I believe my physic and God's grace has made you well again.'

'Thank you.'

'Do not thank me. Now I am no longer in your debt.' William stood up. 'You should give thanks to God for your deliverance. I thought not to see you again.'

'That would have disturbed you very greatly?'

William leaned closer. 'What happened in those mountains, Templar?'

'When my captors saw the *paizah* and learned I was a Christian ambassador with the sanction of Khubilai, they released me. They have great regard for the lives of envoys in these parts.'

'Then where is the *paizah*?'

'I must have dropped it.'

'Who were they?'

'Bandits. They attacked us hoping for profit, nothing more.'

'I thought I saw the witch among them.' William said.

Josseran shook his head. 'You were mistaken,' he said and turned his face to the window. 'Sartaq and his Tatars have treated you well?'

'He has not cut my throat and boiled my innards for his supper and for that I give thanks to God.'

'I feared you had moved on to Khotan or Osh.'

'After the ambush Sartaq ordered us to return to the fort. Since then we have remained here, behind these walls, but I have no idea why. Perhaps it was to await your safe return. Since these people cannot speak the language of civilized men and only gibber like monkeys, it is impossible for me to know. Sartaq wishes to speak with you, by the way, as soon as you are recovered.'

'I am tired. I will see him tomorrow. For now I just need to sleep.'

'Then I shall leave you.' William paused at the door. 'When they brought you here you were in a delirium. You babbled like a child.'

'What did I say?'

'It was something about your father,' he said. He went out, the heavy door shutting behind him.

✝

It was not until the next day, when Josseran was recovered enough to receive a visit from Sartaq, that he learned the real reason the Tatars had returned to the fort. After the ambush Sartaq had sent a message to Bukhara, asking the regent of the Chaghadai khanate, Organa, to reinforce his escort. While he waited at Kashgar for a response, he received a message on the *yam* that Organa had been deposed by Ariq Böke's ally, Alghu, and was given orders from Khubilai himself to remain where he was until the situation was resolved.'

'So who laid the ambush, Barbarian? Whose soldiers were they?' When Josseran hesitated, he answered for himself: 'Qaidu sent them.'

'Yes.'

'What happened to the others who were taken with you?'

'They were executed.'

'Did they die well?'

Josseran wondered how he should answer him. Would a Tatar consider boiling a good death? 'They were beheaded. It was quick.'

'You are sure?'

'I saw it with my own eyes.'

Sartaq seemed relieved. 'That is at least a blessing. Dai Sechen,' he said, using Drunken Man's real name, 'was my brother-in-law.'

'He died like a man,' Josseran said and looked away. It was kinder than telling him they had made soup out of him. It was a falsehood, but then there were some truths it was better not to know.

PART VIII

The Silk Road

*Kashgar to Bukhara
in the year of the Hejira 638, and the year
of the Incarnation of our Lord 1261*

CXX

✠

THE CRISIS IN the Chaghadai khanate had trapped them in Kashgar for the winter. Now Sartaq told them it might be years before they were able to safely cross the Roof of the World. But arrow riders of the *yam* continued to appear at the fort almost every day on their way to and from the east. It was not difficult to imagine the plotting now taking place in Qaraqorum and Shang-tu.

One day Sartaq confided to Josseran that the Son of Heaven had found a way around the impasse. 'There is a caravan on its way to Bukhara from Ta-tu,' he said. 'Alghu has promised to send soldiers as escort. We will join the caravan when it reaches here. But we will have to wait until spring to cross the Roof of the World.'

'So Khubilai has reached an accommodation with the Chaghadai khan?'

'In secret.'

'What is in the caravan? Gold?'

Sartaq smiled. 'Gold can be spent. It is a woman. One of the Emperor's daughters is to marry Alghu. A judicious alliance, for it will ensure harmony between the house of the Emperor and that of the Chaghadai khanate.'

'What is the princess's name?' Josseran asked, though he suspected he already knew the answer.

'It is Miao-yen,' Sartaq told him. 'Princess Miao-yen.'

✠

To the north the mountains, barrier to new and undiscovered lands; to the west the medinas and murmuring poplars of Samarkand and Bukhara; to the east the pavilions and rustling bamboo of Cathay; to the south the howling winds of the

Taklimakan. And here, at Kashgar, crossroads of the Silk Road, the paths of his life converged.

He watched from the walls of the fort as the caravan snaked its way across the oasis. The camels coughed and complained; the horses held their heads low, beaten by the long crossing of the desert. There were two squadrons of cavalry, their gold helmets reflecting the sun. The green and white standards of the Son of Heaven whipped in the wind.

The wooden gates of the fort were flung open and the vanguard entered, in single file. Behind them came a gilt sedan, bearing the princess, rocking on the back of a wooden cart, followed by two more wagons for her maidservants. When they were safely inside the fort the women climbed down from the wagons and clustered around the princess. He sensed immediately that something was wrong.

A few moments later he saw soldiers carry the princess Miao-yen out of the courtyard on a litter.

He thought of the fragile creature he had walked with in the Garden of the Refreshing Spring. Of course her porcelain loveliness would not withstand the rigours of such a journey. He said a silent prayer for her to a merciful God, if there was such a being.

CXXI

✠

It had been his regime to rise for prime with William, eat a breakfast of pilau and then train at wrestling with Angry Man. The Tatars were very fond of wrestling, and very skilled, and Josseran became an avid student. The exercise helped him regain the strength in his wounded shoulder. He had yet to score a victory over Angry Man but at least the falls had become fewer.

Every morning they practised on the maidan but after a dozen falls Josseran always held up his hands to signify his surrender. But he was determined that one day he would win.

Angry Man – his real name, Josseran had learned, was Yesün – was short, stocky and bow-legged, like many of these Tatars. Most of them had learned to ride even before they could walk and the bones in their legs had grown to accommodate the shape of a horse. Angry Man's body was fleshy rather than muscled, but when he charged it was like being hit by a small bullock. He wrestled barechested, and with his body wreathed in sweat it was like trying to hold on to a greased pig.

Angry Man had showed him many holds, and how to break them; but it was not just a matter of learning holds, the art of the sport was combining many different moves in a blurring of arms and legs, overpowering an opponent with a combination of speed and brute strength and bullying confidence.

One afternoon he finally managed a throw; he took Angry Man off balance for a moment and put him on his back in the dust with spine-jarring force. Josseran was as surprised as his opponent by this development and he hesitated before following through on his success. Before he could pin him to the ground Angry Man held up a hand, his face creased in a grimace of pain.

'Wait,' he gasped. 'My back!'

'Are you hurt?'

'You've broken my back!'

Josseran hesitated. With one movement Angry Man kicked his legs away and Josseran found himself staring up at the sky, all the breath jarred from his chest. Angry Man jumped on top of him, threw him over and put his knee in the small of his back. He put his hands on either side of his head, and twisted. Josseran heard sinews crack.

Angry Man roared in triumph and jumped to his feet. 'Never show mercy!' he shouted. 'It is another lesson you must learn.'

Josseran would have cursed him but he could not catch his breath.

'Remember, surprise and feint. Your greatest weapons.'

He walked away, laughing. Josseran spat the dust out of his mouth, his body hammering with pain. It was a lesson well learned. One day he would use it.

+

The morning after Miao-yen's arrival they were again in the maidan, at practice. They circled each other in a makeshift ring that Angry Man had marked out in the dirt with a mulberry branch. He made a sudden charge and feint; Josseran reacted too slowly. A blur of movement and he found himself on his back on the hard ground under a stinking press of heaving, sweating Tatar. He had lost again.

Angry Man laughed uproariously and jumped up. 'If all barbarians are like you we will rule the whole world!'

Josseran grimaced and slowly forced himself upright. Because of his physical size he was unaccustomed to being defeated like this in trials of strength. It had never happened to him in his whole life and regular beatings at the hands of this nuggety Tatar made him seethe.

'Again,' he said.

Angry Man circled him and then they came together, their hands on each other's shoulders, using their legs to try make the fall.

Josseran heard someone calling his name. 'Barbarian!'

Josseran looked around and Angry Man took advantage of his lapse in concentration to throw him on his back. 'Will you never learn?' he hooted.

Sartaq ran over. Josseran sensed something was terribly wrong.

'Where is your companion?'

'Most surely on his knees somewhere. What is amiss?'

'It is Princess Miao-yen. On the way across the desert she sickened with some malady and now she will not wake.'

Josseran had heard much whispering among the maidservants and officers who attended her quarters outside the western tower. He had asked to see her but had been refused without explanation. He had not known until now the severity of her illness.

'I am distressed to hear this news,' he said. 'But what does it have to do with our good friar?'

'The shamans who accompanied her on this journey have done all they can. I thought perhaps your holy man . . .'

'William?'

'After all, he made you well.'

'William has no power to heal. God alone performs such miracles.'

'I do not care who cures her, whether it is your god or theirs. But she must not die. She is under my jurisdiction now and I would be blamed.'

Josseran shrugged his shoulders. It could no harm, he supposed, though he also doubted that it would do any good. He could persuade William to say a few prayers, at least. 'I shall ask him to assist you, if that is your wish.'

'Fetch him to me as soon as you can,' Sartaq said. 'Without her, there is no alliance with Alghu and then perhaps we will not leave Kashgar before our hair turns white!'

CXXII

✠

Fergana Valley

Smoke rose from the yurts scattered across the valley. The Roof of
the World was hushed with snow.

The three riders rode slowly past the shocked faces of their
clansmen. Their scalps and parts of their faces were scorched and
blackened; glistening white bone was visible through the charred
flesh. One had lost his eye, another a good part of his nose. It was all
they could do to remain upright in their saddles but they did not fall
until they reached the door of the khan's yurt where one of them
finally slipped from his horse and lay unmoving in the snow.

✠

'It was Ariq Böke himself who helped put Alghu on the throne in
Bukhara. And as our Great Khan wished, I sent a delegation to him
to ask for a share of his taxes to buy our Khaghan's army supplies
for the fight against the traitor, Khubilai. And what does he do? He
says he will pay his share in precious metals and has molten gold
poured on the heads of our envoys.'

Qaidu was in his yurt, his sons on his right, his favourite wife and
his daughter, Khutelun, on his left. Blue smoke drifted lazily from
the fire through the hole in the roof.

'We should withdraw further into the mountains,' Tekudai said.
'Alghu has one hundred and fifty thousand soldiers at his back.'

'Withdraw?' Qaidu muttered. He turned to Gerel. 'Do you agree
with your brother?'

Gerel did not have time to answer for Khutelun could not keep
her peace any longer. 'If we run now, we run forever, and we will
never see our fields and pastures again!'

'So what would you have us do?'

'We cannot defeat Alghu on the battlefield. But we can strike when he least expects and hide in the mountains before he has the chance to retaliate. When he turns his back we can strike again. We should never give him a moment's peace. We will wear him down like a wolf with a bear, nip at his heels moon after moon, year after year, until he is hamstrung and exhausted. One day, when we have gathered other wolves like ourselves, then we can take him down.'

Qaidu smiled. His daughter, the warrior, the shaman; Chinggis Khan returned in the body of a mare. The spirits had toyed with him in his life and their joke had been to make his greatest son a woman.

He considered a moment. Finally, he said: 'I agree with Khutelun. It suits my temperament rather better to be a wolf than a sheep. But we must first seek the wisdom of the gods to know their wishes. Khutelun, you must meet the spirits and know their counsel. Then, and only then, shall we decide.'

CXXIII

✠

Kashgar

Through an iron-bossed doorway, studded with brass, along a narrow walled courtyard where roses climbed the brickwork; under an arch with a broken Kufic frieze, grape blue on white. Finally, up narrow, century-worn steps to a tower.

It was a strange delegation that made its way down the dark corridor of the western barbican. The Tatar lieutenant in his gold-winged helmet led the way, behind him a sallow-faced man in a black-cowled robe and behind him a bearded giant in the *del* and stubby boots of a Tatar. At the summit of the tower they stopped outside one of the chambers. A bevy of Chinese maidservants hovered outside a carved walnut door, their heads lowered.

William took Josseran to one side. 'What am I to do?' he moaned. 'I cannot pray for a heathen!'

'Pray then, for a human soul in distress.'

'What you ask is impossible!'

'Will you mortally insult our escort by refusing them? Do whatever you will and hope for the best, then, for I believe the result will be the same.'

'What does he say?' Sartaq snapped.

'He fears he may fail you.'

'His magic worked well enough on Mar Salah. Besides, nothing else has helped her. Remind him that if the princess dies, we may be forced to linger here for fifty winters.'

'I cannot do this!' William repeated.

'Is he ready?' Sartaq said.

'He is ready,' Josseran answered.

Sartaq opened the door to the chamber and Josseran steered William through the door. The room must have once served as the private quarters of a Mohammedan prince or princess, Josseran thought, for it was wondrously appointed, unlike his own bare cell. There was a ribbon of Arabic script around the arched windows, and the mud-brick walls were decorated with a ceramic frieze of geometric design, ox-blood on wax yellow.

Miao-yen lay on a bed in the centre of the room, apparently asleep. She seemed lost in this vast chamber. There were braziers lit in the corners, but the crackling poplar branches could not take the chill from the room.

Sartaq refused to step over the threshold, afraid of the spirits that hovered around Miao-yen's body. Josseran stood back and William went alone to her bedside. He looked around, alarmed. 'Where are her physicians?'

'Sartaq says they have failed to heal her so he has banished them.'

William licked his thin white lips. 'I tell you I cannot do this! She has not received the sacrament of baptism.'

'We cannot offend our hosts! Is it so great a burden to ask you to pray for her? You spend enough of your time on your knees!'

What had so unnerved him? Josseran wondered. Did he fear contagion himself? But if her sickness was of a kind that was spread by her vapours then surely all of her maidservants would be swooning by now?

Josseran looked at the tiny figure in the bed. She deserved better than to die here in this lonely oasis, while yet a child. In some unfathomable part of his being, he still believed that the supplications of a priest, even those of such a vicious cleric as William, were worth to God a hundred of any commoner's prayers.

'Do what you can for her,' Josseran said and turned for the door.

William caught his sleeve. 'You are leaving me here?'

'I am no shaman. It is up to you now to work the miracle.'

'I told you, I cannot pray for her! God will not bestir Himself for a heathen!'

'She is not a heathen, as you yourself know. She is just a young girl and she is sick! You can make the appearance of compassion, can you not?' He went out, closing the heavy door with a crash that seemed to echo through the entire fort.

CXXIV

✠

WILLIAM KNELT BESIDE the bed and began to recite the paternoster. But he stumbled on the words and could not finish. The Devil was here in this room, in all his stinking subterfuge. He saw him smirking from the shadows, knowing too well his thoughts before he knew them himself.

He moved closer to the bed.

In sleep there is the resemblance of death, and in death the victim is forever silent. The thought came to him unbidden: he could do anything he wished with this woman; should he reach out and touch her no one would know.

Impossible now to contemplate the Infinite, to concentrate his thoughts on anything but his own compulsion. He looked around to reassure himself that the door was closed, the room empty. He tentatively reached out his hand. It was as if it was no longer a part of him. He watched it, horrified as if it was some huge, pale spider making its way across the coverlets.

His finger touched the marble flesh of the girl's arm, and then jerked away suddenly as if it had been scalded.

Miao-yen did not wake; the shallow rhythm of her breathing did not change. Again William glanced guiltily around.

Motes of dust drifted through the yellow chevrons of light from the latticed windows.

His fingers pinched Miao-yen's earlobe before jerking back again; then they grew bolder; they stroked her hand, even pulled at some of the tiny, golden hairs on her forearm until they came away from the skin. But still she did not stir.

William stood up, agitated, and paced the room, continually glancing at the door. No Tatar but a shaman would enter the room of a sick person, Josseran had said. And even they had been banned from her presence.

'I did not ask for this,' he said aloud and wrung his hands in prayer. But there was no answer from God and the demons that had haunted him now came to take total possession.

Fergana Valley

The trance was brought on with hashish smoke and koumiss. Khutelun danced alone in her yurt until the spirits came and carried her with them to the eternal Blue Sky. Freed of the bonds of the earth, soaring through the air on the back of a black mare, she rode with the barbarian warrior, Joss-ran; she felt his arms around her as they plunged into the yawning embrace of the clouds.

She dreamed that they rode above the mountains to a high pasture where she joined with him in the long rich grass of summer. It was an image so real that even as she lay on the thick rugs of her yurt, lost in her reverie, her nostrils quivered with the foreign smell of him, and she opened her arms to receive his embrace.

Something moved inside her and she groaned and thrashed in pain; a bloodied child slipped from her body, bronzed like a Person but with the gold-red hair of the Christian.

'Joss-ran.'

It was morning when she woke from the dream. It was dark and the embers of the fire were cold. She sat up, shivering, and stared around the yurt, disoriented.

She had entered the world of the spirits at the behest of her father, in order to discover the will of the gods concerning Alghu and Ariq Böke. But the image of Josseran and the child had drowned out the whisper of every other intuition. She could not comprehend what she had just experienced.

Her skin was slick and there was warmth and dampness in her loins. She rose unsteadily to her feet and stumbled outside.

A broken moon hovered above the snow-white hills. He was still out there somewhere. She knew now without question that there was a silver cord that joined them, and one day the wind would blow the seed towards the flower and they would meet again, after all.

CXXV

✣

Kashgar

It was clear to William that the princess Miao-yen was near the end. How many times had he come to this room, how many prayers had he whispered in her name? She was dying. God was not about to bestir himself for a painted heathen.

She looked dead already. Her breath was barely discernible.

His fingers slid over her skin, smooth as ivory, hot with fever. Emboldened by familiarity with its sweet terrain, it continued its explorations, settling finally on the bud of the girl's breast.

Some barricade within him crumbled down; there was no one to ever see, no one to ever know. Even the object of his desire would not be witness to his fumblings. This fragile princess with her painted face had been offered to him on this altar as his private plaything, his to possess without consequence. Soon she would give up her spirit to the darkness and whatever sins he committed would be buried with her.

Or so the voice in his head reasoned.

He reached beneath the silk of the gown and gasped when his fingertips touched the hot and supple flesh of her thigh. He hesitated, before continuing his exploration. His hand was shaking uncontrollably, his mouth was dry, his mind empty of anything beyond the sensations of the moment, blind to salvation or even reason.

He set aside his Bible and lay down on the bed beside her. He placed her compliant arms around his shoulders and kissed her painted cheek. And as the shadows crept across the room he gave himself over to the terrible urgings of his soul.

CXXVI

✠

Josseran had all his life trained regularly in martial discipline, in close combat and in horsemanship. So he overcame the boredom of the long winter months of inactivity with a self-imposed regime, maintaining his sharpness in the saddle as best he could.

Every afternoon he took his horse to the maidan below the fort and drilled alone with sword and lance. A discovery he had made in the local bazaar had helped him immeasurably. The local merchants stored watermelons by hanging them in slings from bamboo poles so that they remained succulent almost through winter. Every day he bought half a score of these fruit and took them out to the orchard on the other side of the maidan and skewered them on long poles. He would then ride at speed between the mulberry trees and attempt to slice cleanly through a melon with his sword without breaking the horse's stride.

When all the fruit had been thus vanquished he dismounted his black stallion and gave her a curry with the wooden blade the Tatars used to groom their horses. It was the same pony Khutelun had brought him the night of his escape from Qaidu's camp. He cared for him well, although he had no particular affection for the beast, for he was irritable and sometimes vicious. He had named him William.

He heard hoofbeats and looked up. Sartaq rode across the maidan, in the distinctive straight-legged Tatar style. When he reached the orchard he reined in his pony and jumped down, picking his way through the skeletons of the trees. When he saw the wreckage of the mutilated fruit in the dust he looked at Josseran and grinned.

'If you Christians ever go to war against watermelons, they should watch out.'

'I pretend the melons are your head,' Josseran said. 'It helps my aim.'

Sartaq grinned again. 'I have good news,' he said. 'Your shaman has proved his power.'

Josseran tried to hide his surprise. William had led him to believe that she was on the point of death. 'She fares better?'

'This Wey-ram,' Sartaq said, using the Tatar pronunciation of 'William', 'for all his strangeness, has powerful magic.'

Powerful magic? Josseran believed the princess would recover or die, as God willed, regardless of the good friar's prayers, but he said: 'I never doubted the efficacy of his powers.'

Sartaq could not hide his relief. At last there was an end in sight to their journey. 'As soon as the snows melt we will cross the Roof of the World to Alghu's court at Bukhara. From there we will send you on your way to the western lands.'

It was more than a year since he had seen Acre. He wondered what had taken place there during his absence. His hosts would tell him nothing, perhaps because they knew nothing themselves. Outremer was another world to them. Had Hülegü made a treaty with the Haute Cour after all, without Josseran's efforts? Or had he swept on? When he and William reached Acre would they find just smoking ruins?

Josseran did not want to go back to Outremer. He knew he would have to face the friar's accusations of heresy and blasphemy in front of the Council. The fact that he had saved the wretched man's life twice would count for nothing with that intractable churchman. He cursed himself now for speaking so freely and making of the friar an enemy.

But the Grand Master would protect him from any consequences. They were Templars, and even these Dominicans could do no more than shake their fists at them. He might not be able to leave the Order straight away, as he had planned, though. Not until William was back in Rome.

He wondered if poor Gérard and Yusuf were still held hostage at Aleppo. They, at least, would be pleased to see them safely returned.

'I can see the prospect of departing Kashgar makes you speechless with joy so I shall leave you to your melons,' Sartaq said. Then, as an afterthought, he added: 'Should you find yourself outflanked, call for aid and I shall send a squadron of my cavalry to help you fight your way out through the figs.'

He laughed and rode back towards the fort.

✝

Miao-yen was laid out like a corpse on her bed, in her robes of red brocade, tiny silk slippers on her feet. The pale light from the window made her skin appear almost translucent.

William sat there for a long time, watching her, not trusting himself to move. Finally, he reached out a shaking hand to touch her forehead. It was impossible. The fever had left her; her skin was cool to the touch.

He thrust a knuckle into his mouth to keep from crying aloud. What have I done?

She stirred and for a moment he feared she would wake. He jumped to his feet and backed away from the bed until he felt his shoulder blades pressed against the stone.

What have I done?

He heard the cries of a Mohammedan priest over the roofs of the town, the infernal song of the ungodly reverberating from the blue and distant mountains until it seemed to fill the room, deafening him.

He had never thought to see miracles in his daily life. Yet here was one, by his own doing. God had laid hands on this heathen princess to refute him and, yes, to punish him.

Why else would God choose to save this woman *now*?

He fell on to his knees and began to pray once more, this time for his own soul, not the girl's. Then he prayed that Miao-yen's recovery would be short, and that she would lapse again into the sweats, for only with her passing could he be sure his terrible sin would be buried forever.

CXXVII

✝

Now MIAO-YEN was well, her maids surrounded her constantly, fussing like hens. She sat up in the bed, the white powder of her cosmetic disguising her deathly pallor. She had been dressed in a gown of crimson brocade with charcoal sash, and there were ivory and gold pins in her hair.

Josseran and William were ushered into the room. They came to stand at the foot of the bed.

'I am pleased to see you recovered, my lady,' Josseran said.

Miao-yen attempted a smile. 'Thanks to the magic of Our-Father-Who-Art-in-Heaven.'

Josseran turned to William. 'She credits you with saving her life, Brother William. She offers you her thanks.'

It seemed to Josseran that the friar received this news with something less than rejoicing. Some humility from him, at last. He clutched a small wooden crucifix in his fist, turning it over and over in his fingers. 'Tell her it was God's will that she lived.'

Josseran turned back to Miao-yen and relayed to her what William had said. Their conversation continued in low murmured voices.

Josseran said: 'Good news, friar. She would like you to baptize her into our holy religion.'

William looked as if he had been slapped. 'I cannot.'

Josseran stared at him. 'You cannot?'

'I have instructed her as far as I can. She must pray and give thanks to God for her deliverance, if that is her wish. But I am not satisfied as to the sincerity of her faith, and so I cannot give her holy baptism.'

'But she wishes you to help her! Here is a soul begging you for the blessings of Christ! She will be your first convert! Is this not what you wished for all the time we were in Cathay?'

'Tell her not to pester me further,' William said. ' I have given you my counsel on this subject.' He turned and fled the room.

There was a startled silence. Miao-yen and her ladies stared at him, bewildered. 'Is Our-Father-Who-Art-in-Heaven angry with me?' Miao-yen asked, finally.

Josseran was too astonished to answer. Finally he stammered: 'I do not know what is wrong with him, my lady.'

'Does he not wish me to worship the Pope, as he has instructed me?'

'I have no idea what he wishes any longer.' Could his brush with death in the desert have tipped the balance of his mind?

'Perhaps you will ask him to come back and see me. I do not want him to be angry with me.'

'I am sure he cannot possibly be angry with you, my lady.'

'Yet that is how it seems.'

Josseran did not know what to say to her. Brother William had such a gift for grasping ignominy from the jaws of triumph. 'Once again, I am very glad to see you so recovered,' he managed.

'So that I can rush to my husband?'

Through the window he heard the bleating of fat-tailed sheep on their way to the market and to slaughter. It seemed to him the Tatar princess understood their predicament.

'After our parting in my father's gardens at Shang-tu, I thought never to see you again,' she said.

'I have missed our conversations.'

'I told you my father would prevail. You see how it is? Already he has isolated his brother. Alghu saw how the tide was turning and my father won him over by promising him the Chaghadai khanate as his own fiefdom and helping him assassinate the regent. What can Ariq Böke offer him? Just constant demands for men and taxes for his army. With Alghu on my father's side Ariq Böke is trapped between their two armies. '

'Alghu is indeed fortunate to have you as part of the bargain.'

'I am merely my father's excuse to cede so much of his kingdom to another prince. It is politics.'

'I hope your new husband will treat you well,' Josseran said.

'And if he does not, my father will still be Khan of Khans and Emperor of the Chin. So what does it matter?' She sighed. Perhaps she was wishing now that they had all let her die.

Josseran stared at the Mohammedan church framed in the south-facing window. A Tatar princess raised in the ways of the Chin now sent to live among Mohammedan princes. Could there be a more lonely life? 'I am sure your new khan will realize he has been sent a gift more precious than gold.'

'Who knows what he will think of a girl with lily feet?' She closed her eyes and laid her head back on the pillow. 'But I am tired. The illness has drained all my strength. You should leave me now. You will speak with Our-Father-Who-Art-in-Heaven, tell him I do not wish him to be angry with me and that I thank him for saving my life?'

'I will, my lady,' Josseran said.

He took the narrow stone steps up to the roof of the tower. It looked out over a maze of alleys and flat mud roofs, and the half-dome of a Mohammedan church. A sandstorm was rushing in from the north. Oil lamps flickered in a thousand windows; the afternoon was pitched into a premature twilight.

Josseran let the wind buffet him. What is wrong with you? he thought. You are not a Chin princess with lily feet. She has no choice that she can make, but you could still take another path in your life. She is powerless, you are not.

So will you accept the same fate, a life of regret and resignation, all for the want of a little courage? Josseran Sarrazini, if you cannot learn to live, then you must learn to die. Whatever way things go, at least you will be free.

CXXVIII

✠

Fergana Valley

The yurts had been loaded on the *kibitkas*, the tent-carts, and vast flocks of sheep and goats and horses raised clouds of dust across the plain. Qaidu sat astride his horse, watching the preparations. His lips were drawn in a line as thin as a bow beneath his grizzled beard. He stared stolidly ahead, the ermine cap with its earflaps drawn down over his head.

Khutelun rode up to greet him on her white mare. She was dressed in the insignia of a shaman: a white-cowled robe with drum and staff.

'Have you spoken with the spirits?' he said to her.

'I have.'

'What did you see in the other world?'

Khutelun could not tell him that her seeing had again failed her, so she told him only what she had foreseen in her mind: 'I saw a war without ending. I saw the empire of Chinggis Khan crumbling away to many kingdoms, as it was before.'

'Do you see us abandoning the Fergana steppe to Alghu?'

'I see us running like the wolf pack, returning at night to carry off the young and the weak and give no one at the Roof of the World a moment's rest.'

Qaidu considered, his face grim. 'Khubilai has sent one of his daughters to Bukhara, as bride. It will ensure the alliance between him and Alghu and keep us all in their grip, like a bird in a fist. At present this princess is safe behind the walls of the fort at Kashgar but soon she will be on her way across the mountains for her marriage. Alghu has sent a *mingan* of his cavalry as her escort.' He gazed beyond the mountains, as if he could see their caravan. 'I would that she did not arrive.'

'Let me do it,' Khutelun whispered. 'Give me five *jegun* of your horsemen and I will stop her.'

'I thought this is what you would say.'

His own yak-tail standard flicked and whipped in the wind. 'You will see to it that Alghu receives his new bride without her head. Can you do that?'

'I can do it,' she promised him.

CXXIX

✠

Kashgar

WILLIAM FOUND JOSSERAN in the stables, sitting on a stone trough, holding his sword and scabbard two-handed, resting his weight upon it. His robe was hunched around his shoulders.

He looked up when he heard the friar's footsteps in the darkness.

'I thought to find you here,' William said.

'How did you know?'

'I have spent much of this last year in the dubious pleasure of your company, so I know a little about the way you think, Templar. Were you going to ride out tonight or would you have done me the courtesy of a farewell before your departure?'

'I have never seen the need for farewells. And you no longer need me, Brother William. These people will not harm you. They will see you safely along the rest of your journey.'

'You were charged with my protection until we are safe returned to Acre.'

Josseran sighed. Yes, that had been his commission and what a burden it had proved to be. 'Why did you not agree to baptize the girl?'

'She is not ready. Your princess pretends to love Christ, but her soul has no understanding of God. She is still a heathen.'

'You have just described almost everyone in France. None of us understand anything about God or religion other than what you tell us to believe. Look, priest, she has asked for instruction and the solace of baptism and you refused it.'

William stayed silent.

'I do not understand you.'

'That is, as you say, because your vocation is war, not religion. For instance I do not understand this sudden concern for a certain

430

Tatar princess. Is that the reason you planned to leave tonight without me?'

A long silence. Vapour from their breath hung in the frigid air. Josseran shivered and drew his cloak more tightly around his shoulders.

'Well?' William persisted.

'I am thirty-one years old. I could return to Troyes, but there is nothing for me there. I have seen and heard things this last year that have forever changed the way I see myself and the world. Besides, the moment I step on French soil you will bring charges against me for heresy, as you have threatened to do almost since we left Acre. The only way I can protect myself from you and your holy brothers is to remain with the Temple, and I have had enough of a monk's life. You want me to help you now, priest, but I know you Dominicans, what you are like. The moment we are back safe in Outremer, you will think nothing of bringing me down.'

'Can you think of nothing but yourself? You have a duty to your Temple and to God. You have been charged with the safe return of the Pope's legate at Acre and you gave your word to Thomas Bérard that you would fulfil it. And what of the truce you have brokered with Khubilai? The fate of the Holy Land rests with us.'

'You may tell the Haute Cour all you have seen and heard, and I am sure they will be glad of your reports. Your voice in the Council will do as well as mine. As for the treaty, Hülegü will do what he wants now. The Emperor has no interest in affairs beyond this war with his own brother. The Tatar empire is breaking into pieces from within. They are destroying themselves without any help from us. Our journey was for nothing. Should we never return, it will make no difference to the history of Jerusalem.'

William was silent. Something rustled in the dark corners, a rat perhaps, foraging through the straw. A pool of water had frozen black on the stones at William's feet.

'They toyed with us, William, from the very beginning. Hülegü already knew the Great Khan was dead. He wished only to play for time, to see if the succession would be contested by his brothers, as indeed it has transpired. The charter we received from Khubilai is lost, but even if we still had it, it means nothing now. Hülegü is free to treat as he pleases, and the Son of Heaven has no authority over him. It is all to be done again.'

'You have sworn an oath before God to see me safe returned to Acre,' William repeated.

'Which God did I swear to? The God of Jerusalem? The God of the Mohammedans? Or the God of the Tatars? I have never seen such gods as I have witnessed in this last year.'

'If you ride out of these gates, they will kill you. You will ride not only beyond the help of Christendom but beyond the help of God Himself.' When Josseran did not respond, he said: 'Stay with me to Acre and I shall stay silent about your heretical opinion and blas-phemies.'

Josseran's horse, saddled to ride, stamped its feet in the shadows.

'What has made you so afraid, William?'

'I am not afraid,' William said but Josseran heard the catch in his voice.

'You are terrified to go on from here without me. What has happened to shake you like this?'

'You flatter yourself. Go, if you must. But remember this. If you ride away from Kashgar tonight you abandon forever your own kind. You will be lost in this world and the next.'

'I fear that I already am, no matter what I do.'

William stepped closer. 'What would your father say if he were here? Would he want you to throw away your life, as he did? What a legacy he left you! If you can find redemption nowhere else, find it there, in making your peace with him.'

☩

Josseran sat unmoving in the shadows long after William had gone. Finally, he got to his feet. He found his horse and rested his head on the poll, breathing in the smell of horse and leather. He felt the pony's withers twitch beneath his beard.

William was right. Qaidu and his bandits would kill him should he return. Was that what his father had wanted for him? Had his ghost followed him all along the Silk Road, as Khutelun had said, his guardian and protector, just to see him die in one defiant but futile gesture? He had to go on, if only to find something to believe in, something to make his father proud, something that would make even heaven worthwhile.

He started to unstrap the girth, defeated by faith, as well as by reason.

CXXX

☩

MIAO-YEN WATCHED the preparations from the window of her chamber, high in the western tower. Men and horses filled the courtyard, mostly Alghu's irregulars in their brown furs, the wooden quivers on their backs bristling with arrows. It seemed they were ready for a fight on the road. Their force was bolstered by the men of her father's *kesig* who had accompanied her from Shang-tu.

In the midst of the preparations she saw the barbarian sitting motionless on his stallion, the holy man beside him, mournful in his black-cowled robe.

Our-Father-Who-Art-in-Heaven had saved her life and yet now he refused even to speak to her. It was all so mysterious. What had she done to earn his enmity?

She did not relish the prospect of another journey. Although she had recovered from the fever, she had a sickness in her stomach and she had not bled this moon. It must be because of the illness. Her breasts were also sore and swollen but she was reluctant to mention so delicate a matter even to her maidservants.

The girls helped her wrap her lily feet for the journey. Two of them removed the embroidered silk shoes on her feet, then carefully unwound the long strips of binding cloth, yards and yards of it. She groaned as it was done and almost wept with relief, as she always did, when the last cloth was removed.

She looked down at the wreckage of her limbs in loathing and disgust. There was not, as men imagined, the feet of a small girl beneath the bindings. Without their coverings they were the feet of a monster. The arches had been crushed and the toes were curled inward under the insteps. Rotting flesh hung from them in long strips.

She whimpered as her feet were cleaned, for the agony did not grow any less with time. During this operation she held a flower to her nose to alleviate the smell. When it was finally done the maids replaced the bindings with a fresh strip of cloth.

So much for the life of a royal princess.

✠

Josseran sat stiffly in the saddle, waiting for the gates of the fort to be thrown open. Their party was pressed tightly together in the courtyard and the smell of the Tatars was overpowering, a pungent mixture of horse and goatskin and unwashed bodies that had him almost gagging, even after so long amongst them. Wild-eyed shamans passed amidst the milling throng of men and horses, sprinkling mare's milk on the ground and on to the polls of the horses. They were filthy creatures with matted beards and hair, their white robes stained with mud, shrieking incantations to the sky.

He stared at William's back. Dark patches stained the rough wool of his robe. He had been at the birch again, it seemed, punishing himself for some transgression known only to God and himself.

How he wished he had never set eyes on him.

The iron-studded gates creaked open and the vanguard rode out. Their officer turned the column to the right, the lucky way, before straightening their line and heading towards the mountains. A cart, covered in silks and furs and white ermine, followed them out, bearing the gilt sedan of Princess Miao-yen and her ladies.

Josseran and William were at the rear of the line with the rest of Sartaq's cavalry. They followed the caravan through the Kashgar oasis, along avenues of poplar, past clusters of mud-brick houses and orchards of apricot trees.

Later that morning Sartaq and his *kesig* veered away to the southwest and the blue gallery of the mountains. The rest of the caravan, Alghu's irregulars and the wagons bearing the princess, continued on, taking the northern route through the pass.

They galloped across a desert of black stones, the impossible mountains rearing ahead of them. Josseran spurred his horse after Sartaq and caught him at the van. Sartaq grinned. 'What is it, Barbarian?' he shouted.

'It is never wise to split your forces,' Josseran yelled at him over the rush of the wind and the drumming of their horse's hooves.

'And if your enemy is also wise,' he shouted back, 'he will never assume that you are foolish!'

'What are you saying?'

'Qaidu's troops are waiting for us in the mountains! We know they are there but they do not know that we know it. So we have set a trap for them. When the caravan reaches the Valley of the Shepherds it will make a very tempting target. But we shall have already doubled back through the passes and we will be waiting on the high ground. If Qaidu commits his forces to an ambush we shall decimate them!'

'You risk Miao-yen's life!'

'Miao-yen is still in the fort! There is no one in the sedan but Alghu's archers.' Sartaq laughed, eager for the battle he had engineered, delighted with his own ingenuity. 'An enemy will see what you wish him to see. We have chosen the killing ground. Once we trap Qaidu these mountains will be safe again for our caravans!'

Josseran fell behind, leaving Sartaq to gallop on ahead. He was impressed with the Tatar's cunning, but a part of him also felt unutterably sad and, yes, frightened. He prayed that if Qaidu did send his raiders into Sartaq's trap, Khutelun would not be among them.

CXXXI

✠

Khutelun and her cavalry waited in the black shadows of the spruce. The brown hills glistened under a blanket of frost that was slowly melting away with the rising of the sun in the eastern sky. A minaret and a stand of poplars rose from the mist at the far end of the valley.

They had waited all that morning but there was no movement on the road, the only traffic a donkey, loaded with firewood, driven along by a barefoot urchin with a stick.

Finally they saw the caravan in the distance, sun glittering on the swords and lances of the escort. As it came closer Khutelun could make out the *kibitkas* bearing the princess's sedans. Behind the wagons came three more *jegun* of cavalry.

Her spies in Kashgar had reported that they had split their force, the better disciplined troops of the *kesig* taking the road to the south. Joss-ran and his shaman were with them. She allowed herself a smile. So, he had survived. She knew he would.

Why had they divided their troops? The passes were steeper at the southern route, and unsuited to wagons, and she supposed they thought to speed the Christians on their way. Whatever the reason it worked to her advantage for now she was pitted against an enemy of similar strength. Surprise would weigh the odds in her favour. Her objective was not to gain ground but to take from them Khubilai's daughter, either by capture or by the sword. They would strike quickly, and retreat to the mountains.

Yet she was unable to shake off a deep sense of foreboding. The premonition was nameless and there was no seeing to accompany it. Perhaps, she thought, it is a foreshadowing of my own death.

She went back to the horses, waiting eagerly under the trees.

✠

Sartaq sat hunched against the cold, his long felt coat hanging in dark folds down his horse's flank. His sparse beard was beaded with ice, his breath frothing white on the air. His warriors waited behind him in the shadows of the gully, arrows bristling from the wooden quivers on their backs. A triangular pennant hung limp from the shining blade of a lance.

They could see Qaidu's raiders waiting just below the tree line on the far side of the valley. Sartaq turned to Josseran with a wolfish grin. 'You see! I told you they could not resist.'

Josseran did not answer. He searched for a flash of purple silk among the distant knot of riders, but it was impossible to make out; they were too far away.

✠

Khutelun sprinkled koumiss from her leather saddlebag on to the ground, invoking the assistance of heaven against her enemies. She closed her eyes and tried again to listen to the spirits, but the unease which had settled on her all that day had dampened her intuitions. She looked up at the Blue Sky, her face creased in confusion. The other Tatars watched her, troubled by her indecision.

'What is it you are trying to tell me?' she whispered.

She jumped into the saddle. The caravan was spread across the valley floor below them. They could not delay the moment.

She raised a fist in the air, the signal for the charge.

CXXXII

✠

THE HORSEMEN STREAMED out of the tree line, and the shriek of their war cries carried clearly across the valley on the frigid air. Josseran watched in grim silence.

'You will stay here,' Sartaq said to Josseran. 'I shall leave ten of my men as escort for you. You will be safe.' Sartaq raised a hand, waiting for the two forces to engage, ensuring there could be no swift retreat for Qaidu's warriors. 'This is for my brother-in-law,' he said.

He gave the signal and the Tatars streamed down the moraine and along the valley, a thousand of them, each in boiled-leather armour, bows across their backs, the steel points of their lances flashing in the sun.

'What is happening?' William shouted.

'Qaidu's soldiers have attacked the caravan. Sartaq has set a trap for them.' He wheeled his horse about. 'Tell me the real reason you would not baptize the princess.'

'Why do you wish to question me on this now, Templar?'

'Just tell me the truth.'

William hesitated, but then it was as if something shifted in him, some great burden of guilt was shrugged aside. 'Why should I bring her to a God who brings nothing to me?'

'William? Do not tell me you have lost your faith.'

'Take your pleasure in my fall, as you will.'

'There is no pleasure in it. I am astonished, that is all.'

'He has abandoned me, Templar! I have borne every suffering in His name, travelled far beyond the known world and endured each and every indignity, and what help has He given me, though I cried out again and again for His assistance to aid my endeavours in the name of His son? Was she to be my consolation for all I have done?

Was that the crumb He threw at me? One convert, and that a mere woman, a heathen woman?'

'She is a soul.'

'One soul is of no account to me! I dreamed of millions!' The wind howled around them, throwing grit and ice in their faces. 'I will tell you the truth of it, if that is what you wish. I do not know what I believe in any more.'

Josseran stared into the priest's face, and saw something there he had thought never to see: fear. It was like watching the sun topple from the sky.

He turned in the saddle and stared at the thin, dark line of horsemen sweeping down the green slope. Then he saw it, the very thing he had dreaded: a flash of purple silk.

Khutelun. His mouth was suddenly dry.

'What did you say?' William asked him.

'Khutelun. I said, Khutelun.'

'What?'

'Khutelun is there.'

'The witch?'

'She is there. Do you see the purple? She is down there!'

'Then she is going to die.'

'Or she may be saved. You may have lost your religion, priest, but I have found mine. This is my faith: I believe in the congress of two ill-tamed souls, of the sacred bond that will make a man do anything and everything for a woman, and she for him. I have no creed to offer, no confession. My heaven is with her, and my hell is when I am not.' Josseran put his hand to his throat, to the crucifix he wore under his silk undershirt. He tore it off his neck with sudden violence, brought it to his lips to kiss it for the last time and tossed it to the priest. 'Pray me for me, Brother William.'

'What are you going to do?'

'I do not know why it so amused God to put you in my path, but I cannot say I shall miss your company when we are apart. Nevertheless, I wish you Godspeed to Acre.'

'Templar!'

'I cannot do my penance. If I am damned, then let me be damned. You will not see me again.' He spurred his horse down the grey moraine, after Sartaq's cavalry.

'Josseran!' William screamed.

Their Tatar escort was taken by surprise. Their attention was focused on the battle taking place just below them. When they heard William's shout they all turned their heads but by then Josseran was already galloping away from them and they were too late to stop him.

CXXXIII

✠

Kʜᴜᴛᴇʟᴜɴ ɢᴀʟʟᴏᴘᴇᴅ ᴛʜʀᴏᴜɢʜ the milling ranks of Alghu's cavalry, her cavalry behind her. Alghu's men had ridden out to meet them but the momentum of her attack had taken them off guard and dozens of them already lay in the grass or in the shallows of the river, slain or wounded by the first volley of arrows. Khutelun and her vanguard rode through and around them, avoiding individual combats, interested only in the prize that awaited them in the *kibitka*.

They were within a dozen paces when the curtains parted. She shouted a warning, but it was lost in the screams and the thunder of hooves. Instead of the princess, all that awaited them within the silk curtains of the royal litter were Alghu's archers.

She tried to wheel her horse around, but it was too late.

She heard the whine of the arrows, and all around her her *magadai* screamed and clutched at their wounds. Several slid from their horses. Her own mare was hit in the shoulder by an arrow and reared on to its back legs.

It took all her skill to stay in the saddle. She put her own bow to her shoulder and loosed two arrows into the archers in the sedan. She knew it was hopeless. The charge had been checked, the impetus lost.

And besides, their quarry was not there.

She spurred her horse away from the caravan. She realized that the unease she had felt all that morning had been more than the premonition of her own death. It was the foretelling of disaster. She looked up the valley, knowing what she would see.

A black line of horsemen was galloping along the flood plain, and in moments it would sweep through their flank. Now she understood the nature of the trap.

All around her, she heard the cries of men suffering and dying, the clash of steel on steel as a hundred different combats took place along the line of the skirmish. She galloped back up the slope of the valley, found her messenger, had him send the retreat arrows singing through the air.

But she knew it was too late, much too late.

✛

As Sartaq's cavalry swept into the battle lines, the tattered remnants of Khutelun's *mingan* broke off and streamed back towards the foothills. Josseran galloped around the mêlée and looked for the purple silk: he saw Khutelun escaping up the face of the mountain slope, gathering the remnants of her soldiers around her. She was heading towards the tree line on the north side of the valley.

Sartaq's warriors loosed volleys of arrows from the saddle as they pursued her. He joined the pursuit, splashing across the ford, just one purpose in mind.

CXXXIV

☩

KHUTELUN TWISTED AROUND in the saddle. The retreat had degenerated into a score of separate pursuits. She was on her own now, with two riders following her up the slope, their lamellar armour identifying them as men from Khubilai's *kesig*. They were gaining ground.

Another arrow slapped into her mare's rump and she screamed and almost fell. She looked back again and saw that a third rider had joined the hunt.

The black shelter of the pines seemed impossibly far.

☩

Josseran's pony was galloping at breakneck speed across the uneven ground. His charge across the valley had taken him almost into the path of two of Sartaq's troopers; he was almost close enough to touch them. He saw the rider nearest him raise his bow to his shoulder and take aim.

Josseran swung wildly with his sword, an act of desperation. The blade slashed across the rump of the bowman's mount. The pony screamed and swerved, throwing his rider's aim. As Josseran spurred alongside him the bowman looked over his shoulder, his face twisted in anger and surprise.

Josseran swept sideways with the butt of his sword and knocked him from his horse.

☩

Just a hundred paces from the tree line now. Khutelun knew she could lose her pursuers there.

And then her horse staggered and went down, hard.

CXXXV

✛

ANGRY MAN HEARD a shout behind him and twisted around in the saddle. The barbarian! What was he doing here? He should be safe away from the battle on the other side of the valley.

'Help me!' Josseran shouted and sagged in the saddle, clutching his chest.

'Get away from here!' Angry Man shouted. 'Are you mad?'

But he stopped and wheeled around. No more than twenty paces away from him the fallen rebel lay motionless on the grass. Her horse tried to get back to its feet, but finally surrendered to the pain and lay her head down on the grass, exhausted. Satisfied he would not lose his quarry, Angry Man trotted back down the slope. The barbarian cried out again and clutched at his horse's mane to keep from falling from the saddle.

'What are you doing here?' Angry Man shouted at him.

'Help me . . .'

'Where are you hurt?' He grabbed Josseran's coat in his fist, jerking him upright in the saddle.

Josseran struck him full in the face with his right fist.

Angry Man fell heavily on his back, and lay there, stunned and only half-conscious, blood pouring from his nose.

'Remember, surprise and feint,' Josseran said. 'Your greatest weapons.'

He slapped Angry Man's mount hard on the rump and sent it cantering away down the mountain. He spurred his own yellow stallion up the slope after Khutelun.

✛

Her mare lay on its side, in its death throes. There was an arrow in

445

the animal's shoulder, another in her belly, yet another in her rump. Blood was streaked along her heaving flank. Finally she lay still, eyes wide in death.

Khutelun lay just a few paces away from her. She clutched at her ankle, slowly easing herself to a sitting position. So, she thought. This is my day to die.

She heard the thunder of hooves and saw another of Sartaq's cavalrymen spurring up the slope towards her. One of Alghu's irregulars by the look of him, in his brown furs and felt boots. She found her sword in the grass and struggled to her feet, ignoring the searing pain in her leg. She would not let them take her alive for their torments and their pleasure.

He stopped his horse a few paces away from her. She recognized the round eyes, and the fiery beard. *Joss-ran!*

He leaned from the saddle and held out his hand. 'Quickly!' He pulled her up beside him.

✝

They galloped through a dark forest of spruce and pine, following the ridge along the shoulder of the mountain. Now they were safe Josseran was overcome with the exhilaration that always came in the aftermath of a battle and he shouted aloud, relief and triumph all mixed up together. His voice echoed from the sheer walls of the gorge. From somewhere below them he heard the rushing of a river in torrent.

She turned around in the saddle and he grinned at her. But she did not answer his smile; her face was pale; there was blood seeping under the scarf. 'Are you hurt?'

'You should not have come back for me, Joss-ran.'

'It was a gamble. I won. *We* won. Didn't we?'

She did not answer him.

They left the trees, emerging into cold sunshine on a stark red ridge, bare of trees and grass. They slowed their pace. The narrow trail became a ledge skirting the edge of a ravine. Suddenly Josseran felt a cold dread settle again in his insides. Spring and the thawing of the ice had brought down an overhang and the way ahead was blocked by a mountain of boulders.

Josseran's stallion turned up the face of the scree looking for a way through. Too steep. Its unshod hooves slipped on frost-cracked rock and lichen, and loose shale clattered away down the slope. They were trapped. There were cliffs on one side of them and a ravine on the other.

'Leave me here,' she said. 'If you stay you only put yourself in danger.'

'If they take you alive, you know what they will do.'

'I will not let them take me alive.'

Below them he heard the rush of black water, a river swollen by the spring floods. Josseran turned his horse, thinking to find some other way around the mountain, but then he heard shouts from the tree line. Sartaq's soldiers had found them.

Josseran saw the dull gleam of lance points, as one by one they emerged from the forest; steam rose from their horses' flanks, ice and mud and blood stained their boots and coats. There were a score of them, most of them from Khubilai's *kesig*, many of them his riding companions from Kashgar. He recognized Sartaq among them.

'Go back, Joss-ran,' Khutelun whispered.

'I shall not leave you.'

'Go back. It is not you they want. Leave me here.'

They were less than a hundred paces away. One of them had put his bow to his shoulder but Sartaq raised his hand and at his shouted command the man reluctantly removed the arrow from the bowstring.

'There is a way out,' Josseran said. He walked the yellow stallion to the edge of the cliff and stared into the foaming river.

'You are mad,' Khutelun said, reading his thoughts.

'I made such a jump once before.'

'This cliff is ten times as high. This time you will die.'

'I may die or I may live. But if I live I will have you. Or I can die and it will make no difference for I do not wish to live without you.' He put his arms around her waist to support her. 'Tell me that you will marry me and live with me the rest of your days.'

'There will be no more days.'

'Just say it then. As a parting gift.'

'They do not want you,' she repeated. 'Go back to them. You do not have to die!'

'Every man has to die. There is no escape from it. But a lucky few have the opportunity to name the time and the place. Today is my chance. So say it! Say you will have me in marriage.'

He turned the horse to face Sartaq and his Tatars. He saw Sartaq shake his head, bewildered. Then he turned his stallion again, back towards the cliff. Sartaq realized what Josseran intended and he gave a shout of surprise and despair. Suddenly Josseran spurred his horse towards the gorge, and then they were falling, falling down towards the brutal judgement of the river.

✝

She had always dreamed she could fly.

She felt the rush of the wind against her cheek and as it had been in her dreams the sky was both above and below her. And she shouted out the words, I would gladly live with you and have your babies and be your woman if that is what you want, but almost at once her voice was drowned by the rushing of the river as it came to meet them.

She had always dreamed she could fly.

CXXXVI

✟

SUMMER CAME AGAIN to Bukhara, and the almond trees were once more in bloom. The honey-coloured bricks of the great Kalyan minaret were framed against a sky of impossible blue. Under the raggle-taggle awnings in the bazaar, the fresh-dyed rugs blazed in crimson and buttercup yellow and royal blues as they hung to dry in the sun. Grapes, figs and peaches set the stalls groaning with their weight and there were scarlet-fleshed watermelons in abundance, the gutters running with their sweet juice leaving the cobblestones of the bazaar ankle deep in rind.

But in the palace of Khan Alghu other seeds had also begun to ripen.

✟

Dust motes drifted through the shafts of sunlight that filtered down from the vault. There was silence in the great hall, a shuffling dread before the face of the khan's anger. The prisoner, his wrists tied behind him with leather thongs, was thrown face-first on to the stone flags, and there was no one in that great company who would not have rather laid open their own veins than swap places with the miserable wreck writhing like some night crawler at the khan's feet. It was apparent he had been beaten over a period of days rather than hours. There were few teeth left in his head and his eyes were almost shut.

William felt his bowels turn to water. He had not recognized the man at first. 'What is happening?' he whispered to the man at his side.

His companion was a Mohammedan, a Persian scribe who spoke Latin as well as Tatar. He had been assigned to him by Alghu's court on his arrival in Bukhara from Kashgar a few weeks before.

'The princess Miao-yen is with child,' the man answered. 'Her maidenhood had been taken before she arrived here. This officer stands accused. As chief of her escort he was responsible for her protection. If he will not give up the culprit then he must pay the price himself.'

William watched, gripped by a terrible fascination. Sartaq was hauled to his feet by his guards and stood there, swaying, blood caked in his sparse beard, his skin the colour of chalk. William imagined he could smell his fear.

Alghu barked out something in his heathen tongue and Sartaq answered him, his voice no more than a croak.

'He denies it was him,' the Persian whispered in William's ear. 'It will do him no good. Whether it was or it wasn't, he was in charge.'

'What will they do to him?' William asked.

'Whatever it is, it will not be easy.'

At a command from Alghu, Sartaq was dragged from the court. He was screaming and babbling, his valour had deserted him in the face of whatever death Alghu had pronounced for him.

No, William thought. No, I cannot allow this to happen.

'Tell Alghu it was me,' William said. 'He is innocent. I am the guilty one. Me.'

But he only imagined he heard himself say the words. Terror had paralysed him and he could not speak, or think. He could not even pray.

☩

That night he dreamed he was falling. Below him was the blue-ribbed dome of the Shah Zinda mosque and beyond, the burning plains of the Kara Kum. His arms and legs kicked frantically at the spinning blue sky. Then the dust of the *Registan* rushed to meet him and there was a terrible sound, like a melon being split with a sword, and his skull cracked open like an egg and stained the dust.

And then he dreamed he was standing in the square staring at the corpse, but it was not his own body lying there below the Tower of Death, it Sartaq's; and it was not a dream.

Sartaq was already raw as a carcass when they tossed him from the minaret, for they had flayed him first, there in the Tower of Death, slicing off his skin in strips with sharp knives and levering it from the flesh with iron pincers. His screams had rung over the city, a call to prayer for all those ever unjustly accused, Mohammedans and unbelievers together. William stood over the tortured and broken flesh with the others who had witnessed his execution that afternoon, and murmured over and over: 'Mea culpa. Mea maxima culpa.'

But no one understood. William knew he had escaped his terrible punishment and now stood condemned a second time for his silence.

CXXXVII

☩

ALGHU SENT A swift message by *yam* to Khubilai to request his further wishes in the matter. The answer was unequivocal.

Miao-yen was sequestered in a tower of the palace with her hand-maidens for the remaining months of her confinement. Alghu's executioner was then given a further and secret charge. Miao-yen was a royal princess and it was not permissible for the blood of Chinggis Khan to be spilled. Another method of execution must be devised for her.

☩

Swallows darted among the cupolas and semi-domes, dipping under the branches of the mulberry trees in the gardens, fluttering into the nests they had built under the jutting beams of the thick-walled mud-brick houses. They are preparing for their hatchlings, she thought, placing a hand on the swell of her own stomach. There is a frantic joy to their busy swooping and wheeling. Yet I wait here in this dolorous tower like a prisoner.

She knew she had displeased her new lord, that she had displeased everyone, and she knew that it had to do with the child growing in her belly. She did not understand how such new life was made, but that it had to do with the lying of a man with a woman. But she also knew, from her conversations with Nestorian priests and with Our-Father-Who-Art-in-Heaven, that a child could be born from a young and chaste woman, and that this was regarded as a great blessing.

The maidservants she had brought with her from Cathay had been sent away and in their place were sullen, silent Persian girls

452

who spoke only their own Farsi and could tell her nothing of what was happening. They did not understand the custom of the lily foot and did not try to hide their disgust when they changed the dressings. She endured her lonely vigil, wondering at the manner of her offence and fearful of the coming birth, of which she was as helpless and as ignorant as a child.

Late that evening, the soldiers appeared, their armour clattering as they hurried through the corridor to her quarters. They were Alghu's soldiers, the first men she had seen since the day of her arrival in Bukhara. Their expressions were cheerless. She turned from the window, expecting some messenger from Alghu or her father, but instead the soldiers took her by the arms and without a word marched her out of the apartments and through the heavy barred door at the end of the cloister.

She was rushed across the hexagonal flagstones of a treed courtyard, the mulberries crunching under the soldier's boots in the grey twilight. Beyond another gateway a *kibitka* with a curtained litter was waiting, and she and two of her Persian handmaidens were motioned to step inside.

They were driven through the streets towards the western gate. Through the curtains Miao-yen saw oil lamps flickering in countless windows. And then they were out of the city, and she felt the hot, fetid breath of the desert.

She wondered what the khan had planned for her. Perhaps, she thought, there is to be no marriage after all. Perhaps they have decided to spirit me away in the darkness, and I am to return to Shang-tu.

But the soldiers had not come to escort her to Shang-tu. She was not even to leave the khanate of her proposed husband. She was instead brought to a lonely yurt on the featureless plains of the Kara Kum, with only her two mute servant girls and a dozen of Alghu's soldiers as company.

She passed the next few days alone inside the yurt, frightened and confused. Outside the wind howled across a barren plain.

Don't let them hurt my baby.

✢

It was dawn when the waters broke. The stab of pain in her belly took her by surprise, leaving her gasping in shock on the floor of the yurt. She cried out for her servant girls but they just stared at her wide-eyed and made no move to help her. One ran off to fetch the soldiers. Moments later the flap of the yurt was pushed aside and when she saw their faces she screamed, for she knew in that moment what her fate was to be.

Not my baby.

They dragged her out of the yurt to where the horses were already waiting, saddled to ride. It was a beautiful morning, the sun not quite risen, the moon still a pale ghost on the desert.

'Why are you doing this?' she screamed. 'Why are you doing this?'

They bound her arms behind her back with leather thongs and threw her on a litter that they had tied between two of their horses. They took her perhaps no more than three or four *li* from the yurt. Then they hauled her from the litter and dragged her across the sand.

She screamed, racked by another contraction, but they paid her suffering no heed.

There was a shallow depression, still sunk in black shadow. It was here they threw her down and one of the men held her while the other bound her legs with rope around her knees and her ankles. Then they applied leather thongs around her thighs and heavier leather ties around her pelvis, binding them so tightly she cried out in pain.

'What are you doing?' she cried at them. 'Tell me what is happening! What have I done?'

They walked back to their horses. Their officer stared at her for a long time, perhaps to ensure that his men had performed their task to the exact specifications, and then they galloped away across the plain.

Miao-yen gasped at the shock of another birth-pain, and when it was over and she opened her eyes again the soldiers were no more than specks on a featureless horizon.

As the sun rose she screamed her protest to the everlasting Blue Sky, shouting over and over the words of the paternoster, taught to her by Our-Father-Who-Art-in-Heaven, for she knew she had never sinned against her father or her husband, and Josseran's priest had told her that the innocent were never punished. *If you will but call out the name of God,* he had said, *you will be saved.*

EPILOGUE

✠

Lyon, France
in the year of the Incarnation of Our Lord 1293

THE MONK'S EYES turned towards the abbot.

'Now you know the most terrible thing I have done. I took her, while she was near death, thinking only the Devil and I would know what I had done. I was wrong.' His eyes followed the shadows of the candle to the corner of the room. 'The thongs they tied around her thighs and her belly would not allow the child to be born. It is a unique punishment among the nomads of those lands. Finally the babe is forced away from the natural path of its birthing, upwards, into the vitals and the heart. It kills the mother and, with her death, the infant dies also. How long it took for Miao-yen to die, no one can know. As no one can ever know how indescribably she must have suffered.'

He paused, and his breath rattled in his lungs.

'The Templar was right, of course. When I returned to Acre history had already overtaken our mission. Soon after we left on our great journey to the East, the Tatar hordes from the north attacked Poland. Lublin and Cracow were sacked, and when he heard the news the Pope proclaimed a crusade against the Tatars. The Holy Father also declared those Christians who had sided with the Tatars in Palestine excommunicate. So the Haute Cour stayed their hand when the Mamluks met the Tatars at Ain Jalut and defeated them, driving Hülegü from Syria. Now of course the Saracens have all the Holy Land and our one chance to defeat them was lost.'

'And the Templar and this Tatar witch?'

'No one could have survived such a fall. Although the water was deep there were great boulders beneath the surface. Even if the rocks

457

did not crush them, the torrent ran so fast they must have drowned. And yet . . .'

The abbot leaned closer. 'What?'

'And yet Sartaq told me when he returned that afternoon that he thought he'd seen two heads bobbing in the water, far downstream. Were they alive or were they dead? He could not be sure. And neither can I be sure, not completely. Ten years later, when I visited Acre for the last time, I heard a story of a Mohammedan merchant who had just returned from Baghdad and claimed he had met a Frank with flame-red hair who was living with the Tatars somewhere at the Roof of the World. Perhaps it was he, or perhaps it was just another of the legends that fly the steppe, without any more substance than the dust devils and the clouds.'

He smiled, revealing rotten teeth. His breath had the taint of death on it. The abbot recoiled from the bed but the monk held on to him, gripping the edge of his robe between his fingers. 'I often picture him. Is it not strange? I lied to him that last night in Kashgar. If he had returned with me to Acre I would certainly have denounced him to my fellow Inquisitors as a heretic and blasphemer. Yet now I think back on him as perhaps my greatest friend. I even smile when I think of him living there beyond redemption, beyond faith, in the arms of his barbarian witch, sire of his own heathen brood.'

He closed his eyes.

'And so hear this my confession, in the year of the Incarnation of Our Saviour twelve hundred and ninety-three. I have slept with my sins these thirty-three years; I can bear them no more. Soon the candle will gutter and die and leave me here in the darkness. I have often looked from this window towards the east and my thoughts have travelled to the places I knew in those days. There is snow on the sill tonight; somewhere there will be snow on the Roof of the World and the Tatars will lead their herds down the valleys once again for the winter. I remember them, my companions, in the days of my glory and my sin. Pray for me now, I beg you, as I go to meet my judge.'

✝

The abbot hurried from the cell. The monk's confession had chilled him to the bone; all this talk of idolaters and strange lands and devil-women on horseback. The ravings of a sinful and enfeebled mind! He believed none of it. He doubted if this old man had ever been any further east than Venice. Yet as he hurried down the darkened cloister he felt a sudden chill on his face, as if a wind had sprung from nowhere, and he imagined he had brushed against the Devil himself.

GLOSSARY

✠

arban: a Tatar platoon of ten soldiers.

argol: dried camel droppings used to make a fire.

Borcan: the Tatar name for the Buddha.

bonze: monk.

chador: garment worn by Islamic women covering the entire body.

chai-khana a teahouse.

darughachi: resident commissioners. Local men employed by the Tatars to administer their government in the area and collect taxes.

del : a quilted wrap-around gown worn by the Tatar.

fondachis: the warehouses of the Italian merchant communes in the Palestine states.

gebi: round flat stones found in the deserts of central Asia.

han: caravanserai located inside a town or city.

iwan: vaulted entrance to a mosque.

jegun: a Tatar military unit of one hundred men, made up of ten *arban*.

karez: a well linked to an underwater irrigation channel; found near Turpan in the Taklimakan desert. The Persian name is *qanat*.

keffiyeh: traditional Arab headdress.

kesig: Khubilai Khan's imperial bodyguard.

khang: raised platform of mud brick under which a fire can be lit and sometimes used as a bed.

khuriltai: meeting called to anoint a new khan after the death of a reigning khan.

kibitka: ox-drawn wagon used by the Tatars for transporting their yurts.

Kufic: Arabic calligraphy used on monuments.

league: three nautical miles.

li: approximately one-third of a mile.

manap: village headman.

maidan: an open field.

magadai: literally 'Belonging to God', a Mongol suicide squadron.

mingan: a Tatar military unit of one thousand soldiers.

muezzin: a Muslim official who summons the faithful to prayer from the minaret.

ordu: the household; by law a Tatar could have four wives, with a household for each, although he could have any number of concubines.

Registan: 'sandy place', central square in a Silk Road oasis.

rod: approximately five and a half yards.

the Rule: the strict laws that governed the daily life of the Templars.

stupa: Buddhist tomb or mausoleum with characteristic bulbous shape.

touman: a Tatar military unit of ten thousand men.

yassaq: the code of laws as promulgated by Chinggis Khan.